Praise for Lorrie Thomson and *Equilibrium*

"Thomson's first novel treats issues of loss, mental illness, adolescence, and sexuality with great openness and sensitivity. Fans of Kristin Hannah and Holly Chamberlin will similarly appreciate this hopeful, uplifting story about family, friendships, and a second chance at love."

—*Booklist*

"An emotional, complex, and deeply satisfying novel about the power of hope, love, and family. I couldn't put it down!"

—Lisa Verge Higgins

"Riveting . . . Very uplifting . . . Romantic, yet heartbreaking all the way through, this novel is a beautiful take on starting over in life."

—*RT Book Reviews*

"Tender, heartbreaking and beautifully realistic. Fans of Anita Shreve will be riveted by this intense and compassionate story."

—Hank Phillippi Ryan

"One beautifully written novel . . . A lovely, heartfelt read that I plan on revisiting soon."

—Heroes and Heartbreakers

Books by Lorrie Thomson

Equilibrium

What's Left Behind

Published by Kensington Publishing Corp.

WHAT'S LEFT BEHIND

LORRIE THOMSON

KENSINGTON BOOKS
www.kensingtonbooks.com

KENSINGTON BOOKS are published by

Kensington Publishing Corp.
119 West 40th Street
New York, NY 10018

All Kensington titles, imprints, and distributed lines are available at special quantity discounts for bulk purchases for sales promotion, premiums, fund-raising, educational, or institutional use.

Special book excerpts or customized printings can also be created to fit specific needs. For details, write or phone the office of the Kensington Special Sales Manager: Attn. Special Sales Department. Kensington Publishing Corp., 119 West 40th Street, New York, NY 10018. Phone: 1-800-221-2647.

Kensington and the K logo Reg. U.S. Pat. & TM Off.

eISBN-13: 978-0-7582-9331-2
eISBN-10: 0-7582-9331-3
First Kensington Electronic Edition: September 2014

ISBN-13: 978-0-7582-9330-5
ISBN-10: 0-7582-9330-5
First Kensington Trade Paperback Printing: September 2014

10 9 8 7 6 5 4 3 2

Printed in the United States of America

For Bill

You are my home.

Acknowledgments

Thank you to my wonderful husband, Bill, for your continued support and enthusiasm—standing by my side during the first launch party, making sure I take bookmarks everywhere I go, and handing them out for me when I hang back. You never once complained about taking me to Casco Bay for all my shoreline research. You may not say much about my writing to me, but I hear tell you're mighty proud you're married to an author. Don't worry, your secret's safe with me.

Thank you to my critique partners, Sylvie Kurtz and Ellen Gullo, for reading every chapter and answering my perpetual question, "Does this make sense?"

A second thank-you goes out to Sylvie for Celeste's Sugar-coated Lemon Blueberry Muffins recipe. Sylvie tried out several recipes, working extra hard to get that sugar coating just right. All I had to do was taste test. What a sweet job. And a sweet friend.

A third shout-out goes to Sylvie Kurtz, who, via Cassie Kurtz, unintentionally researched a medical scene.

To my agent, Jessica Alvarez, of BookEnds, thanks for your insight on motivation and the first chapters—the biggest challenge. It's nice to know you're in my corner every step of the way.

To my editor at Kensington, Peter Senftleben, thanks so much for believing in me and my characters, and making sure we make sense. You're the best! (And also my Kensington go-to guy.)

Kensington designer Kristine Noble once again created a gorgeous cover, evocative of the story and the characters' inner journeys. Thank you.

Landscape architect Jerry Guthrie sat me down and patiently answered my questions about labyrinths and the steps needed to undertake a landscaping project. Thank you for that and for the specific suggestion that each project tells a story.

Innkeeper Carol Emerson of Edgewater Farm B&B in Phippsburg, Maine, provided the inspiration for Briar Rose B&B. Carol ran me through her daily drill and shared the trials and joys of running a bed-and-breakfast. Thank you for the candid talk, delicious breakfasts, and comfortable accommodations. Research is such hard work!

Cheryl Aldrich, aka my forever roomie, inspired the novel's inciting incident and, thankfully, lived to tell.

Tuxedo cat Snoopy Jr. "Buzzy" Grummon provided inspiration for Abby's gray tabby, Sadie. Thank you to my children—Ben, Josh, and Leah. Without you, I couldn't have imagined the enormity of Abby's loss.

CHAPTER 1

Abby Stone refused to look at her son's photos.

If Abby strained her imagination, she could almost convince herself today was like any other Valentine's Day at Briar Rose B&B, a Saturday celebration replete with lovers feeding each other chocolate-dipped strawberries and toasting their unions with her best champagne. That nearly five hours ago, half the town hadn't followed her home through high winds that rattled her truck, buffeted snowdrifts, and narrowed Hidden Harbor, Maine's shoreline roads. That Monday morning, she hadn't wrapped a blanket around herself to bandage the shaking, while she typed apology e-mails and issued rain checks for her six guest rooms. That Sunday afternoon, her only child hadn't died.

One misstep and her son's daredevil climb between dorm-room windows had ended in a three-story, neck-breaking, heart-stopping plunge to the unforgiving ground.

Abby's heartbeat fluttered and flared in her throat, and her fingers trembled.

She imagined Luke's friends trampling down three flights of stairs. She imagined their footfalls and panicked voices echoing in the stairwells. She imagined them finding Luke splayed in the courtyard and knowing he was already gone.

The *Hidden Harbor Gazette* had called Luke, "Spiderman."

Luke would've loved that.

The small-town reporter couldn't have known a younger Luke had worn his paper-thin Walmart Spiderman getup three Halloweens in a row, in lieu of Abby's offer to sew him a handmade costume. Each year, the hemline inched up his pale legs, and the top rose to reveal a longer swatch of belly. The better for tickling, she'd tell him. Before she was ready, Luke had grown from a round-cheeked toddler clutching Abby with a sweaty grip, to a little boy eager to slip away from her.

I want my son back.

She'd never spanked Luke, but right now she wanted to take all five foot eleven inches of her full-grown son over her knee and give him what for. *Don't you ever scare me like that again!* Even under normal circumstances, the idea would've been preposterous.

Abby's oldest and dearest friend, Celeste, stood with her back to Abby, her shoulder muscles working, hands buried in the double sink. Water sprayed the white-tiled backsplash. Steam rose, and Celeste slipped a white serving platter between the slats of the wooden drainer.

Abby's chest rose in a pressurized wave, as though a hand were trying to shove her heart from her body. She sipped the seltzer Celeste had forced on her. Her throat clenched around the bubbles, and she coughed into her elbow.

Celeste shut off the faucet and leaned a hip against the counter. The uncharacteristic gray half-moons beneath Celeste's auburn lashes made her eyes appear greener than usual. In the last week, Abby and Celeste had held each other and cried more than they had in their entire lives. Celeste had insisted on staying at Abby's to boil water for herbal teas, which Abby could not taste, and pop romantic comedies that Abby could not follow into the DVD player. Sleep had been sporadic. Celeste couldn't afford to continue the Abby-watch, with two energetic children to chase, a bakery to run, and a husband in need of occasional attention. Besides, nothing had made Abby feel better. Nothing.

"Ten minutes?" Abby said, trying to blanket her exhaustion with a thread of optimism.

"Ten minutes, buddy, and I kick them to the curb. Hand to heart." Celeste's gaze held tight, but her voice wavered.

Earlier, Abby had taken Celeste aside and made her promise to gently enforce the reception's visiting hours, a task Abby knew she could never do herself. In the fifteen years since she'd owned the B&B, she'd never rushed a single guest out the door. Didn't matter whether she'd known them all thirty-seven years of her life, or they were newly acquainted. Abby lived by the motto gracing her front door: *Enter as strangers, leave as friends.*

"Hand to heart," Abby said, "and that includes you. Go home and take care of that husband of yours." Abby tugged at one of Celeste's shiny braids.

"Oh, yeah?" Celeste's weak smile twined two parts curiosity with one part genuine concern. "Want me to kick Charlie out, too?"

Abby sputtered on her second sip of seltzer. Her eyes watered, and she wiped her mouth with the back of her hand. As Luke's parents, Abby and Charlie had sat together in the front pew of the Congregational Church; their hands clenched white in solemn solidarity. As kids, they'd been best friends before they were sweethearts. After Abby had gotten over hating Charlie, mostly, they'd renewed their friendship and indulged in what she liked to call leap-year sex, although not necessarily on the leap year. And Charlie always turned to Abby when life got rough.

"He's not moving back in." Directed at Celeste, Abby immediately regretted the defensive edge to her voice.

"Not judging, just worrying."

"Our timing has never been right," Abby said, offering up

the same simple answer she'd given Luke whenever he'd asked why his parents weren't together.

"Present situation included."

"Agreed." Abby stared at Celeste, questioning the wisdom of having shared her every Charlie slipup, but Celeste's brows remained knit. "I thought you loved the guy."

"Of course I love Charlie. Everybody loves Charlie."

Celeste yanked off the dish gloves. She plucked one of her prize-winning mini blueberry muffins from the center island, sighed, peeled the liner.

The muffins' fruit-and-sugar aroma rumbled Abby's stomach. What had she eaten today? A packet of apples-and-cinnamon oatmeal she'd choked down to keep Celeste from fussing over her? Coffee, gone cold in the mug between her hands? Abby considered the muffins, Luke's all-time favorite pastries from Luke's all-time favorite bakery. Clear as a noon sky, she could see Luke returning home from Celeste's bakery, Sugarcoated, his teeth and tongue suspiciously blue, the waxed bag containing far fewer muffins than she'd requested.

Yet, Luke was gone.

At Tuesday morning's private funeral, she'd watched his casket lower into the ground. She'd tossed dirt onto its lid. She'd stared into the black hole, willing the earth to swallow her, until Abby's mother and Celeste had gripped her by either arm and urged her away from the edge. Nearly nineteen years ago, those same strong hands had held Abby's arms for support while, terrified, she bore down and Luke slid from her body, a screaming, slithering miracle.

Her pulse raced, the room grayed, and she thought she might faint.

I want my baby.

Celeste popped the rest of the muffin into her mouth, covered the chewing with her palm. "I still can't believe . . ."

Abby nodded, but she couldn't meet Celeste's sad-eyed

gaze. "We'll be okay," Abby said, using the plural pronoun that had eased her through her teenage pregnancy with Luke. This time, girlfriend togetherness couldn't soothe her.

In lieu of a touchstone, Abby rubbed her forefinger against her thumb. Her sight cleared, but her heart refused to settle. She arranged half a dozen rolls along the lid of a Crock-Pot of chicken soup for her mother. Lily Beth hadn't been eating well. Leftovers would provide a week of easy dinners. Abby carried the soup into the dining room. She'd scan the room, see who needed her, and busy herself with whatever they needed. Anything to keep herself from thinking about her son.

"Luke thought the pavilion looked like that Swedish hotel! He said, after graduation, he might open his very own ice hotel right here in Maine." Lily Beth, an honorary local, was regaling two born-and-bred lobstermen with tales of her last Hermit Island nature walk with Luke. Lily Beth's mouth quivered with the memory of her grandson's words. But her eyes shone, as though Luke's memory also gave her solace.

Over the Christmas break, Abby's eighteen-year-old son and fifty-four-years-young mother had strapped on snowshoes for a trek down Island Road. Five hours later, they'd returned red-cheeked, and talking overly loudly in the way of people who'd shared an adventure.

Abby wished she'd joined them, rather than staying behind to do what? Cooking? Laundry? Greeting guests? The minutia that went into running the B&B had taken up the better part of her life since Luke had entered nursery school. The days flew by in a blur. She'd prided herself in showing him how even a single mom could turn a run-down, bank-auction farmhouse into a thriving business. Luke had been both her motivation and her muse. She'd learned bookkeeping, carpentry, and the art of hospitality. For her son, she'd refused to fail.

I want my son back.

Abby's heart tapped an off-tempo beat she chose to ignore,

and she forced herself to lift her legs, no longer meant for walking. Her skittish rescue tabby, Sadie, darted across her path, a streak of gray fur. Abby's knee buckled, and she hobbled with the soup the rest of the way to Lily Beth. "Sit down, baby. You've been standing all day." Lily Beth, eyes red-rimmed from crying, should've been sitting herself.

"I'm okay, Mom," Abby said, her standard answer for today, and pulled out a ladder-back chair for Lily Beth. No fair adding her grief to her mother's burden. Luke was Lily Beth's baby, too. She'd supported Abby's decision to keep him, although her pregnancy must've felt like a cruel déjà vu. Abby hugged Lily Beth and marveled at the smile that rarely left her mother's face. Lily Beth's motto practically radiated from her pores: *Whatever doesn't kill you makes you stronger.* "Sadie startled me," Abby said.

"Blame the cat."

"That's right."

Lily Beth sat with a sigh, and her black cardigan slipped down her arm, as though the weight of the day had rounded her shoulders. Sometimes Abby forgot her force-of-nature mother was human, too. Abby tugged her mother's sweater, bent, and whispered into her blond curls. "I'll be fine. I promise. It's okay to go home."

Lily Beth took Abby's cold hands between her own icy fingers. "Celeste?"

"Staying one more night," Abby said, a lie for Lily Beth's own good—her mother couldn't sleep away from home—but the fib still sat like a stale doughnut in her gut. "I'm going to lie down, and so should you." Abby gave her mother's fingers a final squeeze.

Someone well meaning, probably Celeste, possibly Lily Beth, had transported the photo collage and its stand from the front of the church and erected the blasted thing at the far end of Abby's dining room. Floor-to-ceiling windows faced the ocean, two unblinking eyes perpetually gazing out to the Atlantic. The view opened her lungs. A strawberry-hued sundown reflected off the frozen harbor. Hidden beneath the ice, unseen, the tides still moved.

Luke had adored that fact.

Luke's girlfriend, Tessa, stood to the side of the offending photo display. Her head tilted toward Charlie, her face a study in concentration, as though she were one of the starry-eyed high-school girls who'd voted him Coolest Teacher.

This morning, Abby had finally met the mysterious dark-eyed Tessa she'd been hearing about for months. At least Luke had prepared Abby with the promise his latest girlfriend was super nice, and way different from the girls he usually dated. In high school, Luke's girlfriends had no more than two holes in each ear, not half a dozen. Their highlights came from the sun, and not a packet of blue dye. But the look on Luke's face when he spoke about his artist girlfriend had tipped Abby off to the biggest difference of all. When he spoke the girl's name, he'd draw out the vowels, his voice making a smoky sound. His gaze lost focus. And his pupils swallowed the soft blue of his irises. Abby's baby had been falling in love.

Likely, Luke's death had short-circuited first heartbreak. Given time, super nice or not, Abby doubted their relationship would've lasted beyond the heated rush of infatuation between polar opposites.

Charlie's laugh punched the air, an unnatural *har-har* that fooled Tessa into laughing along with him, but told Abby that Charlie was barely hanging on, too.

He caught her gaze, held it. Even though she'd known Charlie since the day she'd let him win a schoolyard race, even after everything they'd been through together, the sight of him still energized her, like the first summer day at the beach. She made her way across the room, a hand raised to her forehead to ward off the glare.

Long ago, nineteen years, seven months, and twelve days ago, to be exact, Abby had believed she could plan out her entire adult life, down to the smallest detail. Despite her doubts, she'd chosen to believe Charlie when he'd promised you couldn't get pregnant if you did it in the ocean, and they'd forgone their usual precaution.

Before Abby had sent Luke away to college, she'd lectured him about the dangers of unprotected sex, drugs, and alcohol. Even Charlie, Good-Time Charlie, had echoed her concerns.

The coroner had found neither drugs nor alcohol in Luke's system.

Which led Abby to the tried-and-true conclusion that drugged or dry, men were impulsive, irrational, and prone to delusions of invincibility. Eventually, they all broke your heart.

Abby touched Charlie's shoulder and turned her back to the photo display. Charlie swung his hair from his eyes, a gesture meant to appear carefree. His left eyelid twitched, a tell Abby doubted Tessa had noticed. "You doing okay?" Abby asked Tessa, but she kept her hand on Charlie's arm.

Abby attempted to see beyond the girl's heavily made-up face. Black lined her top and bottom lashes. Gold gilded her lids. And highly reflective gloss shellacked the center of her lower lip. Only the very young would intentionally try to look so hard.

"Uh-huh." Tessa tried for a nod, but then her dark eyes filled, and she shook her head. "I didn't want to let him go."

The back of Abby's neck broke into a sweat, like when that first Luke contraction had clenched her body. She hadn't wanted to let Luke go then. She didn't want to let him go now. She never wanted to let him go.

Abby wiped Tessa's tears. Black mascara smudged her thumbs. Up close, only the insides of Tessa's irises were brown. Green and gold constellations brightened the outer halves. "Luke cared a great deal for you." Abby's voice tangled around her son's name, and she took a slow breath. "He would've been thrilled you kids drove up from Amherst. And thank you so much for forwarding me the article about the UMass memorial."

Celeste poked her head out from the kitchen and held a hand in the air, fingers outstretched. Five minutes.

Tears, watercolor black, streaked down the sides of Tessa's face. "I'm wicked sorry!" Three sharp shrugs of her shoulders, and Tessa made a run for the couple she'd come with: a petite girl and her built-like-a-wall boyfriend. The girl embraced Tessa, and then, moments later, grabbed Tessa's coat from the chair back.

Abby jolted forward, and Charlie took her by the arm. "Let her go, Abby."

"She's hurting!"

"So are we," Charlie said, his voice barely a whisper. He looked down and shook his head.

"Charlie." Abby brushed the dark-blond hair out of his eyes, her own self-soothing gesture, and her gaze caught on the photo display: Luke's six-year-old grin pressed between her and Charlie's sun-drenched faces, three look-alike blondes. They'd spent the day at Popham Beach, and a passerby had snapped the photo. Luke had insisted. "Just like a family," he'd said, and Abby's heart had bottomed out. Her little romantic.

"I loved him so much."

Charlie followed her gaze to the photo board.

Their baby in his car seat, his eyes closed, pink lips pursed in his sleep. A blurred image of Luke on the high-school basketball court, nailing a jump shot. Luke on break from college, winter camping in the yard. The tent's canvas framed his beaming face.

She gazed into Luke's eyes. Luke stared back. Background conversations faded to a hum. Perspiration prickled her hairline.

Whatever doesn't kill you makes you stronger.

All day she'd cycled between the numb out-of-body experience of observing herself from afar and this strangling intensity of in-your-face grief. When the person you'd built your life around was gone, where did that leave you?

Last night, she'd lain in bed, doing the math. If she lived to eighty-six, she'd have another seventeen thousand six hundred and one days to endure. That was no way to think, certainly no way to live. She ached, as if someone had run her over with an eighteen-wheeler, thrown the rig into reverse, and ground her flattened remains into the asphalt.

If she didn't find something else to build her life around, losing her son was going to kill her.

In her peripheral vision, the two lobstermen made their way to the front door. The ladies from the town hall crossed the dining room. A throng of Luke's high-school basketball buddies who'd been hiding out in the library peeked into the dining room and then made their awkward exit. A dozen girls who'd spent their high-school careers adoring Luke and the last two hours hugging in the entryway sent Luke's senior prom date to offer Abby their final condolences.

The room tilted on its axis. A slip of frozen white harbor. The sun glinting off the chandelier's crystal prisms, glancing off the pale turquoise walls. Lily Beth across the room, and then her mother up close, Crock-Pot at her feet, shrugging into her wool coat. "Celeste's going to follow me home, in case I need help shoveling my way to the front door."

"Call if you need me." Abby tried for a reassuring tone, but her voice came out foreign and far away, as though filtered through a bad phone connection.

Lily Beth leaned in for a peck on Abby's cheek and then hurried for the door, leaving the earthy smell of snow and salt in her wake.

Celeste bustled into the dining room, wearing her puff jacket and smelling like powdered sugar. Her gaze honed in on

Charlie. Arms folded, he stared out to the harbor, swallowing repeatedly. His breathing betrayed a ragged edge. "Oh, holy hell," Celeste said, loud enough for Charlie to hear, and Abby walked her to the door.

"I can come back. I can stay. Really, no big deal." The note of panic in Celeste's voice was reminiscent of the first time Abby had gotten back with Charlie.

"Mama Bear." Abby's nickname for Celeste whenever she'd wax overprotective never failed to make them grin. "Don't worry. I'll give him tea and sympathy and send him on his way." She sighed. "He needs me," she said, and something deep inside her eased a tiny bit. She couldn't build her life around Charlie, but she could keep herself busy a while longer.

Celeste's eyes widened at the thought, and Abby hugged her. "Love you." Abby slipped a piece of paper from her apron and edged it toward Celeste's jacket pocket.

Celeste grabbed her wrist. "What're you doing?" She pried open Abby's fingers and shook her head at the spa certificate for Simple Indulgence. "I can't accept this."

The sudden look of reproach in Celeste's eyes tugged at Abby's resolve. "Come on. You deserve it. I know how hard you work. Wouldn't hand and foot massages feel great?"

"You're losing money this week." Celeste glanced at the spa certificate. "Those don't come cheap."

"I get a discount."

"Discount doesn't mean free. Besides, *you* could use a massage. When was the last time you treated yourself? Wouldn't a massage make you feel better?"

"No." Lying exposed on a massage table and letting a stranger dig fingers into her tangled muscles was not Abby's idea of a treat. Bad enough she'd let Celeste see her at her worst. Abby pressed the spa certificate into Celeste's hand and turned her toward the door. "Don't make me grovel," Abby said, earning a half giggle.

"Don't let Charlie move in," Celeste said over her shoulder, and the front door clicked shut. Two consecutive engines revved and screeched in protest of the cold. Snow tires ground from her driveway. When Abby returned to the dining room and caught sight of Charlie, she could've sworn she heard the crash of the surf from the open ocean, pacing the roar of her heart.

Charlie rocked on his heels, the same unconscious tick he'd displayed at Tuesday's burial until Abby had held his hands in hers.

She took his hands now, held tight, and settled the movement. For a long moment, he pressed his lips to the top of her head. Then he stepped back. The look of regret in his hazel eyes, Abby knew all too well. He was such a great dad Abby sometimes forgot he'd slipped in and out of Luke's life those first three years. Right when she'd thought she'd gotten it together on her own, he'd slipped in and out of her life, too.

"I miss him every second," Charlie said. "Kept thinking I'd see him sitting with his high-school friends, you know? Kept looking for him at the church . . . at the cemetery . . ."

Luke's swim team and basketball trophies lined the entire top shelf of the library's bookcase. His old Matchbox cars collected in a wicker basket to entertain the B&B's younger guests. Three concrete handprints sat sentry before her perennial garden: Luke's hands at five, small and pudgy; stretching out at twelve; man-sized on his eighteenth birthday.

Wind rattled the windowpanes, but the cold couldn't touch her. She had the urge to kick off her shoes, traipse through the snow-covered yard, walk straight into the iced-over bay, and let the frigid water numb her heart.

"Everywhere I look—" Charlie said.

"Stop it!" Abby wasn't sure whether she was talking to Charlie or herself.

Charlie's eyes clouded, the color darkening from green to gray. His lips gently shut. He mouthed, *Okay,* and lowered his gaze.

When he pulled her against him, she rested her head on his chest. The unique-to-Charlie musk of his skin filled her nose. If she closed her eyes, she could make herself believe they were seventeen years old again, their whole lives ahead of them, nothing decided. The heady beat of his heart thrummed through her head and resurrected a string of major life firsts. First kiss, fast and fumbling and stolen, by her, in the tide pools at Joe's Head. First sex, equally fast, and initiated by Charlie in his parents' den, while his little sister slept upstairs. First-breakup heartbreak: ongoing.

And now this.

Abby shifted her head, and his breath hit her in the face, hot with a sting of Scotch, one of Charlie's occasional indulgences. To his credit, Charlie would never have sneaked a nip from her liquor cabinet if he were planning on driving himself home.

Abby's stomach muscles convulsed. The edges of her mouth twitched upward. Nothing was funny, nothing at all. Yet her shoulders shook, and she struggled against the grip of hysterical laughter.

Charlie pulled away from her. "What is it?"

Tears wet her cheeks. "Johnnie Walker," she said, a reed-thin squeak.

"Ah, you got me. Did a couple shots." Charlie nodded, rubbed her arms until her hysterics subsided. His chin dimpled, but he did not cry. Scotch could do that.

She sighed, wiped her cheeks, held a hand to Charlie's face. His handsome, heartbroken face. "Presumptuous of you."

Charlie took her hand and kissed it, slow, heated pressure reminiscent of the time she'd taken him in after his divorce. He gilded her with his warm gaze. His I-know-you-better-than-you-know-yourself gaze. His Abby-can't-say-no-to-Charlie gaze. His maybe-this-time-will-be-different gaze. "Was I wrong?"

She could make Charlie a care package of sandwiches, teas, and muffins. She could drop in one of her hand-sewn lavender sachets encouraging soothing thoughts, sweet dreams, and smooth sailing through life. She could drive him home and make him promise to call her in the morning.

And left to her own devices, she could walk straight into the iced-over bay.

Abby took a deep breath and rubbed her forefinger against her thumb, skin-on-skin friction loud enough to hear. She shook her head, and brushed Charlie's hair from his eyes. Her fingers wove into his hair, thick and silky, and boyish, just like the rest of him.

Charlie's eyelids drifted to half-moons. He edged closer, his gaze lighted on her lips. His shadow fell across her vision.

She turned her head, and Charlie's lips brushed her cheek.

Abby hadn't lied to Celeste. She wasn't about to invite Charlie to move back into her home or her heart.

"Okay," Charlie said, and he sounded not like himself, strangled and small and unsure. "Okay," he repeated, and a sob muffled his voice.

"Shh, shh, shh." Abby hugged him close, wrapped her arms around his waist, slid her hands along his perspiration-moist lower back.

Abby hadn't lied to Celeste. But she hadn't told Celeste the truth either. She couldn't send Charlie on his way.

She didn't trust herself to be alone.

Abby's hands shook, her fingers numb at the tips, as though ice shards had jammed beneath her nails. She closed her eyes, absorbed the shock of Charlie's sobs. And then a different sensation rippled through her. Charlie's stomach rumbled, growled, convulsed, but not in laughter.

Charlie jerked away from her. He slammed his hands on the dining table, hung his head, and retched into a discarded soup bowl.

Three fingers of Scotch could do that to you, too.

"Sorry, Abby," he croaked. "Sorry."

She took him by the hand and led him from the dining room, past the library, and down the hallway to one of her vacant guest rooms. She sat him down on the bed, wriggled off his shoes, plumped the pillows beneath his head. She made him down two ibuprofens and laid an ice-water-soaked washcloth across his fevered forehead.

Abby hummed under her breath, the way Sadie sometimes purred to comfort herself. But her fingers were no longer shaking. Her breathing came even, the air flowing unobstructed for the first time in days. Focusing on Charlie had taken the edge off her pain. Way healthier than walking into the frozen bay.

Charlie's eyes drifted shut, blond lashes settling against the curves of his cheeks. His breathing softened. His chest rose and fell beneath the quilt's wedding ring pattern. Abby pressed her mouth to the warm pulse of Charlie's temple, the way she used to kiss Luke good night.

I want my son back.

The backs of her knees spasmed, and her legs went out. She leaned against the bed.

On the day Luke was born, she'd reached between her legs and placed her hands on the top of his head, so he'd feel her touch when he took his first breath. So he'd never be alone. She'd once told Luke that someday, in the impossible distant future, when she was old and gray, she wanted him to hold her hand when she breathed her last.

Yet she'd been miles away from her baby when, alone, he'd fallen. And she hadn't even known. She hadn't felt a thing.

Fully clothed, she turned down the quilt, slid in on top of the blanket, and switched off the lamp. She crossed her arms. In the dark, her teeth chattered. Beside her, Charlie snored. She got up on one elbow and set a pillow between them, in case Charlie woke in the night with renewed energy and the wrong idea.

As if sex were the only way Charlie could get to her.

Charlie was to Abby as partying with the boys, poor investments, and broken promises were to Charlie.

Oh, holy hell. Celeste was right.

Abby was going to hate herself in the morning.

Chapter 2

Rob Campbell refused to look at Bella's dog run.

Instead, he backed his truck into the driveway that was no longer his driveway, jogged up the no-longer-his walkway, and fumbled for the key he'd returned to Maria back in February. Then, remembering, he cursed and rang the bell. The beautiful woman who was no longer his wife opened the door. "It's time," she said, and stepped back to let him pass.

Inside the Victorian's formal entryway, he gave his spring-muddy boots a cursory stomp on the mat, but didn't bother taking them off. He wouldn't be staying long.

"How's she doing?"

"Hardly ate yesterday, trouble sleeping last night, kept waking up howling." Maria's bottom lip trembled.

He held up his hands. "Wait a second. What's this 'hardly ate'? I thought you said she didn't eat. A bad day doesn't translate to 'it's time.'" When two people loved each other, a bad day didn't mean you should get a divorce either. Campbells never gave up. Too bad his ex-wife didn't share his born-and-bred philosophy.

Maria sighed and shook her head, her gaze weary, yet determined. "Not one bad day, many bad days. Can't remember what a good day looks like anymore."

He could.

Coming home after dark had never bothered him. He liked finding his way to the front door by the post light, the satisfaction of creating one of his landscape designs giving him a natural high. The ache of hard work humming through his muscles. Bone-tired, he liked bounding up the stairs, climbing into bed, and finding his college sweetheart, Maria, by his side.

Pretty much summed up Maria's reasons for divorcing him.

Tears shone on the tips of her lashes. Rob jammed his hands in his pockets to quell the urge to brush them away. No longer his wife.

"You promised. We're not putting her through a third round of chemo. We're not prolonging her suffering."

"I know what I said." He also knew Maria had fought him on the first two rounds, each yielding months-long remissions.

"Where's the old girl?" he said, expecting Maria to head into the kitchen, where Bella's flowered doggie bed sat next to her food and water bowls for easy access.

Maria let out a laugh and angled her chin toward the stairway.

"Grace?"

"Yeah, couldn't stop her. Freakishly strong, like her father." Maria sliced her face away from him and started up the stairs, as though she were embarrassed by the expression's association with Rob. Pride in their daughter was a given.

"Hope that doesn't earn her a freakishly strong hernia," he said, imagining his eighteen-year-old daughter trudging up the stairs, carrying their seventy-pound golden retriever in her arms like a baby.

Rob followed Maria up the stairway he could navigate in the dark. His hand skimmed the salvaged mahogany banister he'd sanded and buffed until it shone. At the landing, morning filtered through the reclaimed stained glass he installed days after they'd closed on the property. The sunlight cast ruby and gold diamonds against Maria's long dark hair, down the curves of female topography his hands knew by heart. If he reached out to touch her, would she stop him?

After twenty years of marriage, how did you remember to forget?

He walked past Grace's hall-of-fame photo gallery, her favorites in a row. Grace's senior prom photo, his daughter beaming in a frilly blue dress, arm linked with her just-a-friend date. Grace in her various sports team group shots: field hockey, basketball, and track-and-field players Rob knew by name.

And then, right before Grace's closed door, instead of Rob and Maria's eight-by-ten wedding portrait, a giant empty space.

"What the hell?"

Maria flushed and held a hand to her cheek.

Rob brushed his fingers across the lighter-than-the-rest rectangle. "Ought to cover it with one of the graduation photos."

Maria offered him a tight-lipped half smile, the same condolence-laden expression making the rounds in answer to news of their divorce. "You're right." She gave the door a single tap with her knuckles and then turned the knob.

A blast of sour-sick dog odor hit him in the face, and his eyes watered.

Grace sat cross-legged on the floor, wearing jeans, a T-shirt, and unlaced Converses. Same outfit she was wearing last night when he'd taken her out for Chinese. Grace's dark hair fell around her shoulders; Bella's face lay in her lap. The old dog opened her eyes. Her brown gaze trained on Rob, as if she'd chosen him from all other humans, same as the day he'd taken her home curled on his lap.

Rob knelt on one knee, offered Bella his hand. "Hey, girl, how you doing?"

"She seems real sad." His daughter's shadowed eyes told him she was speaking about herself as much as their dog.

Worst feeling in the world.

Rob nodded and stroked Bella's head. He thought of the day he'd handed the warm bundle to Grace, the joy in her six-year-old eyes.

Best feeling in the world.

Rob breathed through his mouth. "Call the vet?" he asked Maria.

Maria leaned against the doorway, arms crossed. She chewed her bottom lip, a nervous habit that had worn away the center pigment. Any other day, lipstick would've covered the blank spot. "He's waiting for you."

Grace's mouth fell open. She shook her head, a subtle side-to-side motion, hinting at the horror of understanding. "No." She clutched Bella, and the dog's forelegs splayed beneath her. A yip scratched from Bella's throat.

Rob tilted his head, peered beneath Grace's hair. "Shh, it's okay. Don't scare her." Grace pumped her lips between her teeth. Rob lowered his voice to a whisper. "If we're calm, Bella's calm. Isn't that right?" Bella rewarded him by licking his hand. "There you go."

Grace's eyes turned glassy with unshed tears, and she nodded.

A picture of Rob's mother flashed before him, Dad taking her by the hand for her last trip to the hospital. "No worries," Rob had promised his mother. "Maria and I will watch out for Dad while you're gone," he'd said, even though everyone—Mom included—had known she wouldn't be returning. Not sure whether the lie had made leaving easier for his mother or those left behind.

Rob eased his hands under Bella's belly, scooped her up. The dog's ribs pressed against his chest, her heartbeat *lub-dubbed* through him, and she let him take her down the stairway.

At the open door, Rob turned, intending to ask Maria and Grace whether they were coming with him. Instead, Grace lifted her house keys from the hook, and Maria scrambled up the stairway, leaving him to deal with the mess. He didn't mind. But he suspected their daughter secretly wanted both parents along for this heartbreak. Grace couldn't hold a grudge forever.

Eight minutes later, Rob and Grace were sitting side by side in the vet's waiting room with Bella at their feet. The dog sat to Rob's left, the way he'd trained her. The reason she'd graduated first in her class, same as Grace. A bitter knot tickled the back of Rob's throat, and he coughed to dislodge it.

Grace stiffened and sucked in a breath, removing all the air in the room. Rob's heart hammered, trying to escape through his ears.

Last chance, last chance, last chance.

They were doing the right thing. They were putting an end to the suffering.

Same melodramatic reason Maria had given him for wanting a divorce.

Grace swiped at a tear, and her hand jazzed across her cheek. She rested her hand on Bella's head. Rob placed his hand on Grace's, and their hands rode the waves of Bella's breath, their dog comforting them.

Rob remembered the first time Grace had strode into the vet's office with Bella in her gangly six-year-old arms and deposited the pup on the metal examining table, proud as a new parent. "Dr. Anderson, look at my puppy!"

Thing was, when Rob looked at Bella, he still expected to see an eight-pound bundle. When he gazed at his daughter, he expected a little girl.

Rob had brought Bella home, ostensibly as a present for Grace. At the time, he'd thought Maria needed the puppy more. She'd wanted to have another baby, about four years after he'd given up trying to convince her. For a while the puppy had worked, and Maria had seemed content. She hadn't complained. He hadn't looked for trouble.

Grace's face paled under the fluorescent lights.

"You okay?" Rob asked.

Grace nodded, but she didn't answer.

Rob's legs stiffened, as if he'd been kneeling, setting pavers and plantings from sunup to sundown. He stroked the dog's back, avoiding her sensitive patches. By the time he'd noticed a swelling in Bella's neck, the cancer had already migrated to her bones.

Silent, insidious killer.

Grace gave Bella a kiss on her head.

Hammering in Rob's ears, hammering through his chest. His whole body ached with warning.

Last chance, last chance, last chance.

Rob's fierce-on-the-field girl struggled to maintain her composure. Her teeth chattered. Grace rubbed the dog's ear, and Bella sighed.

Rob stroked the length of Bella's back, warm beneath his sweaty-cold hands. He took hold of Grace's right hand, and his daughter squeezed. Freakishly strong, just like her father.

Crazy, but Rob silently asked Mom to look out for his dog, as if Bella were headed for an eternity catching Frisbees and chasing seagulls along a dog-friendly beach. Power of suggestion, the hammering in his ears softened. He inhaled through his nose, deep and measured.

Through Grace's long hair, the tips of her ears glowed red. She rubbed Bella's ear, squeezed Rob's hand.

Good-bye, old girl.

"Do you think she knows I love her?" Grace said.

"Oh, yeah. She knows. She definitely knows."

Grace's right foot shook. The reverberations trembled against Rob's chair, up through his body, tingled the chords of his neck.

"Do you think she's scared?"

"No, sweetheart, she's not scared."

"Do you think—?" Dr. Anderson's vet tech angled in the door between the waiting room and the hallway to the examining rooms.

Rob and Grace startled, exchanged a look.

The vet tech tucked her short blond hair behind one ear. Rob caught her eye, and her expression morphed: open and curious, glad to see you, sorry to hear the news.

Story of his life.

Rob stood and turned to Grace. "You coming?"

Grace shook her head. She examined the vinyl flooring. Her right leg trembled, but her left foot pointed toward the door to the examining rooms.

"Sure?" he said. "I think you'll regret it if you don't. I think you'll wish you had," he said, borrowing the theme from his daughter's valedictorian address.

Less than a week ago, he and Maria had sat next to each other in a row of sticky plastic folding chairs strung across the Morse High School football field and listened to their amazing daughter urge her classmates to dream big, no regrets. According to Grace, a boy who graduated last year from Hidden Harbor High, one town away from Bath, had inspired her speech. Kid had lived his whole life in Hidden Harbor and then died tragically over the winter in western Massachusetts, a freshman in college.

Among the clamor of applause, ladies dug in their purses for tissues and men cleared their throats. Even Rob, a transplant from New Hampshire, had taken a moment to glance to the sky and thank God for his good fortune.

He couldn't think of anything worse than losing a child.

Bella may not be human—he sometimes wondered—but she was a member of their family.

At least he and his daughter could be with Bella at the moment of her passing. At least they had the choice.

Grace raised her gaze to Rob and stood. "Okay." She nodded, chewed at her lip, same spot Maria had worried to white. "I'll come in, for Bella."

"All right, then." A turn of his left hand, and Bella stood. Head held high, she strode through the doors. The vet tech gave Rob a pulled-across-the-face smile, and he passed before her brown scrubs, cartoon drawings of cheerful cats leaping over flowers with fat petals.

He was not a fan of cats.

The vet tech handed Rob her clipboard. "Some papers for you to sign," she said.

Without reading a word, he scrawled his signature, agreeing to the euthanasia of his dog. A few months ago, he'd signed a similar paper to dissolve his marriage. Same as before, he tried to wrap his mind around what was happening, but couldn't get a handhold.

The vet tech took the clipboard and led them down the hall.

Rob placed his open hand against Grace's back—sticky and throbbing with heat—and they followed.

He wished he could make this hurt all better. Wished he could take away the pain of losing Bella. He was really going to miss their sweetheart of a dog.

And in the fall, his sweetheart girl was headed to Plymouth State. He was really going to miss her, too.

Rob's mind trundled to an argument with Maria, one of their many disagreements.

She'd claimed his work was the only thing he cared about.

Wasn't true then, wasn't true now.

Yet, after Maria had served him with the divorce papers, he'd tossed a mattress into the bed of his truck and headed to his office, a second-floor walk-up in town. A couple of rooms above a bakery suited him just fine. Every morning, he woke to the smell of coffee and muffins wafting through the floorboards. And in the moment before he opened his eyes, he imagined he was home. Maria and Grace making breakfast in the kitchen. Bella darting around their legs. He imagined the footfalls in the shop below were the sounds of Maria headed up the staircase to bring him coffee in bed. Because after twenty years of marriage, they were still like two kids, crazy in love.

The last part always jolted him to reality.

Then he'd open his eyes, take in the bare walls, his mattress squeezed beside a bank of filing cabinets. He'd peer out to the main office. Monitor and keyboard sitting on a yard-sale-find desk he'd refinished, drafting table he'd had since college. He'd remind himself he should talk to Maria about putting their dream house on the market. And he'd wonder what the hell had happened. What came next? Because everything he'd worked for, everything he cared about, was either slipping away from him or already gone.

The vet tech headed past the open examining room door.

Inside, Dr. Anderson was waiting for them.

Last chance, last chance, last chance.

The door clicked shut.

CHAPTER 3

Abby resented Celeste's blueberry muffins.

Third try in a row, Abby set her index finger at the beginning of her newly acquired desk toy, a two-sided sand labyrinth she'd casually admired at Lily Beth's shop, Heart Stone, and then purchased on a whim. She pushed her finger through the grit of sand along a winding path that thus far had fallen short of the promise to quiet her mind.

She needed something bigger to move her whole stressed-out body through.

Who was Celeste to say she should distance herself from Charlie? Abby couldn't tell him to stop calling her every night and take away his touchstone of comfort. Charlie would always be Luke's father; she would always be Luke's mother. She shouldn't have to explain herself to Celeste. Caring for Charlie had kept her semi-sane for the last four months.

Abby's index finger jostled from the labyrinth path, spilling sand onto her desk. She sighed and swept the spilled sand back onto the toy. Peace was highly overrated. Unfortunately, Celeste's prize-winning muffins deserved every ounce of praise that had earned their starred spot on Abby's breakfast menu. Also unfortunate, the fact Abby had let Hannah, the chambermaid she usually sent for the muffins, leave early.

Abby slid her feet back into her sandals and took her straw tote down from its hook. Within the last hour, she'd checked her favorite couple, the Sanchezes, into Room 3, made dinner reservations for the sisters in 5, dismissed Hannah, and completed most of the preparations for tomorrow's continental breakfast.

That left one more task before she could walk into town.

Outside, Abby breathed in the remains of the day. The heady warmth of the lowering sun baked the recently mowed grass. Sharp green notes accented the subtle scents of the sea. And the newly blossomed lupine—purple and blue cones—waved from the perennial bed.

Luke had thought the lupine smelled like grape soda.

She sat on her heels, smoothed her skirt, skipped her fingers across the first two handprint stepping-stones. If any of her guests glanced out a window, they'd see only the back of her head. If anyone strolled outside, it would seem she was gazing past the yard and across the bay, lost in prayer. Close enough to the truth.

Abby lowered her hands to the third stepping-stone and settled her fingers into Luke's sun-warmed handprints, the end of his life's short path. The dry skin of the stone roughed her fingertips. Before her, the waves tapped the shore. Farther off, a bell buoy clanked. The high call of children's voices drifted from across the neighboring peninsula. She marveled how much bigger her son's hands were than hers, how much stronger they'd been. When she closed her eyes and tilted her chin to the sun, she imagined Luke's warmth bathed her face.

"You're back home now," she said. "Back home for the summer. Probably, you're staying out too late and making me worry." She laughed. "I know you're making me worry."

She let the sentence vibrate in the air before her until she could taste the bittersweet memories from last summer. Luke had one foot in Hidden Harbor, the other jutting into the future. He'd spent his free days with his buddies, playing volleyball on Head Beach, hiking over the sharp edges of Breakwater Point, and jumping into the high-tide thrill of the Bath Tub. Nights, he'd stayed out hours past curfew and returned home smelling of beer and bonfires, his pockets lined with girls' phone numbers Abby would later discover in the wash. "But then you apologize. You kiss me on the cheek. You work extra hard weeding and mowing, anything I ask. And even though I want to get angry—"

Her fingers trembled, lifted from the print. Her hands fisted atop the stone. The side of her forefinger rubbed the flesh of her thumb. "I can't stay mad at you," she whispered.

Abby opened her eyes and blinked against the light. She brushed off her skirt and turned to find her guests out on their balcony. Greg Sanchez stood behind his wife, Jenny, his hands wrapped around her waist; his face rested in the crook of her neck.

Abby's heart startled at the sight. The beautiful, perfect sight. She raised a hand in greeting, slow, tentative, not wanting to interrupt the couple's perpetual honeymoon. Ongoing for five years straight.

Jenny waved back. "Thank you for the beautiful flowers!" she called across the yard.

"My pleasure!" In addition to the lupine, the small perennial garden included day lilies, irises, violets, and lavender for drying. The snow-white beach roses transplanted from her childhood home had given the Briar Rose B&B its name. Pretty to look at, but not enough for a cutting garden.

As a thank-you for all of her referrals, Blossoms by the Beach gifted Abby with a few free arrangements a year. Abby loved sharing with the couple who'd first come to her bed-and-breakfast as newlyweds and returned the same weekend every year, as predictable as her lupine. She'd taken extra care with the suite, arranged a dozen white peonies in a cut-glass vase, washed the windows with vinegar and newspaper, spritzed her softest sheets with homemade lavender mist.

"No one gets out of this life without a little wear and tear," Lily Beth often said.

Abby hoped that wasn't true. Others' misfortune didn't ease her sorrow. The fringe benefit of working in hospitality was that she got to both augment and share other people's happiness. And her guests had no clue about her life.

How perfect was that?

Abby race-walked through the yard and down the driveway. Her sandals bit into the pea-stone drive with ferocity she didn't understand. Gravel flew in her wake. She turned down Ocean Boulevard, arms pumping, scooting to avoid the poison ivy edging the sidewalk.

Less than ten minutes later, she stood in the shade beneath the awning at Sugarcoated, her reflection screaming at her like a madwoman. Wrinkles filigreed her filmy white skirt. Most of her hair had escaped from a once-tidy ponytail. And a blond halo frizzed around her face. She wrangled her hair, steeled herself for Celeste's green-eyed disapproval, and pushed into the near-empty bakery.

Above her head, the door-top bell jingled. The smell of fresh-every-half-an-hour coffee and hot-from-the-oven pastries, and the toffee-colored walls wrapped Abby like a warm hug, direct from Celeste. Softened her, despite not wanting to be softened.

A dark-haired man sat at a table with his back to Abby, looking too tall for the bistro table and chair. He leaned against the wrought-iron chair back. Long, denim-clad legs stretched to the side of the table, crossed at the ankles. A laptop stood open and angled sideways, away from Abby's line of vision. The man gestured. His hand, held palm up, sliced the air, as though someone were sitting in the empty seat across from him. A laugh, deep and un-self-conscious, had Abby thinking of thick woods and privacy, the amber tones of maple syrup, the intimacy of familiars.

A slight turn of the man's head revealed a curve to the side of his mouth, his face creased in a grin. A flash of blue eye directed affection toward the empty chair. "How much stuff are you planning on taking with you?" he asked. "Far as I can remember, they do have stores in New Hampshire."

Abby's sandals tapped across the wooden floorboards. The man turned his head fully in her direction, as though responding to the sound. He caught Abby's gaze, and his chin lifted. Half a nod, as if in greeting, although she didn't think she'd met him before.

Good-looking man a few years older than her with energy that reached across the room. No, she would've remembered meeting him. Even in her Luke-obsessed world—a state strangely similar to new motherhood—she would've remembered.

The man touched a finger to his ear, a half cringe of explanation, and Abby smiled. Earbuds and a wire. Skype. She should've guessed.

"Gracie girl," the man said, his gaze still trained on Abby. "Yeah, you're a goofball. You get it from your dad." He was speaking to his daughter—gentle, teasing, self-deprecating sense of humor. One of the ideal-guy qualities Abby had once written on a wine-fueled, Celeste-encouraged list.

Top of the page.

Abby dropped her gaze. Her heart pounded in her belly, hollow and echoing. She window-shopped the contents of the pastry case she could recite in her sleep, ran a fingertip along the heat of the lighted glass. Apricot-glazed fruit tarts, caramel-topped cheesecake cups, and powdered sugar-dusted cannoli watered her mouth. But when she swallowed, maple syrup flavored her tongue.

The man chuckled. "Okay, all right already. See you tomorrow." He lowered his voice. "Love you, too."

An image of Luke rose up and crashed over her like a rogue wave and squeezed the air from her lungs. Over the past four months she'd discovered the course of grief was unpredictable, random, and completely unfair. One minute she could be chatting with a guest over a plate of Belgian waffles and discussing the difference between organic and free-range eggs; the next she'd have to casually excuse herself, feigning the need to check on something, anything, in the kitchen.

If only she had a Skype connection to her son.

"That was embarrassing," the man said.

A buzz of warning trickled up the back of her head, as though the stranger had seen inside her and called out her pain.

Abby slipped on her innkeeper face, stepped forward. She squared her shoulders and offered her hand. "Abby Stone," she said. "I didn't mean to eavesdrop."

The man stood, all six foot something of him, and took her hand in his. Grip firm, but not crushing. Grin genuine and glad to meet her. His bright blue eyes shot her full of light and made her throat ache.

The first time in months she'd felt alive.

"Rob Campbell," he said. "I didn't realize anyone was hanging in the eaves."

She laughed, and his light pulsed through her chest.

"Care to sit down? My imaginary friend went home."

"Oh, uh, I was just waiting for Celeste," she said, gesturing toward the kitchen. Which must've sounded insane.

"Celeste's in back making coffee for me. My usual evening cup of decaf."

Usual evening decaf? As opposed to his regular morning cup of caffeinated brew? The name Campbell sounded familiar, but she didn't think Celeste had mentioned him before.

Abby's gaze wandered to Rob's laptop, open to a series of three-dimensional technical drawings.

"I'm working on a labyrinth for the elementary school,"

he said, and the technical drawings clarified into the mazelike pathways she'd navigated with her desk toy. Until a few days ago, she hadn't paid much attention to labyrinths. Now, they were popping up everywhere. "Celeste got me the gig."

In Celeste's spare time, she was president of the elementary school PTO; it proved the saying, if you want to get something done, give it to the busy person. Had Celeste mentioned a labyrinth project for the school? Abby hated to think Celeste had shared this with her and she hadn't paid attention.

Worse, she hated to think Celeste had deemed her so overwrought she hadn't bothered to share in the first place.

Abby's desk labyrinth had attracted her with images on the box of full-scale versions of a formal park in Barcelona, and the casual grounds of Kripalu, a yoga and health center in Lenox, Massachusetts. But she hadn't considered an in-between version, small enough to fit into the limited acreage of the Hidden Harbor Elementary schoolyard.

Or the backyard of Briar Rose.

"You a fan of labyrinths?"

"You know what? I think I am. I own a bed-and-breakfast, Briar Rose, and I'd like to put a labyrinth in the backyard," she said, deciding right there and then. The idea of a grand project that required envisioning and planning simultaneously filled her empty spaces and lightened her. Free time was her enemy. Not that she had much of that.

"What kind of scale are we talking about?" Rob pulled a chair out for her, and Abby lowered herself to the seat. He angled his laptop in her direction, and sat down beside her, close enough for her to inhale the just-showered clean menthol smell of his skin. Close enough for her to notice a tiny star-shaped scar beside his right eye and imagine pressing her lips against its raised surface. "This here is a simple three-circuit design I'm working on for the school. They've about an eighth of an acre to work with, give or take. How much open land do you have to play with?"

Abby pictured her perennials, Luke's stepping-stones, and the flat green expanse that dropped into the ocean. Maples and pines covered the rest of her property. "About a quarter acre," she said. "Give or take."

Rob rubbed a finger against the center of his chin. "You could easily fit seven circuits. What kind of materials are you interested in? A grassy path with plantings? A stone walkway? Any sort of theme?" His passion for his work drew her closer.

Abby shook her head, grinned. "I haven't really thought about it."

"The elementary school's labyrinth is also a butterfly garden," Rob added.

Butterfly garden, thank goodness. That project Celeste had mentioned.

Celeste came out from the back, carrying a stainless-steel coffee dispenser. She wore a blue cupcake-covered apron and matching handkerchief. Her son and daughter trailed behind her. Four-year-old Phoebe, wearing a miniature version of her mother's apron, shot across the café. Abby grinned, eager to catch her wild-haired goddaughter in her arms. But then the tiny firecracker leaped onto Rob's lap and landed with a thud that sent a flutter to Abby's throat.

Ever since Luke had died, Celeste had worried spending time with her seven-year-old son, Elijah, would be too hard on Abby. But sometimes what you'd never have hurt more than what you'd lost.

Celeste nodded at Abby and Rob, and her gaze narrowed. A flicker of a smirk, and Celeste turned to place the carafe on the counter. Elijah stocked the coffee lid dispenser, reminding Abby of how Luke used to love helping her set up for breakfast buffet.

The always-cautious Elijah waited for Abby to wave to him before he came over to Abby and gave her a slender-armed hug. Celeste often wondered aloud whether she'd given birth to a little old man, but in some ways her dark-haired son was more like her than her daughter. He noticed everything. Abby hugged Elijah back, breathed in his damp-necked little-boy scent. Remembering hurt, but forgetting was even worse.

Rob bounced Phoebe on his knee. She clutched his shirt and squealed with laughter.

Good with kids. Another fine quality on Abby's ideal-guy list.

Celeste wiped her hands on her apron, poured and capped a large decaf, and delivered the coffee to Rob. "I see you've met my new old neighbor," she said to Abby.

"Hey," he said. "I'm not that old." He aimed a teasing smile at Celeste, and Celeste returned the favor.

A pang ran through Abby, as if she were some teenage girl who'd laid claim. As if she and Celeste were in a competition for Rob's attention. Irrational, since Celeste was happily married and her business-friendly banter shouldn't bother Abby.

These days, Celeste and Charlie were competing for Abby's attention.

"Rob liked his office upstairs so much he decided to move in full time," Celeste said.

"Can't beat blueberry muffins every morning for breakfast. Thanks to Celeste, I think I've gained ten pounds." Rob patted his belly, conspicuously flat beneath his fitted T-shirt. Phoebe slid from his lap, and Celeste lifted her onto her hip.

"You live upstairs?" Abby said. "Is that even legal? It's zoned commercial." Really, she'd no idea, but Rob inspired teasing. "I could turn you in. I could have you arrested." She could enact a citizen's arrest and frisk him herself.

Celeste was right. Going without sex made you think

crazy thoughts. But after the last time Abby had allowed a man in her bedroom, she'd vowed to padlock the door.

"Why do you think Celeste's getting a deal with the PTO project?" Rob asked.

"Don't let him fool you," Celeste said, a phrase she'd used many times in reference to Charlie, and Abby tensed. "He donated the time and gave us a deal on materials before he moved in."

"I work for muffins."

"Oh! Muffins! Almost forgot." Abby shook her empty straw tote and turned to Rob. "Excuse us for a moment?"

"Sure thing."

When Celeste started across the room, Phoebe wriggled from her arms and ran behind the counter. Elijah gave Abby's arm a pat, sighed, and followed after his little sister. Celeste was right. Seven going on seventy.

Abby set her tote on the counter's worn butcher block, and Celeste dashed behind the glass bakery case. "Hannah told me last night you'd be coming by for her," Celeste said.

"She hadn't even asked me yet!" A mere two hours ago, Hannah had leaned against the doorjamb to Abby's office, sighing with anticipation for her date and their plans to listen to the blues at the Chocolate Church in Bath. Abby doubted the girl knew the difference between blues and jazz, or cared to learn, for that matter. At nineteen, a date was all about the boy.

At any age.

"Hannah knows you're a softie. Besides, how can you deny her one true love?" Celeste wove her fingers together and pumped them back and forth, heart beating out of her chest.

"You mean her boyfriend of the week?" Abby said.

"Same difference." Hands inside the bakery case, Celeste scooped muffins into two brown boxes and then secured them with pink-and-white twine. Elijah fit his hands over Phoebe's and helped her cut the twine with the heavy-duty scissors.

"Why, thank you," Abby said, and dropped the boxes into her tote.

Celeste leaned across the counter, lowered her voice to girlfriend-personal. "Talk to Charlie last night?"

Abby's shoulders ached, as though Celeste and Charlie were engaged in a tug-of-war and she were the rope.

What was so wrong with Charlie calling to check in? Their son had died. Abby both looked forward to and dreaded the day when the hard truth of their loss ceased to color their every breath. Sometimes she and Celeste had to agree to disagree, but arguing with Celeste drained her. "You're not the boss of me, sistah."

"You're right. I'm not the boss of you. Charlie is."

Abby blew out through her lips. "Now, I know you don't mean that." Abby held Celeste's gaze. In the periphery, Elijah handed Phoebe a picture book, and then sat down beside her with the hardcover copy of *Harry Potter and the Sorcerer's Stone* Abby had given him on his birthday.

Celeste blinked first. "I'll call you later," she said, and kneeled to straighten a line of perfectly straight rum balls. As much as Abby hated being at an impasse with Celeste, Celeste hated it even more.

Abby nodded and went over to Rob. "Very nice to meet you."

"Same here," he said.

Abby headed for the door.

"Abby," Rob said, and she liked the way her name sounded sweet and sure coming from his lips, as though he'd known her forever. "If you need an architect for that labyrinth project . . ."

Her landscaping skills were amateurish at best. But as far as hiring a professional, did she really have the funds? What with Luke's—

She was no longer helping her son pay for tuition, room, and board. No college, no future, no Luke.

Her baby was gone.

Her eyes misted, and she drew her mouth into a grin to ward off the railing in her head. Unpredictable, random, and completely unfair.

"Do you have a card?"

Rob dug a business card from his laptop case and held it out to her. She read the inscription's crisp lettering: CAMPBELL LANDSCAPE DESIGN. Nothing flowery. Direct and to the point.

"I can come by to take a look at the site you have in mind, get started on a plan, work up an estimate."

Abby nodded, hoped he didn't notice the slight tremble to her bottom lip. "When?" she said, thinking of her office computer and the calendar she lived by, her endless scheduled hours.

"Now works for me."

"Now?" She admired Rob's fast talking, his not wanting to lose potential business. She got that. But she couldn't help but wonder whether the trait carried through to his personal life. Not that she minded, exactly. She flicked her gaze to his bare-of-a-band ring finger. That meant nothing. Some men worried about getting their rings caught while working with their hands. Some worried about getting caught, period.

Rob probably didn't have a wife squirreled away above the bakery. What he more likely had was baggage, like the rest of mankind.

"I don't want to steal you away from Celeste."

"I believe we're done for today," he said loud enough for Celeste to hear.

Celeste popped up from behind a pastry case. "Oh, yeah. I'm done with you," she said, infusing her words with a playful lilt.

Once again, that irrational pang of girlhood competition hit home.

Rob Campbell traveled light.

The walk back to Briar Rose passed more quickly than

Abby's lone walk into town, as if the half mile had shortened in her absence. A gentleman, Rob walked on the poison ivy side of the walkway. He carried a legal pad in one hand, a pencil in his back pocket. All he'd claimed he needed for an initial sketch of the labyrinth site. The laptop, he'd run up to his apartment. The coffee, he'd forgotten at Celeste's.

"This is it," Abby said, gazing from the backyard of Briar Rose out to the ocean. The sun set low in the sky, a pretty pink ball lowering itself into the water and forecasting another hot-for-June day.

"Wow. I wouldn't even need to regrade." Rob's face glowed, as if he'd swallowed the sun. "Mind if I do a little exploring?"

Abby sat on the grass, one hand resting against Luke's third stepping-stone, the warmth evaporating with the day. Rob set down the legal pad, paced with his long-legged stride. He whistled to himself, totally comfortable in his work, and completely off-key. Seven times he circled before her, seven circuits to a classic labyrinth, seven passes in front of Luke's stepping-stones.

"Huh," Rob said, and plunked himself down on the brink of her personal space, arms slung over his knees. His nearness tingled her cheeks with warmth, tightened her throat, tweaked her pulse. He picked up the legal pad and slid a pencil from his back pocket. "First up, I always ask my clients their goals for the project. So . . . Abby, what do you want from the labyrinth? What sort of experience?"

"For real?" she said, because what kind of a man asked you what you wanted and then took notes?

Rob shot her a high-cheeked grin with a twinge of mischief. "Why not?"

She shook her head, thought of her hopes for the desk toy, the sand flung on the floor, the frisson of energy trapped in her body. "Peace." She took a breath to shore up the unexpected ache in her voice. Flip of the switch, she revised her focus, and the constriction in her throat eased. "A mind-quieting peaceful place for my guests to relax," she said, as though she had no needs of her own. As though her grief weren't lurking a fingernail's scratch beneath her skin. "A feature that would enhance their stay."

Rob touched her shoulder, waited until she looked him in the eye. "No, Abby. What do *you* want?"

Her vision blurred, like gazing through privacy glass. Without thinking, she reached down to the stepping-stone, slid a finger across Luke's name.

Rob followed her gaze, read the inscription. "Luke Connors is your son?" he said, and she nodded.

"We could easily work the stepping-stones into the design. Is Luke eighteen now? My daughter, Grace, is eighteen. You know, my imaginary friend? Did Luke graduate this year? Luke Connors from Hidden Harbor. The name sounds familiar." He tapped pencil against paper, chuckled. "I thought the name—"

"Last year," she blurted out. "Luke graduated last year."

Abby watched the realization settle down on Rob. A crease formed between his brows. His head tilted. She read a flicker of understanding in the slight widening of his eyes, a micro-twitch of his lips, and then, just as fast, the deliberate forced return to a neutral expression. He searched her face, and heat flamed her cheeks. She wished she could disappear.

"Your son," he said, the tone somber, the volume set at one notch above a whisper. "The boy who . . . ?"

She traced the *L* in Luke, down-across-back up, pressed her fingertip into the rough edge until pain shot up her hand. "Passed away."

"I'm so sorry for your loss," he told her, the words you said when there was really nothing more to say. "I can't begin to imagine." His lips twisted, his eyes turned down at the corners.

The look on his face shifted from pity to empathy, as if, in fact, he could understand the vastness of her loss.

A couple of years ago, she'd given a talk at her local B&B association about chatting with guests. No Debbie Downers, positive spin, and for heaven's sake, lighten up. They're on vacation. She straightened, cleared her throat, and willed her tone to strengthen. "Tell me about your daughter, Grace, your recent graduate. Is she going away to college? I believe I heard you say something about taking stuff with her . . ."

Rob gave her a sideways look, and his mouth clenched. Unsure whether he should allow her to change the subject or relieved? "Going to Plymouth State to study outdoor ed. My little girl wants to be a forest ranger." Rob took on the same loving tone as when he'd spoken to his daughter at the bakery, and his gaze relaxed. Abby's hand splayed against the steppingstone. "Totally my fault," he added.

"You sound like a proud papa gearing up for day trips to New Hampshire. White Mountain National Forest, right? Planning on bagging a few peaks?"

"You know it."

"Moosilauke, Liberty, Franconia Ridge," she rattled off, another innkeeper fringe benefit. If you paid attention to your guests, you learned about people and places vastly different from your world. And added to your really long bucket list.

"Oh, yeah, Franconia Ridge. Incredible views. Stayed at the Greenleaf hut with Grace and her mother. Long time ago." He swung his pencil above the legal pad, batting the air. "Anyway. The labyrinth." He gave his head a slight shake, as if to clear the memory. "Where were we? Goals for the project!" With a flick of the wrist, he tapped the paper three times with his pencil. "Give me a minute," he said, and a shiver laced her shoulders.

Rob glanced out to the bay, the day melting into the ocean. He let out a breath, nodded, scratched pencil against paper.

"Every design tells a story, conveys a theme with subtle details. What do you say, Abby?" Rob turned the legal pad in her direction so she could read the side-by-side words: *Peace* and *Luke.*

"Is this what you want?" he said.

More than anything.

She skirted his gaze, swallowed, studied the lupine. The sturdy purple cones pointing to the sky would wither by summer's end. Day in, day out, she served breakfast to bleary-eyed guests, taking into account half-a-dozen different dietary restrictions, their random preferences. She answered the phone and made reservations with a smile in her voice. She laundered white cotton sheets, ran her hands across the smooth heated fabric, warmth missing from her own life. The two-sided longing never left her. And yet no one saw. No one saw her.

Peace and Luke.

She raised her gaze to Rob's. He'd never looked away.

The ability to withstand life's storms without flinching earned Rob a third check for Abby's ideal-guy list.

Did he see that, too? "Where do we start?" she asked.

Rob patted Luke's stepping-stone, as though inviting her to sit down, take a load off her feet, and settle in for a long stay. "This, right here, is where we begin."

CHAPTER 4

Ever since eighth grade, Tessa Lombardi had always wanted whatever her best friend, Dina, had. Two parents who lived in the same house, slept in the same bed, and never bickered. A mother who gave a shit. A boyfriend who didn't cheat.

For a few short months, she thought she'd finally gotten the boyfriend part right.

Now, Luke was dead, it was all her fault, and her life was over. *Be careful what you wish for.*

It totally pissed Tessa off that one of her mother's favorite sayings had actually come true, like a broken clock, right twice a day.

That was one of her father's favorite sayings.

Tessa swung her legs over the edge of the bed, planted them on the apartment-issue rug, and gazed wide-eyed through a skim of tears. The room appeared magnified, the walls canting, the dresser looming, as though she were swimming through salt water.

Since Luke had been gone, she cried every day, and not just about stuff that made sense either. The endless stream of posts on Luke's Facebook wall did her in. Girls Luke hadn't really known, or cared about, posted dumbass stuff like, *I'm going to wicked miss you,* as if Luke were spending a semester in London and would return in the fall, sporting a cockney accent and a fondness for clotted cream. All the girls who posted were pretty, if you believed their duck-face profile photos, which Tessa did not.

She knew better than anyone how you could put on a different face during the day to trick the world into thinking you were someone other than who you were and then wash it off at night. Luke had known that, too, without needing an ounce of makeup to pull off the prank.

Or maybe she wanted to believe the worst. If she believed the worst, then she wouldn't have to remember all she'd lost.

Tessa waited until her sight cleared and then tiptoed across the bedroom. The apartment was a bargain, as long as management didn't find out they'd crammed two beds and three people into a one-bedroom.

Morning light sneaked through the blinds of the off-campus summer rental and threw flickering leaf patterns across the blue-blanketed mass. Two figures crammed into a single bed no bigger than the twins from the dorms. Dina's linebacker boyfriend, Jon, lay with his broad back to the room. One large hairy leg flung atop the covers and clamped around Dina.

Nestled against Jon's arm, Dina looked like a little girl with her face awash in a golden-glow night-light, rather than a nineteen-year-old sleeping off strains of last night's birthday beer bash. Dina's hands clasped together beneath her chin, and she sighed, not a care in the world. If only.

In a snap-quick slip of the wrist, Dina-and-Jon and Tessa-and-Luke had become Dina-and-Jon and tagalong Tessa.

Tessa closed the bedroom door behind her. At least Dina and Jon had the decency to sleep, only sleep, when she was in the bedroom.

Since Luke had been gone, Tessa hardly slept at all.

Not due to weekends of staying up late, after-hours dance-till-dawn parties. That used to be her thing. Now, at the end of a beaten-down-tired day, she'd slide into bed early, only to find herself awake again three hours later, Pink Floyd's "Wish You Were Here" playing over and over in her head, Luke haunting her. He'd introduced her to the band, musical taste he'd claimed was handed down from his father. Tessa and Luke had sat on his dorm bed, backs up against the painted brick wall and legs out in front of them, holding hands, at first zoning to the music and then tuning into each other.

Bags of chips gaped open along the coffee table, a dank smell tainted the air, and red plastic cups a quarter filled with beer decorated the kitchen table. Tessa's cup sat at the table's head, her name spelled out in black Sharpie, the beverage completely drained.

Since Luke had been gone, Tessa had lost her taste for beer.

Tessa yanked open the porch slider and stepped into the fresh air. Her hand grasped the wrought-iron railing. "Same shit, different morning," she mumbled.

"Kiss your mother with that mouth?" Dina stood on the cement balcony, her hands jabbed on her hips. Dark-blond hair tumbled around her shoulders, as though she'd arranged it that way. Jon's favorite football T-shirt came to the top of Dina's knees. White letters stood out against the black background. *How do you want to be remembered?*

Tessa tried to glare at Dina before tears sprang to the corners of her eyes.

"Oh, God. Sorry, I'm an idiot."

"You said it," Tessa said, but she'd no fire behind her words. And when Dina came in for a hug, Tessa didn't resist. She never talked about her mother with anyone but Dina, so even a momentary lapse stung. She supposed it wasn't Dina's fault she couldn't relate. She didn't have to rely upon thrice-yearly cards sent from Europe, on Christmas, Easter, and Tessa's birthday, to pinpoint her mother's latest location.

Last birthday, Tessa's mother had thought she'd turned eighteen for the second year in a row.

Jon stumbled into view and tickled Dina from behind, making her jostle against Tessa.

"Quit it," Dina said, batting a hand behind her. Tessa untangled herself from her friend so she wouldn't have to feel Dina let go first.

"Uh, sorry," Jon said, as if he hadn't noticed Tessa, and lumbered into the kitchen. How could she simultaneously be both the talk of the campus and invisible?

"What are you going to do?" Dina asked, same thing she'd been asking Tessa daily.

"I have no clue," Tessa said, and headed for the bathroom with her cell. Behind the door, she reviewed the text from her father, philosophy professor Noah Lombardi, requesting her *presence* for a breakfast date. The message was no small feat considering her father's newest phone was an old-fashioned flip job where every letter required three jabs of the thumb. Tessa tapped in, *ok,* and hit the shower. She must've been desperate to resort to talking to her dad, but what choice did she have? Even she was sick of hearing herself talk to Dina. The same conversation wound in mazelike circles with no way out.

Fifty minutes later, Tessa sat across from her father at Dad's favorite Amherst haunt, Lone Wolf. Midmorning, and the restaurant was packed with students Dad ignored, sprinkled with a few faculty members he acknowledged with a lift of his chin. The din of conversations, the clang of silverware against plates, created a buffer of privacy. The server placed Dad's regular order on the table before him, lox and latkes, his way of remembering his Jewish mother. Tessa's order came next, challah French toast, because she was so hungry she thought she might hurl.

Tessa slathered the toast in butter and drenched it in maple syrup until the sticky liquid pooled around the stack. She shoved the first bite in her mouth, smiled through sweet relief.

Dad took his time, slicing and dicing lox and latkes, and

examining Tessa in preparation for stabbing philosophical inquiry. "Present," he said. Her father's way of asking her to lay out her opposing arguments totally threw her off, since all she could think about was the past and the future.

"I can't do this," she said, and burst into tears over her French toast.

Her father became Professor Lombardi. He tilted his head and blinked at her, as if she were one of his freshmen who'd failed to grasp the basics of debate. The way he chewed his lox—steady and sure—made her want to tear the breakfast from his lips.

He took off his glasses and folded them beside his coffee mug. "Tessa, Tessa, Tessa," he said. "It's a little late for tears, don't you think?" He let out a put-upon sigh. His gaze softened, as if he were about to, for once, talk to her like an adult. "Just like your mother."

That only made her cry harder. Did he honestly think he was being helpful?

"Life is a matter of priorities and proper focus. Your mother's *artistic* attitude"—Dad said, pausing to draw a set of quotes in the air—"doesn't work in the real world. We all have to get up at a certain time, go to a job or school. And when you have a child, he or she is your main priority. I blame myself for thinking your mother was ready for motherhood at twenty-two. Some people's temperaments aren't suited for the job, no matter the age. Simple as that. Stop overthinking. Right now, college should be your priority."

Tessa remembered Dad focusing his nails-on-blackboard logic at her mother in response to Mom's last great rant about needing the richness of foreign soil to grow creativity. Tessa remembered Mom's final summation that her father was heartless.

"Meredith, Meredith, Meredith," Dad had said. "One *can* have everything, just not necessarily at the same time."

What he'd meant was, not necessarily with a husband and a kid.

Her father had met her mother's tirades with calculated logic, her heat with ice.

No wonder Mom had left him. But why did she have to leave Tessa? What had she done wrong?

The last time she'd seen her mother, Mom had stood in the doorway to Tessa's bedroom, her face blotchy with spent tears. Dark eyes shining, she'd offered up her usual bedtime rhyme. "Sleep tight, don't let the bedbugs bite, see you in the morning light," she'd chirped.

"Promise?" Tessa had said, and Mom came to sit on the edge of Tessa's bed. She'd gathered Tessa's hands in hers. She'd looked Tessa in the eye. She'd promised.

She'd promised.

Tessa had never again seen her mother in the light, morning or otherwise.

Dad scrubbed a fist across his close-cropped dark beard, and set down his fork. "Have you registered for fall classes yet?" he asked, as if she had a choice. She could already see him formulating his arguments, his gray gaze drifting from hers, lengthening the distance between them.

Tessa struggled to catch her breath, and then blew her nose in her napkin. "I can't let go of Luke." As if to prove her point, Tessa's throat hugged his name. Her heart beat double time, her body working to resurrect the boy she loved.

Dad raised his gaze to the ceiling, a sure sign of exasperation with emotional displays, immature students, her. "Clean breaks are best. You have a chance to move on, get your degree. No need to compound the tragedy."

Tessa shot her father a questioning look. She knew what he thought about her completing her bachelor's degree in studio art for the express purpose of painting. If she'd no interest in an MFA and a professorship, she might as well have majored in coloring with flat-bottomed Crayolas, building with Legos, and sculpting Play-Doh.

"Take advantage of your opportunities."

"I have an opportunity—"

"To do what? Ruin your life? You're nineteen. I'm not going to support you forever." His gaze bore into her, the x-ray vision of disapproval simultaneously scorning her outer appearance and assuming all of her mother's inner faults. Flighty, impulsive, irresponsible. Tessa had heard them all before. She didn't care to hear them again.

After Luke's death, her father's negative opinion of her had solidified, clay in a kiln. Why bother trying to change it? Heat flushed her hairline. It wasn't her fault she looked like her mother. That much she knew. "Mom was right. You are heartless. I wish she'd taken me with her." Tessa hated the way her voice sounded, thin and pinched and prepubescent, same as the first time she'd hurled the phrase.

Dad didn't even flinch. He never did. Instead, he regarded her over the rim of his coffee, set down the mug, and tapped his napkin twice against his lips. Seeing his nostrils flare wasn't half as thrilling as Tessa had hoped. "Leaving you with me was the only unselfish thing *that woman* has ever done in her life."

So now he thought Tessa was selfish? She couldn't untangle that inside-out logic. The din of background conversation rose; the sharp tone jumbled her insides. Not only had she inherited all her mother's faults, but she'd also managed to sidestep her mother's single crumb of goodness.

Tessa hadn't been willing to forget Luke and move on with her life in February. Why should she do it now? She still loved him. That constant would never change.

When her mother had left, her standoffish father had taken a giant step backward. He'd prepared dinners, where the two of them chewed and swallowed without exchanging a word, and she'd assumed he was angry with her. He'd wished her a good night's sleep, without the benefit of a rhyme or a hug, and she imagined her adolescent development explained Dad's sudden shyness. A year ago, he'd congratulated her on her art scholarship. Yet, last week he'd refused to visit the Herter Gallery, where her painting hung beside her mother's, Professor Meredith Lombardi.

Her father might act as though her mother's leaving hadn't touched him at all, but Tessa knew better. For once, his little act didn't fool her. "I have three choices," she said.

Her father swirled a bite of latke in sour cream, popped it into his mouth, and held up his index finger. He might as well have flipped her off with the middle one instead.

"Luke's mother would understand how I feel," Tessa said, remembering the way Abby had dried her tears at the post-memorial reception, one hand resting on Luke's father's arm. Luke's parents had never married, but Abby still loved Luke's dad. It wicked showed.

Dad shook his head, his slow side-to-side gesture meant to erase the silly misguided thoughts of silly misguided children. "Complications, Tessa. Keep things simple and straightforward."

A laugh burst out of her. Her life had spiraled way beyond *complications* months ago. "Are you freaking kidding me?"

"Language." Dad's eyes jostled from the effort to keep them from flicking around the restaurant. Heaven forbid he looked bad in front of faculty, or worse, his students. One must maintain decorum at all times.

Screw that to hell.

Tessa pushed to standing and yanked her handbag off the chair. She made sure to use her best pronunciation and project across the crowded restaurant sharp enough to slice the heads off conversations. "Sorry, Dad. What I meant to say was, are you *fucking* kidding me?"

Dad's mouth stopped mid-chew, and Tessa headed for the door, expecting her father to chase her out to the sidewalk and convince her to stay. But when she peered through the glass, her father unfolded his glasses and bent his head to study the bill.

Tessa slammed her handbag onto the passenger seat of her car. She considered going back to the apartment to pack. Last time she went out for the morning and returned early, she'd found Jon's baseball cap hanging on the bedroom door. The murmurs and moans from beyond the door would've explained the not-so-subtle symbol, if she hadn't already known. Dina and Jon were going at it. That had only made Tessa miss Luke more.

She'd never again feel Luke move inside her.

Tessa tapped *Recently Found* on her GPS and scrolled back until Briar Rose B&B showed on the screen. She pressed *Go,* and hit the gas.

She thought of the last time she'd seen Luke's mother, the way Abby had gazed straight into Tessa's eyes without any preconceived notions about her flaws or failings. She remembered running to Dina. But in her peripheral vision, she'd noticed Abby starting after her. She imagined Abby embracing her, giving her one of those cheek-to-cheek hugs, the kind that reverberated deep in your bones. The kind that told you that you were special and loved and too precious to leave.

Something shifted inside Tessa, unleashing a hot flood of tears down the sides of her face. She dug into the box of tissues she kept on the passenger seat, came up empty, and flung the box onto the stupid floor.

Since Luke had been gone, Tessa really missed her mother.

In the short span of four weeks, Rob Campbell had figured out how to drive Abby crazy.

He'd taken her to North Creek Farm in Phippsburg to introduce her to his favorite beach rose, a showy strawberry-blond blossom he called Agnes, and Abby could've sworn he was trying to make her jealous.

He brought her to test-drive three different coastal labyrinths. An all-brick patio bordered by formal statuary. A casual sea rope path that meandered through a grove of oak trees. And a grass trail, lined with privet shrubs and unabashedly feminine pink paving stones that shimmered with ocean-reflected sunlight.

Instead of uncovering her particular brand of mind-quieting peace and authentic style, Abby studied the wide expanse of muscles in the sweet valley between Rob's shoulders. She ogled the just-right-uplifted shape of his buttocks, and imagined the round feel of his flesh in either hand. And on post-field-trip nights, she discovered a near-forgotten knot of tension between her legs that scared away sleep.

Without ever having touched her, Abby could've sworn Rob was trying to make her remove her bedroom's virtual padlock, along with every shred of clothing.

Worst of all, on each and every date that wasn't a date, the conversation had meandered from groundcover, paving stones, and statuary, and inexplicably wound around to reveal pieces of their lives. This afternoon's not-a-date lunch had included glasses of sauvignon blanc and lubricated Rob enough to admit that when he'd married his college sweetheart, he'd assumed the union would last forever. And Abby had shared that because she hadn't married her high-school boyfriend, she'd vowed to never again assume.

He wasn't saying, and she wasn't asking, but Abby could've sworn she and Rob were in a relationship.

Rob's double-cab pickup, sporting a *Campbell Landscape Design* decal, crunched into her driveway and parked beside her Toyota single cab, *Briar Rose* looped across the driver's side in cobalt script.

"Well, this was a nice midday distraction from work. Thank you for distracting me."

"The pleasure was all mine," he said. A hint of mischief lit his eyes, and then he dropped his gaze. He tapped the steering wheel, a forefinger drum roll, nodded, and bit his bottom lip. "There's something I'm forgetting . . ."

Finally. She smiled, thinking he was ready to call what they were doing, dating, thinking they would finally end a date with a kiss.

"We need to see what the labyrinth site looks like from inside your house."

"We do?"

"Oh, yeah, it's time." He swiped a notepad from the backseat, and then came around and opened the passenger door.

"But you've seen the view," she said, her voice notched higher, for no reason she could detect.

"Only from the public areas," he said, and understanding prickled the back of her head.

Midweek, she'd asked Rob into the dining room for apple pie and coffee. Last week's excuse was popcorn and a movie in the Briar Rose library.

Since Luke had died, no one—not Charlie, not Celeste, not even Lily Beth—had ventured beyond the public areas of the bed-and-breakfast. No one had asked, as if they sensed she'd erected an invisible fence to keep back the world.

She didn't want to be that person.

"Right this way."

No guests were chatting in the front-of-house sitting area. Casco Bay informational brochures and Maine magazines remained in tidy piles, the way she'd left them earlier. Her display of lavender sachets piled in a large wicker basket on the coffee table before the pineapple-patterned love seat. Beside the basket, the honor bowl contained only the seed money she'd planted. The guest book was open to the most recent entries, thanking her for waffles and fresh fruit, soft sheets and plush bath towels. A silver dinner bell stood beside her leather-bound guest book, a necessary evil for guests checking in to alert her to their presence. On this midsummer mid-Saturday, her rooms were full, and she wasn't expecting any new guests.

Abby slid the wooden pocket door aside to reveal her private living room. She glanced inside, checking for Luke's size eleven sneakers blocking their entry, his cereal bowls with pools of day-old milk, cast-aside beach towels. A couple months after Luke had left for school, she'd gotten away from the habit. But in recent months, the habit had returned. And in that split second of forgetting, she allowed herself to hope.

"Tada!" she said, loud enough to mask the quiver in her voice.

Her gray tabby, Sadie, raised her head from atop a tufted throw pillow on the couch. The cat stared at Rob with her big golden unblinking eyes.

"Don't take Sadie personally. She's shy," Abby said, expecting her cat to dash from the pillow and duck beneath the couch's sheltering skirt.

But when Abby closed the door behind Rob, her shy girl jumped from the couch and made her way across the room, her shoulders rolling, taking her sweet time. She wound around Rob's denim-clad right leg and rubbed the length of her body against him, from the pink triangle of her nose to the dark gray tip of her tail.

Sadie pressed up against Rob's left leg, and her purring vibrated the air. "She likes you. She likes you a lot."

"Looks that way." Rob grinned down at Sadie, but he didn't offer his hand for a sniff or a pat.

"You don't like cats?"

"More of a dog person."

Abby imagined Rob lying on a four-poster bed, play-wrestling with a big dog. A retriever or a husky or a Samoyed, one of those notoriously loyal outdoorsy breeds. Abby imagined Rob lying across her bed, no dogs in sight. She imagined lying on top of him, nose-to-nose, chest-to-chest, and winding her legs around him.

Rob took a step closer, and warmth climbed Abby's neck. "She's marked you with her scent. She owns you now."

"I thought cats were aloof."

"Not this one. Girl's got some definite opinions."

"Not unlike her owner."

And then, right when Rob's gaze held hers and lingered. Right when his hand rose, as though he might touch her hair she'd purposely left down for his touching, a photo on the side table caught Rob's attention. Charlie and three-year-old Luke squishing cheeks, a kind of father-and-son reunion after Charlie's college graduation. Out in the open for years, the photo of Luke barely rattled Abby. But Rob tucked his hand into his pocket, and his face darkened. She'd seen that look before. A couple of times, Rob had noticed Charlie's name pop up on her cell's caller ID. Letting Charlie go to voice mail hadn't altered Rob's expression.

"Sadie's never cared for Charlie," Abby said.

"Never rubbed against his leg?"

Never rubbed against any man's leg. "No way. She used to leave Charlie presents by his shoes." Especially when Charlie's shoes slid beneath her bed. That tidbit of information she didn't share.

"Animal skins?"

She shook her head, scrunched up her face. "Litter box presents."

A slow smile curled Rob's lips. "I may have to rethink my opinion of cats."

How much had she told Rob about Charlie? That, years ago, he'd left her to fend for herself and then returned? That to this day, they remained close friends. She supposed that alone was enough to bring a wicked grin to Rob's face, if he were jealous of Charlie. Was he?

"Beautiful view. And this room is all you. Kind of like the rest of the house, but more personal." Rob bunched up his mouth, as though words were jammed behind his lips. "But I was hoping to see more of Luke."

Her heart thudded in her chest, one deep, resonating note. "Oh?"

Rob touched her upper arm, his hand warm against her skin. "Luke's things. You know, stuff that was important to him."

They'd discussed this before. The labyrinth would commemorate her son's life, and Luke's prized possessions could provide the telling details.

The reason she hadn't stepped foot in Luke's room since she'd chosen clothes for his burial.

Rob wasn't trying to get into her bedroom. He was requesting entry into her son's.

An audible breath slipped through her lips, too late to take it back. "You want to see Luke's room."

"We don't have to."

The intensity of his gaze drew tears to Abby's throat. "I'm embarrassed to admit it, but I haven't gone in there for months. Not since—" She'd stood in the center of Luke's bedroom, box cutter in hand, tearing into the boxes of Luke's belongings delivered from Amherst. She'd run her hands over each article of clothing, the rims of his Red Sox caps, the rungs of his leather belts. His shirts she'd held to her face, trying to extract a remnant of scent, disappointed when, instead, laundry soap burnt her nose. "This must sound nutty."

"Not at all. When my mother died a few years back, Dad took to sleeping on the couch in his office. Six months straight, he couldn't bring himself to go back into their bedroom without her." Rob shrugged. "At least, according to my brother."

"Not your take on it?"

Rob widened his eyes, his mouth set in a smile-frown of resignation. "Who knows? My father and I aren't exactly on speaking terms."

"Why not?" Abby had known people who'd burned through family relationships with their selfish demands, their me-me-me attitudes, but Rob wasn't one of those people. She'd only seen him give. If she'd known her father, if the subject wasn't the one topic her easy-going, nature-loving mother skirted, she'd hold on tight and never let him go. Even when she'd been small, she hadn't bought into Lily Beth's fable that her father was a merman who'd returned to the sea. Even a merman would've come back for her.

"Dad's got it in his head I had something to do with my mother's death."

Abby held a hand to her heart, unable to imagine Rob doing anything to a fly, other than opening a door to shoo it out.

"When Mom knew she was sick, when she knew the cancer—" Rob shook his head, jammed his free hand in his pocket. "Ticked Dad off when she gave me power of attorney instead of him. Ticked Dad off worse when I enacted the DNR. But, hey, what can you do?"

"Your mother trusted you to honor her last request. In my experience, the strong people get the tough jobs. Tough isn't easy."

He shrugged again, and his vulnerable expression blanked out, a deliberate numbing. "Got any more of that apple pie?" he said, and she thought of herself standing at the kitchen counter, middle of the night, fork in hand, filled with the hollowness of missing Luke. She'd eaten three quarters of an apple pie before the pain had hit her in the gut. Satisfied, she hadn't stopped until she'd swallowed the last sticky crumb.

"I thought you wanted to see Luke's bedroom." She drew herself up taller, stepped closer to Rob. She forced back the impulse to press her lips against the tanned star-shaped scar to the side of his right eye, to soothe whatever hurt him.

Many a night, she'd considered going into Luke's room alone, but then she'd talked herself out of it. She knew exactly what she'd find in his room, could picture bedding and photos and boyhood artifacts. But she had the irrational fear that if she opened that door, if she stepped inside, she would unleash something remarkable, something she could never put back.

She'd considered going into Luke's room with Charlie. With Charlie, she wouldn't fall apart, because she'd be too worried about Charlie's mental state, too set in her role of the emotionally strong one. But if all she was worried about was Charlie, she wouldn't feel a thing. She wouldn't feel Luke.

Lately, even joy didn't feel the same, as if on the day Luke had died, she'd taken out all of her emotions and wrapped them in gauze. You couldn't filter out pain without also filtering out joy.

But with Rob, her new dating-but-not-dating friend Rob, maybe the experience wouldn't be too much for her to handle or too little to make a difference. Maybe the experience would be just right.

Rob took her hands in his, stilling her unconscious habit of rubbing her thumb against her forefinger. Inside of his warm grasp, her fingers stilled.

"We don't have to, if you're not ready," he said, but she was already moving toward Luke's door, one foot in front of the other, Rob's hand in hers.

She opened the door, and they stepped inside.

Sunshine warmed and illuminated the room. Behind Luke's bed, the wall glowed with photos of Luke and his friends. Luke kayaking out on the bay with his high-school swim team co-captain. Luke cheering with his dorm buddies in the stands at a UMass football game. And at the center, the photo Abby had taped to the wall, sent from Amherst, in a box of Luke's belongings: a shot of Luke and his girlfriend, Tessa, sitting on a cafeteria tray atop a snow-covered hill somewhere on campus, getting ready to let go and fly.

"His friends meant everything to him." Ever since Luke had turned thirteen, it was like someone had flipped a switch, turning his attention away from his family and toward the world.

Rob squeezed her hand. "Last fall, Grace asked a friend to help troubleshoot a car problem, instead of me."

"How'd that turn out?"

"Not so good. The kid didn't know as much about automotive maintenance as she does."

She laughed. "You've taught her well."

A gnarled branch of driftwood decorated Luke's night table. Sea glass filled a glass jar, along with assorted rocks and spare change. On the shelf above Luke's desk, a glass aquarium displayed Luke's collection of starfish and sand dollars. Two boogie boards and a skim board leaned against the ends of his bed. No curtains covered the French doors that opened to a small flagstone patio, allowing a clear view to the yard, the perennials, and the future labyrinth site. Luke's memorial.

Best of all, she inhaled the brine of the ocean, the rubber of Luke's basketball sneakers, the singular scent of her son. Had he returned to her? She could almost feel Luke's presence in the room, filling the hollow places inside her. A shiver traveled up her arms and bunched her shoulders.

"You okay?" Rob asked.

A grin, a silly one at that, ached her cheeks. She could tell because whenever she was thinking how proud she was of her son while in her son's presence, he'd call her out. He'd tell her to quit smiling so hard, while he mirrored her grin. "Better than okay," she said, and gave a plump section of Luke's dark blue down comforter a pat. The fabric compressed, and then re-inflated with air, like a living, breathing thing. "But I think this is enough for one day. Baby steps, you know?"

Rob pressed his lips together and nodded. In his gaze, she saw the reflection of the tears in her eyes.

Still holding Rob's hand, they left the room, but Abby didn't bother closing the door behind them. "Thank you. I needed to go in there. I needed a little push."

"You're thanking me for making you sad?" he said. "I'm thinking you should smack me."

"Shows how much you know about women," she said.

Rob angled her a sideways smirk. "Never claimed expertise in that particular field."

She turned toward him and ran a hand down his forearm until she held both his hands in hers. Until he was smiling so hard his grin surely mimicked hers. "I was thinking," she said, rising up on her toes, "I should kiss you for making me happy."

He bent his head to hers, close enough so his words whispered against her lips, and her pulse tickled her throat. "You can't do that," he said, "if I kiss you first."

Before she could mock-protest, before she could fully close her eyes, his lips brushed hers. His hands ran the length of her back, sweet and soulful, sweeping her closer. She held his face between her hands and leaned into the kiss. The firmness of his mouth upended her stomach, as though she were standing on the edge of a cliff. The nub of his tongue edged her hips nearer to his. The unmistakable scrambling sound of Sadie dashing from the hallway opened her eyes.

Sadie raced around the room, the same driven-by-Luke's-energy school-morning routine the cat had insisted on following, while Luke slurped cereal and gobbled toast, gathered his books and backpack, and readied for classes. Strange, so strange, because she hadn't done that since.

Abby placed a steadying hand against Rob's T-shirt, and his

chest moved beneath her hand. His pulse beat into her palm. "What took you so long?" she said.

"I didn't want to scare you away," he said, and he kissed her again.

A tinkling sound issued from beyond the closed pocket doors, the dinner bell she left in the entryway for guests to beckon her.

Sadie jumped onto the couch and meowed, a long string of vocalizations.

"Sorry, sorry." Abby untangled herself from Rob's embrace, slipped his hands from her waist. "Somebody needs me."

"I need you," he said, a dare-laced statement, and he tapped a finger to his just-for-show pout.

Abby backed away from him, shaking her head and wagging a finger. She took a few steadying breaths to soften the flush of her cheeks, stiffen the wobble in her legs, and set her back in the land of the living.

Abby slid aside the pocket door.

A girl sat on the sofa behind the wicker basket of sachets. Her eyes widened, and she grinned at Abby, her mouth quivering, unsure. The girl's brunette hair hung past her shoulders, dark, without an ounce of blue. Her face appeared younger, the beneficiary of a light, rather than a heavy, hand of eye makeup. More unsettling, her cheeks were rounder, the cheekbones less pronounced than the last time Abby had seen the girl retreating through her door.

The girl stood. Her hot pink camisole hugged her full breasts and clung to her protruding belly, about six months along. About six months' pregnant. About five months since—

Abby's eyes watered, her heart raced in her throat, and her windpipe narrowed around the pulse.

She remembered the ache in her arms the day Luke was born when Lily Beth had whisked her son away to clean him up. But five minutes later, Lily Beth returned her son to her, instantly soothing the ache. She remembered dropping Luke off the first day of nursery school and standing outside, a hand pressed to her mouth. Two-and-a-half hours later, Luke had barreled into her open arms, knocking the wind from her lungs and steadying her pulse.

She remembered last February's phone call from Amherst, the day she learned when your world is pulled out from under you, you do, in fact, fall to your knees.

The girl blurred at the edges. Her mouth moved as if she were talking, but all Abby could hear was a high-pitched whir. Abby's arms twitched like a marionette. Behind her, Rob firmed his hands on her shoulders.

Abby opened her mouth, intending to say *Tessa*. "Luke's," she whispered, and the room went black.

Chapter 5

One week after their high-school graduation, Abby and Charlie sat on the checkered couch in Charlie's parents' den while his sister, Kate, slept upstairs. Abby's knees pressed together, Charlie's arm wound around her shoulders. *Forrest Gump* played in the VCR, the volume set to mute because they'd seen it at the movies. The windows were open, the sound of crickets thick in the air. Off in the woods a bullfrog croaked, deep and ridiculous. Abby jumped, jostling Charlie's arm, and his beer bottle bumped up against his teeth.

"Ouch!" He rubbed his mouth, set his beer on the side table. "Thanks a lot, Abby." She'd been jittery all day; the cottony words she wanted to say to Charlie lined her throat. And in the mix, something akin to thrill, because this was good news, right? Ill-timed, years too early, shocking, but good and real and meant to be.

In the low light of the television, Charlie's eyes glowed. He wended a cool hand beneath the hem of her T-shirt, his touch sweet and familiar. "Want to mess around?"

Abby held her hand to Charlie's, took its placement on her lower abdomen as a sign. She leaned into his touch. In the kitchen, the clock ticked, the refrigerator hummed, and a fresh batch of ice cubes clinked into the waiting tray. Her pulse revved. In this moment, she loved Charlie more than ever, maybe even more than a year and a half ago when, on the reverse side of the couch cushion, he'd opened her with his fingers, unzipped his jeans, and pushed himself inside her for the first time. Making love had seemed like an afterthought because she'd loved him forever.

Would he love her after today?

Charlie's gaze went half-mast, his face leaned in to kiss her, his hand slid lower.

Abby cupped Charlie's face. A smile tugged at the corners of her lips, a fragile twine of fear and hope. "I'm pregnant," she said, and Charlie froze, his fingers caught beneath the band of her underwear.

"Charlie?" she said.

Charlie let out a breath. He stared at her until his chin trembled. He stared at her until her smile fell and her hope faltered.

Charlie yanked his hand from her shorts and tore into the kitchen. The clink of bottle against bottle, Charlie riffling through the beers his dad kept in the crisper but never counted. One beer wasn't enough?

Abby sat up and folded her arms over her stomach. On the TV screen, Jenny asked Forrest to marry her. Across the room, a framed eight-by-ten portrait of the Connors family hung on the wall. Twelve-year-old Charlie sat on a studio bench beside his father, fake pine tree in the background. Baby sister, Kate, balanced on Mrs. Connors's knee. To this day, Mrs. Connors referred to Kate as her little miracle. Charlie called her annoying. He only volunteered to babysit so that he could get his parents out of the house and get himself into Abby's shorts.

But Charlie had told Abby he wanted kids. She hated Charlie, but she hated herself more for believing him.

Charlie stood in the dark doorway, beer in hand. Mist billowed from the bottle's open mouth.

"We're keeping the baby," she said, because sometimes Charlie needed her to state the obvious, to make their plans, to break them down into manageable bites. Last week, they were planning on going to the University of Maine. Now, they weren't.

Charlie came into the room. He got down on his knees before her and laid his head in her lap. Out of habit or love or insanity, she stroked his hair, worried the satin-soft strands between her trembling fingers. The yeasty beer aroma hooked in her throat, tugged queasiness from her belly to her mouth.

Charlie raised his head and offered Abby the open beer. "Maybe," he said, "we should drink on it."

You drank a beer while pregnant if you didn't give a damn, or worse. If you wanted the pregnancy to end, you drank quite a few.

Abby took the beer from Charlie, the bottle cold against the web of her hand. The words on the label blurred, and her hand shook. Sometimes stating the obvious wasn't enough. Sometimes she had to show Charlie their plan.

"Get off me," Abby told him, and shoved him from her lap onto the shag rug.

"What the—?" Charlie said, and then flinched.

Abby stood and hurled the beer bottle past Charlie and against the far wall, smashing the glass of the Connors family portrait.

The pom-pom throw pillow behind Abby's head let her know she was lying on the love seat in the entryway of Briar Rose. The bittersweet aftertaste of a memory filled her mouth, and her hands covered her belly. The warmth of someone else's hands covered hers.

She opened her eyes, expecting Charlie.

"Hey, sleepyhead," Rob said, and everything flooded back. Tessa. The pregnancy. Luke's baby, but no Luke.

Luke's baby.

"I found some apple juice. But I didn't see any straws anywhere." Tessa stood over Abby, one of Abby's juice glasses in hand. Tessa's nose was red, as if she'd been crying, but her eyes were dry. She shifted from foot to foot.

"Put it on the table," Rob said, his tone sturdy and take-charge above an undercurrent of concern.

Abby had better get it together before her guests returned to find their innkeeper laid out in the parlor, Rob staring at her as if she'd just woken from the dead. The only time she'd ever fainted before was when she and Celeste had locked themselves in the upstairs bathroom at Celeste's parents' house, two eighteen-year-olds cracking up over the absurdity of peeing on a stick. Minutes later, Abby had read two solid pink lines and promptly forgotten how to breathe.

Rob helped her up, propped the pillow behind her back. Her body moved at half-speed. "I'm fine." Abby reached for the glass of juice with a trembling hand.

"She's a terrible liar," Rob told Tessa. He held the glass to Abby's lips, and she bent her head to take a sip. The juice scratched going down. She took another sip, got the same result.

"Better?" Rob said, and she nodded. "Liar."

Abby grinned. "How long was I out?"

"Couple minutes."

"Really? Felt like hours." Abby sat up the rest of the way herself and turned to Tessa. "So . . . how are *you* feeling?"

"Okay, I guess."

"Five hours is a long drive." Abby angled her head toward the door with the pink hand-painted Powder Room sign. "Do you need to use the restroom?"

"Pretty much all the time," Tessa said, and they exchanged a brittle smile before Tessa headed across the room. From behind, you couldn't even tell she was expecting. Abby had carried that way, too. Or so she'd been told. As a pregnant teenager, she'd felt anything but inconspicuous.

Abby's smile cracked. "Oh, God," she whispered. "This is not how I imagined the afternoon. I am so sorry. Mortified, actually."

"My fault. I should've warned you about my superior kissing skills. Many a woman has swooned."

Abby laughed, and Rob pecked her on the cheek. The sweet gesture spoke the language of intimacy. Did Rob feel that way about her? "Kidding," he said. "You were my first."

A balloon of hysteria welled in Abby's stomach, threatening to burst, and she breathed through it.

What was it with teenage pregnancies in her family? Lily Beth had warned Abby, to no avail. And Abby had passed along Lily Beth's admonition to Luke. *If you can't be chaste, for goodness sake be careful.* Yet, she'd always imagined Luke fathering beautiful children. Towheaded boys with ruddy cheeks, quick smiles, and a weakness for Abby's oatmeal raisin cookies. Blue-eyed girls who were equally at home digging in the sand or standing on a stool before Abby's kitchen counter. She already loved them. She'd told Luke as much. But in her fantasies, she imagined the pitter-patter of Luke-related little feet years and years in the future. Not while her baby was still a teenager. Definitely not after Luke had died.

Abby filled her cheeks with air and blew out a breath. Charlie called her habit, Abby's little blowfish. She called it, releasing excess stress. Or attempting to do so.

How could Abby spring this shock on Charlie? Or Lily Beth, for that matter? Charlie still needed to call her most every day. And Abby knew Lily Beth had been middle-of-the-night widow walking since Luke's death. Lily Beth would admit to nothing, but the dark circles under her mother's eyes told the tale.

Abby tested the steadiness of the floor, found it lacking.

"She should've warned me," Abby said, imagining how Lily Beth might've reacted if Abby had announced her pregnancy six months after the fact, instead of days after she'd known. In front of Abby, Lily Beth had called her pregnancy a blessing. But late at night, the muffled sound of Lily Beth's behind-closed-doors tears had spoken of something darker.

Yet, Tessa's pregnancy was a blessing. A miracle that had knocked Abby off her feet.

"Five hours," Abby said. "Why didn't she call first? What if I wasn't even home?" Irresponsible behavior got you pregnant, but then you had to grow up and smarten up for the sake of the baby. Abby's pulse throbbed against her eardrums, and she ordered it to slow down.

"She's . . . ?" Rob said.

"Luke's girlfriend," Abby whispered.

"Thought so."

Tessa came out from the restroom, her hairline wet, as though she'd splashed water on her face.

"Did he know?" Abby asked.

Tessa met Abby's gaze. She squinted across the room. Her lips opened and rounded, as though translating *he* to *Luke*. Her brow relaxed, and she shook her head.

If Luke had known, he'd have called Abby right away, and they'd have talked it out. They always talked things out. But to what end? She wouldn't have wanted Luke to drop out of school. He'd worked hard to get there.

Yet, that's exactly what she'd expected of Charlie.

She'd also expected Charlie to marry her, but only because he'd asked her years before the pregnancy. This situation was different. Luke hadn't been ready for that kind of commitment.

While in high school, he'd never dated a girl more than a few months before the outgoing calls would cease and the incoming calls would commence. Tearful pleas for Luke to call back, because he was the love of her life. She couldn't live without him. Oh, the unnecessary drama.

Yet, that wasn't fair, because what each girl felt was real. "What did I do?" Luke would ask Abby after the latest rash of calls.

"You made her fall in love with you," she'd tell him.

And then he'd lose interest.

"Luke was good with kids. Did you know that?" Abby asked.

"Drink some more juice," Rob said.

I'm okay, Abby mouthed. He nodded, but his hand slid to the small of her back and stayed.

Tessa sat down on the wing chair beside Abby, a two-step process. Lower to cushion, shift to relative comfort.

"He used to babysit for my friend Celeste. He was the only male sitter she'd allow. Her kids loved him." Luke would help them build couch cushion forts in the living room, igloos in the yard. He'd make cocoa they claimed they liked even better than their mother's homemade hot chocolate. Celeste was wise to ignore the empty packets of Swiss Miss in her trash.

"He never mentioned babysitting."

"No? He took an early childhood ed class in tenth grade. The one where he had to carry a baby doll around with him in a Snugli? And the doll cried until Luke changed its wet diaper or gave it a bottle?"

Abby pictured Luke carrying a real baby, his baby, a smooth round cheek resting on Luke's shoulder. She lifted the apple juice from the table. The enormity of what Luke had lost—his whole beautiful life—made her want to smash the glass against the wall. Slowly, carefully, she set the glass down.

Tessa shrugged. She clasped hands on her thighs, making herself look like a shy schoolgirl, if you could ignore the pregnant belly backdrop.

At least when Abby was expecting Luke, she hadn't been known as that pregnant freshman girl. No, she'd been that pregnant girlfriend from home who called and talked to Charlie's roommate every Friday night while Charlie was out partying.

And then she'd stopped calling.

An ache pressed her temples. Rob took her hand, as if they were in this together, whatever *this* was. Tessa had waited months to let her know of the pregnancy. Why hadn't Tessa simply called to tell Abby she was carrying Luke's baby? "Only two other boys took the class with Luke. When Luke figured out they were only there to meet girls . . ." Not that Luke's motives had been any more pure. "When the boys didn't take too well to twenty-four/seven child care, Luke charged them for doll sitting. He did pretty well for himself at ten dollars an hour. Kind of cornered the market."

Rob squeezed Abby's hand. "An entrepreneur, like his mother."

Tessa let out a laugh and a hiccup, and she covered her mouth. "That sounds like Luke."

Good. Abby had set Tessa at ease. Took guts to drive herself from Massachusetts to Maine, no clue what kind of reception she'd receive. Act first, think second, if at all. Unfortunately, she could well imagine Luke doing something similarly impulsive. Tessa probably hadn't anticipated the fainting. That made three of them.

Tessa's fingers unclasped and jittered in her lap.

"Do your parents know you're here?" Abby asked.

Tessa hiccupped again.

"Let me get you some water." Abby stood up. Brown dots played before her eyes and she sat back down.

Rob shook his head at Abby and rested a hand on her shoulder. "I'll get the water. You, stay."

"Woof," Abby told Rob, and Tessa giggled. Rob walked from the room. Abby's gaze zoned in on the back of his jeans, the angle of his hips.

The sensation of being watched turned her to Tessa. "Your parents?" Abby asked.

"My father knows." Tessa's gaze scurried to the ceiling.

Abby had seen that expression before on her son's face, the squirm of a half-truth. "Really?"

"Uh, well, he will when I phone to tell him."

Thought so. "And your mother?"

Tessa sucked her lips into her mouth. "She's . . . she's out of the country." Her expression turned numb with a tinge of defiance around her eyes.

Was her mother also out of Tessa's life?

"Does she know about the baby?" Abby asked.

Tessa shook her head, and her eyes misted.

Abby took a slow, deep breath. How horrible for Tessa's mother not to know about the existence of her own grandchild.

How horrible for *Abby* not to have known. Until Tessa had, on impulse, landed on her doorstep.

Abby drew her hands to her chest, one overlapping the other. "Why didn't you tell me sooner?"

"I don't know." Even though Tessa's gaze did not scurry and retreat from Abby's, Tessa sat up taller. She shifted into a subtle defensive stance. And Abby still didn't believe her.

Rob returned with a glass of ice water and handed it to Tessa. "There you go." He sat next to Abby, and the sides of their knees bumped.

"Thanks." Tessa hiccupped and gulped down the water, as if she hadn't had anything to drink in hours. Did she know the dangers of dehydration? As soon as Abby had discovered she was pregnant, she'd worried about the baby's health. She hadn't realized how much harder it would be after Luke was born.

Between middle school and high school, Luke had sprained the same ankle twice playing basketball. Broke his wrist executing a back flip on a frozen pond. Suffered a concussion during a sledding accident because he'd refused to wear a helmet. Each injury had chipped away at the fallacy she could keep her child safe from harm.

"You have a bag or suitcase I can haul in for you?" Rob asked.

"Just this." Tessa gave the handbag at her side a poke.

Was she staying somewhere else and she'd already dropped off a suitcase? "So . . . what's your plan?" Abby asked.

"I guess I have three choices?" Tessa's hand settled over the swell of her belly. "I could, you know, keep the baby?" she said, and her gaze wandered around the room.

Heat prickled the back of Abby's neck. She hadn't asked Tessa about her plans for the baby. She'd assumed Tessa would raise the child.

What else would you do for the child of the man you'd loved and lost?

Tessa's gaze fell to the floor, and she shook her head. "Probably a dumb idea. I've never even babysat. I'm not good with kids. I have school and—" Tessa took a couple of long, deep breaths before she met Abby's gaze. Her mouth turned down, as though she might cry, and her brow furrowed. She tried for a smile, the same shaky optimism Abby had seen before she'd fainted. "I could give you the baby."

The words thrummed between them, pounded through Abby's chest. Beside her, Rob shifted in his seat. She ushered her hair over one shoulder. Her hand came away sticky with sweat. Beneath the apples-and-cinnamon scent of her home, she detected a milky newborn scent. Beyond the shushing crash of waves, the memory of an infant's cries tickled her ears. And instead of the carved-out feeling that had plagued her since she'd touched her lips to her son's cold cheek, warmth, soul-warmth, filled her head to toe.

I want my son back.

Abby glanced at Rob, and he offered an encouraging nod-grin that didn't touch his eyes.

Abby stood up. Her legs did not shake. No spots danced before her eyes. And her vision did not waver at the edges.

"Thank you, Tessa. Thank you so much." Abby bent and gave Tessa a hug. The girl reached up to touch Abby's hair, looped a finger into a curl, the way Luke had when he'd been small. Tessa swallowed and pressed her cheek to Abby's. Abby had prayed for a second chance. Maybe this wasn't a miracle, but it was pretty darn close. Abby let go first and swiped at the wetness beneath one eye. "You at least have to stay the weekend."

Tessa's wide grin withered, and her bottom lip puckered into a pout.

A sudden knowing panic gripped Abby's chest, a close cousin to the sensation she'd experienced months ago when the University of Massachusetts had flashed on her caller ID. "What? What's wrong?" Abby said, her voice high and tight.

Tessa shrugged and shook her head. "I'm sorry, Abby. It might be better for me to give the baby to someone else."

"Better?" Abby said, her voice wavering, a hairbreadth below hysteria. "Better for whom?" Abby searched the girl's face, looking for malice or madness. But all she found was a nervous smile and a gaze that hid from Abby's glare.

Did Tessa think this was some sort of game? Why would she come all this way to offer Abby Luke's child and then, seconds later, snatch the baby away? How horrible for Tessa's mother not to know she had a grandchild on the way. But Abby would gladly trade places if the alternative was knowing Luke's baby existed somewhere in the world, in a stranger's house, a stranger's arms. And she would never hold him.

She might never hold her grandchild.

Luke had told Abby that Tessa was nice. As compared to what? A monster?

"I don't know," Tessa said. "I'm not sure. I honestly have no clue."

Rob made a sound behind her, a grunt of disapproval that Abby wholeheartedly agreed with.

Honest, or one of its derivatives, was one of those words kids used when they weren't. Once a mother, always a mother. She wasn't that long out of practice. And Tessa was not at all sorry.

"Then you'd better stay," Abby said, "until you decide."

The sticky-sweet smell of Belgian waffles and blueberries, Sunday breakfast at Briar Rose, flipped Abby's stomach on its head. She ducked inside the pantry, folded a saltine into her mouth, and washed it down with tap water. Too much thinking and too little sleep had resulted in a worry hangover. In short, she felt like crap. She'd managed to wake with the sun, complete food prep, and set the tables before the first bleary-eyed guest stumbled into the dining room for coffee. She'd set herself on autopilot, forbade her mind from wandering to the girl who slept in Luke's bedroom, wrapped in Luke's blankets and around Luke's baby. But maintaining focus had zapped her meager supply of energy.

One couple was finishing up and lingering over coffee, and another awaited the delivery of their meals. The rumble of their voices scraped across her tattered nerves. Not their fault. But more than anything, she wanted to return to her bedroom, dive under the covers, and hide from the plans she'd made last night with Charlie. She'd called and asked him to meet her at Percy's for an ice cream, a safe spot to tell him about Tessa. She'd felt like she was lying to Charlie by fabricating a sudden ice-cream craving. She'd felt like she was cheating on Rob, the man she craved.

Abby balanced two breakfasts across her arms and made

the delivery. "Here we are," she said, and set the warm plates before the gray-haired couple.

"Excuse me, Abby?" Lisa from Room 1 motioned her over to where she and her husband, Ronnie, sat before empty plates, oversized servings consumed. Lisa and Ronnie weren't newlyweds, but the childless couple in their thirties acted the part. They sat on the same side of the four-top, ate from each other's plates, made a point of finishing each other's sentences and each other's food. Earlier this week, Abby had to knock on their door and drop not-so-subtle hints about the thin walls, although nothing at all was wrong with her home's insulation. Some people—Lisa—liked to make sure everyone knew when they were having a good time.

"More coffee?" Abby asked.

"We'd like some eggs."

"Eggs?" Abby asked, her mind working to come up with a polite answer that wasn't a lie. She had plenty of eggs, all needed for tomorrow's eggs Benedict. She always explained breakfast service, a different meal each day. Coffee or tea? Apple juice or orange? Canadian bacon or sausage? Half an hour ago, those were the only choices she'd offered.

Lisa nodded. "Two scrambled, dry please."

"Of course." Abby might still have enough for tomorrow.

"Sunny side up for me," Ronnie said.

Never mind.

In the kitchen, she eased two cast-iron frying pans from their hooks and fired up the gas burners. She slid a carton of eggs from the fridge and cracked one over the bowl before she realized she'd forgotten the bowl. "Really?" she told the egg oozing across the gray granite. "Are you kidding me?"

"Who are you talking to?" Hannah bustled in for her shift, light brown hair piled wet on her head, arranged like one of Celeste's sticky buns.

"Please." Abby motioned at the egg mess, and Hannah

snapped up a sponge from beside the sink. Abby shook her head. She cracked two eggs onto the surface of an oiled pan, two more into an actual bowl for scrambling.

Hannah rinsed the sponge in the sink and then scowled at Abby's kitchen chalkboard menu planner. "Those don't look like waffles to me."

"They most certainly do not. Some people think rules don't apply to them." Abby whisked the eggs harder. "I explain the rules about breakfast, rules I've thought out, planned out. How am I supposed to plan if, at any given moment, someone can just walk into my home and change my entire life?" Egg sloshed over the rim of the bowl.

Hannah rushed in to wipe up the drips. "You need me to pick up eggs for you at Rooster's?"

Eggs sizzled in the frying pan. Abby turned down the heat, sprinkled her Briar Rose recipe seasoning mix. She added some to the scrambled eggs and poured them into the second pan. "Some people do whatever they want, no thought to the consequences, or who they're hurting. I mean, I love eggs. Love them. You know that, right?"

"I guess."

"I always thought that I'd have more."

"I can run out after my shift."

With her right hand, Abby flipped the eggs, landing them sunny side up. Left-handed, she scrambled eggs in the pan. "One thing's for sure, I do not take well to teasing."

"That makes two of us." Charlie stood in the doorway to the kitchen, over an hour early and in the worst possible location.

Abby's heartbeat kicked her in the ribs. She gazed around Charlie, making sure a certain young lady wasn't heading his way to take him out at the knees. "What are you doing here?"

"You sounded stressed on the phone."

"You have no impulse control."

Charlie shrugged. "That, too," he said, but his expression caught the brunt of her insult.

Sorry, she mouthed, and ushered him in. She slid the egg orders onto the waiting plates and turned to Hannah. "Deliver these to table three?"

Hannah glanced at Charlie and back to Abby. Abby didn't make a practice of sharing her personal life with her employees, but Hannah had worked for her long enough to piece together their history. "I'm on it." She slid a half apron from its wooden peg, tied it around her waist, and snapped up the orders.

Abby turned off the burners, but heat flushed her chest. Her lips tingled. All she could do was shake her head, give herself a moment before she upended Charlie's life.

"Don't do that, Abby. What is it? What's wrong?" he said, his voice taking on the tinge of her mood.

"Do you remember Luke's girlfriend, Tessa?"

"Sure, of course, hot girl with blue hair."

Abby laughed, the perfect antidote for her tension. Leave it to Charlie to sum up a woman by the color of her hair and where she hit on the hotness chart.

Hannah breezed into the kitchen. "Just passing through." She slipped the apron from around her waist and backed out the door so she wouldn't miss a thing.

Abby waited for the sound of Hannah rifling through the broom closet. "Tessa's pregnant," Abby said.

Charlie tilted his head. He stared at her, long enough to remember why she loved his changeable hazel eyes. Long enough to remember Celeste's warning to keep her distance. Long enough for her to wish she could forget.

His eyes brightened from gray to green. "How far along?"

"About five, six months. I'm not sure, I—"

Charlie let out a whoop. "We're having a baby!" He grabbed Abby around the waist, lifted her in the air, and swung her in a circle, the kind of over-the-top reaction she'd wanted when she'd told him she was expecting Luke. Crazy, irrational, but she'd wanted it anyway. She'd been a teenager. She'd been in love.

Abby held on to Charlie's shoulders, widened her eyes at him, a little thrilled and a lot horrified. "Put me down! What's wrong with you?" She cut her gaze to the dining room, filled with guests waiting to gobble up a juicy piece of local gossip and spit it out across town. Or, worse, spew bits of misinformation at the gift shop she recommended to all of her patrons: Lily Beth's Heart Stone.

He set her back down, closer to him than when he'd lifted her from her feet. "We're having a baby," he repeated, slow and sweet and caressing every syllable.

"I'm not pregnant, Tessa is."

"Would it be weird if I were proud of our kid, in a you-the-man kind of way?" Charlie said, referring to Luke. "You know, along with an appropriate amount of parental disapproval."

She was about to tell Charlie he was a complete ass, but truth be told, he wasn't. If Luke had been alive, she could well imagine Charlie lecturing him from here to next Thursday. And then, after the baby was born, pounding him on the back and sharing a cigar.

"It wouldn't be *that* weird."

"What do we do now? Road trip to Amherst?"

"Not necessary." Abby told him about Tessa showing up on her doorstep and everything that followed. "She might want to give the baby to someone else," Abby said, and the cracker she'd eaten hardened in her belly. "I'm keeping the baby."

"I'll talk to her," Charlie said, and his airy confidence rubbed Abby the wrong way. "She's just a kid. She's scared," he said, as if Tessa were a damsel in distress, rather than a young woman who'd come here with a hidden agenda. "How can she know whether she's ready to raise a child? She's probably spent the past few months trying to avoid the issue." Charlie's voice filled the kitchen, taking on the resinous tone of Charlie the caring objective teacher. No relation to Charlie the one-time absentee father.

"Is that what you did?" she said, hating the raw edge to her voice, but powerless against the pull of the past. And sleep deprivation stripped away every defense.

"Never."

"No?"

Tessa stepped into the kitchen, her face flushed, her pink camisole wrinkled from sleep. The fabric gaped, revealing an inch of bare round belly. "You sound just like Luke. I thought you were Luke." The disappointment in Tessa's eyes wound around Abby's heart and tugged her toward the girl. Then Abby remembered Tessa's list of options for Luke's baby, and she stood her ground. Tessa knew what they'd all lost. How could she threaten Abby with more of the same?

Tessa tugged the jersey down over her belly. She hung her head, and tears ran down her cheeks.

"Hey, don't be like that." Charlie opened his arms to Tessa and ushered her closer. "Tessa," he said, drawing out the syllables, the way Luke had done. "We should be celebrating."

Tessa ran into Charlie's arms. She buried her face in the shoulder of his white polo shirt, no doubt soaking the fabric, as if she'd known him forever. "It's going to be okay. We're here for you. We're going to figure this out. No worries." Charlie rubbed Tessa's back, and her shoulders rose and fell with her tears.

All Abby had ever wanted from Charlie those many years ago.

Abby ducked into the pantry and clamped a hand over her mouth to quell the cottony swell, the urge to scream. Did Charlie think he could sway the girl? Convince her to leave Luke's baby with Abby, just because he said so?

What you wanted and what you ended up with weren't necessarily the same.

Luke had worried Abby with his devil-may-care attitude toward sports and all manner of physical dares. Her son was all-boy, all the time. With Luke, Abby had at least understood what she was up against. Girls in general, this girl in particular, were something else altogether. Charlie was no match for passive-aggressive girly crap, especially in the guise of a beautiful girl who was carrying their grandchild.

Abby focused on a row of spices—rosemary, thyme, oregano—and bit the soft flesh of her palm until pain bloomed and the panic in her belly receded.

Back in the kitchen, Tessa clung to Charlie's shirt. Above the girl's head, he mouthed, *No worries,* to Abby. But Abby Stone wasn't a schoolgirl he could charm with his good looks and pretty words. She'd seen too much to believe in easy answers. Happy ever after had died with her son.

Abby put water on for peppermint tea. She poured batter into the waffle iron and peeled a banana for slicing. The baby needed nourishing. The girl needed convincing. If Tessa were anything like Abby had been while pregnant, breakfast would lead to second breakfast and slide right into lunch. Abby wished she could rewind the clock to a time when her fondest wish had been four straight hours of uninterrupted sleep. Back to one perfectly ordinary mid-March, middle-of-the-night newborn feeding. Back to a time when she hadn't appreciated her good fortune.

She'd thought she'd be in that room forever. Late-winter winds battered the nursery's windows and banged shutters against the siding. A CD played "Little Boy Blue," a loop of warm sound. The song's steady backbeat mimicked a human pulse, but the ersatz heart didn't fool her son. Luke had kicked off his blanket, his arms and legs flailed for her, twitches of movement in the darkened room. His thin cries pierced her chest. Abby lifted him from his cradle. Before she could fully settle into the rocking chair, before she wedged the nursing pillow beneath her forearm, Luke clamped on to her nipple, hard enough to snatch the air in her throat. He'd always known how to get what he wanted.

A grandchild. A piece of her son alive in the world. She'd lost her child once and survived. Losing again would kill her.

CHAPTER 6

Tessa couldn't stop looking at the photo centered above Luke's bed.

Dina had taken the shot of her and Luke in December, when they'd gone sledding, right before finals week. A last blowing off of steam before they locked themselves in books and laptops to memorize facts they'd forget five minutes after the doors of the lecture halls snicked shut behind them. She and Luke sat on an oversized cafeteria tray at the peak of the hill by their dorm. Top of the morning, top of her life.

After breakfast, they'd hiked the paved trail up Orchard Hill. Tessa was falling behind, savoring the strange feeling between her legs. The secret ache told her hours ago, everything had changed. Luke, who could've had any girl, had chosen her. He thought she was beautiful. He thought she was special.

Boys were so easy to fool.

The sun's rays bounced off the snow-covered hillside, blinding her. Luke jogged back down the hill, and she climbed onto his back. With a battle cry, he raced up the hill, Tessa grasping the fabric of his ski jacket for dear life, her body bouncing mercilessly against Luke's. The solid feel of him pounded against her chest. Clear blue sky with a whisper of white cloud skittering across it. Snow-dusted tree branches.

Groups of kids along the path. As she and Luke bounded past, their voices touched her, like high-fives of celebration. Joy bubbled from her center. Luke deposited her at the top of the hill, with her stomach muscles tight from laughter, her cheeks chapped from the cold.

She was smart to have made him wait a few months to have sex. A calculated risk, but worth it. Because he'd held her hands and dusted her face with kisses. He'd told her to open her eyes. He'd said it might hurt. But that night, it hadn't hurt at all. Not in any way that mattered.

Tessa hummed the first line from "Wish You Were Here," slow and ethereal. Luke's cat, Sadie, poked her head out from under the bed. The cat had slept there all night. She'd refused to come out, even when Abby had waved a rainbow wand of curly ribbons by her face. Not even when Abby had tumbled aluminum foil balls the cat supposedly could not resist past the bed. *Fine,* Abby had said, when Tessa could tell the sleeping arrangement—for Tessa and the cat—was anything but.

Tessa clucked her tongue. When Sadie wound around her bare legs, she scooped the cat into her arms and planted a kiss in the soft fur behind her ear. In the photo, Tessa faced forward, legs crossed. Luke's legs wrapped around her waist. He gazed out to some unknown point, or some unknown person. A girl, most likely. That tall blonde from Central who was always hanging around, waiting for the latest breakup? How long could a relationship last when there was always some girl, or girls, waiting in line for you to fail?

"Who do you think Luke's looking at?" Tessa asked. "Hmm?" Inside Tessa, the baby squirmed, and Sadie leaped to the floor. Tessa pressed both hands to her stomach, as though trying to hold the baby inside her.

On that day on the hill, she'd longed for Luke, as though he were already gone. If love felt so much like grief, how could you tell the difference? Tears sprung to her eyes, and a familiar congestion filled her chest.

A handled shopping bag from yesterday's shopping spree sat on the floor, and Tessa set to unpacking the contents. She'd dashed out after breakfast, giving Abby and Charlie privacy, she was certain, to talk about her. At Mama Land boutique, the saleswoman had cautioned Tessa against purchasing too many items at once. She'd assured Tessa that just when she'd thought she couldn't get any bigger, she'd grow exponentially. But what the heck? She had Dad's credit card and his sort-of blessing. At Abby's urging, Tessa had called to tell her father her location, and she'd taken his rather pronounced sigh from the other end of the phone as all the permission she needed. "You don't listen at all, do you?" he'd asked, not expecting an answer. No, she did not listen. And neither did he.

But Abby would listen to Tessa. She'd make sure of it.

Tessa laid out her purchases across Luke's bed. Two pairs of not-too-short shorts, the denim low-cut, if you didn't count the stretchy beige fabric that cradled her growing belly and reached all the way to the underside of her bra. Three T-shirts, longer in the front than the back. A sundress with navy stripes running vertical. Each item was cleverly designed to camouflage the fact she was a freaking freak show. From the bottom of the bag, Tessa retrieved half a dozen pairs of underwear, the worst of the worst. Underwear with a secret baby belly, in case she were trying for the sexy prego look.

She couldn't imagine letting any guy see her undressed, not even after the baby was born. She only wanted Luke.

Luke, taking her by the hand, dragging her into his study carrel, and locking the door behind them. Luke's voice in her ear, telling her how sweet she tasted in his mouth. He'd known exactly what he was doing, an expertise born from years of fooling around with other girls.

She wished she'd been his first. She wished they'd been high-school sweethearts. Like Dina and Jon, and Dina's parents. Like Abby and Charlie. Luke had told her his parents were best friends before they dated.

How romantic was that?

Had Luke loved her? For real? He'd said the words, breathless soft-sweet mumblings, uttered when he was about to come. But everyone knew that didn't count. Everyone knew that wasn't romantic.

She wished Luke were here, right now, with her in his bedroom.

Luke had told her his mother was strict. She'd never allowed girls in his bedroom. But even as he'd told Tessa, she'd detected the undercurrent of a smirk. Luke had been an adrenaline junkie. That was for sure. How easy would it have been for a girl to slip from the night and through the French doors? How easy would it have been for Luke to lead a girl by the hand into his bed?

How easy would it have been for Luke to cheat on her while they were going out? Wouldn't *that* have given him the ultimate adrenaline rush?

Sunlight bathed the aquarium on the shelf above Luke's desk. Starfish and sand dollars stood out in stark relief. She could imagine Luke finding the treasures in the sand. His warm hand reaching down to make them his own, the way he'd claimed her.

Tessa took the stack of hideous underwear across the room to Luke's dresser and opened the top drawer. No tightie-whities, no boxers, no balled-up crew socks. Instead, two photo albums filled the drawer, one atop the other. She carried them to Luke's bed, feeling as though she'd unearthed buried treasure, clues to Luke's secret sacred self.

At the UMass memorial, Father Thomas had spoken of

how Luke was taken too soon. He'd assumed Luke's untimely death had them all searching for answers. But Tessa had been searching since the day she'd met Luke. Luke's death had only made him harder to unravel.

She cracked open the album, flipped past a teenage-looking Abby holding Luke in her arms, a blond-haired woman at her elbow. Abby and chubby-cheeked Luke holding hands before the entryway door of Briar Rose. Would her baby have eyes like Luke's, so intense you thought he saw inside you, even if he didn't know you at all? She'd thought they'd have more time. Why did she always make that mistake?

Heat flooded her face, and her breath came in wet gulps.

A preschool Luke in overalls stood on a stool before the center island of the Briar Rose kitchen. A mixing bowl with a wooden spoon sat on the counter. Flour overflowed the bowl, dusting the counter, Luke's apron, and Luke. Abby beamed at Luke, but little Luke stared straight ahead. His right hand extended before him, reaching for someone or something out of his grasp.

Tessa touched a fingertip to Luke's tiny photo hand. Strange thought, she loved who Luke was before she'd even met him. Her left hand slid to her stomach, caressed the curve beneath her belly button. Not so strange, she already loved Luke's baby.

Loving meant loss.

"What are you doing?" Abby's voice, breathy and strident, startled Tessa's hand from her belly.

Abby stood in the doorway, staring at the photo albums, or, more specifically, in their general direction. Six o'clock in the morning, and Luke's mother looked like she'd been up for hours. Hair pulled back in a ponytail. Face scrubbed and shining, with just a hint of makeup. A natural beauty, Tessa's mother would've called her. As if takes-two-hours-to-get-ready Meredith Lombardi would know anything about that. Some women needed a little assistance, Mom had told Tessa, and then she'd taken twelve-year-old Tessa out to shop for blush, lip gloss, and mascara.

"He was so cute all covered in flour." Tessa slid her finger from Luke's photo hand to his little boy face, traced the curve.

Abby's cheeks pinked. The corners of her mouth turned down, and she shook her head. Gaze hovering somewhere above the bed, Abby closed the pages of the photo album, without even looking.

She couldn't, Tessa realized.

Add that discovery to the Abby Stone file, the one Tessa had only just begun.

"I'm sorry, Abby," Tessa said, even though she wasn't sure what she was apologizing for. The fact she'd opened the albums, or that Abby couldn't.

Abby sighed, and folded her arms across her chest. "Luke loved to bake."

"For real?" At school, they'd taken most of their meals in the cafeteria. Luke's dorm room boasted the world's smallest microwave and a dorm fridge that, last seen, housed crunchy peanut butter, grape jelly, and a hot dog of questionable vintage. No one would claim the dog, so no one dared to toss it.

"Everything and anything."

Luke Connors liked to bake. Add that to her Luke Connors file, the one Tessa had started on the day she'd met Luke.

"Hungry?" Abby asked.

"Only when I'm awake."

"Go wash up. I'll get you something to eat before I put you to work in the kitchen."

Tessa imagined working alongside Abby, elbow-to-elbow in batter, and knee-deep in conversation. Then Tessa imagined screwing up so badly Abby sent her away before she could learn more about Luke. She imagined losing her opportunity to know Abby. "Are you sure? I need to shower. I don't want to hold you up."

"Twenty minutes," Abby said. "You've got plenty of time."

The last time Tessa had made breakfast with her mother, Tessa had scalded the hot chocolate, burned the pancakes, and accidentally set the kitchen on fire. Three weeks later, Mom was in Paris, sipping champagne and nibbling crepes, free from a daughter who'd tried too hard to please.

Coincidence?

"But, Abby, I don't know what to do. I'll only get in the way. I'm no—"

"Breakfast service starts at seven for the guests. If you're family, you're expected to help out." Abby flashed Tessa the smile she'd shared after Luke's memorial, the one that had drawn her closer then. The one that drew her now.

If you're family.

Was that an offer or a dare?

To Abby, cooking eggs Benedict was a dance requiring two in-sync partners, an almost clairvoyant communication between like-minded individuals, a give-and-take that could upend the most kitchen confident individuals. When Hannah called in sick, Abby could've managed breakfast alone. Whisk and cook hollandaise sauce, poach eggs, warm Canadian bacon, toast English muffins. She'd done it before. She'd been planning on doing it again.

Until she'd checked in on Tessa and found her poring over Luke's photo albums, eyes puffy, expression determined to punish herself. If left to her own devices, Tessa would've stayed in Luke's bed, turning the pages of Luke's life, pressing a thumb into her ache to freshen the pain.

Why else would Abby have hidden the albums away from herself?

"Stir until bubbles form. *Until.*" Abby grabbed a pot holder and moved the simmering hollandaise sauce in front of Tessa to a cold burner, seconds ahead of an unsightly, and wasteful, curdling.

"Sorry."

"That's okay." Abby slid English muffins from the toaster, slid slabs of Canadian bacon from the pan, scooped poached eggs from their bath. "Now, you drizzle the sauce over the eggs."

Tessa grabbed the hollandaise sauce pan by its metal handle. "Youch!"

"Pot holder."

Tessa held her hand by the wrist, face set in a grimace.

Abby inhaled the savory ham and eggs, shook her head, and ran the tap. She held Tessa's palm under the cold water and then patted it dry with a dish towel. "Better?"

"Much," Tessa said, even though she looked as though she might cry again, when that was the last thing Abby had intended. "I bet Luke never burned his hand," Tessa said, and Abby had the urge to place a kiss in the center of her palm, the way she had when Luke had tried a similar stunt.

"Sure he did."

"You're just saying that to make me feel better."

"Yes, and it's also true." Pot holder in hand, Abby drizzled hollandaise over two sets of eggs Benedict and placed them on a serving tray.

"I told you I'd get in the way. I warned you I didn't know how to cook or—"

Abby passed the plated breakfasts to Tessa, forced cheer into her voice. "Deliver these to table one, please!" Tessa wasn't going to learn how to cook by whining about her inability. And she wasn't going to get over her grief by wallowing in it either.

The thought conjured Lily Beth, her voice loving, but her

expression take-no-prisoners serious. The day Abby long feared had arrived. Sure enough, she'd become her mother. Soon, she'd be bathing crystals in sea salt and spinning fairy tales.

"Table one?" Tessa asked.

"Couple by the window, practically sitting on each other's laps," Abby said, and a grinning Tessa headed into the dining room.

After Charlie had left for college, Abby had done her share of wallowing until Lily Beth had dragged her from her bedroom and back into the world. The baby she'd been carrying should've been enough to give her purpose, but all she knew was that the boy she'd loved forever was gone. She'd thought her life was over, instead of beginning anew.

Abby prepared two more plates of eggs Benedict and delivered them to the guests at table three, a young couple spending their first visit at Briar Rose. "And here you go," Abby said, sliding the plates before appreciative *oohs* and *aahs*.

Tessa stood talking to Lisa and Ronnie at table one, a hand at her back, arched, as if to make sure they noticed her pregnancy, despite the vertical stripe camouflage of her sundress. They hadn't touched their food. Their breakfast sat before them, their eggs growing cold, and their forks remained atop their folded napkins. They leaned slightly forward, necks craned, elbows on the table, listening to Tessa.

A buzz of warning hummed in Abby's ears. "Enjoy your breakfasts," Abby said, and she headed across the room for the coffee carafe, conveniently situated next to table one. She slid the carafe from the warming plate.

"I didn't know I was pregnant until a couple of weeks after my boyfriend died." Tessa's hand went to her belly. The expression on Tessa's face, two parts regret with one part awestruck pride, flashed a wave of sadness through Abby's chest. The carafe of hot coffee trembled in Abby's hand, and she breathed through her nose.

"Wow." Lisa widened her eyes, and she tilted her head to the side. "How long were you and the boy together?"

Abby had forgotten to give Tessa the employee talk, to explain to her the difference between public and private information, to install privacy settings on her mouth.

Never let the guests see you grieve. Rule number one on Abby's official list of appropriate B&B employee behavior from this day forward.

In the last five months, she'd only had to tell guests about Luke's death a few times. Each time, the guests had been blessedly respectful, allowing her to briefly describe what had happened and then change the subject. Each time, she had the nagging worry that brushing over her loss diminished it. And then she'd buried the uncomfortable feeling under a pile of chores.

"Only a few months," Tessa said, "but we wicked loved each other."

Ronnie nodded. "I get it. Fell in love with Lisa on our first date."

"So romantic," Tessa said.

Good, turn the conversation back to the guests. Abby moved to table one and refilled Lisa's and Ronnie's mugs. "How are you two doing this morning?"

"Fantastic, as always," Lisa told Abby, but her gaze remained on Tessa.

Ronnie covered his wife's hand with his own. "So, Tessa, how do you know Abby?"

The humming in Abby's ears roared. She and Tessa hadn't shared a clairvoyant connection in the kitchen, but she tried for one now. *Please don't tell them, please don't tell them, please don't tell them.*

Tessa glanced at Abby, the whites of her eyes indicating her belated awareness of the faux pas. "Luke?" Tessa said.

At last year's Ronnie-and-Lisa visit, Luke would've been

getting ready for college, dashing through B&B chores en route to his friends and the beach. Last time Ronnie and Lisa had visited, her son might've served them breakfast, pausing at their table to inquire about their lives, and thereby drawing them into his own lighthearted flirting.

He was the polar opposite of Tessa sucking the guests into a melodrama that included Abby.

"Friends with Luke!" Lisa said to Tessa, and a grin spread across her face. She turned to Abby. "How's that handsome boy doing?"

"We keep meaning to ask you," Ronnie said. "Why haven't we seen him?"

Lisa nodded. "Such a nice boy. Is he home for the summer? Last year, I remember, he was all excited about starting school in the fall."

"Got into every school he applied to," Ronnie said.

"Decided on HRTA at UMass."

"Wanted to work in hospitality, like his mom," Ronnie added.

Inside Abby's apron pocket, she rubbed her forefinger against her thumb, wishing for a pencil to break, a box of pencils. Her beautiful boy should've been reaping the rewards of having studied himself to the top of his high-school class. He should've finished his first year of college. He should've come home to her with a long list of dinner requests and overflowing bags of stinky laundry. He should've come home to her. "Luke's not home."

"Stayed on at school, then?" Ronnie said. "First summer after I started school, I didn't want to—"

"He's not at school."

Lisa lifted her coffee mug, as though intending to take a sip. Then, her gaze caught Abby's, and something in Abby's face made her set the mug down. Lisa shifted back in her seat, as though trying to skirt the impending blow.

Ronnie's gaze slid from his wife to Abby and then back again.

The week Luke had died, Abby e-mailed scheduled guests to say there had been a family emergency. That was as close to personal information as she'd wanted to get. Months later, when guests who hadn't known Luke asked about her year, she gave general positive pseudo private information. She'd updated her menu to include vegetarian and vegan selections. Mid-winter treat-your-sweetheart packages were now posted on her website. She'd joined a wine-of-the-month club. She'd finally learned how to knit. Well-thought-out tidbits led guests to think they had a connection, when they didn't know her at all.

Abby's cheeks tingled. She probably looked as red-faced as Tessa. The phrase, *Luke died,* played in her head, but she couldn't coax it to her mouth. "I lost—" she started, but that word seemed all wrong, too.

You lost sauce-splattered handwritten recipe cards in the confusion of a busy kitchen. Socks worn thin at the heel went missing in the dryer. A child's nubby red mitten fell from an open backpack.

You lost your way.

Lisa nodded for her to continue, the woman's expression turning grim.

Abby cleared her throat. "There was an accident," she said, and the statement sounded like a lie, an impossible horror that happened to other people. "Luke was Tessa's boyfriend."

Lisa's hand fluttered to her mouth, and she shook her head. "Oh, Abby. How horrible." Her sad-eyed gaze slid from Abby to Tessa, and the corners of her mouth trembled upward. "And wonderful, too. At least you have the baby to look forward to," she told Abby, and Ronnie nodded in agreement. "Lots of visits. Lots of baby love." Lisa directed her statement to Tessa.

Tessa's hand fell from her belly. "I don't know if I'm keeping the baby," she said, even though no one had asked.

No one had asked.

Abby's cheeks stung, third-degree burn. Sun poisoning.

"Oh." Lisa's voice trailed off. Her gaze drifted to Abby, lingered, deposited the dreaded pity. Ronnie glanced at his wife and then offered the straight-lipped grimace-grin of discomfort.

Tessa stared at the table.

"Why don't we let Lisa and Ronnie enjoy their breakfasts?" Abby placed a hand on Tessa's back to prod her along, but Tessa didn't budge. Instead, her breathing deepened, and she shifted from foot to foot.

"I need your help in the kitchen," Abby said, hoping to head off hysterical crying, an outburst, whatever was brewing behind Tessa's shifting countenance.

"I'm so sorry, Abby. We didn't know," Lisa said, her eyes turning liquid before Abby. Ronnie rolled his lips into his mouth until they disappeared.

Heat flushed Abby's chest, the sensation of her heart breaking wide open, in public. "Of course not," she said, and she excused herself to go back into the kitchen, leaving Tessa behind.

Abby lifted the cast-iron fry pan from the stovetop and set it to cool in the sink, hoping the muscle required would stop her hands from shaking. She ran the water until it burned the tips of her fingers, and then, gloveless, wiped the cooked-on ham grease.

A hand touched Abby's shoulder. She shut off the water and spun around, expecting Tessa.

Instead, Lisa stood in her kitchen, pink-faced and teary-eyed. Wrong person. Wrong place. Wrong expression for a vacationing guest, if Abby wanted return business.

"I apologize, Lisa. Tessa shouldn't have said anything. I don't want to make you sad."

"Don't be ridiculous," Lisa said, and her tone strode across the line separating a polite guest from a concerned friend. "I only wish you'd told us sooner about Luke." In one swoop, Lisa took Abby into a bear hug.

Abby let out a faint yelp of surprise, and Lisa released her grip. "Ronnie and I have always looked forward to seeing Luke. Don't know if I've told you before, but we tried to have kids for years, even tried a few rounds of fertility treatments." She shrugged. "But it never happened for us."

Abby had assumed Lisa and Ronnie's childlessness was by choice. She knew they lived in a suburb of Boston. That Lisa had relocated from Connecticut for her job in banking. That Ronnie had family in West Palm Beach. But she'd never known of their greatest disappointment. She'd never considered they were anything but dual-income, no kids, who enjoyed walks on the beach and indulged in loud sex that shook the walls of the B&B. She never knew anything other than what they chose to show her.

That made them more alike than she cared to admit.

"We used to say, if we had a son, we would've liked him to have been like Luke." Lisa's gaze went soft, as though she could see Luke in her mind's eye, too.

"You and Ronnie used to say that?"

"He was such a part of this place. He had such great energy—"

"Yes."

"Such a way of making everyone feel special."

Abby's mouth trembled, and she brushed away a tear.

"I'll never forget how Luke brought flowers up to the room for me last summer," Lisa said.

"He did?"

"I mentioned I liked lupine, just mentioned it. And that night, I found a bunch outside the door to our room."

"He never told me." Abby imagined Luke taking the pruners to his favorite flowers, the impulse to please overriding his aversion to cutting. She imagined Luke knocking on Lisa and Ronnie's door, ducking around the corner, and then waiting to hear her appreciative squeal. The image warmed her cold places. The image made her want to run to her room and sob into her pillow until her chest ached. She took a slow, deep breath to clear her head. "Thank you for sharing that story with me."

Lisa gave Abby a long stare. "You were lucky to have had a son like that," Lisa said, and then left the kitchen, the word *lucky* trailing behind her.

Lucky wasn't a word Abby had associated with herself in quite a while.

All over the evening news were stories of overwhelming luck. Just last week, a three-year-old boy fell from his bedroom window and came to a soft landing in a thick patch of overgrown shrubbery, bruised but otherwise unharmed. A six-year-old girl pushed through a window screen, ten stories above a city sidewalk, and a bus driver with unusually fast reflexes and strength happened to be walking by and caught the child in his arms.

Where was luck when Luke had fallen?

Tessa slipped into the kitchen, gaze wary, but chin held high.

Abby's heart skipped a beat, a palpitation connecting her to the grandchild this stranger carried.

Abby supposed she'd been lucky to have become pregnant at eighteen, if you considered that many couples battled years of infertility and never conceived. She'd been lucky to carry her son to term, to have instinctively known she never would have survived terminating her pregnancy. She never would have survived cutting him out of her life after he was born either. To that end, she was lucky to have had Lily Beth's support.

"Close the kitchen door," Abby said for the third time in her life. The first time was when, years ago, she'd had to fire a chambermaid for stealing a Rolex from a guest room. The second time was when, months ago, she'd called Hannah into the kitchen, told her to take the rest of the week off, and then thrown up in the sink.

"Sit down."

"You're mad at me."

"Not exactly." Abby pulled out a chair and sat down next to Tessa. She shook her head. "When I was pregnant with Luke, my mother told me to hold my head high, not to be ashamed."

"I'm not ashamed—" Tessa said.

"Let me finish." Abby held a hand up. "That doesn't mean I volunteered information."

Abby also hadn't needed to explain her pregnancy, because she'd lived in one place her entire life. And like it or not, everyone had known her business.

"I want you to understand I'm not going to pressure you to decide what you want to do with the baby," Abby said. "It's a big decision, probably the biggest you'll ever make. I don't want you to ever look back on this time with regret. If you decide to keep the baby, I will support you. If you decide to give the baby to someone in your family, I will support you."

And if Tessa decided to give Abby's grandchild to a stranger, she wouldn't lie down and take it. She would drag her into court. She would fight her on it.

She didn't tell her that.

Tessa started toward Abby, and for the second time, Abby raised a hand for her to halt. "But, what I will not do. What I refuse to do," she said, and she pressed a fist to her chest, "is audition for the role of mother to Luke's child. I have proven myself, over and over. I have done the work."

Tessa's big brown eyes filled with tears, but they did not fall. Her whole body trembled with the effort. "I'm wicked sorry, Abby. Please, Abby. Don't make me leave. I have no place to go, no one I can talk to. I've got nothing left."

Really, Tessa? From where Abby sat, gazing at the swell of Tessa's belly, she had everything.

Everything that Abby wanted.

Why would Tessa jump to that conclusion? "I'm not asking you to leave," Abby said. That was the last thing she wanted. Abby wiped the tears from Tessa's cheeks with her thumbs, the way she had on the day of Luke's memorial service. "You can stay as long as you want."

"For real?" Tessa's voice caught on the hiccup of a laugh-cry, and tears spilled down her cheeks.

Abby hugged Tessa close, pressing the girl's wet cheek to hers. That made Tessa cry harder, like a little girl lost.

Abby's heart skipped a beat, a palpitation connecting her to the stranger who carried her grandchild.

Don't play me.

If luck was what happened when opportunity knocked on your door and found you prepared, then Abby would welcome luck with open arms, even if she had to do so through gritted teeth. Even if luck came in the form of a girl with the face of a child, the body of a woman, and the ability to toy with her heart.

CHAPTER 7

Rob barely recognized the house he'd once called home.

His truck made a sharp turn and the tires ground into the pea-stone driveway, kicking up dust in the dry summer heat. He'd taken Bella's dog run down months ago, sent over a couple of guys to aerate and seed the lawn. Maria still hadn't gotten around to listing the house, part of their divorce settlement. But per a realtor friend's suggestion, Rob had instructed his summer hire to unhinge the fire-engine red front door and paint it a "warm and welcoming" yellow. Last day off, he'd trimmed the arborvitae himself until the bubble had centered on the level. The property looked tidy, well-maintained, and organized.

Unlike his life.

Sweat cooled the back of his neck, a sticky concoction of summer heat, hard work, and mad-as-hell. He tugged at the cotton fabric beneath his arms, stepped from his truck, and brushed the gray dirt from his knees, evidence of the soil he'd been kneeling in before Maria's call. He flexed his fingers because he'd promised Maria he'd come over to talk with Grace and have a discussion with the boy his ex-wife had found in bed with their daughter, and Rob liked to talk with his hands.

Maria met him at the door in a crisp white blouse and black shorts, her hair slicked back in a ponytail. If it hadn't been for the crease between her eyes, the way she was gnawing at her bottom lip, he would've thought he'd imagined their phone call.

"Tyler took off," Maria said before Rob could fit through the door, and the boy's name once again forced the image of Maria finding his daughter and her just-a-friend beneath the sheets of Grace's bed. Rob shook it off, and more pleasant Tyler images settled. The scrawny kid used to come over every Sunday night for dinner, gobble down Maria's mashed potatoes, marvel at the fact they ate together as a family. He and Grace liked to play on the swing set in the yard, hang upside down from the monkey bar until their faces turned red. They played ultimate Frisbee, Tyler against Bella and Grace. The game always ended in a tie. Everybody won.

Long time ago.

The unnatural chill of air-conditioning raised the hairs on the back of Rob's arms. He'd forgotten how much he disliked the closed windows. And shades drawn to keep out the heat darkened the home's interior, a stark contrast to the place he was supposed to be in less than two hours. "Coward," Rob said. "I wasn't going to hurt him. Much."

Maria gave him a tight little smile.

All the way over from the Hendersons' place, he couldn't stop thinking about Abby's unexpected guest, Tessa, not much older than Grace, and a few months away from having a baby. What would he do if his Grace got pregnant? What would he want her to do?

All he knew was that he didn't want Grace to ever be in that position. He never wanted her to have to choose between the life she'd intended and the one coming her way. That thought had him racing from Phippsburg to Bath, praying his way through yellow lights, red lights clipping the cab of his truck.

"Where's our baby girl?" Rob asked, but the joke misfired, tightening his chest.

Maria blinked back tears and her voice came out weighted and water-logged. "Upstairs in her bedroom. Locked the door," Maria said, "after she slammed it on me."

That didn't sound like Grace. His girl was level-headed and, unlike her mother, not prone to melodrama. She'd never gone through a boy-crazy phase, found most boys ridiculous and immature, a sentiment Rob wholeheartedly agreed with. As far as he knew, until Tyler, his girl hadn't slept with any boys.

And if Maria's manicure appointment hadn't been cancelled, they wouldn't have known Grace was sleeping with Tyler either.

"What did you say to her?" he asked, remembering Maria's urgent call, her hard-to-comprehend rambling that slipped into the Italian of her childhood, ranting about their daughter behaving like a *puttana*. A whore. Had Maria said that to Grace?

Maria was like an old-fashioned pressure cooker, slow to anger, and then she blew.

"Nice girls do not have sex before marriage," Maria had told him. But Rob and Maria had. Did she regret that, too?

Maria met his stare, and her gaze narrowed to a point. "This isn't my fault," she said. "I did everything right. I was always home after school for her, always had dinner waiting on the table." Dinner that Rob had missed those last years of their marriage, more times than he cared to admit. Maria never missed an opportunity to throw that one in his face.

Maybe he hadn't done everything right, but neither had she.

"Tell her she shouldn't have slept with Tyler," Maria said. "If he cared for her, he would've waited. He wouldn't have pushed."

As Rob recalled, back in college, Maria had resisted his pushing, for about five minutes.

Rob stopped at the bottom of the stairway, hand on the

newel cap, and pinched the bridge of his nose. "You asked me to come here and talk to her. Now, let me."

Maria started after him.

"Alone," he said, and left her at the bottom of the stairs, staring up.

He glanced at Grace's sports team photos. His pretty tomboy wore Morse High School blue and white, her dark hair pulled back, her expression sports-serious. Then his gaze caught on the portrait of Grace and Tyler taken at the prom, as if he'd never seen it before. Grace's long hair hung in loose waves around her shoulders, and she aimed a high-voltage smile at the photographer. Excited about the dance or moony for her date? Tyler's arm wrapped around Grace's back. Muscle had replaced scrawniness. Confidence now overrode little-kid awkwardness. When had the neighbor boy become a man? When had Grace's just-a-friend turned into something more?

Rob knocked on Grace's door. "It's Dad," he said, and Grace opened the door to let him in. Windows were open wide; a fan moved sheer white curtains. Even on this shirts-stick-to-your ribs muggy day, his daughter couldn't tolerate artificial anything, just like her dad.

"Hey, Gracie girl," he said. "How's it going?"

"She's taking a hissy fit," Grace said, borrowing an expression of Rob's. "That's how it's going."

To Rob's relief, Grace was fully dressed, wearing cutoff jean shorts and a tight-fitting green T-shirt. The blue-and-green polka dot spread she'd had since middle school covered Grace's bed, and a row of throw pillows leaned against her headboard. That didn't stop Rob from imagining rumpled sheets beneath the spread, Grace on top of the sheets and Tyler on top of his daughter. That didn't stop Rob from imagining picking up Tyler by the shoulders and throwing him against the wall. A line of perspiration ran down the center of his back, and he flexed his fingers.

"How was your mother supposed to act?" he said. "How do you think it would've gone down if I'd found Tyler in your room? Or any boy, for that matter?" Grace took a step back from Rob's rarely used harsh tone.

Pink splotches bloomed on Grace's cheeks. Her gaze lowered to her arms, folded over her chest. "Not so well."

"Not so well," he repeated. The edge to his voice cut both ways, tensing his jaw.

Grace shifted her weight from foot to foot. Her bottom lip jutted out, as though she might cry.

That's what happened when he let Maria rile him, when Rob let his ex-wife's wild emotions replace his common sense and reason. Shaming words—Maria's—and an angry tone—Rob's—would only drive their daughter away. Shaming words and anger would do nothing to keep her safe.

Rob turned his head from side to side, worked out a kink in his neck. "Oh, no, you don't." He sat down on Grace's bed and patted the seat beside him.

As if she were still a little girl, Grace slid beneath his arm and fit her face into the crook of his neck. He wrapped his arms around her and kissed the top of her head, the way he had when she'd been small. But instead of sharp angles and hard bones, a woman's curves pressed against him, and he shifted away from them. Instead of fly-away hair, smelling of No More Tears shampoo and strawberry detangling spray, a mix of vanilla and flora hit his nose. And, when Grace raised her head from his shoulder, instead of the mortified gaze of a repentant child, a woman's wide eyes met his and her long eyelashes refused to blink.

"So . . . old buddy Tyler's your boyfriend now?" Rob said.

Grace shrugged. "Guess so."

"Since when?"

"We never, you know, decided to go out. It just sort of evolved." She flexed her hands to reveal open palms.

"At the prom?" Rob asked.

Grace laughed, shook her head. "Way before that."

"When were you going to tell me?"

"I was kind of hoping I wouldn't have to. Kind of thought it was obvious," Grace said. Rob started to shake his head and then paused. What had he missed?

Last winter, Tyler had asked Grace to troubleshoot a problem with his car, even though his uncle owned a garage in Phippsburg. A few times, Rob had swung by for an impromptu visit after work and found Grace and Tyler in the living room, books and schoolwork spread out across the coffee table, the two of them sitting on the couch, tight as a secret.

Grace tucked her hair behind one ear, revealing a diamond stud and a pearl. Since when did Grace have two holes?

What had he missed? What hadn't he missed?

He'd come here intending to lambaste Tyler and Grace with his words. To threaten Tyler with bodily harm.

Truth was, they were both eighteen years old, the same age Rob and Maria had been when they'd started dating. Ducks-in-a-row Grace had had her life planned out since she was ten. Study biology in undergrad school and then apply to veterinary school. Overachiever Tyler had his sights set on law school. Kid was mature, for a boy his age.

Truth was, Tyler could still hurt her, in so many ways.

"What's going to happen in a few weeks, when you go away to different schools? Not great timing to start a relationship, kiddo."

"Cell phones, instant messaging, Skype," Grace rattled off. "It's a brave new world."

"That's not what I mean."

"Yeah, I know." Grace turned toward the window, and a corner of her bottom lip tucked into her mouth, a trace of her mother.

Had to admit, Grace might favor him in temperament and

athletic ability, but she was Maria's daughter, too, prone to spikes of emotion. When Rob first moved out, Grace had refused to talk to Maria for a week. And after Maria took their wedding photo off the wall, Grace dug it out of the closet and set it on her bureau. If Maria wanted to talk to her, she'd make her come into her room, where the photo of what she'd denied Grace could bear witness. Making herself stare at that photo day after day, night after night, must've hurt Grace worse.

"We're not going to see anyone else for the first semester," Grace said. "And when we come home for Thanksgiving, we'll reevaluate."

For Rob, first semester at school had been a free-for-all. He'd never been a big partier, but that hadn't stopped him from propping a beer in his hand while he'd scoped out the cutest girls at the dorm parties. That hadn't stopped him from bedding more than his share of freshman girls, until he'd met Grace's mother. Until she'd somehow made him care.

"Devil's advocate," Rob said, a term he'd used when Grace had been knee-deep in college acceptance letters and weighing each school's pros and cons. "What if Tyler wants to see other girls? You'd be okay with that?"

"He won't—"

"Oh, Gracie girl, your dad's here to tell you, guys are different. It's not the same for them. It's not all emotional."

"It?" Grace said, and she tilted her head. Her eyes widened—*Are you serious?*—but her grin said she forgave her dad's discomfort.

"Okay. *Sex* isn't the same for boys." As he recalled, he'd also had more than his share of girls, who, come Monday mornings and the return of reality, wanted more from him. He wasn't proud of it, but he'd broken plenty of girls' hearts, too. "Guys don't have the same concerns, honey. Guys can't get pregnant."

"Daddy!" Grace pressed both hands over her mouth, a move Rob suspected was more about embarrassment than slapstick.

"Don't you dare tell me you and Tyler hadn't thought of that." When Maria had called Rob, that's all he could think of. "You are being careful, aren't you?"

"We're not stupid!"

"Answer the question, Grace."

"Yes, Daddy, we're being careful." Grace angled him an impish grin. "What about you? Are you being careful?"

"Come again?"

"Heard from Tony DeCaprio you've been going out with a blond babe, bringing her for fancy dates at his uncle's shop."

Rob's stomach muscles clenched, as if his daughter had spied his schoolboy crush. He laughed a little too loud. "Her name is Abby; she's a design client. And for the record, visiting a garden center isn't a date. That was business."

For the record, he wasn't exactly dating Abby either. They were two adults, exploring their options. Options that, with the arrival of Abby's unexpected visitor, had suddenly narrowed.

Talk about lousy timing.

If he knew anything about the beginning of relationships, nothing challenged them more than adding a baby to the mix. When he and Maria had first gotten married, the woman had baby on the brain. Fresh out of college, the notion of a wee one almost sounded like fun to Rob, too. Want to go on a camping trip? Tuck the tot in a sleeping bag. Need a weekend ski getaway, sun shining on white powder to clear out winter cobwebs? Strap the kid to your back.

That should've been his first hint that he didn't have a clue.

Days ago, he'd thought he'd wanted to start over with Abby, because she made him feel like a stricken teenager.

She made him feel.

But he had no intention of ending up like one of the foolish middle-aged men pictured on the covers of gossip rags at Shaw's checkout, starting new families in last-ditch attempts to reclaim their youths. Or, closer to home, Dan Mulligan, fifty-year-old owner of the family restaurant Bait-N-Switch. Guy divorced his wife after their three grown boys had finished college and took up with a woman half his age. He heard Dan and the new missus were expecting twins.

Heard the whole town laughing out loud and whispering about Viagra.

Rob wasn't anywhere near as old as Dan, and Abby wasn't as young as Dan's wife. But still . . .

Rob was looking to start over with the right woman, not do over his entire life.

Grace waggled her eyebrows. "So your design client Abby's a blond babe?"

"She's an attractive woman with blond hair. I don't think she'd appreciate the term *babe,*" Rob said, although late at night, alone in his apartment, he'd imagined whispering the term *baby* over her earlobe, and then exploring the rest of her bare curves. First time, fast and furious. Second time, slow as sin. Rob's neck heated, a sudden sunburn.

"Ha! You like her. You like her a lot," Grace said, reminding Rob of what Abby had said about her cat taking a shine to Rob. What was the beast's name? Sophie? Sadie? Until now, Rob hadn't considered Abby might've been letting on how she felt about him. "Hello, hello!" Grace used to say. "Light dawns on marble head." Until now, Rob hadn't considered that his daughter could turn a conversation around on him.

"How about you and Tyler?"

Grace's smugness faded. She scrunched up her mouth and shook her head, a slow side-to-side refusal.

Rob got up on one knee, raised his hands over his daughter. "Gracie girl?" he said, giving her less than a second before he went in for the kill, aka the tickle attack.

Grace squealed and flopped over. She folded into a ball for cover. "Uncle."

"Can't hear you."

"Uncle!" she yelled. "Uncle, already!"

Rob let her catch her breath and sit up. "About Tyler?" he said.

Grace nodded and spoke like a woman who knew her mind. "I like Tyler. I sure do like him a lot."

And Rob liked Abby a lot. He owed it to his friend Abby to come clean. He owed it to himself to be realistic about what he really wanted, not a subject he'd spent much time pondering of late.

He wanted to take Abby out on real dates. He wanted to get to know her better. He also wanted to get inside her pants. And he wanted to support her, even if Abby wanted to convince Tessa to let her adopt her son's baby.

If Abby got what she wanted, Rob couldn't see a future with her.

That didn't stop Rob from still wanting to get inside her pants. That made him worse than Grace's friend-turned-boyfriend Tyler, starting a relationship when they were headed in different directions. Starting something he knew he couldn't finish.

On the day Luke was born, Abby had awoken to chalk-white skies, snow drifts edging her bedroom windows, and a pressure that wracked her body and had her calling out for Lily Beth.

Today's overcast skies couldn't hamper Abby's mood.

"Rain's coming." Lily Beth squinted past the guests sitting in the rows of teak folding chairs before Luke's handprint stepping stones, and gazed out to the water. "Listened to the weather service on the drive over," Lily Beth added, even though she and Abby knew full well the ways to predict a storm without the benefit of radio waves. Same as Abby, surely Lily Beth had awoken to a dewless lawn, a sky free of fog, and the sensation of wanting to jump out of your skin, like the fish dimpling the surface of the harbor.

"Fortuitous for a ground-breaking ceremony?" Abby asked, because she knew that would be her mother's next proclamation. Lily Beth grinned and squeezed Abby's shoulder.

They could use a good downpour, something strong and soaking, to soften the dry soil and open it up for the rows of plantings and stones that would edge the grassy path of the labyrinth. For now, white lines painted the temporary path until the real thing came along.

Charlie strolled around the side of the house, carrying a bouquet of red roses in his right hand, yellow roses in his left. He caught Abby's gaze and broke into a broad grin. Without slowing down, he made an exaggerated sweep of her body, head to toe and back again, and then drew his lips into his mouth and emitted a low wolf whistle of appreciation.

"For me?" Lily Beth said, fingertips to her chest.

Charlie winked and gave Lily Beth a kiss on the cheek. "The whistle, not the blooms. These are for my girls," he said.

It took Abby a beat to realize he meant her and Tessa. It took Abby a moment to shake herself out of déjà vu: the memory of a teenage Charlie stopping by Lily Beth's to bring Abby drooping grocery-store roses and stale chocolates in a heart-shaped box. Charlie dropping in to say his good-byes.

Abby took the flowers from Charlie's hands. "Classy," she said. "The flowers, not the whistle. You do know this is my place of business?" Abby said, even though no Briar Rose guests were attending the gathering.

Without qualm, Charlie leaned close and directed his gaze to Abby's cleavage. "If you didn't want me to whistle, then you shouldn't have worn that dress."

Heat rose from Abby's center, a confused mix of anger and embarrassment that Charlie could, so easily, draw a reaction from her. She buried her nose in the red roses, inhaled partway.

Lily Beth flipped her hair with the back of her hand. "Oh, that old thing?" she said, twisting a line from one of her and Abby's favorite movies. "Abby only wears that when she doesn't care how she looks. Isn't that right, baby?"

"That's right." She didn't care, at least not about Charlie's opinion. She'd chosen the low-cut turquoise dress for Rob. After spending half an hour ruling out several more conservative contenders, she'd decided to trot out her secret weapons. Rob had come by yesterday with a crew to spray paint the labyrinth on her lawn and erect a simple arbor at its entrance. The first time she'd seen him all week, and she couldn't get him to look her in the eye, let alone gaze at her cleavage. He'd been all business. Fine by her, as long as he dropped the act when they were alone.

She wanted to get him alone.

That wasn't about to happen with a yard full of guests.

Celeste tiptoed over the lawn, perching on the balls of her feet so her high heels wouldn't dig into the grass. She held a tray of Luke's favorite cupcakes, Death by Chocolate. Two short helpers—daughter, Phoebe, and son, Elijah—held on to Celeste's skirt. "Where's your new best friend?" Celeste asked, referring to Tessa.

Abby widened her eyes. "That's the precise reason I haven't let you come by."

"What, *that?*"

"That comment, that look on your face." That overprotectiveness Abby loved and appreciated. "Mama Bear," Abby whispered, and Celeste took down her snarky shield.

Lily Beth waved at Phoebe, and she ran across the lawn, a streak of red curls. Abby's mother knelt in her long skirt and caught Phoebe in her kayak-paddling-sculpted arms, then hoisted her onto her hip and spun her in a circle, putting a grin on Abby's face. Her mother did not act like a soon-to-be great-grandmother. Then again, she'd never acted like a traditional mother or grandmother either.

Seemed to work for Tessa.

On Tuesday, Abby had let Lily Beth drop in for a casual meet and greet—as casual as the circumstances allowed. She brought Tessa a bottle of Earth Mama Body Butter, a drawing tablet with an egg-in-a-nest cover, and the last sand dollar Luke had given her.

Seemed to work for Lily Beth.

But then Lily Beth sat in Abby's driveway behind the wheel of her lime-green Beetle for a good ten minutes before she'd keyed the engine and headed for home.

Abby played at swiping a cupcake from Celeste's tray. "Heard there's been a rash of cupcake robberies," she said, and her stomach dipped. Tone, cadence, word choice. Without meaning to, Abby had channeled Luke.

"Don't you dare!" The tilt of Celeste's head, the rue in her grin. One glance from Celeste let Abby know Celeste had heard it, too.

Abby brought her voice back to a normal range. "They look delish." No regrets, no sadness allowed. Want to share funny Luke stories? Go right ahead. Talk about a prank he played, even complain a little? Go to town. But no tears. Not today.

Celeste set the tray on Abby's quilt-covered table, right next to Luke's favorite drink.

Extra-tart lemonade filled an etched glass beverage dispenser, and a dozen matching glasses awaited the beverage. Elijah studied the arrangement and then turned each glass right-side up.

Abby gave Elijah a thumbs-up. "Good job. Why didn't I think of that?" she said, and he grinned at the table.

No adult beverages or fancy finger sandwiches. Abby had

invited her closest friends and instructed each person to bring a dessert. Homemade cider doughnuts balanced in a pyramid. Blueberries melted atop a two-layer cheesecake. Bite-sized carrot cakes with cream-cheese frosting rounded out the selection. Today was all about a boy and his sweetness.

Now and again, Abby could stand a lesson in sweetness, at least as it pertained to Charlie. He was the only person she knew who could, knee-jerk, get a rise out of her. She tucked the bouquets under her arm and touched Charlie's shoulder. "Thank you for the flowers. I'll go put them in water. They'll look lovely on the table."

"Not as lovely as you."

Abby took her hand from his arm, straightened her posture. "What are you doing?"

Charlie laughed. The sharp burst of air sent a shiver up the back of her neck. "Trying to pay you a compliment," he said, and his tongue darted out to lick at his bottom lip. A slight tilt to his chin, and Charlie locked his gaze on hers. Too serious, too loving, too inappropriate for their friendship.

"Well, don't!" Abby said. "I don't want to owe you anything."

"Abigail Pearl," he said, full-on crooning. "You'll always be my jewel of the sea."

What madness was this?

If Charlie had suggested they duck behind a bush for a quickie, she would've known he was kidding. Kidding, but hoping she'd take him up on the offer. If he'd asked her to mess around, complete with an obscene arm-pump gesture, she might've even laughed. But for Charlie to go soft on her, speaking to her as though they were still teenage lovers who'd never stopped loving . . .

Why now? To what end?

A heat churned in Abby, bringing her dangerously close to tears. Tears that she didn't understand, which really ticked her off. She shook the flowers at Charlie. "I'm going to go put these in water," she repeated, "and when I get back, I expect you to act normal. Think you can manage that?"

"Not a chance, Pearl."

Abby opened her mouth to protest Charlie's term of endearment, but nothing came out. At the house-side flagstone path, she turned to find Charlie staring after her. He nodded, as if he'd gotten exactly what he'd intended.

Charlie's madness couldn't hamper Abby's mood.

Instead of taking the flowers into the kitchen, Abby headed to check on Tessa. She wasn't overly surprised by Tessa's tardiness; that girl took forever getting ready. But Rob was supposed to have been here half an hour ago, and he'd never been late before. When she'd invited him to stand by her side and say a few words about labyrinths, he said he'd be honored. But what if he felt the invitation too personal? What if personal was the last thing he was interested in?

Abby slid open the pocket door, cocked her head not so much toward as against the racket. The song "If I Die Young" reverberated off the walls of her living room, a thick rope of sound that lashed out from Luke's bedroom and noosed Abby's heart.

"Tessa!" Abby yelled, but all she could hear were the lyrics. The smell of roses sharpened in her nose and clogged her throat, a vile reminder of the days after Luke's funeral and the bouquets that had riddled her home.

When Luke was eight he'd, quite accidentally, discovered Abby's vulnerability to sad songs. Charlie had recorded some favorite music for him, a mix CD that included, of all things, Irish ballads. "Kilkelly Ireland" told the tale of an Irishman whose son immigrated to America, and thirty years of unrelenting loneliness that ended with the father on his deathbed. Nice story for a child.

Luke had loved it.

Boom box in hand, he'd chase Abby around the sofa, while Abby attempted to outrun the father's sorrow.

"If I Die Young" was a heck of a lot harder to outrun. The song reached down through the still waters of Abby's hard-earned tranquility and scraped the soft, sandy bottom of her loss until grief clouded the water and muddied her impossible-to-hamper mood.

Abby tossed the bouquets on the sofa and raced into Luke's room in time to hear the lead singer for The Band Perry claim she'd had enough time. Enough time for whom? Abby certainly hadn't had enough time.

Tessa lay on her left side atop Luke's bed, hands cradled around her belly.

Abby's senior year in high school, there had been a car accident where three football players had died, juiced up on beer and testosterone. Because no matter how many videos the guidance counselors played in drivers' ed of mangled cars and bloody wrecks, no teenagers really believed they were mortal. Or, if they did believe it in the vaguest sense, they saw death as a song, where you looked down on your friends, legs dangling from the vantage point of a white fluffy cloud.

They saw death as romantic.

If you died when you were a teenager, you'd never experience the disappointment of watching your dreams fall short or suffer the indignities of old age. To Abby, those lost boys were forever young, brimming with beauty and potential. Brimming with life.

For those left behind, life was a heck of a lot more complicated.

Abby went to Tessa's iPod she'd attached to Luke's dresser-top speaker and twisted the volume knob until it came off in her hand.

Tessa sprang to sitting. "I was listening to that."

Electricity thrummed through Abby's body, curled her

toes, hunched her shoulders, and beat a drum at the center of her bottom lip. A slow, deep breath only quickened her pulse. Abby understood Tessa's behavior, she really did, but that didn't mean she'd facilitate it. "No, what you were doing was having a pity party for one, the timing of which is completely inconsiderate, seeing as I've invited a couple dozen guests over for sweets and happy Luke remembrances. No time for melodrama today. No time."

Despite Abby's speech, the sad song played in her head, sweet lilting country vocals about a mother burying her baby. Flash of identifying Luke's body. Flash of picking out Luke's casket. Flash of touching her son's face for the last time. The drumbeat at her lip spread to encompass the rest of her body.

Don't think, don't think, don't think.

Tessa's eyes widened. To her credit, they did not roll. "The song makes me feel better," she said, her voice even, the tone disarmingly reasonable.

To Abby's utter mortification, tears ran down the sides of her face. She swiped at them with her palms. "Well, it doesn't help me."

"You sure about that?" Dry eyed, Tessa held Abby's gaze. The intensity was like staring at a mirror.

"Abby?"

Charlie stood in the doorway, and a whimper escaped Abby's lips. Fifty years from now, he'd still remind her of the son they'd lost. No matter how many happy memories they shared, the sight of Charlie would still hurt. "It never ends, does it?" she asked.

In two steps, Charlie swallowed the space between them, and sobs wracked her body, waves of heat and pain. The mesh of his shirt pressed into her cheek. The song played on in Abby's head, a background track of torture. Charlie's chest moved beneath her, deep, measured breaths. He adjusted his stance so that for once, he could comfort her.

What madness was this?

One last shuddering breath and Abby opened her eyes to find Tessa gone, Abby and Charlie alone in the low light of a cloud-darkened bedroom. Born on an ocean breeze, the low rumble of conversations drifted from the yard and through the screen, a whole world outside the door waiting for her to enjoy. A whole world that had moved on after Luke had died.

Heat from Charlie's chest moved through hers. Notes whistled from outside, the tune growing louder as someone neared the side of her house. Sunlight slanted through the French doors, an in-between-clouds reprieve, and glinted off a red-handled shovel, a bow tied at the handle, slung across a broad shoulder.

A turn of his head, a white-toothed grin, a glimmer of pale blue eye, a split-second glance. Disappointment darkened Rob's gaze.

And then he was gone.

CHAPTER 8

Ever since Abby was small, she'd look to the summer sky for guidance. Clear skies meant spending the day outdoors beneath the blistering sun, slathered in sunscreen, arms pumping to keep up with Lily Beth's long-legged strides. At low tide, they'd stroll along the beaches of Hermit Island and scramble over the rocky shoreline, Lily Beth bending to point out the creatures the tides had stranded. Bits and pieces of sand dollars. Small chipped snails. The single sharp hook of a crab's discarded leg. Abby would examine the specimens, searching for clues with a child's eyes, not realizing she wasn't looking at life, but turning over the empty shells of what was left behind.

Overcast skies alone had never scared Lily Beth and Abby indoors, unless the wind kicked up and shaped a vertical cloud. Unless a multistory structure with an anvil top threatened to slam the harbor, pummel the shores, and spoil their plans.

Well, I'll be damned.

Abby peered out her living room window and shook her head at the clouds. Dark and at a distance and not anvil-topped, but nevertheless, on their way. She'd taken five minutes to freshen up her tear-stained face, harness her mood, and attempt to convince Charlie to head out to the gathering ahead of her. Instead, he'd hung close, waiting for her outside the bathroom door like a lovesick suitor, and then arranged her hair across one shoulder.

Charlie rubbed the back of her hand, trying to get her to take his, as though today were a continuation of their son's memorial service. One really, really long day. Abby adjusted the spaghetti strap of her dress that didn't need adjusting. "We can't do this."

"Bad timing again?" he asked, but the rejection didn't register in his eyes.

"Sort of," she said. She and Rob hadn't made any formal commitment to each other, but before this week, she'd thought something special was growing between them, something she wanted to nurture. Now, all she wanted was to get outside and attempt damage control before the skies opened up and rained out the groundbreaking. Walking outside holding Charlie's hand wouldn't exactly help her cause.

Charlie's gaze slid to her chest. "You're twisted." Charlie plucked the silver locket from where it rested in the notch of her collarbone, a curl of Luke's baby hair nestled within, and turned it over. He took his time sliding the necklace's front-migrated clasp to the back of her neck.

"I'm sort of seeing someone."

"Oh?"

"Rob Campbell?" she tried, when Charlie's hands rested at the nape of her neck. "My, uh, landscape architect?"

"I know who he is."

Rob could certainly pick Charlie out in a crowd. He'd noticed the photo in her living room; he'd pretended not to notice Charlie's image when it popped onto the screen of her cell phone. But she'd been careful not to mention Rob's name in front of Charlie. Why invite unnecessary awkwardness? Until today. "How? How do you know him?"

Charlie shot her a wicked grin. He stepped back and

tapped the face of the Cartier that, days post-divorce, had cost him more than a month's teaching salary. "Ticktock. Guests are waiting."

"Joe from Percy's?" A couple of weeks ago, Luke's friend from high school had scooped two medium-sized pistachio ice-cream cones for her and Rob, and then remarked how unusual it was for more than one person to request that flavor, his eyebrows raised with unspoken meaning. But that made no sense. It was one thing to offer cute commentary on her and Rob's ice-cream compatibility, quite another to share that insight with her son's father.

Who would stand to gain from gossiping about her and Rob to Charlie? "Suzette from Spinney's?"

The former student of Charlie's had a terrible crush on him. When she and Charlie used to come in for dinner, Suzette would request their table and make a point of leaning over Charlie to arrange the place setting, so that her multiple charms—a heart, a cross, a diamond-encrusted starfish—toppled head over heels into the deep valley between her breasts.

"Time's a wasting." Charlie tried to grab Abby's hand and then laughed when she shoved him away, as though they were reenacting a scene from when they were ten.

Abby came around the house a couple of strides before Charlie to find half the guests nibbling desserts around the buffet table, the other half devouring the after-ceremony treats at their seats. Celeste and Tessa stood to the side of the table, chatting as if *they* were each other's new best friends.

Stormy weather made people act strange and out of character, as if a low-pressure system had invaded their internal ecosystems.

Elijah straightened a stack of napkins and studied Tessa from a safe distance, nothing unusual there. But his little sister, Phoebe, clung to Tessa, a mass of red curls resting against Tessa's side. The child's open hand traced a lazy trail over Tessa's pregnant belly. Tessa placed her hand over Phoebe's and guided her to a spot just beneath her belly button. When Phoebe's hand jostled, she raised her head and giggled up at Tessa. Elijah startled and fell back onto the grass.

Tessa had yet to invite Abby to feel the baby move.

That explained why Abby had the ridiculous urge to walk up to Tessa and place her hands on her belly, taking possession without bothering to ask. Ridiculous because if Luke's baby moved beneath Abby's hand, she'd fall into what she and Celeste called insta-love and never be able to let him, or her, go.

Celeste met Abby in front of the cider doughnuts. "I thought everyone should start on the treats, since it doesn't look as though the weather's going to last much longer. Plus, you were MIA for a while . . ." Celeste glanced at Charlie, making short work of the mini carrot cakes. "Did I overstep?" she said, the same thing she asked whenever she'd overstepped.

"It's fine."

"You look flustered," Celeste said. "And what's with your hair?"

Abby touched a hand to the warmth of her cheek. She glanced down at the do Charlie had created and shoved her hair from her shoulder.

"Oh, holy hell," Celeste said.

Charlie turned from the buffet table, as if Celeste had spoken his name. He popped a brownie bite into his mouth and grinned through his chewing.

"You need a twelve-step program," Celeste said, "a freaking intervention. He can't be that good. No one is."

"It's not what you think."

"It usually is."

"Not this time." Abby peered past the perennials and found the only person for whom she was inclined to offer an explanation. Rob stood beyond the arbor, propped against the red-handled shovel and talking with Lily Beth, as though they'd already moved from introductions to fast friends. They angled their heads to the sky.

"Excuse me. I need to get this show on the road," Abby said, and she headed for Rob.

"Looking fierce," Lily Beth said upon Abby's approach.

Abby wasn't sure whether she was referring to the weather or the electricity energizing her stride. "I, uh, just need to borrow Rob for a minute. To discuss our little speeches?"

"Of course." Lily Beth's eyes lit with the knowing look she'd mastered round about Abby's thirteenth birthday. "Don't take too long figuring out what you want," Lily Beth said, and she joined Charlie at the stepping-stones.

Rob repositioned the shovel, digging it into the grass between them. He set his grin to neutral. "So . . ."

"I'll, uh, say a few words about why I decided I needed a labyrinth in my backyard, our plan for the rest of the afternoon. Labyrinth walk, whatever's left from the dessert table. And then I'll introduce you."

"Like we discussed over the phone," Rob said.

"Like we discussed." The wind kicked up, ushering pine scent from the treetops. Abby's dress fluttered around her legs. She held Rob's gaze, but his amazing blue eyes offered nothing in return. "I'd like to explain," she said. "About Charlie. What you saw—"

Rob made a sound at the back of his throat, more of a dismissive grunt than a laugh. "You don't owe me an explanation. Charlie . . ." he said, and he scrunched up his mouth, as if to chew on the name. Rob shook his head. "It's none of my business."

Abby blew out a blowfish breath. "Really? Are you sure? Because I was kind of hoping it *was*."

Rob's grin did not shift from neutral, his stiff stance did not alter. And when Abby searched his face, the man barely blinked. A cover-up for hurt feelings? Or had she misjudged him, built up their relationship larger in her imagination than in their reality? For all she knew, he was seeing someone else. Of course, why hadn't she considered that? She was acting like a silly schoolgirl vying for a boy's attention. A silly schoolgirl wearing a low-cut dress.

The first droplets of rain dampened her cheeks, light and insubstantial as sea mist. But, make no mistake, a storm was on its way. Tip of a summertime squall line.

She adjusted her expression to match Rob's. All business. "Let's do this, then. Before we run out of time," she said, and race-walked across the lawn.

In front of the stepping-stones, Charlie rocked back and forth on the heels of his docksides. His hands jiggled in his pockets, as though weighing the change. "Fortuitous," he said, most likely echoing Lily Beth's weather report, but his focus locked on Rob.

"Rob, I'd like you to meet Charlie Connors, Luke's father. Charlie, Rob Campbell, my landscape architect." There, that should do it. Relationships defined and explained, even though it was none of Rob's business.

Charlie took his hands from his pockets, and the two men leaned in for a handshake. They clasped hands, paused in grip hang time, exchanged strangely exuberant grins.

The breeze blew hair across Abby's vision.

Lily Beth tucked Abby's hair behind her ear. "Ready, baby?" Lily Beth said, the same thing she'd asked of Abby on the zero-visibility roads-closed morning Abby had gone into labor with Luke. "Ready or not," Lily Beth had said, when, in lieu of an answer, Abby had doubled over in pain and stained her sheets scarlet.

In front of the rows of seated guests, Abby summoned her public speaking voice. "Looks like a storm's coming, so I'm going to begin our little ceremony," she said.

Conversations twittered to a close. Guests lingering by the

dessert table wandered over and shuffled into empty seats or stood off to the side. Celeste and Elijah joined Lily Beth and Charlie. Phoebe dragged Tessa by the hand to an empty seat in the front row, and then climbed into her lap.

"Thank you all for coming today. It's been a while." Abby took a moment to absorb the warmth emanating from the crowd of friends, a subset of those who'd attended Luke's memorial. "A few of you have asked what compelled me to decide to put a labyrinth in my backyard. What possible purpose would it serve? It's not as if I've nothing else to occupy my time, right?" she said, and a few people chuckled in agreement. "A couple of months ago, labyrinths weren't even on my radar, until I came across a miniature sand labyrinth at Heart Stone, my mother's gift shop."

The public speaking classes Abby had taken stressed looking your audience in the eye, and she directed her gaze to Lily Beth. "My mother always told me that certain people come into your life when you're ready for them. She calls it synchronicity. My mother's always had a lot of wisdom to share." Abby paused for more chuckles of agreement, and Lily Beth wagged her finger at her, but her mother couldn't look cross.

"No sooner had I decided the lap labyrinth was too small for my needs, I met a man ready to help me move the vision from mind and paper to earth, stone, and plantings. The first time I approached Rob, I had no idea what I wanted from a labyrinth, no thought that a design should contain a theme, tell a story." This time, Abby slid her gaze to Rob. "But Rob guided me through the process, taking the time to ask important questions about what I really wanted, taking the time to really listen. When it comes to design work, Rob Campbell is an excellent listener."

Abby returned her attention to the front row, where Phoebe was playing with Tessa's hair. "His wisdom led me to realize what I wanted more than anything was the peace I'd lost with the death of my son, but most of all I wanted the labyrinth to be a reflection of Luke.

"To that end, after the groundbreaking portion of our celebration, I'd like to invite everyone to take a turn walking the labyrinth. And when you do, this one time, I'd like for you to think of Luke. Not how he died, but how he lived. Exuberant and unafraid and sometimes a little bit scary. Like the time he and Aaron Cohen dressed up as scarecrows for Halloween and sat in lawn chairs outside of Aaron's house, waiting to surprise the trick-or-treaters. Or how, when Luke heard the Maine Seaside Children's Hospital had run out of funds for their playground, he organized the Popham Plunge to raise money because he thought sick kids needed to play, too." A twinge ran through the soles of Abby's feet, as though she were still standing barefooted in the torture of February sand, feet aching with cold, heart aching with pride.

Good friend and neighbor Stu Donovan called out from the front row. "How about the mud wrestling championship?" he said, referring to the summer tradition of wrestling in the clamming mud flats of Hermit Island.

"I said, happy stories, Stu." Abby's mind trundled back to Luke trying, unsuccessfully, to sneak back into the house, and how easily she'd followed his muddy trail.

"Kidding!" Abby said. "Luke was really proud of winning five pounds of steamers. He would've been really excited about making and walking the labyrinth, too. To that end, I'd like to introduce you to Rob Campbell, my landscape architect. Rob holds a bachelor's degree in landscape design from Cornell University. And since moving Down East several years ago, he's made a point of getting involved in the local community, dedicating his time and resources to a different cause each year." God bless the Internet. "Last year, through the AMC, Rob and his crew adopted not one, but two trails in the Maine Woods. And this year, he's working on a labyrinth butterfly garden for the Hidden Harbor Elementary School. I honestly don't know where he finds the time.

"I've asked Rob to provide some additional information about labyrinths. What they are and how to navigate them. So, without further ado, Rob Campbell."

Polite applause all around. Charlie clapped at half speed, a universal sign of grudged tolerance.

Rob came to stand beside Abby and touched her shoulder. His expression reflected the warmth of the gathering.

"Thank you for the generous introduction," Rob told Abby, and then he cleared his throat. "For the past couple of months, in order to give me an idea of the young man whose spirit she'd like the labyrinth design to reflect, Abby has generously shared many, many stories about her son. Luke's likes, his dislikes, his favorite things. I imagine this couldn't have been easy for her." Rob glanced over at Abby. "I know that it wasn't," he said.

"I've been privileged to get to know Luke Connors. A secondary benefit of learning about Luke has been getting to know Abby as well. You probably already know, she's one strong lady. You probably don't already know how much her strength has inspired me."

A feeling of fullness crept from Abby's chest and heated her cheeks. She'd had no idea.

"So . . . about labyrinths. A popular misconception is that they're a kind of maze." Rob shook his head. "Nope, not even close. From the outside, they may look similar." He flicked his gaze to Abby. "But sometimes things aren't what they seem. A maze is a game, intended to trick you. A labyrinth is a journey along a simple circuit, no trickery involved. You walk into the center, turn around, and walk out again. Easy. As you walk, you might reflect on your life, you might reflect on your son. Or maybe you clear your mind and think nothing at all. But for any labyrinth, whether indoors or out, each walk is different.

Because every time you walk the labyrinth, each time you begin anew, you're a different person. We're all a little different today than yesterday.

"I really like outdoor labyrinths, especially here in New England, because each time that you walk the path, the changeable weather impacts your experience, too." A far-off rumble of thunder. "Speaking of the weather," Rob said.

Abby stepped forward. "I think Mother Nature has provided the perfect segue to an abbreviated groundbreaking. If you could all follow behind," she said.

Abby paused before the arbor, turned to Rob.

"Your party," he said.

"Your design," she countered, and together, they passed beneath the arbor to where Rob had laid the red-handled, beribboned shovel on the grass.

Abby raised the shovel. "To peace. But most of all, to Luke," she said, and plunged it into the ground. The tip barely broke the surface.

"Like some help?" Rob asked.

When Abby nodded, he placed his hands over hers and adjusted the angle of the shovel. "Ready?" Rob directed his energy through her, and they plunged the shovel into the earth, breaking ground.

A smattering of applause from the guests. Charlie tapped his foot, arms crossed, stance wide. Abby's pulse raced, a buzzing at her solar plexus. How would she feel if their roles were reversed? She should've asked Charlie to help. She should've given him a role.

Even from half a dozen feet away, she could see the color in Charlie's cheeks. The skies grumbled, that deep rumbling that seemed to come from the earth itself and enter your body at the soles of your feet.

The tops of the treetops shook. Abby's hair whipped around her shoulders. And a shiver laced her arms. Twelve o'clock, straight up over the harbor, water droplets had formed a multistory anvil. Big and green and ready to roll. "Cumulonimbus," Abby whispered. She raised her voice for the crowd, but her gaze remained focused on the sky. The ominous green-tinged monster stirred energy in her belly, and her fingers tingled. "I'd like to invite everyone to return another day for a labyrinth walk. Right now, I think it's time we took the party inside. If everyone can please grab a dessert on your way inside and reconvene in the dining room. Many thanks!"

A few squeals from ladies. The deep, booming voices of men. Laughter grew distant as the guests made a run for the dessert table and hurried for the cover of her home. The winds picked up, rattling the branches of pines and maples, and setting leaves aflutter. A second rumble of thunder took her back to a long-ago morning of cold whistling through a drafty house, white-washed skies, and the rarity of thunder snow. The morning Luke was born.

Abby had backed up against her pink-painted headboard, knees raised, head turned to the side. A white sheet draped over her legs, but just for show. A part of her floated above her body, above the pain, aware that she should be mortified Lily Beth was reaching between her legs, checking the progress of her labor. Lily Beth's hand emerged, but the pain remained. "Six inches! You're almost in transition," Lily Beth said, and Abby started to cry.

"What is it, baby? What do you want? What can I get you?" Lily Beth said, but it was useless. Even if Lily Beth called Charlie, even if he still loved her, he wouldn't make it here in time. Instead, Abby had asked for Celeste.

A hand gripped Abby's upper arm, and she startled.

"Shouldn't you be headed in?" Rob said.

Abby gave herself a shake to bring herself back to the present, but the past held tight. The memory of Celeste snowshoeing a mile in the storm, and then, snowshoes still on her feet, she'd clomped into Abby's bedroom and told her that her timing sucked the big one.

The anvil-topped cloud grew, becoming more defined, gathering strength, and blotting out the sun. The low light simulated sundown, a sunglasses tint that crisped images, simultaneously darkening and defining.

Luke had never let a little weather get in his way. Any weather was camping weather, although he liked winter camping the best. A blizzard necessitated a nature walk, a day on the slopes, a day living. And if Luke were alive, he'd be standing here, not wanting to miss a thing.

"I want to walk the labyrinth before the lines wash out," she told Rob.

Rob's close-cropped hair rippled in the wind. His pale blue eyes shone with both amusement and concern. "Wild woman struck down by lightning."

She laughed because that was the kind of warning she would've given Luke if he'd been alive and, despite her efforts to drag him to the sidelines, he would have insisted on remaining in the epicenter of a storm.

"Wild woman, huh?" Abby said, an expression not usually associated with hard work and responsibility. An expression not associated with someone who put off living. An expression not usually associated with her.

"You coming?" Abby said, and Rob followed her into the labyrinth.

Nowhere to go and nothing to do.

The phrase Lily Beth recited to invite a meditative state played in Abby's head. The shade-enhanced grass appeared too green, fluorescent. Each blade stood out in stark relief, a whole world unto itself. She thought of Luke the teenager, jumping off the cliff of the Bath Tub at Hermit Island, Abby standing by as a spectator to his joy. Luke winter camping in the yard, Abby ducking into his tent to bring him a thermos of hot cocoa and chocolate-chip cookies, warm from the oven. He'd encouraged her to stay and pull up a sleeping bag, but she'd never taken him up on it. Why? What was she waiting for? For her body to grow too old to withstand the physical rigors? For her mind to grow too stodgy, too scared, too set in its ways? From the time Luke was born, he'd always been reaching for something, arms outstretched, eager to experience more. Eager to experience life.

The wind gusted, ushering a sideways burst of rain and a howling high in the treetops. She answered the wind's fury with a girlish giggle, a grin that stretched her cheeks.

"Abby."

Abby glanced over her shoulder at Rob's rain-spattered face, and put a finger to her lips. Quiet in the meditation room.

Two more circuits to experience.

Rain pelted Abby's chest, soaking her dress, enlivening her skin. She blinked up at the sky, now darkened from sea mist to hunter green. But tension grew in her belly, a holding back, as though the storm were just winding up and getting started.

Center of the labyrinth.

A deep boom of thunder rattled the earth. A crack of lightning threaded the sky. And Abby lit from within. Energy charged her, from the vibrating soles of her feet to the ache at the base of her throat. For a vertiginous moment, she thought she'd been struck. That a bolt of lightning had jolted her heart. For a vertiginous moment, she didn't care. Nowhere to go and nothing to do, but be here now, loving every minute.

"We made it." Rob shot Abby a rain-slicked grin. His jeans clung to his hips and followed the long line of his legs. His light-blue button-down melted across the expanse of his arms and chest.

Storm force, low-pressure madness, regression to her teen years. Abby wanted to slip a hand beneath his shirt, taste his skin, and work her way down. She wanted to taste all of him.

Rob's bright-eyed gaze slid down her neck to the wet fabric clinging to her breasts, and then returned to her eyes. *Wow,* he mouthed, and then reached out to take her hand. "Abby—"

"What the—" Something struck her behind. Not rain, too hard for rain, more like a stick or a rock. A direct hit jostled her shoulder.

"Ouch," Rob said, as though something had hit him, too.

"Hail!" they both yelled. Rob pulled Abby against him, chest to chest.

Ping, ping, ping, ping, ping.

Luke would've loved this snowstorm in July.

Marble-sized hail splashed the harbor, battered the shore, and slapped their bodies. The assault stung Abby's skin, sending shivers through her limbs, a bass-deep ache between her legs. She laid her head against Rob's chest.

On the morning Luke was born, ice-laced snow had pinged off her bedroom windows, a *tap-tap-tapping* background track to her moans. Celeste held her hand, refusing to flinch when Abby dug her fingernails into her palm, creating a red semicircle record of contractions.

Lily Beth stood at the foot of Abby's bed, hands on her hips. "Give me a minute alone with her," Lily Beth told Celeste. Seconds later, Lily Beth loomed over Abby's face, barking orders for her to sit up, quiet down, and get serious.

"It hurts!" Abby had protested.

"Of course it hurts. It's supposed to hurt. Otherwise you wouldn't know a baby was coming."

Lily Beth taught Abby how to settle down. She taught her that labor pains had an anatomy, with valleys and crests and durations, same as ocean waves. If Abby rested in between the contractions and saved her energy, she could listen for the approaching wave and get on top of the pain. If she paid attention, she could work with the pain, and ultimately make the pain work for her.

Fifteen minutes later, her son had been born.

Rob yelled to be heard above the hail racket. "Let's make a run for it!"

Stones rained from the sky, hitching Abby's shoulders. She trailed a hand to where Rob's hand rested at her waist, and held tight. "One more minute!"

And sometimes, when the waves wouldn't stop coming, when no valleys offered a respite, when the intensity rendered you mute with agony, well, sometimes, pain was just something you had to get through.

Because pain was so much better than feeling nothing at all.

CHAPTER 9

Tessa's usual stress-buster wasn't busting, and she totally blamed Abby. Instead of being able to simply lie down, revel in "If I Die Young," and marinate in the music, she was sitting on the edge of Luke's bed and listening, really listening, to the words. And, damn it all, they had nothing to do with Luke.

For starters, the dead kid in the song was not only a girl, but also a virgin. According to Luke, his virginity was something he'd given up at sixteen, along with wishing on chicken bones, eyelashes, and the first star in the night sky. Those dumbass lyrics had Tessa imagining Luke up in a heaven, where he took his pick from a harem of fair-haired virgins and got laid every night. After all, wasn't heaven supposed to be whatever got you off?

In Tessa's heaven, she'd get to relive a certain day in January when she and Luke spent every moment together, their post-holiday-break reunion celebration. They'd started out downtown at the bookstore Food for Thought, Tessa consciously avoiding her father's bore-me-to-tears collection of philosophy essays and dragging Luke by the hand to find the romance novels. There, at least, the stories guaranteed her a happy-ever-after. They'd lunched at sun-filled Judi's, Luke reaching across the table to feed Tessa bites of his popover, Tessa licking the apple butter from his fingers. Then they'd gone back to Luke's dorm room and made a baby.

According to Luke, anything that felt that good was worth taking a risk.

Everyone—Dina, Jon, even her father—had told her to take grief one day at a time, as if the days without Luke didn't stretch as far as the shifting horizon. How was she supposed to get through something that never ended? With each passing day, grief didn't get better. It got worse.

Sometimes, here at Abby's, Tessa half-expected Luke to walk into his bedroom with that can't-help-but-love-him smirk on his face. Then Luke would tell her that the last five months had been a game, a practical joke gone terribly wrong.

Then Luke would need her forgiveness instead of the other way around.

A familiar tightness gripped her throat. Her hand gravitated to her thigh. She squeezed the hemline of her shorts until the top of her shoulder twinged, and the tightness in her throat spread across her chest.

Tessa imagined laying her head against Luke's bed pillow, her body at rest, sinking into the oblivion of sleep. Instead, she lifted the egg-in-a nest drawing tablet from the dresser top, and rifled in her purse for the Baggie of art pencils Dina had sent along with her makeup and prenatal vitamins. She considered taking the picture of her and Luke from the wall. In lieu of a live model, she usually needed a photo to refer to when drawing a face. But Luke, beautiful Luke, she could sketch with her eyes closed.

Outside, Tessa squinted through the glare. The sun baked the top of her head, as though yesterday's crazy hailstorm had never happened.

After Tessa had taken cover inside the house with all the other normal people, she'd pressed her nose to the glass of the dining room slider and watched Abby, on-schedule, house-rules Abby, go crazy. What else would explain refusing to come in from thunder and lightning, oh so frightening? What else would possess Abby to stand her ground in the center of the labyrinth site, hail pounding her like a stoning? What else would compel Abby to hang all over Rob, judges-you-in-a-glance just-like-Tessa's-father Rob?

Abby belonged with Charlie.

Charlie had waited for Abby by the slider, bath towel in hand. Love and disappointment, two sides of the same coin, had twisted his features, reddened his eyes, but he'd stood his ground. And when he'd wrapped a towel around Abby, something electric had passed between them. Just like in a romance novel.

Tessa scanned the yard for a patch of shade.

Oh, crap.

Abby was kneeling before Luke's stepping-stones and talking out loud to no one that Tessa could see, as if crazy hadn't ended with the storm. She couldn't quite make out the words, but like a good song, the emotion in Abby's voice sent a shiver up the back of Tessa's head.

When Tessa ducked under the shade of the nearest maple tree, a warm breeze ushered the sweet purple scent of grape soda and the green bite of seaweed, and clarified Abby's words.

"The groundbreaking for the labyrinth went well yesterday. That is, until the storm washed away the painted lines. And did you see that storm? Did you see it, Luke?" Abby paused, as though waiting for a response.

Tears pressed at the backs of Tessa's eyes.

She used to walk around campus, having in-her-head arguments with Luke she still couldn't win. Being alive had seemed like an unfair advantage. Then, after she'd found out about the baby, she'd asked Luke for advice. A sign or an omen, a bird crapping on her head.

But the difference, the major difference, was that Tessa

never talked to herself out loud. And even if she did, she sure as hell wouldn't expect a response.

So why was she waiting for one now?

"Hail the size of marbles fell from the sky," Abby said. "Just like snow in July. Piles of it! Didn't last long, but still. You would've loved it. I saved a couple of prime specimens in the freezer. Remember how you used to make me keep a few snowballs every year, and then we'd take them out in July? You'd get so excited, looking forward to winter." When Tessa turned eleven, her mother had given her an I Dream of Winter Barbie doll, a blonde in a glittery blue evening gown. Tessa hadn't the heart to explain she'd outgrown playing with dolls by the time she'd turned ten.

What if Luke hadn't been all that thrilled with the summer snowballs? What if he'd only acted excited to make his mother happy? What if Abby remembered everything wrong?

If the way Abby remembered Luke made her happy, did it really matter?

Abby crawled onto Luke's stepping-stones, pressed her hands to a paver. "There's something I have to ask you. Something I've been wondering for a long time. I'm sorry," she said, and she bent her head.

Under the shade, Tessa's face flushed hot and cold at the same time. She pulled at the sticky soft hairs at the back of her neck. Dug her fingers into the maple's trunk until bark bit beneath her nails. A sharp intake of breath, and she did it again.

Abby wanted to talk to Luke about his baby. What else could she possibly dread? What else would make her sit still for so long that Tessa thought she must've changed her mind and decided to keep her question to herself?

"It's about your fall . . ." For a breath, Abby's words hung in the summer-humid air. Then their meaning hit Tessa, as clear as the sound of Luke's body smacking the snow-slick ground.

Abby's words reverberated in Tessa's throat. Tessa lowered

herself down to the grass. Her heart slammed her ribcage, hard and fast and painful, same as the day she'd raced down three flights of dorm stairs to get to Luke, the prayer *Please God* sounding in her head.

Abby swept her long hair off her neck, gathered it on top of her head with both hands, and then let it spill back onto her shoulders. "What happened?" she said, and her voice splintered. "Why were you climbing out your window?" A noise came out of Abby, a cross between a bark and a wail, and she covered her mouth. "Why, Luke? What would make you do something so stupid? What in the world was worth risking your life?"

What or who?

Tessa's palms slid against each other, as sweat-damp as the day Luke had fallen. Her fingers slid beneath the hem of her shorts. She pressed into the flesh until her fingers fatigued. But her thigh still tingled.

Abby brushed off her bare knees, shook out her skirt, and stretched to her full height.

Tessa scrambled in the grass for the drawing tablet. She opened it to the first page and tried for a casual leaning-against-a-tree pose. Knees bent to support the tablet and pencil raised in the air, as though she were awaiting inspiration instead of Abby's approach.

"Hello, there!" Abby said, her voice taking on that now-familiar innkeeper lilt, the assumption of happiness. "What are you up to? Been here long?" Under the too-bright sunlight, Abby's face betrayed no traces of guilt, no hint of the meaning beneath her words. No attachment to any particular response.

"Just got here." Tessa heard a similar tone in her own words, the faux-sincerity of a liar. She fanned herself with the drawing tablet. "I wicked needed some shade."

"Mind if I join you?" Abby flopped down on the grass beside Tessa. She hung her head back, and her long blond hair glowed like spun silk, like the surreal soft curls of a princess in a fairy tale. "I'm questioning my decision to start wearing my hair down again," Abby said. "I think one of those hailstones hit me a little hard in the head, maybe shook something loose."

Tessa laughed, managed a full breath. She stretched out her legs. Maple-shade patterns played against her calves, climbed to the hem of her shorts.

Abby's smile dropped, and her voice flattened. "What's that from, Tessa?"

Tessa's abdomen hardened, pressing on her bladder. "Huh? What's what from?" She covered her thigh, in case Abby hadn't already gotten a good look. She was an idiot, a stupid careless idiot. A fact she hadn't intended to share with Abby.

Abby shifted onto one hip, turned her body toward Tessa. The skin around Abby's mouth dimpled, as though she might cry. And her eyes, so much like Luke's, made Tessa almost forget who she was. Made her think, maybe, just maybe, she could be somebody else.

No, she couldn't tell. She couldn't stand to see a mirror of her own disgust on Abby's face. She couldn't let Abby hate her as much as she hated herself.

Abby set her hand on top of Tessa's, sending a shuddery shock to Tessa's throat, her mouth, the center of her chest. No one had touched Tessa, not like that, since Luke had died. No one had made her want to give herself away, risk everything, and ruin her life.

"It's okay. Let me have a look at your leg," Abby said, as though Tessa were a little girl who'd covered up a scraped knee.

"It's nothing," Tessa said, which was mostly true. It was nothing that mattered. Not anymore.

Abby angled her head so her face was closer to Tessa's, her

expression an open and caring invitation. An opportunity for Tessa to lose.

"Honestly, it's nothing!" Now, Tessa sounded like a little girl, too. That only made her fingers tremble. That only made her more disgusted. That only made her want to take off, get behind a locked door, and make her thigh stop tingling.

She wouldn't do it. She'd promised.

Abby slid her hand from Tessa's, and the back of Tessa's hand went cold. "If it's nothing," Abby said, "you won't mind me taking a look. Right? Not a big deal. I just want to make sure you don't have an infection."

Tessa's heart raced. *I can't, I can't, I can't, I can't, I can't,* pulsed between her ears. She clenched her teeth, the way she used to when she was small and her mother would take her to the pediatrician for a shot. Sometimes, Tessa would drop down from the examining table and hide from the nurse beneath her mother's chair, the smell of rubbing alcohol thick in her mouth, her bony knees raw against the floor. But they always found her. No matter how many times she'd wished herself invisible, she'd always get caught.

Tessa hung her head and her hair fell before her face, like a night-darkening shade. Was this what it felt like to be dead? In perpetual darkness and hidden from sight, but also safe, because the worst had already happened. You had nothing left to lose. Her whole body shook, a last-ditch attempt to hang on, hold on, never let go.

Abby tucked Tessa's hair behind her ears. Sunshine flooded Tessa's face, Abby in the center of the light. "Shh, shh," Abby said, soothing, as if she already knew. As if it really didn't matter. "It's okay if you're not ready. I can wait."

A staccato burst of air released from Tessa's mouth, an almost laugh. Luke had given Tessa the same speech, verbatim, when she'd told him she was still a virgin.

Tessa had always been a sucker for other people's patience. Crouched under the plastic examining room chair, she'd grow bored of staring at her mother's jeans-clad legs, the nurse's green scrubs, the faces that cajoled and pleaded. Finally, they'd bribe her with red lollipops, waving the candy beneath the chair the way Abby lured Sadie with rainbow ribbons.

Luke had had his own methods of whittling away Tessa's resolve to delay intercourse, making love to her in every other way possible, until her virginity was nothing but a technicality.

Out on the bay, the sun gleamed off the navy water, and Tessa imagined herself swimming. The cold numbing her body. Her arms straining against the tides. Then she'd crawl from the water onto a sandy beach and collapse, utterly, blissfully, spent. Then she'd feel nothing.

Tessa slipped her hand from her thigh.

This time, a burst of air came from Abby, a sober, reverent "Oh." More than Luke had uttered in response to seeing Tessa naked for the first time. He'd treated her scars the same as the rest of her body, kissing every inch to make them all better, no questions asked.

The clang of a bell buoy punctuated Abby's sigh. "Why, sweetheart? What made you want to injure your precious body?"

Sweetheart, precious, terms of endearment. Not a single word of disgust was directed toward Tessa. Not a hint of anger laced Abby's tone. Head down, Abby focused on Tessa's thigh, as if Abby were a magical princess, willing her gaze to heal the ugly lines Tessa had carved into her flesh.

"I don't know," Tessa said, which wasn't exactly true. But whenever she'd posed the same question to herself, the reasons led her down the same twisted path and made as little sense to her as when she'd first held her father's purloined razor blade over her perfect, unmarred skin.

One glance from Tessa, and water edged Abby's eyes.

Was Abby crying for her? That made no sense, since Tessa

had gotten exactly what she'd deserved. She'd tried to erase the scars, slathered vitamin E oil over the bumpy surface. But then her thigh would glow, the oil highlighting the raised flesh instead of erasing it, the skin reddening beneath her touch. Her father was right. Some people created their own problems. And others—Tessa—made everything worse.

Abby lifted her chin to the sky, the same cute way she'd scanned the horizon for yesterday's storm. "When was the first time you cut yourself?"

The pulse in Tessa's thigh jumped to life.

Tessa had been worried about this moment for years. She'd always known she'd do something careless. Slip on a bikini for the beach and fail to add swim shorts. Change in front of Dina and forget to turn to the wall. But she'd never imagined anyone asking for details. She'd never thought anyone would want to hear her story.

Pretty much the reason she'd done it in the first place.

"Um, I was thirteen, I guess."

"Wow," Abby said. "You were just a baby."

"Not really," she said, but then she considered one of her prized possessions.

When Tessa's mother had taken off, she'd left behind the family photo albums, as if Meredith Lombardi had been trying to cast off not only her daughter and husband, but all of their memories. Whenever Tessa rifled through the albums, she'd focus on the last pictures of her mother. She'd wonder at Meredith's seemingly genuine grin; she'd search for traces of sadness in her mother's dark eyes. But she'd barely noticed herself at her mother's side. Mouthful of braces, hair hanging in two sloppy French braids, and half a head shorter than her mother. At thirteen, she was always craning her neck and trying to catch her mother's attention. Tessa had never put the two together.

Her mother had given up her baby.

"What happened?" Abby asked, jolting Tessa back to the pink-tiled bathroom Meredith had hated.

Tessa had rifled through her father's side of the medicine cabinet, not caring if she was making a mess. Not caring if her anal father actually counted the replacement blades for the fancy shaver her mother had given him for Christmas, and found one missing. At first, she'd sort of hoped he did.

"I didn't mean to," Tessa said. Closer to the truth, she hadn't meant for it to continue for so long. She hadn't known the secret thing that was all hers, the one thing she'd thought she could control, would spiral out, until the cutting controlled her.

When Tessa tilted her head, the maple's branches and leaves spun in a circle. Sunlight glinted into her eyes. She bent her head to her knees, wrapped her arms around her legs, held on.

Beside her, Abby secured her filmy white skirt around her knees. "Tessa, no. I meant, what happened to you before you hurt yourself? Was something going on in your life that upset you? Was someone bothering you?"

"My mother," Tessa blurted out, and then wished she could take it back. Just reach out to the air in front of her, grab the words she'd spoken, stuff them in her mouth, and swallow them back down to her center. Keep them with the rest of the lies she told herself. The truth was, Meredith Lombardi had stopped being her mother the day she'd booked a flight across the Atlantic. So what if, nineteen years ago, she'd managed to squeeze Tessa out from between her legs? That was totally irrelevant.

Mother was a verb, too.

Abby's eyes bulged a tiny bit, her mouth set in a grim line. "Did she? Did your mother hurt you?"

"No. I mean, yes. I mean, she promised she wouldn't leave. . . ." It sounded so stupid. Who cared if her mother had broken a promise? Everybody lied.

"And then," Abby said, "she left?"

Tessa had awoken to the smell of the Belgian waffles Meredith cooked every Sunday. She didn't cook a lot, so when she did, she made a big deal of it. Meredith cheated with Aunt Jemima mix, but she always heated real maple syrup, browned six sausages in a fry pan, and set the table with cloth napkins.

Dad had set the table and warmed the syrup. But a stack of waffles sat on a transparent-from-steam paper plate, drooping and cold, as though they'd come off the iron hours ago. And four shriveled sausages lingered in the coated fry pan, stale-smelling and sticky with congealed grease.

That day, Dad had become Professor Lombardi, a pontiff who'd stated the facts and clarified the new reality. Tessa's mother was gone. Other than that, nothing had changed. Then Tessa had watched, transfixed, while her father choked down his breakfast and left the dirty dishes in the sink for her mother to scrub.

According to her father, Lombardis put their heads down, got their work done, and never whined. Who needed a mother when you had every advantage?

Tessa yanked up two handfuls of grass, tossed them on the ground. "Yeah, she left. She never came back. End of story."

"If that was the end of the story, then why did you cut yourself?"

"Because," Tessa said. "That was the only way I could tell."

Abby's gaze dropped onto Tessa's scars. Several were white with age. But one stood out, pink-hued and angry and screaming for attention.

"I stopped a long time ago," Tessa said. She knew that other girls in her grade would rush home from school, lock the bathroom door, push their jeans to their ankles, and steal a few precious minutes of self-service relief. That wasn't her thing. Who would've thought, after everything that hurt, slicing through your flesh would come as the biggest relief of all? Who would've thought something that relieved her stress would create her greatest shame?

Until ninth-grade art class.

Who would've thought telling stories through sketches and painting would feel better than carving her flesh? She'd even tried her hand at sculpting reliefs, cutting stone to give the illusion of elevation. Those reliefs she didn't have to hide.

Abby's nostrils flared, as though sniffing out Tessa's lie. "Are you sure about that? Because, if you're still cutting . . . Sweetheart, it's not good for you. I can get you help."

"I'd never—" Nausea prickled the back of Tessa's throat, the lining of her mouth. Her hand drifted to her belly. She knew she was losing her mind, because she was thinking of the last time that she and Luke, and Dina and Jon had played their favorite drinking game.

I never had sex in the university library. Chug. *I never went down on my boyfriend while he was driving on Route 116.* Chug.

"I'd never hurt my baby," Tessa said.

"I know that," Abby said. "I know that's not what you'd want."

Why should Abby believe her? The evidence was as obvious as the pink welt on her thigh, a long slash above all the others that pointed straight to the day Luke died. Blood dripping down her leg and pooling in her boots, she'd hobbled down Orchard Hill to Health Services. She'd begged them not to tell.

Three weeks later, she'd returned for prenatal vitamins.

"Right after Luke died, I didn't know I was pregnant."

"I know, Tessa. You told me that before."

"Right after Luke died," Tessa repeated. "That was the last time I did it."

Abby squinted, and then her features broadened with understanding.

"I'm not crazy," Tessa said. But wasn't that exactly what a crazy person would say?

"Want to know a secret?" Abby said. "After Luke died, I thought I was going crazy. I was feeling desperate. It's hard to be the one left behind."

"After. After I knew I was pregnant, I was freaking out. I thought I was being punished and I was going to lose the baby, too. But I never told anyone about the, you know, what I did." Tessa waved at her thigh, wished it were that easy for her to dismiss the hideous scars, the pathetic story of her life. "I came close to telling my best friend, Dina, but I couldn't go through with it. I didn't want her to think I was bat shit."

"You're not bat shit, Tessa. It makes sense that after Luke died, you turned to something that once made you feel better. Even though that something was really, really bad for you."

Tessa inched closer. "Promise?"

Abby held up her pinkie.

Tessa wrapped her pinkie around Abby's, and a shiver skittered up her spine. "Did you and Luke used to pinkie swear when he was little?"

"If by *little,* you mean when he was old enough to shave. Then, yeah. Luke was a big fan of the pinkie swear." Abby secured her arm around Tessa's shoulder and gave her a squeeze, as though welcoming Tessa into the Luke-and-Abby pinkie swear club.

Tessa rested her head on Abby's shoulder, inhaled her hair. Sunshine and summer sand, and something she could only describe as a deep blue sadness. She touched a fingertip to one of Abby's shining princess curls. "Your hair's pretty," Tessa said, and then she started to cry.

"Sweetheart," Abby said.

That only made Tessa cry harder.

The day she'd cut herself too deeply, she'd stripped down and made herself stand in the shower under burning hot water, gritting her teeth so that her dorm mates wouldn't hear her cry out in pain. Then she shut off the water and leaned against the dirty shower stall, shivering, until brown dots no longer danced before her vision and she was reasonably sure she wouldn't pass out. She slapped a gauze pad on her thigh and immediately soaked through it, but the wet cotton provided enough of a cushion so she could struggle into a pair of sweats. Through the darkness, the light from Health Services shone like a beacon, a promise of relief.

A stocky nurse with lipstick on her teeth tore the bloody pad from Tessa's leg and exposed her shame to the sting of the air. "Well, well. What do we have here?" she'd said, widening her eyes to take in the horror show. "I hope you're pleased with yourself, young lady."

Now, Abby rubbed Tessa's back, rocked slightly to a rhythm both foreign and familiar to Tessa, like hearing a song you used to know. Heat came off Tessa's body, waves and waves of heat that prickled her skin, coated her with sweat, and lightened her even better than creating art. Her pulse relaxed, settled. Lemons and summer sand. The curve of Abby's neck. The pressure of Abby's hand between her shoulders.

Who would've thought telling Abby about the second-to-worst thing Tessa had ever done would give her so much relief?

CHAPTER 10

The sadness of the day lingered, sticky as the homemade peppermint-candy ice cream Abby and Tessa had churned under the shade tree. Abby told Tessa the treat was for Briar Rose guests, too. That wasn't a lie. But the chore was primarily a means to an end. Half an hour of rocking wasn't nearly enough time to offset years of Tessa's emotional and physical scarring.

In lieu of lunch, Abby and Tessa had gobbled ice cream, racing against the melting. Then they'd taken a long, leisurely walk into town, both of them unusually quiet. Abby sensed that Tessa had had enough sharing for one day, and they hadn't spoken again about the cutting. But even now, Tessa's revelation niggled Abby, like a canker your tongue couldn't resist worrying.

Why would someone hurting you make you want to turn around and hurt yourself? After Luke's memorial, Abby had been in that dark place, wanting to drown out her pain by drowning herself. She knew she'd never allow a friend—or a stranger, for that matter—to contemplate such selfish foolishness. Why was it so difficult to show yourself the same compassion?

Abby wanted to sit cross-legged in the middle of the floor and have herself a good cry until she'd drained herself of every emotion. Instead, she'd taken a long shower, fluffed and arranged herself into her version of a bombshell. A bombshell looking forward to her date with Rob and a little no-drama letting off steam.

That thought doubled the pressure.

Abby wore her hair down, thanks to copious quantities of summer curl-taming gel and spray. Gray eye shadow, once relegated to the back of her medicine cabinet, now graced her lids, highlighting her blue eyes. Mascara darkened her pale lashes. And she'd made sure she'd brushed the lint off the berry lipstick that lived at the bottom of her pocketbook before gliding the balm across her lips. She wore a hot-pink give-the-girls-some-attention sleeveless T-shirt and tight dark-wash jeans she'd purchased last summer.

She eyed the shoe choices. Flats were all wrong, but wear too high of a heel and you ran the risk of crossing the line from slightly sexy to seriously slutty. Considering she hadn't had sex in two years, she didn't want Rob to accuse her of false advertising. With that in mind, she shrugged into the white short-sleeved cardigan she'd, moments ago, slung across the arm of her bedroom's peach club chair beside the seat's pile of rejected T-shirts and blouses. On the dresser, her cell buzzed. Celeste smirked at her from the photo window, perpetually on the cusp of speaking her mind.

"Heels or flats," Abby said, not bothering with a hello.

"Inch and a half. Two at most," Celeste said.

"You think three inches is too slutty?"

"Too much for you to handle," Celeste said. "But take off the damn cardigan."

Abby clasped the sweater's cotton neck, exaggerated a gasp. "I feel like you've known me forever."

Abby had known Celeste long enough to be certain she was smiling through the phone. "Is that your best line?" Celeste said. "Is that what you're going to use on Rob to seduce him on your first official date?"

"Yeah, I'm having a little trouble with that part."

"What do you mean?"

Abby conjured the image of Hailstorm Rob, rain-soaked and sexy. When she pictured the way he'd deliberately run his gaze over her body, her T-shirt tightened against her chest and her back arched into a luxurious stretch. She wanted more. "Well . . . if this is our first date, then polite dinner conversation should lead to a polite truck conversation. Which leads to a walk to my front door and a good-night kiss. Absolutely no tongue permitted. But since we've kind of sort of actually been dating for over a month . . ."

"And his tongue has already familiarized itself with the inside of your mouth."

"Right."

"Huh," Celeste said. "I see your dilemma."

Sadie peeked out from under the pile of Abby's castaway tops and jumped to the floor. The cat glanced up at Abby and then launched into a full-throated purr. She wound around Abby's jeans leg, no doubt marking the dark-wash with several long gray hairs. *You're mine,* she seemed to say.

If Rob didn't work out, at least Abby still had Sadie. No matter how many men came and went, Abby could always depend on her cat to love her unconditionally. As long as Abby plied Sadie with foil balls, rainbow ribbons, and chicken-and-brown-rice kibble, no one got hurt.

"You still there?" Abby asked.

"I'm thinking! Okay, here we go. You need to seek a middle ground. More than a kiss, but less than full-out boinking."

"Can you be more specific? I mean, there are a lot of middle ground options."

"Hand jobs, bl—"

"Celeste! I meant, above or below the waist?" She couldn't fault Celeste for regressing to high-school talk and not realize Abby had slid down that slippery slope all the way into middle-school rhetoric. Abby's cheeks tightened, and a flush bloomed across her chest. She yanked off her cardigan and tossed it onto the rest of the discarded tops. Sadie dashed for the sweater, pounced atop the pile. "Never mind. I'm probably worrying for nothing. Rob's a complete gentleman."

"Sure, Rob's a gentleman, emphasis on *man*. I've seen the way he looks at you."

"Think he's noticed my secret weapons?" Abby said.

"Girlfriend," Celeste said, sprinkling a dash of city attitude. "Yesterday, everybody noticed your secret weapons. But that's not what I meant. Whenever Rob talks about you, he gets this goofy grin on his face. He's got a thing for you, Abby."

And she had a thing for Rob. Then why was she holding on to the bed post and rocking? She bit the flesh at the base of her thumb, thought of Tessa, and let go. She rubbed the smudge of lipstick off her thumb. "Can I ask you something?"

An oven timer dinged in the background, one of the many bells and whistles that kept Celeste's bakery running and her shelves stocked with pastries. "You've got ninety seconds."

Abby sighed.

"Eighty-five."

Abby looked to the ceiling, exasperated with herself, not Celeste. "Do you think Rob's seeing anyone else?"

"Nope."

"You answered awfully fast."

"Seven days a week, Rob comes down for coffee and muffins at seven. Unless he's out with you, he returns twelve hours later for his decaf. No one goes into his apartment, no one ever comes out. Kind of like Willy Wonka's factory. Oh, yeah, except for that one time he brought his daughter by. Definitely a daddy's girl."

"You met Rob's daughter?"

A buzzer thrummed through the phone line, then the creak of a stainless-steel oven door opening on its hinges.

"Do me a favor and just go with it," Celeste said, one of the phrases Abby herself used time and again over her many years of dating. So why was she getting all worked up about this one date? Why was she wondering when *she'd* get to meet Rob's daughter?

"I liked dating Rob unofficially better. Official means I could mess up. Official means I have something to lose." Abby usually felt better when she came clean with Celeste. This time, her stomach tensed, as though trying to regain the balance of pretending not to care.

"You're not going to mess up."

"How do you know that?"

"Because," Celeste said. "Rob's the real deal, one of the good guys. That said, if you do end up boinking Rob, tell me all about it."

"I most certainly will not!"

"Boink or tell?" Celeste said.

"Love you," Abby said.

"Love you more." Celeste hung up the phone, leaving Abby with a goofy grin on her face.

Abby stepped into the one-and-a-half-inch heels, opened her closet door to check out her reflection, and frowned. She kicked off the low sandals and strapped her feet into the three-inch heels, turned from side to side. The extra inch and a half straightened her posture, lengthened her legs, and boosted her confidence.

"I'll show Celeste how much I can handle," Abby told Sadie. "But the cardigan stays." Abby eased the sweater out from under Sadie's belly and past her swiping paws. Sadie angled Abby her best look of reproach. "Lily Beth always said a girl should leave something to the imagination."

Abby slipped her pocketbook onto her shoulder, the sweater over her arm, and opened her bedroom door to find Tessa with her fist raised to knock. "Sweetheart," Abby said, as if she'd been calling Tessa that forever.

The only thing that felt strange to Abby was the fact it didn't. "I was about to go hunt you down."

Abby had been looking forward to her date all day, but she wanted to make sure Tessa was all right. Abby understood Tessa had last hurt herself during a time of extreme stress. She believed Tessa when she'd told her she wouldn't do it again. But Abby also understood how hard it must've been for Tessa to share a secret, after having kept it to herself for so many years. And, frankly, the fact Tessa had chosen to share with her, of all people, humbled Abby. The sharing, the emotional responsibility, made her feel like a mother again.

Tessa glanced at Abby's pocketbook. "You're going out?"

A pang tightened Abby's stomach, even though she was sure she'd told Tessa about her date. "I have plans, but I can cancel them."

Tessa leaned against the door frame, reminding Abby how tired she'd get when she'd been expecting Luke. Not normal end-of-day fatigue. That would've been a pleasure. More like, scrape-self-off-chair-and-drag-to-bed-at-six exhaustion.

It was already six-thirty.

"Come in before you fall asleep standing up." Abby moved aside, and Tessa slipped into her bedroom, where Sadie occupied the only chair. "Servant to a cat," Abby said, and she patted her bed. "Second-best seat in the room?"

"Oh, uh. I'm kind of on my way out, too. Just came to tell you."

"Really?" Abby said. Tessa had pulled her hair into a high ponytail, and her face glowed, freshly scrubbed, as though she'd washed up for bed. Only a skim of gloss shined her lips. She wore Bermuda-length shorts, a pink hoodie, and sparkly pastel flip-flops, her usual hang-around outfit. "Going anywhere special?"

"Spinney's?"

Then she was dressed appropriately. "Food's always great there. And they've a nice view. You may want to avoid anything fried, though. Not great for indigestion. Going with anyone special?" Abby asked, thinking Hannah the most obvious choice. She'd noticed the girls chitchatting by the dining room fireplace after Hannah was off work. And she'd seen them actively noticing Jordan, a good-looking young man in his early twenties who'd been visiting the B&B with his middle-aged parents.

"An older guy," Tessa said, and her entire countenance brightened.

"J-Jordan?" Abby said, tripping over his name. Somewhere in her mind Abby acknowledged that one day Tessa would get over her son and find another man to care for. But not today. Certainly not while she was carrying Luke's child.

"No! Jordan's cute. But this guy is way older."

Abby should call Rob, tell him Tessa needed her. Clearly the girl time they'd had this afternoon hadn't been enough after their tree-side conversation. Tessa needed a lot more of her attention. Abby would find a suitably sweet romantic comedy, she'd pop popcorn, encourage Tessa to open up about her father.

"C'mon, Abby," Tessa said, putting on a fake air of annoyance. "You know who he is. Guy's old enough to be a grandfather."

"Charlie!" Abby said, not because her brain had finally sputtered to life, but because the *older man* was standing in the doorway to her bedroom. A doorway through which, ever since Charlie's two-years-ago expulsion, Abby hadn't allowed anyone to trespass.

Until Tessa.

"Divider was open," Charlie said. "Hope you don't mind, I let myself in."

Abby had asked Tessa to close the pocket door when coming and going from the private wing of the house. She'd forgotten how conveniently forgetful teenagers could be when it pertained to house rules that inconvenienced them.

Probably not fair, since Charlie wasn't any good at following her rules either. Yesterday, he'd taken her dress selection as an invitation to ogle her, their shared grief as an opportunity to try and take her hand, their history as justification for throwing a towel over her and ushering her away from Rob.

To the untrained eye, it might've looked as though Charlie had been acting the part of the overprotective mama bear, rather than the part he'd played for years. Never more interested than when Abby wasn't.

The crease in Charlie's weekend khakis was fresh-pressed. His hair appeared casual and windblown, although Abby knew he bothered with hair gel to get that effect. He didn't wear cologne, thank goodness. But, today, his aftershave carried a hint of lime, the spray scent he'd worn when they were teens.

Charlie whipped out two boxes from behind his back. He handed the smaller beribboned tan box to Tessa, the larger to Abby.

Abby untied the ribbon and flipped open the lid to reveal two dozen gourmet truffles. The type made with good dark chocolate and heavy cream, infused with vanilla, and finished with crystallized ginger. The variety she'd told Charlie she preferred when he'd, instead, presented her with that pathetic red heart-shaped box of waxy chocolates. Who the hell was dumb enough to give his pregnant girlfriend a jumbo heart when he was leaving her?

She'd shared that thought with Charlie, too.

"Better late than never?" Charlie said.

Abby looked to the ceiling, making sure no tears would fall. She didn't need Charlie's too-little too-late apology. But she would've liked to travel back in time to give the-girl-she'd-been a big hug. Better yet, she would've liked to expel that girl from her heart and soul. "Thank you. You've quite the memory."

"Not as good as yours," Charlie said. "My warning to you, Tessa. Never cross Abby. She holds a grudge like nobody's business. She never forgives."

"That's not fair."

Charlie pressed a hand against the door frame, as though he might step into her bedroom, and Abby blocked his path.

"Not fair," Charlie said, "but it's true."

Tessa came up behind Abby and placed a hand on her shoulder, as if to comfort her. Then Tessa stood on tiptoe and kissed Charlie on the cheek, as though she were trying to placate him, too. "Thanks for the truffles," she said. "They look awesome."

Despite Abby's and Charlie's promise to put Luke before them, Luke had, time and again, ended up between them, trying to bring them back together.

Was that what Tessa was attempting?

Abby had told Celeste there was no Team Rob. But was Tessa rooting for Team Charlie?

It was obvious, now that Abby had figured it out. Tessa was the gossip who'd told Charlie about Rob. Abby had a spy in her ranks, sure as the days when Luke had, upon Charlie's not-so-veiled requests, chronicled her personal life.

"Truce," Charlie said. "Would you like to join us for dinner? We could agree to disagree about your lack of forgiveness and your propensity for unfairness. All while overeating."

"That's quite an offer. Thank you, but I have a date." Abby didn't mean to sound spiteful, but the tone crept into her voice, and she couldn't say it displeased her.

"Rob?" Charlie said, and Abby nodded.

With one glance, Charlie took in her outfit and reflected his disapproval. So his next comment threw her off. "He's a lucky man," Charlie said, diffusing her anger. And then he pulled her into a hug, a ploy to whisper in her ear. "Temperature's dropping fast. If I were you, I'd wear the sweater."

That was all Abby needed to leave the damn cardigan with Sadie.

Abby sat across from Rob at the Lobster House, hiding behind her menu and trying to ward off the late-day chill and errant nerves with covert gulps from her glass of Sam Adams. The rich aroma of seafood and drawn butter filled the air. Cold beer sluiced into her stomach, and the alcohol rocketed to her brain, lending a hazy quality to her thoughts and reminding her how little she'd had to eat today.

A wagon-wheel chandelier hung above her. She wasn't worried the fixture would fall, but she couldn't shake off the awareness of a heavy weight hanging over her head. She couldn't stop thinking about Tessa going off with Charlie on a Sunday visit, as though she were a child of their divorce. Or, as Luke had been fond of saying, a product of not-together parents.

How easily Charlie had stepped into his role of the father. How easily Tessa had stepped into the role of the daughter.

Where did that leave Luke?

Abby didn't know how she felt about that. She took a gulp of beer and cared a little less about untangling the knot of her emotions. Tiny white lights were strung around the room's perimeter. In an hour or so, the sun would set and the dim bulbs would fire to life. For now, the sun hung low over Casco Bay, shining way too brightly for what she had in mind.

Rob leaned his tanned forearms against the table. His direct gaze tumbled her heart. "Thirsty?" he asked, and then he sat back and took a conservative sip from his glass of beer, as if to both gain a wide view of her swigging and show off his restraint.

Abby set down the menu. So much for her cover. "Uh, hum." She took a slightly smaller sip, and a shiver jostled her shoulders.

"Cold?"

"Not really." A second twitch shook her frame.

"Got an idea." Rob got up from his chair, slid onto the bench seat beside her, and slung his arm around her shoulders. With a slight flex of his bicep, he gave her a squeeze. His body heat warmed her arms, trickled through her chest, pooled in her jeans. She ordered her hips not to move. That only cranked her imagination into overdrive.

Abby pictured peeling off Rob's jeans and lowering herself onto the wooden bench beneath him. She imagined the electric sensation of Rob moving inside her, his energy coursing through her veins. Ridiculous, there wasn't enough room on the bench. Abby's throat and tongue went dry. She took another swallow of beer and gazed out over the bay, rather than risk looking Rob in the eye.

Horny?

Their waitress, Janet, came to take their orders. One of Phippsburg's seasonal residents, Janet taught high-school English, and found summer waitressing relaxing by comparison. With her hair piled on top of her head and her big smile, Janet looked closer to thirty than the fifty years she admitted to.

Abby considered asking for a shot of tequila. Instead, she settled for the mussels. Rob chose the lobster dinner and, just as Abby was finishing her first beer, ordered them two more.

"Warming up?" Rob said. His voice made Abby think of campfires and wood smoke, deep warmth in the chill of a night forest.

"Starting to." Of course, she could sit on top of him. That would take care of the space issue, and save her tailbone from the abuse of the wooden bench.

Rob liked to talk while he worked, that much she knew.

Did that mean he'd also like to talk during sex? Would he take verbal notes on the grade of her body, the way he'd mapped her yard? Would he ask to view her from every angle, the way she wanted to study him?

"So, about yesterday," Rob said, and Abby stiffened. She thought they'd put their little Charlie misunderstanding behind them, between their cryptic speeches and the mind-clearing, hail-pelting labyrinth walk. Then he'd asked her out.

"Sorry about getting to your place late. I'm usually ridiculously punctual."

"That's okay."

"It's not. I don't let my crew get away with being late. Ever. Kind of have a thing about it."

Something in Rob's voice made her look him in the eye. Not quite a catch in his voice, but a slight alteration to his usual breezy tone.

"Was something wrong?"

"Kind of. Not really." Rob took a swallow of his beer. More than a sip, but short of a gulp. He ran his thumb over the edge of his beer label.

"Rob?"

He gave a slight chuckle, but she wasn't buying it. "Ex called me to the house again . . ."

Through her beer buzz, Abby noted the use of the word *again,* the antecedent *the* in place of the possessive *her.* Did Rob still consider his ex-wife's house his home? Abby seemed to remember a previous call when the electricity had inexplicably failed or a circuit breaker had tripped. Or was it the plumbing? Rob's ex sure seemed to consider *her* house *their* home.

"Maintenance issue?" Abby asked.

"Grace."

Automatic, Abby's heart dashed to her throat. "Is she all right?"

Rob rubbed her back. "Oh, yeah, she's fine. It was just . . . ex overreacts sometimes, as in a lot. Grace had a boy up in her bedroom, and Maria walked in on them."

"Oh, wow. That must've been a shocker. Hard to underreact to that one," Abby said, remembering the time she'd walked in on Luke and noticed a pair of tan feet with ten bright-blue toenails poking out from beneath his comforter. Then, a few months later, Abby had gotten down on her knees and invited the high-school principal's shaking daughter to come out from under Luke's bed. Different girl, pink toenail polish.

Sure, Abby had been frazzled. But clearly not as horrified as she should've been. She'd slipped a box of condoms into Luke's college trunk. She'd threatened to give a demo, if he had no idea how to use them. Yet, a small voice at the back of her mind had played the ill-conceived reassurance. Boys being boys couldn't get pregnant.

A girl being a girl was still someone's daughter. She should know.

How was Tessa's father handling all of this? Abby had been planning on giving him a call. But, frankly, she was hoping he'd phone her first.

Rob took a deep breath, held the inhalation a beat before the exhale. "Yeah, Grace has a good head on her shoulders, but I still came down on her pretty hard."

Rob shared the tale with Abby, from his ex-wife's overwrought call to his daughter's relationship with the buddy-turned-lover. Behind Rob's words, Abby saw a dad having a hard time watching his only baby grow up. A dad struggling with the inevitable letting go.

Not the same as losing a child, but Rob could relate. Once a parent, always a parent.

"I'm not sure who was more embarrassed, me or Grace. But I had to let her know I'm worried about her getting pregnant." Rob turned his gaze from the label he'd one-handed shredded into table scraps. "Worried about her getting hurt, too."

"Ah, my visitor's story hit close to home."

"Guess so."

"It's not every day your late son's pregnant girlfriend lands on your doorstep." Sadness washed over her, overriding her attempt at a flippant tone. "Grace is lucky to have you for a dad." Tessa hadn't shared much about her relationship with her father, but Abby could bet it wasn't this sweet. Not sweet enough to keep her from leaving.

Janet brought the side salads, cloth-covered basket of warm rolls, and second bar order. Rob poured Abby's beer into her glass and then filled his own. Abby bit into a tomato and chased it down with a healthy gulp of beer. Her fingers tingled, her head floated. Her gaze went to Rob's forearm, the sun-bleached hairs, and she rubbed his arm. The conversation was taking them down a serious road, too serious, as though her heaviness had seeped into Rob.

Rob kissed the top of her head.

Abby wriggled out from under his arm. She took one look at the strangely sad look on his face and swallowed against sudden reflux. "What's wrong?"

"I don't want to hurt you."

"Then don't," Abby said, and her words came out in a breathy whisper. Was he breaking up with her on their first official date?

"I know how much you want to adopt Luke's baby."

"Of course." The ambient noise of restaurant conversations buzzed in her ears. Two tables over, a young mother cut up a chicken finger for her pig-tailed toddler. Beside her bearded husband, a school-aged boy slid his peas one by one onto the tines of his fork. How would the couple feel if someone walked in and stole their children? Abby's situation was no different. "Luke's child is my child. I can't let Tessa give the baby away to someone else. I can't let her make a terrible mistake. I can't—"

Lose Luke again.

Rob caressed her cheek with a calloused finger, sending a shock through her center. "I admire what you're doing," he said. Abby thought of his blush-inducing words from yesterday's groundbreaking. Her strength had inspired him. Then why did she still feel as though he were trying to give her the brush-off?

"But?" Abby said.

To Rob's credit, he didn't miss a beat. "But I think it's only fair to let you know, at this point in my life, I've no interest in becoming a dad again."

This took a couple of seconds to sink in. Then, "I'm not looking for a baby daddy," slipped from her brain through her lips. An amalgam of relief and annoyance flashed through her. Or maybe it was just the alcohol. Celeste was right. Abby was Little Miss All or Nothing. Either buttoned-up or give everyone an eyeful of her secret weapons. Celibate as a nun or hankering to throw caution to the wind and launch herself at Rob.

At the moment, Rob didn't exactly look as though he were predisposed to catching her.

Rob angled away from her, and his expression went from guarded vulnerability to simply guarded.

Another Little Miss All or Nothing-ism. Get a little buzzed, and Abby tossed her tight-assed filter out the window.

Okay, she was a little more than buzzed.

Janet brought their dinners and set their plates before them. Lobster, baked potato, coleslaw, and corn for Rob. Mussels in a broth of garlic and white wine for Abby. Slices of crusty bread edged the generous plate. Her stomach rumbled in appreciation. "Anything else I can get you?" A frown pulled at the corners of Janet's grin. She looked from Abby to Rob and back again.

"I'm good," Rob told Janet, although he clearly was not.

Abby ordered a rum and Coke.

She placed her hand on top of Rob's. "Hey, I'm not angry with you. I appreciate your honesty. It's just, this situation." She shook her head. "I'm having a flashback."

Why else would she have ordered her favorite cocktail from twenty years ago?

Rob leaned in the tiniest bit, and the line between his eyes softened.

The first summer after Luke had been born, Abby manned the register at Heart Stone. An ocean sounds CD piped through the shop's sound system while Luke napped behind the mesh of his Pack 'N Play. Summer boys looking for seasonal hookups would stroll into the shop, zip past the candles with inlaid shells, the collections of mermaids and aquamarine, and head straight for the blonde wearing a snowdrop anemone behind her left ear and a knowing smile.

Until they figured out that the baby behind the counter was Abby's, and not Lily Beth's.

"When Luke was about four months old, I started to date again and . . ." Abby shrugged. "What would you expect from guys in their late teens and early twenties?"

"You got the same reaction?"

Abby pressed a finger to her nose. "Not all of them, but a lot. I used to work at Lily Beth's shop. Got a lot of boys parading in and out, so I developed a strategy."

Abby launched into her routine. "Hi, I'm Abby, and I have a baby. I'm not looking for a baby daddy. My son already has a father. But if my having a kid still freaks you out, then we'll pretend you didn't just ask me out. Skim boards are ten dollars. Boogie boards will cost you fifteen." Unfortunately, the feelings returned along with her practiced speech. Anger and hurt and injured pride. She'd wanted to make sure the door hit those boys on their way out. She'd wanted to stand in the doorway and call them back to her.

Abby looked straight at Rob. She softened her tone and rephrased to avoid the rude expression from her youth, but the sentiment remained the same. "I'm not looking for a father for Luke's baby." She didn't need anyone to save her. She'd operated as a single parent her entire life, managed to raise a great kid, managed to grow a respected business. Eventually, even those boys looking for summer hookups had grown up, married, and divorced. Men weren't as squeamish about her having a kid once they had a few of their own.

So what if she was starting over with a new baby? So what if that status once again deemed her untouchable? She had a lot going for her. Like the rum and Coke Janet had delivered to the table, for instance. Abby gave the alcohol fumes a moment to play with her nose before she gulped down a third of the drink. Straight to her head, just like old times. She scooped a tender mussel from its shell, popped the morsel in her mouth. She savored the juicy shellfish, the bite of garlic, and sunk her teeth into the crusty bread.

She was going to make one hell of a cat lady. A fat, drunk cat lady.

Rob put down his fork and offered Abby his hand. "Hi, I'm Rob, and I'm a complete horse's ass."

Abby took his hand and cursed the relief clogging her sinuses.

Rob leaned close until his nose nuzzled her hair, his mouth warmed her ear, and his choice of words played a mean game with her heart. "If you'll have me," he said, "I'd like to start over."

Chapter 11

Tessa nestled into the supple leather of Charlie's cherry-red Jeep, the ocean-scented breeze blowing her hair, straight out of a song about endless summer. Early evening was as bright as midday, but the chill in the air betrayed an undeniable truth. Even July contained a trace of fall, Maine's way of reminding Tessa she'd better not get too comfortable.

Nothing good lasted.

When Tessa had been a kid, she'd spent every July fourth at the UMass Alumni Stadium with her parents. Dad would busy himself spraying Natrapel mosquito repellent around the perimeter of their striped scratchy wool blanket—DEET-free, so that no person or plant would be harmed—and Meredith would sneak Tessa caffeinated soda, so she could stay up late to watch the fireworks. Lying flat on their backs, Tessa and Meredith would try to memorize the great bursting chandeliers of electric light and color breaking the night sky, and Dad would go and ruin the experience by pronouncing the summer nearly over.

Come winter, a snow day would land Tessa, Dad, and Meredith at Hospital Hill for sledding and hot chocolate. But then, after a good three-person tandem run where Tessa's heart was racing and her mouth was sweet with cocoa grit, good old

Dad would squint through the glaring sun and make an off-handed quip about the upcoming mud season. And right when Tessa had been starting to enjoy carrying a part of Luke inside her, she'd grabbed her father's hand and pressed it to her belly, so he could feel the baby somersault. A light had flickered in Dad's eyes, but then it was gone, replaced by his insistence she figure out what the hell she was going to "do about it."

Tessa could've forgiven her father if he hadn't called her baby *it*.

Charlie slowed to look for a spot by Spinney's, a white clapboard building sporting an ad with a strawberry ice-cream cone, a porch overlooking the ocean, and a full parking lot. He continued down a peninsula and looped around another lot edging the sea.

"Coming up on your right," Charlie said, deepening his voice to sound like a tour guide, "is Fort Popham. Used in the Civil War, Spanish American War, and World War I. The massive granite structure, hugely expensive, was never attacked, proving the age-old adage that strength deters intruders. But, many years later, the fort made a really cool playground for little boys who liked to play hide-and-seek with their dads."

Charlie glanced Tessa's way. When her mouth slackened in understanding, his jaw tightened, his chin did a peculiar little dance, and his gaze returned to the road.

"Little boys like Luke?" Tessa said, although she already knew the answer.

Charlie's Adam's apple bobbed. "E-yup."

On their left, a big-ass old person's car backed out of the spot in front of a Porta-Potty. A yellow smiley-face ball bounced on the car's silver antenna. "Bingo! Prime real estate." Charlie raised a hand in greeting to the elderly driver. "Thank you, marvelous Millie!"

The car paused, as though the driver were momentarily

dazzled by Charlie's greeting. A smile flashed from beneath a head of gray curls. Just for a second Tessa could see beneath the woman's lines and wrinkles clear to the girl she'd once been.

Charlie jogged around the Jeep to open the door for Tessa. At the restaurant's entrance, he held open the door to let her pass first. And when the hostess asked where they'd like to sit, he deferred to Tessa. Then, on their walk to their table with a view of the harbor, he stopped at a table where three women around his age were working on a pitcher of beer, and introduced Tessa as his friend. Big smile on Charlie's face and personalized compliments for all, and three women jockeyed to gain Charlie's attention. Three women tried not to notice Tessa's belly, and failed. Tessa was sure that three women wondered why a local high-school teacher was hanging out with a pregnant teenager.

Their waitress—a former student of Charlie's with strawberry-blond hair and freckles across her nose—flushed when she called him Mr. Connors, poured two waters, and left them to consider the menu.

"You can tell everyone who I am," Tessa said. "I don't mind."

Charlie jostled his glass of water in a circular motion, so the ice cubes swirled. He took a sip, gave his head a slight shake, and set the glass down on the how-to-eat-a-lobster place mat. He crossed his arms and leaned across the table, close enough for Tessa to mentally erase the tiredness beneath his eyes and the faint lines bracketing his sad smile. Close enough so that, for a whole second, instead of staring into Charlie's eyes, she was gazing into Luke's. "What? You're not my friend, Tessa?"

"Obviously. I mean, we're practically related," she said, her tone laced with disappointment, because as soon as he opened his mouth, he turned back to Charlie. She must've been delusional when she'd first heard Charlie's voice from across Briar Rose and imagined he sounded like Luke.

Charlie's voice was smooth, where Luke's voice carried

subtle underlying huskiness. When Luke was excited, he'd talked too fast. The words had spilled out of him faster than his brain could edit. In contrast, Charlie kept an even keel, even though you got the distinct feeling he had barely contained energy just below the surface. You could almost see Charlie reining himself in. And the way Charlie said Tessa's name, succinct and to the point, as though he were calling on her in his class?

Nothing like Luke.

The gravel of Luke's voice would stroke the two syllables of Tessa's name, stretch the second syllable into a third, and nearly make her come.

If that hadn't been love, then why had it felt so good?

Luke had been her only lover. But, according to Dad, having a baby set her in the camp of the terminally slutty. Her father hadn't needed to say it out loud for her to know that's what he was thinking. Over the years, Dad had never missed an opportunity to point out a teen mom picking up a gallon of milk at Cumberland Farms, strolling along Pleasant Street, or riding the PVTA. Fodder for Dad's how-to-ruin-your-life lectures. Now, Tessa had become his favorite cautionary tale.

"Aren't you worried about gossip?" Tessa swept a finger through her ice water's condensation, drew and erased an etched-in-glass heart.

Back in Amherst, everyone knew her story. Clearly, everyone in Hidden Harbor and the surrounding towns would, in about the next five minutes. No matter where she lived, no nice boy would ever love her again. Location didn't matter.

Charlie sat back in his chair, cocked his head to the side. "You don't owe anyone an explanation. People gossip, with or without your help. Why make it easy for them?" He sucked his lips between his teeth, released. "I learned that lesson a long time ago. You got that?"

"Schadenfreude?" Tessa said, although she sensed she was missing some crucial point. "People love making themselves feel better by gossiping about how much my life sucks. It's like I'm providing a public service." She knew how weird people were—kids, adults, everyone. When Tessa had started telling people she was pregnant, this wow look flooded their faces. Not wow, as in, how'd you get so lucky? The wow look suggested they were sad and sympathetic. But also, the wow look meant they were also oddly thrilled.

Who didn't enjoy a super-sad tragedy?

Charlie drummed his fingers on the table, glanced to the side. He leaned forward and lowered his voice. "You have nothing to be ashamed of," he said, as if he could see the worst thing Tessa had ever done. As if he could forgive her.

"If Luke hadn't died, I would've married him. I wouldn't have thought twice."

"Thank you, Tessa. You're a good girl," Charlie said, and Tessa warmed under his gaze.

Of course that was ridiculous. She was ridiculous. But, right this minute, she totally loved Charlie. She was having a silly romantic fantasy where Luke was alive, they'd had their baby, and they were getting married in a barefoot ceremony down the road on Popham Beach. Charlie would be Luke's best man. And Abby would be Tessa's matron of honor. Matron, because six months before Luke and Tessa's wedding, Abby and Charlie had gotten married, too.

Improbable wasn't the same thing as impossible. Different words, different meanings.

See, Dad, I'm not an idiot. Or a moron. She even knew that was a difference of twenty-six IQ points.

Her father wanted her to register for the fall semester, glean meaning from the musings of dead writers like Shakespeare and Chaucer, and finagle an independent study project using green goods and found objects to make a relevant statement about society. Wasn't growing a whole entire person in her body enough of a statement? Couldn't preparing to give birth imbue her with more knowledge than picking apart the literary bones of the dead?

"I really like it here with you and Abby," Tessa said.

Why couldn't she stay in Hidden Harbor until the baby was born? The tiny seaside town was about as far away from academia as you could get. A week of breathing in sea and sand, and falling asleep to the lull of waves had already done her good. Even with the added baby weight, she felt lighter, stripped down, and closer to her center. Closer to Luke.

Why shouldn't she stay with Abby and Charlie?

"I just, you know—" Tessa hiked her shoulders to her ears on a sharp intake of breath, dropped them on an exhale. "Wish Luke was here, too." Tessa searched Charlie's face to see whether he'd gotten the Pink Floyd reference, but his expression didn't waver.

Charlie tapped two fingers against his chin. "Friends are straight with each other," he said, and she wasn't sure whether he'd asked her a question, so she didn't bother answering. Charlie unwrapped his silverware from the paper napkin, set his fork, spoon, and knife in parallel rows. "Abby and I are really excited about the baby. Things have been rough, and you've made us happy again."

Tessa nodded. She noticed the way Charlie made it sound as though he and Abby were still a couple.

She translated *things* to *the-fact-our-son-is-dead.*

The fried-clams aroma from the next table tickled the back of her throat. She sipped her water. Ice cubes bumped up against her lips, shot pain through the gum line above her front teeth. Another stellar side effect of pregnancy. Right when she needed to feel less, she felt more. Tessa ran her tongue along her gum line, numbing the ache.

"You know Luke was a surprise, right?"

"I did the math," Tessa said, sounding totally bitchy, and not caring how she sounded.

It didn't take a genius to figure out Charlie and Abby hadn't tried to get pregnant when they were seniors in high school, any more than she and Luke had tried to get pregnant in college. But late one night, Luke had shared a heck of a lot more about his parents.

Alone in Tessa's dorm room, Luke had laid his head on her stomach and told her everything about Abby and Charlie. Not just about their on-again off-again relationship, but about how it had affected him.

That had been the second most important thing Luke had ever given her.

"When Abby first told me she was pregnant," Charlie said, "I didn't take it well. I was getting ready to head off to college, and the idea of a baby freaked me out."

"You didn't want to change your life," Tessa said, thinking of how her father didn't want Tessa to change hers either.

Half of Tessa wanted to hear Charlie's side of the story, the other half wanted to stick her fingers in her ears and sing, *La-di-da, I can't hear you.* Charlie's story was messing with Tessa's what-if-Luke-were-alive fantasy. The one where Luke found out she was pregnant and didn't bolt.

Charlie's hand wavered above the place mat, as though he were tempted to strike the table with the heel of his hand. "No excuses. I acted like a jerk."

The regret in Charlie's eyes swelled Tessa's throat. "Okay," she said, and her voice came out muffled.

"Okay."

Their waitress stood over the table, held a pencil over her ordering pad, and regarded Tessa and Charlie sideways. "You guys need a few more minutes?"

"A few more. Thanks, Suzette." Charlie gave Suzette a glance-nod before she turned to leave.

Charlie's gaze slid back to Tessa, but she had the sense he

wasn't seeing her at all. "The thing was, near as I could tell, Abby never freaked out. She took the whole thing in stride and adjusted her plans." Charlie tapped his chin again, gave a half chuckle. The forced tone reminded Tessa of the way Charlie had laughed after Luke's memorial. "She tried to adjust our plans," Charlie added.

"Sounds like Abby."

Charlie flashed a grin, big and broad and full of love for Abby. "You're getting to know her, then."

"I am." Abby had held Tessa while she'd cried, stupid selfish tears, grief for having slashed her own body. Abby was kind and patient and everything Tessa was not. No wonder Luke had told Tessa that Abby was a great mom. How many boys talked that way, unless they were trying to be ironic?

"So it makes sense that Abby would want to adjust her plans again. It makes sense that, as soon as Abby found out about Luke's baby, she wanted to adopt him." Charlie tapped his chin. "Or her. Whatever, as long as Luke's baby is healthy."

"Totally makes sense," Tessa said. *Her* baby. The baby was hers, too.

"Abby's a great mother. I don't get why you'd consider giving the baby to anyone else. Can you help me out with this, Tessa? Help me understand." Charlie sipped his water, raised his eyebrow over the glass.

Tessa's heart kicked into defensive gear. Mr. Connors had slipped her a pop quiz, and she'd no idea she was about to be schooled. Tessa had never understood the logic of giving the baby to a stranger. That option had been forced on her by her father, Mr. Logic himself. Or so she'd thought. "I want to give my baby what I don't have to give."

"Which is?"

"Two parents."

Charlie raised a closed hand by his head. He unfurled, furled, unfurled his pointer finger. "When Abby adopts Luke's baby, he, or she, will have two parents. Me and Abby. Same as Luke, and he did fine."

"Call me old-fashioned," Tessa said, "but I think parents should be married. I think Luke was old-fashioned, too."

Charlie tilted his head. A smile tugged at his mouth, but he didn't look pleased. "That doesn't sound like Luke."

"I knew him pretty well." Maybe Luke wasn't ready for marriage, but that didn't mean he was opposed to the practice.

Lying in the dark with his head on her stomach, Luke had told Tessa that during his junior year in high school, Charlie moved into Briar Rose, and Luke thought he'd finally gotten what he'd always wanted: two parents who lived together and never bickered.

Instead, he'd gotten two parents who lived together.

That night in Tessa's dorm room, Luke had told her he considered the day his father packed his bag and moved out of the B&B the end of his childhood. That night, he'd kissed Tessa's belly, and shown her his broken heart. That night, Tessa had realized she and Luke weren't so different after all.

After Charlie moved out, Luke had done some stupid things. Stolen a bottle of Johnnie Walker from his mother's liquor cabinet and smashed it on the rocks of Head Beach. "Borrowed" Abby's truck and driven six friends into Boston, two months before he'd earned his license. Given his virginity to an eighteen-year-old girl he didn't love, maybe hadn't even liked.

Not all in the same night, but still . . .

Tessa couldn't bring Luke back to life, couldn't undo everything she'd done wrong. But maybe she could make sure one of his childhood dreams came true. It was practically a mandate. Love never died. "Luke always wanted you and Abby to get married."

Charlie sputtered on his water, coughed into his fist, swallowed hard. "I know that, Tessa."

"He would've wanted you and Abby to raise the baby as a married couple."

"Maybe so." Charlie offered Tessa a sad little smile. "But did Abby seem ready to run off with me tonight?" he asked. "I don't know. Give the lady chocolates, and she nearly clocks me."

The baby tumbled, a slow, strong head-over-butt roll. Tessa's hand went to her belly, the baby pressed against her hand, and she grinned like a fool. A fool in love.

"What is it? You all right?"

"Come quick if you want to feel the baby move." Tessa laughed. "He, or she, is practicing fetal gymnastics."

"You don't have to tell me twice." In a flash, Charlie was beside her, down on one knee, a hand on her belly.

Charlie scrunched his face, as though trying to listen. "I don't know," he said, and then a smile stretched his face.

When Tessa first met Luke at a dorm party, she'd brushed by him on the way to the keg, slowly, twice. On their first date, she'd worn skinny jeans, high-heeled boots, and a low-cut camisole that gaped whenever she leaned over. *Oops.* And even though she'd waited months to dare taking off her jeans, that hadn't stopped her from unzipping Luke's.

If you wanted to catch a guy and keep him interested, you had to give him a taste of how much he had to lose.

Giving the baby to single-mom Abby was a reasonable second-choice option. But if Tessa wanted to give Luke his childhood dream, she'd better convince Charlie she preferred her father's shit-for-logic contender.

"How would *you* feel if I gave your grandchild to someone else?" Tessa asked Charlie.

Charlie's smile fell and his jaw set. His eyes gave a single blink of panic before they blanked out. That felt even worse than Tessa had imagined.

Tessa's thigh tingled. She pictured slicing through her flesh and red beads bubbling from the scar. She imagined never hurting another person as long as she lived. But a girl had to do what a girl had to do. For Luke. "Luke would've wanted you to get back with Abby," she said. "There's a baby to consider."

Charlie stood up and brushed off the knees of his pants. "We've tried, Tessa, and it always ends up badly. Why do you think this time would be different?" His voice sounded tired, but Tessa also heard hope.

"Because this time," Tessa said, "you're not going to bolt."

Any card-carrying, red-blooded male would've killed to be in Rob Campbell's sneakers.

Rob parked his truck in front of Sugarcoated, grateful the bakery's lights were out, Celeste's Closed sign hung in the door, and the baker's white Forester had vacated its spot for the evening. Abby and Celeste were like family to each other. And from the way Celeste watched over her kids, Rob doubted she'd let him get away with bringing Abby back from a date drunk. Besides, he really liked Celeste's mini blueberry muffins.

He opened the passenger door for Abby. Even though summer folks wandered the street with soft-serve cones and lobster tans, Abby slid from her seat straight into his arms. Her breasts brushed his chest during descent, giving him a good idea what they'd feel like cupped in his hands—perfect—and making him wonder how they'd respond to his mouth.

"Sure you don't want to bring me back to Briar Rose?" she asked for the second time, letting Rob know she didn't realize she'd had too much to drink. A sober Abby wouldn't have wanted to return to her place of business sloppy-drunk, even though she also looked tastier than any of Celeste's desserts and hot enough to take right here on the street.

He could've blamed his heightened interest on going without sex for longer than he cared to remember. But Rob knew better. His heightened interest was all about Abby.

"Cup of joe, then I'll take you home," Rob said, even though Abby had passed on Lobster House coffee and dessert. Did coffee actually sober? Or did caffeine only keep you wide-awake while you buzzed? Wasn't the supposed coffee cure one of those myths he'd picked up in college and never bothered to debunk? Considering he couldn't remember the last time he'd picked up a can of Folger's, maybe a tall glass of ice water would serve to dilute the alcohol.

Abby stepped up onto the raised sidewalk and turned to face him. Her blond hair glowed in the setting sun and formed a golden nimbus around her face. She wrapped a finger around a curl. Her hand slipped slowly, slowly through her hair, fell across her collarbone, and then barely brushed her left breast. The tip of her pink tongue glossed over the swell of her bottom lip. "There's something I've wanted to do for a long time. Come closer."

Rob's face heated, which should've been impossible, since the lion's share of his blood had already flowed in the opposite direction. "Abby," he said, as if to protest, but then he stepped till his sneaker brushed the curb, his body responding to the stroke of her voice.

The heel on Abby's sandals and the raised sidewalk evened their heights, and he found himself staring a straight line into her eyes. Blue, but different than his, more hazy and gray and prettier than the richest granite and—

Abby clasped his face between her hands, leaned forward, and pressed her lips to the scar by his right eye.

Her kiss, soft and warm against his cheekbone, had him imagining what her lips might feel like pressed against another part of his body. Her hair tickled his nose. He inhaled her lemon meringue aroma all the way to his toes, now curling in his sneakers.

"Let's go inside," he whispered, and then nearly tripped stepping onto the curb. Two beers with dinner hadn't registered on his buzz meter, but he still wondered whether he could manage his key in the lock without fumbling. Circulation to his brain had ended.

The entry door to his apartment was to the right of Sugar-coated, leading to a stairway that climbed to his office.

"What's your star from?" Abby said.

Rob paused, key in the first door. "My what?" he asked, and then he realized what she'd meant. "My *scar.*" He touched the raised skin beside his eye, chuckled. Grace used to call it his star, too. Used to say it twinkled at her, like the star in the children's rhyme. "Jumped out of bed in the middle of the night and tripped over Bella." The lock gave, and he gestured for Abby to go up the stairs before him.

Abby bent and slipped off her sandals. She craned her neck, looked over her shoulder. "Who's Bella?" she asked, and her voice took on a worried tone. Either worried or jealous.

"My dog."

"Oh, good!" Abby straightened. She dangled her sandals from one hand and scampered up the stairs, giving Rob a perfect view of her ass-hugging jeans.

For the first time in his life, he wished he were denim.

"Pooch used to sleep on the floor, right up against my side of the bed," Rob said. "Until the night Grace woke up from a nightmare, calling for Daddy, and Daddy went flying. Ever see a tall guy topple? Smacked my head against the side of the dresser. Ever hear a head smack against a dresser?"

Campbell Landscape Design was located to the right of the staircase. Rob turned the key.

"Poor baby." Abby rubbed his back, as though trying to soothe his old injury. "You never told me you had a dog. Why don't you bring her around? Bring Bella *and* Grace."

"Bella died. Had to put her down months ago. Cancer," Rob said, thinking of his golden girl in her heyday, running back and forth on her line in the yard whenever his truck had pulled into the driveway, and he'd stepped from the cab. Then he thought of his mom, trotting out to his truck whenever he'd bring Maria and Grace by for a visit.

He didn't want to think about that right now.

The door swung wide.

Abby hugged him from behind, her breasts pressing up against his back. "Poor baby," she repeated. She didn't seem to be going anywhere fast, so he twisted around, lifted her by the waist and over the threshold.

Abby let out a high-pitched squeal, letting Rob know he'd found at least one of her ticklish spots. When her feet found purchase, she quieted, took a moment to look around his office, and then slid into his desk chair.

"Comfy." Abby twirled in his oversized chair, like a kid at the barber. Grinning, she stood and steadied herself against the desktop. "I shouldn't have done that. Think I need to lie down. Where's your . . . ?" Abby's gaze slid to the door, open to his bedroom, aka the smaller room where he housed his overflow filing cabinets and slept on a single mattress with his big feet hanging off the end.

Abby dropped her pocketbook on his desk chair and stumbled to the darkened doorway of his bedroom. She leaned against the door jamb, breasts stretching the fabric of her pink top, hair tussled and shining against the darkness. "I don't like when things spin," she said, but it sounded like *sin*. "You coming?"

Nearly.

If his heart were revving any louder, he would've had a case of the spins, too. Any red-blooded male would've said, "Yes, ma'am. Show me the way." Instead, he said, "Why don't I get you a glass of water?"

"Suit yourself," Abby said, and dove onto his bed.

Closest thing to an out-of-body experience Rob had ever had. Because while he was pouring Abby an ice-cold glass of water from the pitcher he kept in the mini-fridge, a lucky act-first think-later Rob clone was making love to the beautiful woman languishing on his bed.

Rob had to follow his gut. And right now, despite the hell-yes firing his pants, his gut was grumbling with complaints. Funny thing was, Rob's gut sounded a lot like his father. The weekend before Rob went away to school, Dad had sat him down and given him warnings about always doing his best work, staying away from drugs and alcohol, and treating girls right. Number one on the treat-girls-right list of instructions? Never take advantage of a girl who'd had too much to drink.

Rob had taken all of Dad's advice to heart.

Rob sat on the edge of his bed and handed Abby the water. "Umm, that looks nice." She pushed herself to sitting, drained the glass, set it atop a filing cabinet, and wiped her mouth with the back of her hand.

"I should take you home." Rob could hustle her into the private quarters of Briar Rose, whisk her past Tessa, deliver her to her bedroom, and then run before his body realized what he was doing.

Abby edged closer. She laid her hand on his lower thigh, slid it higher. That was all it took for his body to sing, *Hallelujah!*

"But you haven't even kissed me yet," she said.

"True," Rob started to say, but then Abby's moist lips were on his, her tongue playing inside his mouth. One hand raked through the back of his hair, sending tremors across his shoulders. The other hand stroked between his legs, firing him to life, and making him strain against the zipper.

"Baby," he whispered against the curve of her ear, a move straight from his fantasy. Then he worked on her neck, kissing her pulse until she moaned. *Bingo!* He'd hit her sweet spot. Rob rolled her onto her back.

Abby gazed up at him, soft grin on her face. Across his pillow, her hair fanned out, like a mermaid's hair floating on water. Her breasts stuck straight up, as if they too were afloat. Inside his pants, he was raring to go.

First, he should take off his sneakers.

"Hang on a sec," Rob said, and turned from Abby to untie his sneakers and wrestle them from his feet.

When he turned back around, Abby was sitting up. Her T-shirt lay balled on the pillow. A lacy pink bra barely restrained her breasts. A bow accented one of those impossible-to-navigate center clasps. As soon as Rob met Abby's gaze, she, one-handed, popped the clasp.

Even better than his fantasy.

Full and round, with perky tips any red-blooded male would die for.

Abby was so much more than a fantasy.

With steady hands, he reached for her breasts, took the clasps in either hand, and pressed them back together with a *snap.*

The sound of the red-blooded males club retracting Rob's membership.

Abby's sleepy eyes flashed open. Her face went from pleasure-me pleased to mortified. "You don't want me?"

"Baby," he said. "I want you. *Sooo* bad."

"But," she said, reminding Rob of their conversation at the Lobster House that had gone down a similar road. One minute they were all lovey-dovey, the next Rob had volunteered for a dunce cap and a seat in the corner.

"But you've had too much to drink. I want you, but not like this. You don't know what you're doing. You can't make an informed decision," Rob said, remembering his father's long-ago lingo. Sex with a girl, or woman, under the influence wasn't playing fair. You needed a clear mind to make life-altering choices. That rule applied to whether a woman was too drunk to consent to sex, or whether cancer and chemo had fogged a woman's brain so she shouldn't have been allowed to give her oldest son power of attorney. Thing was, Mom hadn't been foggy the day she'd signed the paperwork. Had she?

Rob didn't want to think about that right now.

Abby snapped her crumpled T-shirt from the pillow. She slipped it over her head. She gave a pinched growl of frustration and then yanked it off to turn the fabric inside-right. Instead, she succeeded in twisting some kind of inner bra contraption around itself. "Maybe I don't know what I'm doing, but at least I know what I want." Abby's voice slurred over *want,* but her clear gaze met his, sending her zinger straight to his heart. Signed, sealed, delivered.

Had to respect a woman who could put him in his place even when sloppy drunk.

Rob lifted the twisted top from Abby's hands, untangled the fabric, and handed it back to her. She shrugged into it and stood up. "Where do you keep your water?"

"In the fridge," he said.

"Where?" she said.

A perfectly normal reaction, considering she was thinking he meant a six-foot-tall appliance you found in most houses and apartments, rather than the mini-fridge he'd crammed beneath his office sideboard. "Under the table against the wall."

Abby nodded and slipped from the room, leaving behind a heady mix of lemons and frustration in her wake.

Rob had to admire Abby's determination to have sex, even if she was too buzzed for him to trust her judgment. Had to admire Abby's resolve to try and adopt her son's baby, too. No matter the risk, Abby always reached for what she wanted. Even if success meant having her life stuck on rewind.

Abby leaned against the door jamb, pocketbook slung over her shoulder, sandals in hand. "Is this about Charlie? Because we haven't been together in over two years. And even when we used to have leap-year sex, it didn't mean anything. But if we were together, it would. It would mean a lot."

Leap-year sex? Oh boy. Abby was going to hate herself in the morning, and not just because of her more-than-likely hangover. "It would mean a lot to me, too, Abby. That's why I stopped." He stroked her cheek, reminded himself not to kiss her killer kissable mouth.

"Drive me home?" she said, not an ounce of slur in her voice.

Rob nodded and stepped into his sneakers.

The sneakers he kept beside his too-short-for-his-body single mattress, in his tiny room, in the office apartment where a mini-fridge hid beneath a built-in table. Not unlike his freshman-year college dorm room.

He had the funds to rent an apartment, even buy a small house. But he'd told himself he should wait until the house in Bath sold, and he knew exactly how much money he had in the bank. Rather than risk a wrong move, he wanted to wait until his financial situation was a sure thing.

Rob left his shirt untucked and lifted his truck keys from a hook by the door. His hand slid to the small of Abby's back. She shot him a look, a little sad and a whole lot disappointed.

Kind of like the looks he'd gotten from too-buzzed-to-consent girls he'd once walked from his dorm to theirs. Not much different than the looks he'd gotten from sober girls who'd stayed the night, only to wake up to his not-really-looking-for-a-girlfriend speech. And a close cousin to the look that had taken his ex-wife years to perfect.

Rob followed Abby into the night air, hunched his shoulders against the sudden chill. He got behind the wheel and shut the door with a *thud*.

If Abby was stuck on rewind, then why was Rob the one living like a college kid, making out with a girl in a shoe-box room, and then taking her home under a cloud of shame? Why was he, once again, uncertain what he really wanted?

He didn't want to think about that right now.

CHAPTER 12

Abby startled awake to Sadie's furry rump staring her in the face, her cell phone buzzing across the bedroom, and a pain that burrowed through the center of her chest. She scooted past the gray tabby, curled like a question mark on the bed's right-side pillow, and scrambled to the dresser. The cell slipped from her hands and jounced against the dresser top. Celeste's image and the time pierced through the mud flats of Abby's brain.

Celeste phoning a few minutes past seven wasn't unusual. They sometimes checked in with each other at the start of a busy workday. The fact Abby was late for the start of her morning shift?

Unusual!

A vise of pressure clamped either side of Abby's head, and her brain leaked images from last night's date with Rob. Guzzling drinks at the Lobster House, going back to Rob's apartment, and unsnapping her bra. That didn't explain why she was now back at Briar Rose and fully dressed.

Abby's voice struggled beneath the weight of boozy slumber and came out in a loud whisper. "Hello."

"I knew it! You're upstairs hiding, you naughty girl," Celeste said, mistaking hangover harried for the huskiness of morning-after-boinking. The sound of Celeste banging on the pipe that snaked from her kitchen at Sugarcoated to Rob's apartment clanked through the phone, pinching the nerves at Abby's temples.

If Abby had been on Skype, Celeste would've witnessed Abby's blowfish breathing, her mane of curls snarled around her head, her makeup smudged gray beneath her eyes. Instead, the above-dresser mirror gifted Abby with the favor. She turned away from the image. "What in the world makes you think I'm upstairs?"

"Oh, I don't know. A certain nice-looking man coming in for a large coffee and twice his usual blueberry muffin order, and then hightailing it out of the shop before I could get in a, 'How's it going?' Rob sure looked like he had some*one* to hide. Did you call Hannah to start breakfast without you?"

Abby had long ago trained Hannah to start without her in the unlikely event she was late for her own breakfast service.

First time for everything.

"I think I'm good," Abby said.

Abby's mouth tasted of rum and mussels and mothballs, nudging her stomach into a lukewarm queasiness. *Drip.* Her brain leaked the image of Rob's apartment, the walls and office furniture spinning by in a blur. Had she twirled in his desk chair? *Drip.* Had she thrown herself at Rob? *Drip.* Had Rob taken one look at her secret weapons and put them back in their pretty pink package?

After Rob had told her how he felt about a second chance at fatherhood, she should've clarified her feelings for him. She should've told him she cared for him, should've given him a chance to respond. Instead, she'd chased her feelings down with rum, and they'd come out in a desperate plea for physical contact. She wanted so much more from Rob.

Had she ruined everything?

The center-of-the-chest pain sharpened, as though she were having a heart attack. "Hang on a sec," Abby told Celeste.

Abby reached beneath her T-shirt and found her bra's hard plastic closure twisted in a knot, a sure sign Rob had refastened the clasp himself. Nothing baffled an otherwise coordinated man more than the unhooking and hooking of a woman's brassiere. Abby unsnapped the clasp, unleashing her breasts, but the pain lingered.

"Celeste," Abby said. "You were right, but not about me staying the night at Rob's." She stared at her reflection. Hung over at thirty-eight after a promising date that had degenerated into a disaster. Her eyes looked tired. Her body looked tired. Her soul felt tired. Why did she bother dating?

I don't want to do this anymore.

Abby's words rushed out on a sob. "I'm at home."

Celeste shifted her tone from giddy girlfriend to Mama Bear-insistent. "Tell me," she said. "Tell me everything."

Abby sniffed. "You were right about the heels. Three inches was too much for me to handle. I got drunk."

"You got drunk because you're not used to walking in high heels?"

"That, plus the fact I'm crazy about Rob and he has no interest in being my baby daddy." Abby understood, really she did. But that didn't prevent her from using the same spiteful words and tone she'd chosen to let Rob know how his choice had affected her. Same as before, resentment cut both ways.

"Come again?"

"To Luke's baby."

"Oh," Celeste said, and then fell silent.

Never a good sign when outspoken Celeste was at a loss for words.

"It gets worse. I think I might've maybe told him about having meaningless leap-year sex with Charlie."

"Seriously?"

"No worries," Abby said. "All I remember is I swigged a few drinks, went back to his place, made myself at home, and started taking off my clothes. But I think I told him about the Charlie thing *after?*"

All she knew was Rob had picked up a supposedly mature woman from Briar Rose and by the time they'd returned, she'd morphed into a drunk-on-her-butt girl. Would the real Abby Stone please stand up? Above her head, the pressed-tin ceiling rotated counterclockwise. She steadied herself against the dresser, swallowed down a swell of queasiness.

"Oh my God, Abby. You didn't sleep with him, did you? If Rob laid one hand on you while you were drunk, I will personally cut off more than his supply of blueberry muffins!"

Clear-eyed boinking between consenting adults was one thing, sex when one party was faced was quite another. Abby laughed, and the pain in her head crescendoed. "Hush, Mama Bear. Despite my best efforts to disrobe, he made me put my clothes back on."

Memory dripped in a sticky, disjointed stream. Abby kissing the tiny star-shaped scar by Rob's right eye. Rob nibbling her neck. Abby stroking his erection. She slapped a hand over her eyes, shook her head at no one. Had they really made out on a mattress on the floor in a dorm-small room? And why was she picturing a dorm fridge?

At dinner, she'd told Rob about long-ago summer boys who'd been put off when they'd discovered she was a teenage mother. She hadn't told him about the boys of summer she'd thrown herself at anyway. She'd reasoned no-strings sex was better than nothing at all. Hadn't believed it then, didn't believe it now. Would she ever learn?

She wanted to climb back into bed, pull the sheets over her head, and sleep through the day. She wanted to wake up and realize last night's fiasco had been a bad dream, born of nothing more than heat, humidity, and late-night snacking. She wanted another chance.

"I told you Rob was a gentleman," Celeste said.

"Excuse me?" Abby said. "That's what *I* told *you*."

"Gotta go! I have a customer. This conversation is to be continued later." Celeste cut off their connection, getting in the last word.

Abby's breath fogged the cell's screen. She drew a heart with her fingertip and then wiped the slate clean. Gentleman or not, Rob couldn't have enjoyed hearing about Charlie. No man wanted to hear about a woman's ex-lover, especially when the ex would always be a part of her life.

Before last night's dinner, she'd thought Rob was becoming part of her life, too.

She'd daydreamed Rob and Abby into the future, imagined leading Rob on a summertime hike over Morse Mountain to the deafening surf of Seawall Beach. She'd looked forward to walking hand in hand with Rob through low tide at Popham, and then letting high tide strand them on the rocks of the Fox Island tombolo. She'd fantasized walking beside Rob and following the path of her completed labyrinth, for many seasons to come.

She'd lost her mind.

In reality, Abby had a bed-and-breakfast to run. Her job as an innkeeper? To set the stage and make her *guests'* fantasies come true. She rubbed her thumb against her forefinger, corralled her fantasies, and got to work.

Seven minutes later, Abby stood in the kitchen with her wet hair wrangled into a ponytail. Light filtered in from the shaded side of the house, nothing compared to the ocean-reflected assault from the dining room. Squinting, she poured batter onto the Belgian waffle iron, added fruit salad to two more plates, directed Hannah to take the plates to her waiting guests, and reminded herself to give Hannah a raise.

Abby inhaled the batter's malt aroma. Her empty stomach complained, but she knew better than to listen to a request for anything sweet. Her hunger could wait. She'd washed the worst of the sour taste from last night's date from her mouth, skin, and hair. Two ibuprofens were bathing her brain. A steaming mug of coffee was bringing her the rest of the way home. All in all, she was in pretty good shape.

"Rough night last night?"

Abby whipped around to find Tessa, fresh-faced, bright-eyed, carrying dirty plates past Hannah to the sink, and obliterating Abby's delusion she'd applied more than enough under-eye concealer. To Tessa's credit, as promised, she'd shown up to help with breakfast every day this week.

Abby held a hand to her cheek. "That bad?"

Tessa's mouth formed a panicked O, and then her gaze narrowed. She shook her head. "No . . . It's just Hannah said you've never been late for breakfast before and I—" Tessa's gaze softened, as though she were listening to a beautiful song. She dashed across the room, grabbed Abby's hand, and dragged her into the pantry.

"What?" Abby said, laughing. "What is it?"

Tessa held Abby's hand to the swell of her belly. Abby's heart kicked her in the ribs and her grandbaby moved beneath her palm. A foot, an elbow, a bum? Didn't matter. One touch drove the connection straight to Abby's heart. Sure as her name was Abigail Pearl Stone, she would've gladly died to protect the tiny person growing inside Tessa.

Oh, Tessa, what have you done?

A memory bubble popped, offering up long-buried memories of Luke as a newborn. Luke's skinny, pale arms twitching in a startled response. His head turned to the side in that fencing position. His tiny chin quivering with dimples. Tears leaked onto her cheeks. She brushed them away with her free hand.

Tessa nodded, and she took on the shrill tone of girly gossip. "Did you talk to Charlie yet?"

"Since last night?" The baby's movement tickled Abby's palm, but she didn't dare move, didn't dare ruin this perfect moment.

Tessa grabbed Abby's free hand and brought it to the opposite side of her belly. The baby tickled that palm, too. "Charlie told me he'd call you in the morning," Tessa said, and her voice went singsong. "He wants to take you out this afternoon. He wouldn't say where. But you're supposed to dress for a hike and bring your appetite." She shrugged, as if the thought tickled. "Sounds romantic to me."

"Charlie and I are just friends."

"Are you sure? Because the way Charlie tells it, I think he's still in love with you. I think he's got it bad."

Love for Luke's baby surged through Abby's hands to her heart, but déjà vu enveloped her. Whenever she'd told Luke she and Charlie were just friends, he hadn't believed her either.

Abby would've had to have been deaf, dumb, and blind not to have realized that she and Charlie had disappointed Luke after their relationship's last failure. But that hadn't given Luke the right to talk to her like one of his buddies. That hadn't given him the right to have pointed out that for two people who supposedly didn't work as a couple, Abby and Charlie sure sounded like they worked great together at night.

That hadn't given Abby the right to refuse to talk to Luke about her relationship with his father.

Abby's belly hummed, as though her grandbaby were inside her womb. For a panicked second she thought she was having a hysterical pregnancy. Then, throat palpitating, she took her hands from Tessa's belly and fished her buzzing cell from the pocket of her half apron.

Charlie.

Had Tessa somehow instigated Charlie's phone call? Abby angled Tessa a sideways glance, and then turned toward the spice rack, breathed in cinnamon and nutmeg. "Hi, Charlie."

"Hello, beautiful."

Abby glanced over her shoulder, but Tessa hadn't taken the hint to give her privacy. Instead, Tessa's eyes gleamed in the low light. She leaned against the cereal shelf, one hand cradling her belly.

"Sorry, sir," Abby said. "You must've misdialed."

Charlie laughed, real and honest and from the heart. Abby grinned. She'd always loved making him laugh. "To what do I owe the honor?" *What gives?* toyed with her tongue.

"I'd like to take you on an adventure this afternoon, if you're up for it?"

"What did you have in mind?" Abby asked Charlie, and her gaze wandered to Tessa. Why was she so invested in her and Charlie?

Tessa nodded and rubbed her belly.

The memory of touching Luke's newborn skin blazed before Abby's eyes. Her face prickled with heat, and she fanned herself with a flatbread. Would she get to hold Luke's child and trace the length of his or her spine with her fingertips, or would Tessa steal that joy from her? Was Tessa unaware of the way her actions were impacting Abby? Was she completely aware?

Would the real Tessa Lombardi please stand up?

"A late picnic," Charlie said, and he sounded slightly breathless.

"Where?"

"It's a surprise."

A chill ran up the back of Abby's neck, the kind you get moments before a thrill, or seconds before a disaster. "How would I prepare for said picnic?"

"Wear said hiking boots and bring a towel."

"Anything else? How about a bathing suit?"

Charlie's tone went from breezy to hushed, adding a layer of intimacy. "Totally up to you. Bathing suit's optional."

The smell of baked-to-a-perfect-crisp waffles hit Abby's nose, and her eyes widened. *Waffles,* she mouthed to Tessa.

Tessa made an exaggerated grimace. On her way out of the pantry, her baby belly brushed the back of Abby's hand, sending a sad ache to her throat.

Abby touched two fingertips to her pulse. "Let's see. An afternoon picnic spot. A hike to the dining area. Bathing suit's optional." Abby knew of a couple of places that fit that description, but only one she'd been to with Charlie. Only one held meaning for both of them.

When you'd known someone for decades, when you'd essentially grown up with someone, it was pretty hard for that someone to pull off a surprise.

Unlike Rob. Everything with Rob was a surprise. Last night, she'd learned he would not touch a drunken woman, even if sex was in the offing. He'd shared his worries about his daughter's emotional well-being and his history of racing to her side in the middle of the night.

Each and every reveal left Abby wanting to know more.

"I'm still going out with Rob," Abby told Charlie. Whether Rob still had an interest in going out with her remained to be seen.

"I'll behave."

Tessa flew by with two plates of food, heading into the dining room. Side view, her jaw was set and determined, her gait sure. Gone was the poky girl, unsure of her serving skills. Or was Abby imagining the transformation?

"I know where you want to take me," she told Charlie. "Off limits—"

"The happiest place on Earth."

"That's Disney's tagline!"

"Nothing bad ever happens there."

No one ever grew old, no one ever died. Their special place had been like Neverland.

The smell of cinnamon and nutmeg morphed into the milky-powdery musk of a newborn's scalp. Was it her lingering hangover or the trick of grief? She felt a little sick. Sick with longing. "I don't know whether I'm up for it," she whispered. "I don't know whether I can."

"Shh," Charlie said. "I'll come by at three. Hiking boots, optional bathing suit, towel. I'll take care of the rest. I'll take care of everything. It's about time."

Abby dropped the phone into her apron, stepped from the pantry and into the light. She took control of the kitchen, busied herself with brewing a second pot of coffee, refilled the creamer, and brought breakfast to the Kincaids. The gray-haired couple finished each other's sentences and each other's food. More impressive, after twenty-five years of marriage, they still flirted with each other. Would she ever be part of such a couple?

No mystery where Charlie intended to take her. Her only question was, *why?*

CHAPTER 13

Abby rocked.

On the front porch of Briar Rose, she settled into one of the three white-washed rockers and pushed off with her feet. The motion soothed, but the glider's whine and ratchet against the timeworn floorboards set her teeth on edge. Nearby, a mourning dove cooed, the cry coming late in the day for a creature whose voice marked the rising of the sun. Inside the entryway next to the dinner bell, there was a note with her cell phone number, an alternate means for her guests to summon her. Standard procedure allowed her to slip out now and again for errands: a carton of eggs, a gallon of milk, a hike with Charlie to the forbidden place. She sipped from a highball glass of mint-decorated iced tea, scooped out a leaf, and sucked the cool juices. The texture roughed her tongue, and the triple cooling of shade, drink, and herb revived her energy. Yet, anxiety hummed from the top of her tingling scalp to the tracks of her hiking boots, as though a hopped-up shadow-Abby were sewed to her, like in *Peter Pan and Wendy.*

She and Luke had found a dusty 1940 edition at Hidden Harbor's used and out-of-print books store, Second Time's a Charm. At night, she'd tuck Luke's block quilt around him, nestle his blue teddy bear between Luke and the wall, and snuggle in beside him to share the story of boys who'd never grow up.

Tessa and Hannah breezed onto the porch, and Abby set her hiking boots to the floor, stilling the motion.

Tessa had volunteered to help Hannah clean the guest rooms while Abby hunkered down in the kitchen, preparing afternoon self-serve refreshments. In the dining room, warm Mexican wedding cookies, cool slices of watermelon, and iced teas awaited her newly checked-in guests. Sweet cooling comforts.

The girls' hair was piled high on their heads, like Celeste's gourmet cupcakes. Hannah's bun was frosted milk chocolate buttercream; Tessa's, dark and bittersweet. The girls wore similar outfits, flouncy-frilly eyelet skirts reserved for the under twenty-five set.

Tessa swung her pocketbook, her expression free as a bird. A bird not sitting on a nest. "Going shopping!"

"Retail therapy," Hannah offered.

Abby nodded. "Have fun, girls."

Tessa and Hannah ambled down the porch steps and practically skipped to Tessa's white Corolla. The outfits, the familiarity, the joy of togetherness, the fact one teen was pregnant. Abby could've been looking at herself and Celeste twenty years ago. The teen pregnancy heritage continued. Why did children refuse to learn from their parents' mistakes?

Tessa slid behind the wheel, yelled through the driver's side window. "Have fun with Charlie! Don't do anything I wouldn't do!"

If Celeste had delivered that warning twenty years ago, she would've meant it.

Charlie's Jeep turned into the driveway. He stopped beside Tessa, lining up the driver's side windows. A moment later, Charlie's and Tessa's hands high-fived between the vehicles. Then Tessa took off, beeping her horn, the sound trailing down Ocean Boulevard.

I have a teenager in the house.

Today, the thought made Abby grin. Would the notion thrill her thirteen years from now?

Charlie pulled up in front of the porch and tooted the horn three times. Who needed a teenager when she had Charlie? Charlie, who wanted to take her back to the forbidden place. The pressure to blow out a breath built in Abby's throat. Instead, she swallowed it down and snapped up her day pack.

Charlie got out of the Jeep, tossed her pack in the backseat on top of his. "Let me guess. Towel, water, and the perpetual fleece?"

He wore shorts Abby didn't recognize, hiking boots with fresh laces. His face was clean-shaven and smooth as a boy's, as though he'd waited till afternoon to do the deed. He'd tried for casual. Despite Charlie's breezy tone, casual wasn't something you could try for.

"Let me tell. Towel, water, fleece, and a bathing suit."

Charlie clutched his chest. "Slain through the heart."

"Funny, I wouldn't have guessed your heart the body part impacted by my choice to wear a suit."

Charlie tossed her a grin, the kind turned down in an apology. "Same diff. You know me better than anyone."

Abby squeezed her eyes shut, shook her head. "I'm sorry, Charlie. I didn't mean that."

"Yeah, you did."

Charlie often used humor to diffuse a tense situation. And her humor often lashed out at Charlie's expense when she should've been shadowboxing. Charlie slid his sunglasses from the console, slipped them onto his face, and silenced his inner comic. Abby folded her hands in her lap. For the short ride, she kept her gaze on the road's heat shimmer, the mirage of a cooling pool of water, just out of her reach.

Charlie pulled over to the side of the road and parked in a

spot meant as a turnaround. "Think anyone will recognize my ride?"

"Bright red Jeep with *Teach* vanity plates? Not a chance."

This time, Abby's joke inspired a genuine grin. Just like old times, Charlie let Abby hit the trail in front of him. They followed the white blazes and wended around slabs of limestone and slate, through the silent thick of pine and spruce, beech, poplar, and birch. Hard to believe so many birds lived in the trees, hidden from sight. Abby listened for the whistle of the wood thrush, the variable tweet of the song sparrow, the tap of a woodpecker. Then, over the crunch of Abby's and Charlie's footfalls, a white-throated sparrow called, the sound rising from a low-lying shrub. Lily Beth had claimed the bird was saying, "Old Sam Peabody, Peabody, Peabody!" The same message, over and over, if anyone cared to listen.

Abby climbed a rock face, pulled herself over the ledge, and squinted against the ocean-reflected sunlight. With Charlie right behind, she navigated the rocky shoreline, jumping from boulder to boulder and darting between bushes heavy with wild blueberries. Countless times she and Luke had picked blueberries along the shore, little Luke eating half his basket by the time they returned home, his fingers stained purple from the juice.

Abby almost wished she could tell people she'd scolded him for their wasted time. She almost wished she could say she hadn't kissed the juice from Luke's sticky fingers. If she knew she'd lost Luke because she hadn't appreciated every moment, maybe, just maybe, she could stop looking for a reason.

Charlie came up behind Abby, clamped a hand on to her shoulder. "Here we are."

The sun burned the exposed back of Abby's neck, and sweat pooled between her breasts. She ripped a page from Lily Beth's rule book, inhaling from her toes in an attempt to settle the beat of her heart. It didn't work. Then, pulse hammering in her throat, they half-climbed, half-slid, down into The Cove.

Same as twenty years ago, the sun shone bright on the secluded beach, no clouds to filter or shadow the ocean's turquoise waves. No sounds of beachgoers drifted from neighboring shores, or even from the other side of the rock face. The wooded shoreline insulated them from neighboring beaches, laden with families, Frisbees, and sunbathers who customarily wore suits. They'd once thought the beach was theirs alone, but then they'd find evidence to the contrary. A dropped candy wrapper. A single sand-covered crew sock. A campfire's charred remains.

After Charlie had left for college, Abby vowed never to come back here. Then, when Charlie had graduated and returned, she'd made him promise, too. Luke's death had elevated The Cove from secret to sacred.

Charlie stared out to the ocean. His mouth tightened, and a noise came from the back of his throat. Did Charlie feel it, too?

"Gotta water a tree." Charlie lowered his pack to the sand and trotted off into the woods.

Abby smiled at Charlie's retreating form and then cast her gaze to the water's edge, the surf breaking a jagged line along the shore.

Ghosts haunted this beach.

Two madly-in-love teenagers liked to come here after dark, throw down blankets, and make love in the sand. One night, the boy suggested they go for it in the water. The girl had her doubts. She'd heard it wasn't as romantic as it sounded. Something about water washing away essential moisture and sand lodging in inconvenient places.

The water was cold, but she deep down knew her shivering had more to do with the boy's suggestion they go without a condom than the Maine-cold waters numbing her ankles.

Then the boy promised he'd love her forever, and she was gone.

What would Abby tell her younger self, if she had the opportunity? Not a damn thing. How could she regret the best thing that had ever happened to her?

Abby unzipped her pack, shook out her towel, and took a seat under the blistering sun. She fished around in her pack's outside pocket, looking for her water bottle, and then pictured it sitting beside the sink at Briar Rose. Capped and good to go nowhere.

No water bottle sat in the netting of Charlie's pack. She unzipped the main compartment and discovered two insulated lunch bags and one chilled wine carrier. From the long pouch, she slid out a bottle of Korbel Brut.

What in the world?

She unwound two champagne flutes from Charlie's blue-and-white-striped beach towel.

Charlie stepped from the woods and into the light.

Abby raised the champagne bottle above her head. The glass iced her hand. "Are we celebrating something? Are we celebrating the baby?"

Charlie jogged over to Abby's towel, knelt, and took the champagne from her hands. He shook his head. "Geesh, Abby. And you tell me I don't have any impulse control?"

"Sorry! I was thirsty. I was looking for water. I didn't think you'd mind." After everything they'd shared, was it any wonder Abby overstepped Charlie's boundaries? In elementary school, they'd shared lunches, sipping from the same box-bound bendy straws. By middle school, they were holding hands and trading spit. Was it any wonder they'd made a baby in high school?

Was it any wonder Charlie was still one of her best friends?

Best friends with benefits?

That's not how she thought about Charlie. But was that the way he thought about her?

Charlie took off his sunglasses, so she could see he was kidding.

"Did I ruin a surprise?"

"I sincerely doubt it." Charlie beamed. The tips of his ears turned red, a sign of uncharacteristic shyness she hadn't seen since the day he'd told her he was getting married. Abby didn't think he'd dated since Luke's accident. So maybe the announcement was job related and he was moving away?

Maine's Teacher of the Year had every right to take his career in whatever direction he wanted. Then why did her organs shift, as though she were sinking in quicksand?

Charlie sandwiched her hands between his. He sucked his lips between his teeth. His gaze met hers, and his left eye twitched.

Abby giggled. "You're scaring me."

"Abigail Pearl Stone, I knew you were special when you kicked my ass at Ping-Pong, and then stole a kiss from me seconds before I was planning to plaster one on you. Any girl with the balls to take advantage of me deserves my heart."

Uh-oh.

"I've loved you forever," Charlie said, and Abby's hands trembled in his. "It's about time we stopped messing around and got serious. Would you do me the honor of becoming my wife? Will you marry me, Abby?"

Charlie held a steady smile, her gaze, and her tender teenage heart.

When the boy you've loved forever managed to shock you, your jaw did, in fact, drop.

With a flick of his thumb, Charlie tipped Abby's jaw shut.

Abby-the-teenager wanted to throw her arms around Charlie's neck and slobber relief into his collar.

Abby-the-adult wanted to know whether Charlie was suffering from sun poisoning, summer flu, or early dementia.

"What's this about?"

"I've loved you forever. It's about time—"

Abby should've known Teach had been working from a prepared script. "Why now? What's changed?"

"What's changed?" Charlie asked, his tone a high squeak missing since eighth grade. "What hasn't changed? Our son is dead, and his girlfriend is about to give birth to our grandchild. I want to be a part of the baby's life, and not just on weekends. Wouldn't it be easier if we were married? This is about us, Abby."

Tessa had told Abby she thought Charlie was still in love with her. She'd chirped with excitement at the thought of her and Charlie going on a picnic. She'd stood by in the pantry, eavesdropping and invested. "Did Tessa put you up to this?"

"Can't I ask the woman I love to be my wife?"

The friend. Abby was the friend he loved, a difference worth noting. "Can't you tell me the truth?"

Charlie swished air around in his mouth. "Tessa wants us to get married."

"Ha! I knew it!"

"She wants Luke's baby to grow up with two parents."

"We're the baby's parents."

"She pulled out the Luke card."

"The what?"

" 'Luke always wanted you and Abby to get married. He would've wanted you and Abby to raise the baby as a married couple.' " Charlie's voice, Tessa's words, and Luke's unfulfilled dream. The triumvirate delivered a sucker punch, straight to Abby's gut.

Abby thought of four-year-old Luke crying in his bed the first time she and Charlie had gotten back together and then broken up. She remembered sixteen-year-old Luke nailing her with an angry glare the last time she and Charlie had failed him. Same as those dark days, regret choked her voice. "That's not fair. It's not like we didn't try for Luke's sake. Over and over."

"Yeah, I know."

"Why do you care so much about what Tessa wants?"

Charlie's eyes tried to smile, but then his gaze fell to their hands and he swallowed through a frown.

A chill climbed the back of Abby's head and oozed over her brow. "What happens if we don't get married? What if we don't do what Tessa wants?"

"Nothing," Charlie said. "Nothing happens." Charlie raised his gaze to Abby's. Same as the day she'd had to tell him about Luke's accident, Charlie's lips clamped shut, but his eyes spoke of loss. The waves tumbled; a breeze ruffled Charlie's hair. When he released her hands, her fingers went cold.

Nothing meant no baby.

"Tessa threatened to stop me from adopting Luke's baby if we don't get married? If we don't agree to her terms?"

"E-yup. Only she wasn't as subtle as a threat. It was, you know, more like a promise."

"How dare she? That's emotional blackmail!" Double emotional blackmail, considering the Luke card she'd pulled from her trick deck. After everything Tessa had shared with her! The story about Tessa's mother leaving. The admission about cutting herself. Abby doubted Tessa had lied about either scar, but had Tessa timed the telling?

"How dare she manipulate you?"

"Really, Abby?" Charlie got down off his haunches and sat cross-legged. He wiped his hands on his shorts. Between the shoreline rocks, water crashed and churned, retreated with a sizzle. "When have I done anything I didn't want to do? You've said yourself, 'Sometimes Charlie just needs a nudge.' Consider me nudged. I want to do right by you. Anything wrong with that?" Charlie's eyes reflected years of disappointment. Abby's, not his. "I want to be the man you've always wanted."

Two years ago, he'd moved back into her home and her heart with a similar plea. He'd claimed he'd changed, that he was ready to give up his vices and follow through with his promises. But then, after she'd planned a getaway weekend for herself and Charlie, an old college buddy of Charlie's had last-minute lured him away with a better offer. A weekend golfing with the boys on a private course. All expenses paid, so how could Charlie resist eighteen holes of golf by day and bar golfing at night?

Just like old times.

Abby hadn't minded letting Charlie live with her rent-free. He was going through a divorce. He was paying another mortgage. And when Charlie asked to borrow money for the attorney's fees, Abby hadn't minded that either. The price you paid for the man you loved. But then, without telling her, the man she'd loved decided to invest her loan in a hedge fund that went belly up months before his divorce was final.

Just like old times.

They'd argue all the time. They'd forget to lower their voices within earshot of Luke. She'd told Charlie he acted like a child. He'd accused her of being all work and no play. She'd figured out the surest way to end their misery. She asked him to marry her.

She'd never corrected Luke's assumption that she'd asked Charlie to leave, so that in his son's eyes, he could still be a hero.

Just like old times.

Abby still wished Charlie could be the man she'd always wanted. But now that phrase only conjured Rob.

Lily Beth was right. Nobody got everything they wanted. Scratch the surface of any so-called charmed life, and you hit reality. Abby should be grateful for what she had. Why waste her precious energy on bemoaning what she couldn't have?

Then why did she wish she could pull a toddler fit and throw herself flat on her back, kicking and screaming until she'd worn out her ability to hope?

Past the breakers, out on the open ocean, a Sunfish floated by, its sail a tiny red speck in the distance. Charlie lifted a tear from her cheek. "Hey, Pearl. No crying. Remember when this used to be our happy place?" Charlie said. "Remember when we used to make each other happy? We could do that again. What do you say, Pearl? Me and you." Charlie waggled his eyebrows, raised to his knees, made exaggerated pelvic thrusts. "Every night till our bones crack from old age."

Abby laughed. Tears ran down her cheeks, and she licked the salt from her lips. "Sex was never our problem."

"I've got an idea. There's something I want to show you, something in the woods you're going to love."

"I've heard that line before, sir, and I'm not buying it."

"I promise I'm not trying to seduce you, Abby." Charlie held up his pinkie.

Charlie only pinkie swore with Luke. And despite all of the ways Charlie had managed to squirrel out of commitments to her, he'd never ever broken a promise to his son.

Abby wrapped her pinkie around Charlie's, and Charlie clamped her hand in his. "Get ready for a trip down memory lane. Close your eyes."

"I'm not closing my eyes!"

"C'mon, Abby. Where's the fun girl I used to know? Where's my playground buddy?"

"I don't play much," Abby said. As though responding to Charlie's taunt, her tone turned petulant, and her bottom lip jutted out. Where had that come from? Nobody forced her to run a B&B. No one set her schedule. If she didn't make time for fun in her life, she'd no one to blame but herself.

Charlie, on the other hand, had never veered from the adage of work hard, play harder. Wasn't that the reason all his students gravitated to him? Wasn't that the reason she had?

"Okay." Abby brushed herself off, stood, and squeezed her eyes shut. The sun's light pulsed red beneath her lids.

Charlie wove his fingers through hers. "Relax. This won't hurt a bit."

"I've heard that line before, too," Abby said.

Charlie turned her around, put her back to the surf, her face toward the woods. The toe of Abby's boot hit a rock and she stumbled. Charlie caught her around the waist. "Don't open your eyes." His hands went to her shoulders, guiding her forward. Light dimmed. The temperature dropped. The green fragrance of pine and birch mingled with the musky scent of decaying leaves and hardwoods. The sun's filtered light warmed her face.

And then, all at once, brightness kissed her eyelids.

"Open your eyes," Charlie said.

They stood in a small clearing of ferns, moss-covered slate, and a downed maple trunk with its center point balanced on a slab of marble.

Damn you, Charlie.

He'd accomplished the impossible. He'd brought them back to the beginning. Back to the time she'd taken her turn on the seesaw with a cute boy she'd noticed but had never spoken to. Back to Abby and Charlie pushing off from the blacktop, hair flying, whoops of joy caught in their throats. Back to the game of chicken, where the winner jumped off and the loser hit bottom, reverberations echoing through the torso.

From the distance of adulthood, the thrill of youth came with the comfort of knowing how easy you'd had it. "I still can't believe you dumped me. What a bully, Charlie Connors!

I was half your size. I bumped two feet in the air. You're lucky I didn't face plant on the concrete."

"The way I remember it, Abby Stone, you dumped me. Rattled my brains so hard I couldn't think straight for a whole year."

Had that been the reason why, after they'd played on the seesaw, she'd needed to let him win their race around the tire obstacle course? Had that been the reason why, midcourse, he'd tripped and fallen?

No, she couldn't have . . . Had she?

Charlie straddled one end of the tree-trunk seesaw. With a big grin on his face, he hardly looked older than ten. Even then, he'd rattled her. He'd rattled her badly. "How about a rematch?" Charlie said. "I promise to play nice this time. I promise not to hurt you. I prom—"

Abby jumped onto the far end of the tree trunk, pushed off and rose from the ground. Anything to hush Charlie's slew of promises. She'd heard them all before. The fact they'd never intended to hurt each other never stopped them from doing so. Even when they were in high school, they'd argued. Under the magnifying glass of raging hormones, slights real and imagined combusted. She'd be the first to admit, if only to Celeste, that she'd once lived for their high-intensity manufactured conflict. Now, melodrama exhausted her.

Real life provided more than enough traumas.

Abby floated to the ground, pushed skyward. Charlie bent his knees and soared higher. "What do you say? You and me and baby make three. We can get it right this time."

Was Tessa so unstable she'd dare give Luke's baby to strangers instead of Abby? Or was Tessa's demand some childish ploy to get her way? After months of staying mum about her pregnancy, Tessa had shown up on her doorstep with nothing but the clothes on her back. On Wednesday, Abby had asked Tessa whether she liked avocadoes. She'd waited so long to answer,

Abby had half-expected her to open her mouth and say, "I don't know. Do I?" Instead, she'd merely shrugged.

Tessa's self-imposed mandate to give her baby to a married Abby and Charlie could wane like the moon.

"I'll think about it."

Charlie whooped and pumped a fist in the air. "Girl of my dreams is going to think about it!" His voice boomed, but the delivery fell short.

She didn't need to overthink the fact she loved Charlie. But years of squabbling had banished him from being the man of her dreams. Years of breaking up and getting back together had worn out Charlie's welcome. These days, when her mind wandered into the hazy-sweet land of daydreams, she pictured a down-to-earth man who, unlike Charlie, couldn't tell the difference between a Cartier and a Rolex, but could name every rose at North Creek Farm, and tell you how best to nurture its growth. A man whose emotional maturity made him even sexier. These days, her mind wandered to Rob and lingered on the man who had no interest in a long-term relationship with a new mom.

If she married Charlie, what did she have to lose?

Truth was, if she didn't marry Charlie, they could both lose their grandchild. Was that a blow either of them could weather? Abby didn't want to find out.

Charlie stopped the seesaw motion, got off, and held on to the tree trunk to let Abby down easy. He came over to her side of the trunk, his tone end-of-day phone call serious. "Got room for a friend?"

"Always." Abby scooted forward on the trunk, and Charlie slid behind her, reminiscent of schoolyard days when they'd double up. At an angle, she slipped back into his arms, got an instant case of the giggles. "I'm squashing you." She started to stand, and he held fast around her waist, pulled her back down. "No worries, buddy. This is cozy. A cozy train," Charlie said.

The image of Abby, Charlie, and Luke snuggling in a seated line along a beach towel filled her until she could feel the heat of Luke's small body before her. She breathed hardwood and pine, and then banished the scent for the memory of Luke's just-showered preschool hair. The lemony-sharp scent of No More Tears burned her nose.

When you lost a child on the brink of manhood, you mourned every stage of his life. The past. The present. And the future denied to him.

"I remember," she said. "I remember everything. Those years without you were hard. When you came back to us, I was afraid, afraid to hope."

Charlie held tighter. "When I was at school, I thought about Luke all the time. Wondered how big he'd grown, whether he liked to play catch or dig in the sand."

"I sent pictures!"

"I know, but it wasn't the same. I regret every single second I missed. I know being around for Luke's child doesn't make up for the time I missed with him. But, I don't know, maybe it would help . . ." Charlie's breath tickled her ear. He rested his cheek on Abby's shoulder, rubbed her arms with his fingertips.

Goose bumps raised along her flesh. Like a partner in a long-standing relationship, Abby provided the tail for Charlie's open-ended statement. Maybe their marriage would help *Charlie.* He wasn't looking for a second chance to do right by her or to honor Luke's memory; he was seeking a means to assuage his guilt. She didn't doubt Charlie loved her. She didn't need to overthink the many shades of love. But, aside from Luke's baby, what would she gain from their marriage?

Even if she adopted Luke's baby without marrying Charlie, she'd lose Rob.

Rob, who'd seen her grief and urged her to channel it into a physical monument to her son. Rob, who couldn't walk into Sugarcoated without Elijah gravitating to his side and Phoebe jumping into his arms. Rob, who couldn't make it through the day without seeing or talking to his daughter.

Abby didn't need a baby daddy. But Rob would make a great second-time dad, a loving and supportive stepdad.

A loving and supportive husband.

Last night, standing in the doorway to Rob's bedroom completely faced, she'd accused Rob of not knowing what he wanted, and he hadn't responded. Because he hadn't wanted to argue with her or because he didn't have an argument?

If Rob didn't know what he wanted, there was a chance he wanted her.

"Remember the junior prom?" Charlie's hands roamed down Abby's arms and stilled on her hands.

"No," she said, but she took hold of Charlie's hands and gave them a squeeze. They'd made it as far as the Peddler's parking lot, when Charlie said he needed a kiss. Half an hour later, they tumbled out of his Corvette and stumbled onto the dance floor, red-faced even before their first dance.

"Be my Abigail Pearl again," Charlie said, "for Luke."

Somewhere along the line, Luke had adopted Abby's dream of marrying Charlie, and the idea had blossomed in his heart. Meanwhile, inside Abby's heart, the dream had withered.

"It's about time I made good on my promise to you. Isn't it about time we got married?"

Wasn't it about time she felt better? That she stopped living half a life? Scratch her surface and she bled grief for her son, same as the day he'd died.

Behind her, Charlie struggled with his breath, and she squeezed his hand. "We're okay," she told him. Same lie as their nighttime telephone check-ins. Reminiscing about Luke made both of them sad.

Abby didn't want to be sad anymore.

Past the obstacle course of leaves and branches, past the beach, a bright red triangle bobbed in the waves, the Sunfish headed toward shore. Its red sail bobbed in the waves, like an erratic heartbeat. No doubt, she and Charlie knew how to make each other happy. No doubt, they knew how to make each other miserable, too.

As a teenager, she'd thought the twin fires of passion meant true love. Sometimes when she was with Charlie, their banter and flirtations, their squabbles and fights, made her feel like a teenager again. Full of angst and fury. Full of passion and uncertainty.

She was hardly a teenager.

The Sunfish turned its bow into the wind and changed course, tacking back to sea. The wind filled its red sail, and the small craft soared.

Thirty-eight wasn't that old, but maybe it was time for her to finally grow up.

Chapter 14

What would it be like to live with family again?

Sundown at Briar Rose meant Abby's time to unwind on the porch. To kick off her shoes, lean back, and enjoy the satisfaction of a job well done. To give herself the proverbial pat on the back. Because, hey, if you didn't appreciate your hard work, who would?

A slight breeze came off the ocean, carrying a hint of lavender bloom. A chorus of cicadas chirped, the hum competing with the roll of the surf, and the Charlie statement she kept rewinding.

You and me and baby make three.

Three sounded so much nicer than one. Abby had a sudden pang for Lily Beth, living alone for the past sixteen years. Sure, her mother spent her days entertaining the public at Heart Stone, invited friends over for dinners on the beach, impromptu nature walks. But visits ended. Friends went home to their own families, their own lives. And nights stretched, long as the late-day shadows.

Briar Rose buzzed with activity. Footfalls of guests, male and female voices, water running in the pipes. The commotion comforted Abby, to a point. She and her guests traded life stories. They bonded over trouble talk. Abby provided lighthearted complaints that skirted real issues. Guests offered earnest divulging. But even strangers who became friends were just passing through her life. Abby had no expectations otherwise. Form a relationship, see you next year. Easy come, easy go.

She scrolled through her cell's missed calls, reviewed the history she'd already reviewed. Rob had called while she was out with Charlie, wanting to know how she was feeling. He'd asked her to phone back. But how could she return Rob's call before she had an answer for Charlie? How seriously should she take Tessa's threat? Fuzzy darkness swallowed the Briar Rose parking lot, night casting a blanket, and no sign of Tessa. To hell with impulse control.

Abby flipped through her list of contacts and hit *send*.

Tessa's father picked up on the first ring. "Professor Lombardi."

"Hi, this is Abby, Abby Stone." Silence. "Luke's mom?" Abby savored the sweetness of the words on her tongue, like a widow who worried her wedding band.

"How are you, Ms. Stone?"

"I'm fine. Thank you for asking. And please call me Abby." She waited for the professor to ask her to call him Noah. "Um, Professor Lombardi . . . I'm calling to let you know *Tessa* is doing well. She's actually been a big help to me."

Professor Lombardi harrumphed, a throat clearing with attitude.

Disbelief? Disgust? Disdain? Tessa had phoned to let her father know her whereabouts. But wasn't he worried about her? "It's just," Abby continued. "Well, frankly, she seems a little confused . . ." The word *lost* belatedly popped into Abby's head. Tessa was on a mission, searching. But for what?

"About?"

"About the baby." Abby flipped a curl back and forth between forefinger and ring finger. Back-forth, back-forth, back-forth. Preschool Luke had loved to play with her hair, thumb planted in his mouth, index finger hooked around his nose.

When he'd outgrown thumb sucking, he still liked to come up behind her and flip a curl, a just-between-them gesture that stood in for embarrassing hugs and kisses. When was the last time he'd done that?

The thing about last times? You never knew when they were happening.

A creak from Professor Lombardi's end of the phone, as though he were rising from an office chair, even though she'd called him at home. Then the hollow tap of footfall and a slow release of air. Either disappointed or defeated. "I apologize for my daughter. I told Tessa she should leave well enough alone. No good would come from contacting you and bothering you with her problem. The child doesn't listen, she—"

Abby's brain hummed, as though the cicadas' song had lit all her neural connections. She jumped to standing. "You told Tessa not to contact me?"

"You've so recently lost your son."

"I'm aware of that fact."

"Tessa obsesses. The child can't let go of anything. I told her, clean breaks are best."

"In what universe?" Abby's voice sounded hushed. Tinnitus pin-pricked her left eardrum and then trailed to nothing.

Did Professor Lombardi imagine giving Luke's child to a stranger would somehow spare Tessa's feelings? Or was Tessa's father suggesting Tessa break off her relationship with Luke?

Instead, Tessa had immersed herself in Luke's life. Sleeping in his childhood bed. Becoming involved with Luke's parents. Taking up the train of Luke's childhood dream that his not-together parents get it together.

Another huff of air. Through the nostrils, Abby decided. Professor Lombardi was exhaling through his nostrils, like a bull. A stubborn, wrong-minded bull.

"You advised Tessa not to tell me about my grandchild? To . . . to . . . to . . ." His nonsense-talk paralyzed her tongue. The phone shook in Abby's hand, a violent wave of tremors.

The screen door cracked open. Abby's guest, Bart Trombly, poked his bald head out to the porch. The retired high-school principal and his wife liked to hang glide and paint watercolor sceneries. Bart met Abby's gaze and retreated inside the foyer, pulling the door shut behind him.

Dial it back, Abby. Dial it back.

Professor Lombardi deepened the timbre of his voice, as if he were speaking from behind a lectern. "I advised my child to do what I thought was best for her."

Abby could've gone through her entire life not knowing a part of Luke was alive in the world. Bad enough Tessa was threatening to give the baby away. What her father had suggested would've been so much worse.

How was wronging another person best for anyone?

Abby's hand slid down the porch railing. She tried swallowing down her anger, but, damn it, she wanted to jump on the bullheaded professor's back. Ride that beast until he realized the error of his ways.

Abby knew the type. The know-it-all truck salesman who'd tried to lure her with payments that fit her budget, conveniently leaving out the fact she'd be paying interest alone. Did he think she was easy prey because she didn't have a husband to handle the blue jobs? A guest who'd used another B&B's coupon and tried to short her on the bill. A plumber who'd called her first cute and then crazy, when she'd dissembled the under-sink pipes herself and discovered his business cards clogging the trap.

Abby had talked the salesman down to size. She'd charmed the guest into paying his bill, plus a huge guilt-alleviating tip. She'd reported the plumber and earned a credit toward a new sink.

"What options did you and Tessa discuss?"

"By the time Tessa told me about the pregnancy, her options were somewhat limited."

Translation: Tessa had been too far along for her father to talk her into an abortion.

Years ago, when Charlie had suggested an abortion, for a split second Abby had let herself consider it. She'd imagined herself and Charlie following through with their life plan. Graduate from college, get married, and, a few years later, start their white-picket-fence life, replete with a golden retriever and 2.4 kids. But how could she have looked their 2.4 kids in the eye, knowing she'd stopped their sibling's beating heart because the timing had been inconvenient?

Seemed Tessa had shared that line of thinking.

Thank God thank God thank God thank God thank God.

"Okay," Abby said. "So abortion was off the table." Abby pressed her forehead against a porch support column, trying to snuff out the unintended double entendre, the image of a woman lying on a metal slab, feet in stirrups. A cold ache slid between Abby's legs, and the backs of her knees softened. Abby lowered herself to the granite steps.

"That left one option," Professor Lombardi said.

"Which was?"

"Giving the baby up for adoption."

To a stranger. It was telling that Professor Lombardi couldn't say that to Abby's face.

"But Tessa felt she had other options," Abby said. A statement, not a question.

From the other end of the phone, an insistent tapping. The professor drumming his fingers on a mahogany desk? Abby didn't press, just waited him out.

"She nagged me for months," Professor Lombardi said.

Translation: Tessa had hoped in vain for her father's approval.

"She talked about either offering the baby to you or keeping it."

An exhalation whooshed out of Abby. Relief? Surprise? Utter shock? Tessa's mother wasn't a part of her life. Her father was a wrong-minded bully. Yet, all on her own, she'd opted to continue the pregnancy, had even considered raising Luke's baby herself.

Her baby. The baby was Tessa's, too. If she chose to take up the gauntlet.

Tessa wasn't Abby's daughter, but could she be proud of her anyway?

"Why not?" Abby said, and her voice lifted on a grin. "Why not encourage her to keep the baby?"

"She's nineteen years old!"

"I was eighteen when I had Luke."

"And you were able to take care of yourself and Luke's financial needs? All on your own? Without any help?"

"Of course not. My mother helped us."

Another harrumph. This one softer than the first, but Abby had heard it. The disdain had come through loud and clear.

"You didn't offer to help Tessa?" No wonder Tessa was running scared. Her father had narrowed her choices, boxing her in a corner.

Just like what Tessa was attempting to do to her and Charlie. The child repeating the mistakes of the parent.

"You mess up, you suffer the consequences."

Clean breaks. From his own child? "Did you threaten to disown Tessa if she kept the baby?"

"Abby—"

"Ms. Stone," she corrected.

"I offered to give her a dose of reality." His voice sounded tired, pulling from the last reserves of a long day. Or a long life. "Tessa has a lot of growing up to do. Who am I to take much-needed life lessons away from her?"

"You're her family." Family stuck together. Family never ever gave up on each other.

Especially a family of two.

"I'm aware of that fact," he said, borrowing Abby's previous statement and delivering it in a flat tone. "Perhaps we have different ideas about the meaning of family."

Headlights swung into the driveway, pulling shadows along the porch posts. Tessa backed into an open space between two cars and cut the engine. A familiar sensation washed over Abby, relief at a loved one's return, an up-shift of contentment.

The way she felt whenever family walked through the doors of Briar Rose. Luke, Lily Beth, and now Tessa.

Tessa wasn't family. Was she?

That decision was up to Tessa.

"Tessa just pulled in. Hang on a second." Abby held the phone to her chest, waited till Tessa made her way to the porch. "Would you like to talk to your dad?"

Tessa set down two big-handled white shopping bags. She squinted at the phone, rocked from side to side. "Do I have a choice?"

"You always have a choice."

Tessa met her gaze, and her chin jutted forward, as though she might cry. But then she took the phone from Abby's hands.

Abby went into the foyer and perched on the edge of the love seat. She straightened her sachets in the wicker basket, held one to her nose, inhaled lavender. Flipped open the white cardboard honor box and counted the cash.

The foyer light leaked onto the porch and lit the back of Tessa's head. "Yes." Pause. "Uh-huh. Dina sent me my vitamins." Pause. "I don't know. Why does it matter? You already paid my rent for the month. It's not like you're going to get it back."

Tessa's father paid her rent, but he wouldn't if she had a baby?

"Not yet. I told you, I don't know. And, really, Abby is none of your business." Tessa sat on the rocker. "Wh-What?" The rocker creaked and moaned, Tessa pushing the chair to its limits.

Tessa burst through the door, stopped short, and thrust the phone at Abby. "Thanks for having me. I'll leave in the morning." Tessa sidestepped past Abby, slid aside the pocket door, and race-walked into Abby's apartment.

What had just happened?

Abby followed behind Tessa, closed the door behind them, and threw on the overhead lights. "What did your father say to you?"

Tessa halted in the middle of the living room. Her shoulders rose to her ears and then fell sharply with a huff, as though Tessa were mimicking one of Abby's blowfish breaths. Tessa set her bags on the floor and spun on her heel. "I don't stay where I'm not wanted."

"Tessa, I haven't asked you to leave!"

"Then why did you call my father?"

To figure out whether adopting her grandchild necessitated committing to Charlie.

Blackmail was a lousy reason for agreeing to marry someone. Whether or not Abby was still the girl of Charlie's dreams, he deserved better. So did she.

"I don't know," Abby said.

Tessa snapped up her bags and huffed into her bedroom.

Luke's bedroom.

Abby tried not to laugh at the absurdity. Abby never believed Tessa when she claimed ignorance either.

"I called your dad to let him know how you were doing."

"Oh my God, you told him! You told him about, about—" Tessa's eyes widened, as if they were trying to escape her face. She slapped her thigh once, twice.

"Stop it!"

Breathing hard, Tessa met Abby's gaze, her hand wavering midair.

"Shh," Abby said. "Hush, now. Nobody's asking you to leave. Nobody's leaving you. You don't have to hurt yourself anymore. I didn't tell your dad about the cutting."

Tessa's mouth twisted sideways, and her eyes watered. "Swear?"

Abby held up a pinkie, and Tessa's expression softened, the hurt draining from her pink cheeks. Her hand floated to her side. "You still shouldn't have called my father."

"You shouldn't have gone behind my back to try to emotionally blackmail Charlie. I'm the one seeking adoption. If you have a question, or a demand, come to me first. Leave Charlie out of it."

"I don't even know what emotional blackmail means."

Not knowing the term hadn't stopped Tessa from excelling at the practice. "It means you set impossible conditions," Abby said. "It means you've threatened to give Luke's baby to a stranger, strangers, if Charlie and I don't get married."

Tessa's lips opened to form an O, and then she smoothed her features.

Abby shook her head, sat down on Luke's bed, and patted the spot beside her. "Come on, Tessa. Did you really think Charlie wouldn't tell me?"

"*Luke* would've wanted you and Charlie to raise the baby as a married couple." With a sigh, Tessa lowered herself to the bed. Her shoulders rounded. "I want what I want for my baby."

My baby. Abby hadn't heard Tessa refer to the baby as hers before. She'd only ever called the child Luke's. Or had that been Abby's doing?

"Who's to say a single parent can't provide a good home? Hmm? Did Luke turn out so badly? He was a pretty good guy, don't you think?"

"He had his good points."

Abby bumped shoulders with Tessa. "He had a lot of good points, and you know it."

"I guess."

Abby wanted what she wanted, too. But what if that wasn't the best choice for the baby?

"What do *you* want for your baby?" Abby asked, and Tessa's pupils jostled on the word *your.*

"I told you. I want what Luke would've wanted."

"I don't think you're looking at all of your options. Your father told me you mentioned keeping the baby?"

"Then he also must've told you he called me out for my foolish little fantasy. Silly, silly girl."

"He did, but so what? I raised Luke myself. Charlie was away at school until Luke was three. If I did it, you can do it, too. If that's what you *really* want . . ."

"What I really want? What I really want doesn't matter. I never get what I really want." Tessa stated the opinion without emotion. Abby would've felt better if Tessa had stuck out her bottom lip. Or, better yet, if she'd thrown herself on the floor and pitched a toddler fit. The fact no emotion bled through the statement let Abby know Professor Lombardi had hammered the fight out of his feisty daughter. She might not have been overly eager to take her father's call, but she still wanted his approval.

Abby wrapped her arm around Tessa's back, gave her shoulder a squeeze, to encourage both of them. Abby had jumped at the opportunity to adopt Luke and Tessa's baby. She could jump just as high for the chance to be the baby's grandmother. Wasn't that the natural order of life? As if it was natural to be a grandmother at thirty-eight, when other women her age were just starting families. "You could take care of your baby. Nothing's stopping you."

If Abby had been able to see Professor Lombardi's expression over the phone after she'd made a similar suggestion, she strongly suspected his face would've looked a lot like his daughter's. Tessa raised her eyes. Then her head turned and lowered until she'd fixed Abby in her what-madness-is-this gaze.

"I don't know about your father, but my daddy doesn't support mess-ups. Professor Lombardi pays for college. After that, you get a job and pay your own way. Why go to school, if you're planning on mooching off your family for the rest of your life? What's the point?"

Abby strongly suspected that some of Tessa's words—*mooching* and *mess-ups,* for instance—came directly from her father, too. Professor Lombardi's mouth to Tessa's ear and back out through her lips. Had the sentiments lodged in the child's heart?

Young woman. Tessa was a young woman. Old enough to make up her own mind, even if Abby didn't agree with her decisions.

"You could live at home," Abby said.

Tessa snorted.

"Just until you got on your feet. You could still go to school. They must have day care on campus." Abby's years-ago fantasy about living on campus with Charlie and a baby played before her eyes, the colors washed out, like an old movie. She'd considered Charlie's original request more than a year after it was already too late. People whom she used to know.

"I'm not lucky like you. I don't have a rich mother," Tessa said.

Abby squeaked out a laugh. "Lily Beth's not a wealthy woman. Her shop is charming. But she makes most of her money during the summer season. Her house is nice, but small. She's a single mom, too. Had me when she was a kid herself."

Damn if Tessa didn't remind Abby of Celeste. Eyes focused, expression open, trying to take in the whole picture. "Then how'd she buy her house? And who paid for all of this?" Tessa's gaze swept Luke's bedroom and lighted on the French doors. Nothing remarkable there. Just run-of-the-mill glass doors that took in a side-of-the-house path that angled around Abby's New Englander and opened onto an expansive yard with a view of the Casco Bay. Not the biggest house. Not the most awe-inspiring view. But big enough and awe-inspiring enough that, even sixteen years ago, the price should've been too expensive for a single mom with a limited income. Expensive enough that Abby should've long ago wondered about the source of Lily Beth's money.

After Briar Rose had become profitable, Abby had sent Lily Beth monthly checks to reimburse her for the down payment. Monthly checks that Lily Beth had called to a halt after Abby had breached the halfway mark.

Lily Beth had never needed the money.

"Luke told me you guys lived with his gran when he was small. I figured Lily Beth was either divorced or widowed or—"

"Never been married."

"So your father sends money."

"There's no father."

"Everybody has a father."

"Not me. According to Lily Beth, Daddy was a merman." A painting of a mermama watching her merbaby playing in the sand hung in the Hermit Island Kelp Shed, where her mother had worked as a teen. Lily Beth had always claimed she and Abby were the artist's inspiration, even though the signature was dated 1931. "My merman father beached long enough to get Lily Beth pregnant, and then swam back out to the deepest darkest depths of the ocean. No merman could survive on land."

Abby had once thought Lily Beth's fish tale couldn't possibly survive into Abby's adulthood.

By the time Abby had turned eighteen, she'd been too overwhelmed with her own teen pregnancy to worry about her mother's. She'd allowed Lily Beth to continue with the mermaid tale, adding chapters to the fable, as fast as mermaid statuary and aquamarine multiplied in her shop.

"Sounds romantic." Tessa's gaze lifted to the Luke-and-Tessa photo above Luke's bed, the image already fading under the barrage of sunlight. A little more each day. Luke's impossible-to-handle childhood photo albums hid in his bureau drawers. But even this photo and the surrounding photos of Luke and his friends used to give Abby a jolt of sadness, a gong struck at her center and echoing throughout her body. But now? Nothing.

That hurt in a whole new way.

"A story doesn't have to be sad to be romantic," Abby said.

Tessa looked at Abby sideways, as though daring her to prove otherwise.

Had the true story about Lily Beth and Abby's father been so horribly sad that Lily Beth had needed to fabricate a fable? As tragic a romance as, say, Luke and Tessa?

Abby didn't take well to lies. What was a story, but a lie artfully told?

Whether Abby raised Luke's baby or not, she'd want the child to know about Luke. The good and the bad. The truth, not the lies.

A child deserved to know his, or her, own father.

It was about time.

If Abby knew her mother, Lily Beth would be sitting out on the deck beside the two-foot-high look-alike mermaid statue and in front of the wooden bowl full of sand dollars, with a shawl draped over her shoulders, her hair cascading over the shawl, and a wineglass in hand. If Abby knew her mother, Lily Beth would, right now, be alternately taking a sip of that wine—white or red, didn't matter—and gazing out to sea. If—

"Hi, baby."

Red wine.

Lily Beth grinned—warm and welcoming without an ounce of surprise—as though she'd been expecting Abby to step out of the shadows and onto the deck. "Beautiful night," Lily Beth said.

"Sure is." An oval waxing moon lighted a silver path across the waves. The ocean brushed the shore, as if someone had unfurled a blanket of blue-black silk. Living all of her life on the Maine coast hadn't jaded Abby. She'd grown up knowing they lived in a vacation town. That most people worked fifty-one weeks a year, just so they could spend one week in Hidden Harbor. That for some people, like those who'd once summered in the cottage Lily Beth owned, Hidden Harbor was nothing but a long-ago dream. Others—Lily Beth—had summered in Hidden Harbor thirty-nine years ago, and never left.

"Glass of wine?"

"No, thank you."

Rough stones lined the deck. Dark blue lapis lazuli for truth, blue-green aquamarine for protection, pale blue moonstone for feminine energy. Working stones, Lily Beth called them. Their jagged edges allowed the properties to emanate, heal the user, and the world beyond. Lily Beth sold a few at Heart Stone, but Abby preferred the bins of tumbled rocks. She'd never been able to resist touching them, digging through the cool, rounded edges, worrying her fingers over the shiny-smooth perfection. But the rough stones stood apart, untouchable.

Not unlike Lily Beth.

Lily Beth knew everyone in town, and everyone knew her. Yet, while Abby was growing up, her mother had never dated. She'd never stayed out late and then come home, flushed with flirtation. She'd never brought men back to the house for drinks, conversation, and the low rumble of pillow talk. And whenever a man had tried to ask her out—from vacationers to locals—she'd put them off with a ready excuse. Sometimes she'd slip a friend's phone number into the gentleman's palm, the way you gave away something you didn't need.

Who didn't need love?

"You look tired," Lily Beth said. "Long day?"

"Aren't they all?" Abby hadn't meant to sound so morbid, so raw. So truthful. The daily grind kept her hands busy, darker thoughts at bay. But come nightfall, darkness seeped back in, filling in the silence with her son's name.

Tonight, Abby's brain tumbled rough-edged questions only Lily Beth's answers could smooth.

Abby lowered herself to the cushioned love seat beside Lily Beth's chair, ran her fingers across the sea-damaged white wicker, the familiar striations. Weak light spilled from the great room, casting a shadow across Lily Beth's features. Even in unflattering light, Lily Beth could've easily been mistaken for a much younger woman, Abby's sister rather than her mother. Growing up, strangers made the mistake all the time. But Lily Beth had never confused their roles.

"Mom," Abby said, "I want to know about my father."

Lily Beth blinked twice. She refilled her wineglass from the bottle on the glass coffee table, swirled, but did not sip. "Why?"

"I have a right to know where I came from."

"Why now? You haven't asked me about your father in years. Did something happen today?"

The last twenty-four hours rained down like a summer storm, sudden and soaking. Snippets of her conversation with Charlie. Her out-of-bounds longing for Rob. Her frustration with Tessa and the girl's unnerving ability to poke at Abby's life and find her weak points. The driving force behind the squall? Abby couldn't lose Luke's baby. Salt, sharp and tangy, swirled across Abby's tongue. Abby's sinuses swelled, like when she'd swim underwater, eyes open, wide strokes pulling herself along the ocean floor.

According to Lily Beth, Abby had taken her first steps on

this beach, her first falls. Lily Beth had held Abby in the water, and Abby had wriggled from her grasp, eager to dive beneath the waves. When Abby had been pregnant with Luke, the salt water had buoyed her, rendering her weightless and free. Then she hadn't felt desperate.

Lily Beth caught Abby's gaze, and Abby pulled her cardigan around her, closed the lapels, wrapped one hand around her waist. Growing up, other girls complained their mothers stood by their bedroom doors, listening in on their calls. Or phoned their friends' mothers, trolling for details. Not Lily Beth. One look, and Abby would bare her soul, a shellfish without its protective shell.

Not today.

Today, Abby only needed to share a select detail. Abby took the chunk of lapis lazuli down from the deck railing, pressed the tip of her ring finger into its sharpest point until her breath caught. She offered the stone to Lily Beth. "Tessa asked about my father."

Lily Beth took the stone from Abby's hands and gave her a half smile, lips pursed, slight nod, sideways flick of her gaze, as if to say, *Well-played*. "What did you tell her?"

"I told her my father was a merman who'd returned to the sea."

"What was her reaction?"

Abby laughed, but Lily Beth didn't break a grin. "She didn't take me seriously!"

"No?" Lily Beth passed the lapis lazuli from hand to hand, keeping it in perpetual motion. "Perhaps she was looking for proof? Details of his existence?"

"That would be nice. I'd like proof. A name? What he did for a living? Why he left?" *Why he left me.*

Lily Beth tilted her head to the side, held Abby's gaze, and Abby's stomach clenched.

Happened every time Lily Beth spoke of Abby's father.

"The first time I saw your father," Lily Beth said, "I was swimming laps off Head Beach."

"And a man with beautiful green eyes followed you into the shallows."

"Only then did I discover, he was more fish than man, he belonged to the ocean."

"That's nice, Mom, lovely as ever. Don't you think I've outgrown your quaint little fish tale? Pun intended."

Lily Beth didn't skip a beat. "Seaweed tangled around his—"

"Legs?"

Lily Beth shook her head, cracked a grin. *"Flipper."* She took a sip of her wine, then got up and exchanged the lapis lazuli for aquamarine. When Abby's fifty-four-year-old mother leaned against the railing and gazed out to the ocean, and the breeze combed her hair, Abby could imagine Lily Beth as a sixteen-year-old. Full of angst and longing. Full of beauty and promise. About to be sorely disappointed by her gift from the sea.

"I untangled the seaweed from his flipper, and he claimed I'd saved his life."

"Sounds like a line to me."

"That meant he had to give me his heart."

Abby scrunched her nose. "Gave you more than his heart."

Lily Beth turned to Abby, a smile in her voice. "He most certainly did."

Darkness and water caused people to raise their voices, so Abby was careful to lower hers. "And then he left you."

Lily Beth's voice lifted, strident. "He was never mine to keep. He was of another world. He belonged to the ocean."

Abby snorted, and she sounded like a juvenile, that unique blend of arrogance and unapologetic need. "Tell me something I don't already know."

"I can do that," Lily Beth said.

A shiver splashed the back of Abby's head, the front of her

thighs. Her ankles ached, as though she'd just emerged from the numbing ocean.

Like a mermaid? No. Mermaids wouldn't feel the sting of cold.

Lily Beth left the aquamarine on the railing and made her way to the love seat, her wide-legged pants swishing like a fin, her gaze fixed on Abby. For a second, her mother looked as if she might cry. Then Lily Beth removed her shawl, wrapped it around Abby's shoulders, and sat down beside her.

The ocean roiled. A buoy clanged. Abby's heart pulsed against her ribcage. *Tell me, tell me, tell me.*

Lily Beth gathered Abby's hands in hers and refused to blink her blue eyes. Blue as Abby's. Blue as regret.

"Mom?"

"Your father," Lily Beth said, "was a healer."

Abby envisioned a blond merman beneath the sea, draped in an emerald velvet robe, and wielding an aquamarine healing wand. She gave her head three quick shakes to clear the fable fog. "Don't." Abby tried to jerk her hands away from Lily Beth, but she held tight.

"Other people needed him more than we did."

"People?" Abby whispered.

Lily Beth swallowed, and her hands warmed around Abby's. "*Mer*people."

"That's enough. I'm going home." Abby wrenched her hands from Lily Beth's, stood up, and yanked off the shawl. "Why can't you tell me the truth? I'm thirty-eight years old!" Abby said, the across-the-ages lament of daughters to their mothers.

"I am. You're not listening. Settle down and—"

"Listen with my heart?"

Lily Beth nodded. She raised her wine to her lips, the glass trembling on its stem.

"You can tell me anything. I'm not fragile. You won't break

me," Abby said, in case Lily Beth was afraid Abby couldn't handle another tragedy after having lost her son.

How could her heart break when it was already broken?

"You're a strong woman," Lily Beth said. "That's how I raised you."

"Then why the riddles?"

"You're not ready." Lily Beth wound her shawl around her shoulders and stood to hug Abby good-bye.

Abby was either going to throw herself into the ocean or toss Lily Beth to the merpeople. What a pair they made. Her mother, living alone on the beach with her rocks and shells and mermaid tales. Abby at her B&B with mouths to feed, rooms to change, yet just as alone.

Abby pulled away and dug her keys out of her jeans' pocket. She hit the red light on her key fob to make sure it was working, flashed a trail toward the moon. "Seat belt, spare tire, car jack. I'm good to go. If I keep to the speed limit, I'll be home in ten."

"I know, baby. You're cautious. I never have to worry about you," Lily Beth said.

Nothing in Lily Beth's tone indicated insult. So why did Abby hear criticism? Why did the statement hang in the air, heavy as the fragrance of the heirloom roses that surrounded her mother's cottage? Lily Beth had told her to settle down. Abby wanted to pick up her mother's house, her mother's life, give it a good hard shake, and see what *settled* out. Maybe a middle-age beach bum who'd contributed half of Abby's genes would tumble from the ceiling and land on the couch. *See, Mom, I listen.*

"Talk to you tomorrow." Abby clamored down the steps, started up her truck, and backed out of the driveway. She switched on the radio, Miranda Lambert singing that sassy breakup song about a mother advising her grown daughter to put on her makeup and put away the crazy. She turned off the radio and rolled down her windows. Nothing but the white noise of the road, Abby's unanswered question about her father, and Lily Beth's parting words.

True enough, Abby had been cautious ever since adding the designation of *innkeeper* in front of her name. She certainly adhered to a daily schedule at Briar Rose. How could she not? Two weeks after losing Luke, she was back in the B&B business, dishing out hot breakfasts and warm smiles. That, above all else, should give Lily Beth proof that she could tell Abby anything. No matter what happened, she might shake, but she would not fall.

Nothing but fresh air, a dark country road, and Abby's headlights cutting through the dark and leading back home. Nope, Abby had never given her mother reason to worry. And Lily Beth had never coddled Abby either. If anything, Lily Beth had always pushed Abby to take bigger risks.

So, if Lily Beth wasn't worried about hurting Abby with the truth about her father, then who in the world was she trying to protect?

Chapter 15

Rob's father had taught him the importance of planning.

You went to college, you studied hard, and you married the girl of your dreams. But at twenty-two, how could Rob have known the difference between the girl of his dreams and the first nice girl who'd stuck around? How could he have understood that even with great timing, he'd chosen the wrong woman?

The opposite of the Abby dilemma.

The heat of the sun branding the back of Rob's neck, the smell of the strawberry-blond beach rose in his wheelbarrow, and the tension of the soil at first resisting and then giving beneath the weight of his shovel told Rob all was right with the world, and his decision to break up with Abby today. No point in prolonging agony. Abby wanted a baby; he didn't. Simple as that.

Until he caught sight of Abby making her way through the yard, and his decision cracked under the weight of wanting her.

Abby's sloppy-drunk words spoken on Sunday night rang true on Tuesday morning. Rob didn't know his own mind.

A sober and sexy Abby made her way through the yard and toward the labyrinth site. She wore a peach sundress and carried a wooden stand and a tray with three glasses of ice water, as if she'd, once again, stepped right out of one of his fantasies and into his life. Her blond curls shone with every bouncy step. From ten yards away, he could tell she smelled better than any beach rose. Five yards away, he knew he wasn't going to break it off with her. One yard away, even a clueless guy could decipher her uneasy smile and know she felt awkward as hell about Sunday night.

That made two of them.

Abby unfolded the stand and set the tray on top. "Sorry to have missed your call."

"Not a problem."

Rob planted the shovel in front of him and leaned against the handle. He called to the two college boys he'd hired for the summer. "Water break!"

The boys sauntered over, dirty and sweaty and red-faced from less than an hour of digging plots for shrubs and trail-delineating pavers. Kids needed toughening up. Rob touched a finger to his forehead, and both boys removed their baseball caps, giving Abby the proper respect. "Thank you," they mumbled, one after another. And then they found shade under one of Abby's ancient maple trees to gulp down their waters.

"Much appreciated." Rob drank half his water without pause, hoping he showed a bit more restraint than the college boys, even though the sight of Abby made him want to park himself at the end of a garden hose to quench his thirst. He set the glass back on the tray. "You're looking well."

"You wouldn't have said that if you saw me hungover Monday morning." Abby cringed and held a hand over her mouth. "It was a doozy."

"Figured as much. Happens to the best of us. You're allowed."

"You're sweet to say that," Abby said. "But I think it's only fair to tell you, I don't usually get falling-down drunk on a first date."

"Can't help it if you're a lightweight," Rob said, remembering how he'd lifted her over the threshold into his apartment. The way her ribs shifted beneath his fingers, the vibration of her ticklish laughter.

"I don't usually throw myself at men on a first date either."

And there it was.

The in-his-mind vision of Abby half undressed. The in-his-body reaction of wanting to finish the job.

Rob shifted in place, forced himself to think of mulch. Fields and fields of dark, weed-squelching bark. "Women don't usually *throw* themselves at me on first dates. Not that I've had a first date in over twenty years."

Did he need to point out the obvious? He hadn't gone on a date since his divorce. No woman had sufficiently motivated him to make the leap. Until Abby.

That wouldn't be fair to tell her.

"It's just . . ." Abby took a step closer. Close enough for him to inhale the lemon meringue smell of her, the sun warming her skin. Close enough for him to want to bend down and taste her shoulder and—

Rob forced himself to envision cedar mulch. Piles and piles of pale aromatic bark.

Abby shook her head, tilted her face to the side. "I guess I wasn't completely honest with you."

Ice water cooled Rob's stomach lining, but the back of his neck broke out in flop sweat. "Oh?"

Last time he'd seen that look, he'd come home late from work to a dark house and the now-ex waiting in the wing chair by the front door. One foot in the door, and Maria had flipped on the reading lamp to reveal her expression, each feature working hard to hold back all she needed to say.

"Tired," Rob had said, and headed for the stairs. "Guest room," Maria had countered, halting him at the landing.

Abby glanced at Rob's two-man crew and then her gaze

held Rob's. "You were up front with me about not wanting to be a dad again. And, well, I told you I wasn't looking for a baby daddy. But I think, maybe, I was avoiding the larger issue. Hence the rum and Coke. Hence the removal of clothing. Hence the—"

"Abby . . ." Rob wanted to call her *baby,* but that wouldn't have been fair either. "Did I seem like I minded?" He shook his head, an exaggerated side-to-side negation, and mouthed a well-pronounced, *No.*

Abby laughed. "You were a gentleman. I guess what I'm trying to say is, I want to continue seeing you." She held out her right hand, palm up. "And I want to adopt my son's child." She held out her left hand, moved both hands up and down, balancing two weights. "So . . . I was thinking . . . maybe we can discuss the issue."

"Discuss dating?" Rob worked a knot at the back of his neck, stretched to ease out a kink.

"Discuss what it will be like for us when my life includes a new baby. We could make a plan, work out what you want, what we both want. Like when you asked me what I wanted from the labyrinth . . . What do you want from *us?*"

"I want to continue seeing you, too."

That didn't begin to explain the way he felt about Abby. Truth was, he'd thought about her constantly since Sunday night. Tossed and turned after bringing her home, the bedding tangling around him, as if even the extra-long sheets no longer fit. He'd thought about dropping by on Monday on the way to a job site to bring her an OJ and an egg sandwich, his days-gone-by hangover remedy. Fantasized about giving her a back rub and working his way down the rest of her body to ease out any residual tension.

Worse, his mind had wandered to imagining living at Briar Rose with Abby. But then she hadn't called him back, and he'd chocked his boyish daydreams up to the offbeat charm of living in his office wearing as thin as the toes on his work boots.

Rob knew what he wanted. Problem was, every time he saw Abby, he forgot. He had no right to go after her, no right to lead her on—

She had no right to look so good. And he couldn't stand knowing he was causing that worried half smile as she squinted against the sun. Rob came out from behind his shovel and gave Abby a hands-free peck on the lips, careful not to smudge dirt all over her dress.

He really wanted to smudge dirt all over her dress.

But he wasn't about to take notes and draw up a plan, set his feelings on a grid and analyze them for proper symmetry. "How about we just see what happens?"

Abby licked her lips, but the worried half smile remained. "I don't think that's working for us." She looked out to the pile of pavers—squares of marble, bluestone, and granite she'd purchased on his suggestion. "Maybe, together, we could come up with something great. Like the paving stones."

Abby had ordered an inscribed granite bench for sitting outside the labyrinth, but that hadn't seemed like enough of a tribute to her son. When Abby had asked about leaving notes and prayers for Luke beneath the bench, Rob had come up with the idea for additional pavers. Plenty of room for friends and family to leave notes and prayers that wouldn't blow away.

Abby's suggestion that the notes and prayers would then become part of the earth, like her son, had made Rob's chest ache, actually ache, for Abby.

"I'm glad you liked my suggestion," Rob said.

"You're a great listener, when it comes to landscape design. When we're talking friend-to-friend? Or whatever we are to each other? You shut down."

Ouch. Hadn't Maria voiced a similar complaint, back when everything he did was for his wife and daughter? Now the sentiment came from the lips of the woman he cared about.

He cared about Abby.

Not the time to think about that.

Tessa came barreling through the yard, headed their way. She stepped between Rob and Abby, as though she were intentionally trying to come between them. "I did something really stupid!" she sang. "I just promised Hannah I'd go to a party tonight on Head Beach."

Abby situated herself beside Rob, forcing Tessa to turn and face them both. "You and Hannah have become friends. What's stupid about meeting her at the beach?"

Tessa shrugged. The single gesture made her suddenly look like a kid, a little unsure of herself, a lot lost, and in desperate need of a good parent. "I'd kind of feel weird. Like I'd have to, you know, explain—" Tessa waved a hand over her belly.

"You don't owe anyone an explanation," Abby said. "But if you don't feel comfortable, tell Hannah you changed your mind."

"I have to go. I promised!" Tessa widened her eyes at Abby, and some kind of girl secret passed between them. Rob was sure of it. He'd seen Grace and her girlfriends share a whole story without uttering a single word.

Female telepathy.

"I should get back to work," Rob said. "I'm on the clock," he added, and angled Abby his own form of telepathy. *We're fine. Let's just see what happens.*

"Wait! Are those the only pavers?" Tessa asked.

"Only?" Abby said. "There's a dozen of them."

"Plantings make a big difference," Rob said. "Pea stones fill in the rest."

"The bench was the splurge." Abby angled Rob her own form of telepathy. "I mean, I'd love to have more pavers. But we can't always have everything we want. We adjust. We make do."

Tessa's gaze slid from Luke's stepping-stone at her feet to the labyrinth site. Back and forth, back and forth. Her smile grew with each pass across the landscape. "I'm getting an idea!" Tessa said. "Concrete isn't expensive. What if we filled in all the empty spaces with these concrete jobbies?"

"Still costs money," Abby said.

"What if we got other people to pay for them? You know, crowd source. People could donate a stone with their hand-prints. And write their names on the stone?"

Abby's eyes watered. "Oh, Tessa, that's a wonderful idea!"

"Really?" Tessa's face lightened, brightened. Reminded Rob of the way Grace looked whenever he'd compliment his daughter for a job well done. Kids thrived on genuine parental praise, needed it like the sun. Without it, they wilted, plantings gone to premature seed.

Rob's back pocket vibrated, and he dug out his cell. *Maria.* He considered letting her call go to voice mail, but curiosity got the better of him. Rob headed toward the water, the ocean skirting the shore, and picked up on the third buzz. "Hey, Maria."

"Can you come over?"

"I'm on a job site," he said, as if he needed to explain what he did all day, what he'd been doing for decades.

"When you're done with work, then."

Normally, Rob would've said fine, just to get her off the phone. But status quo didn't seem to be working for him these days. "What's going on?"

The college kids' voices were growing louder. The boys gave each other playful shoves. Too long of a break and their bodies would lose the rhythm of digging, their legs stiffen up. Half a day's work would take all day.

"Can you make it fast?" Rob asked, when silence met his request.

Maria sighed, long and drawn-out. "I want to put the house on the market," she said finally.

"And I want you to put the house on the market. So what's the problem?"

"There's no problem. It's just, you're friends with Larry from Coldwell, and Nancy just started with Brown Realty. She's on her own. This is her first job since the divorce, and I'd really like to support her."

Abby and Tessa kneeled before Luke's stepping-stones. When Tessa pressed her hands inside Luke's handprints, Abby hugged the girl around the shoulders.

Rob didn't trust Tessa. The way she'd shown up on Abby's doorstep without so much as a warning smacked of callousness. But weren't all teenagers self-centered, to one extent or another? Abby seemed to have gotten over the shock. And Tessa's presence at Briar Rose was supporting Abby. Couldn't deny the girl—and the baby she carried—were helping Abby move through her grief. Abby was moving forward because she had something to look forward to.

"So support her," Rob said. "Doesn't matter to me who lists the place. Your decision. Just get it done."

Maria acted as if she hadn't even heard him. "Grace is so busy getting ready for college. We need to go shopping for bedding. She and her roommate have been texting. I don't feel right wasting her *last days* at home packing her life away in boxes." Maria's voice cracked. "Please come over. I don't feel right, Rob. I can't sell our family home."

Clean breaks. Wasn't that the point of their divorce? The sooner the house sold, the sooner Maria would stop calling him for little things. Water running in the downstairs toilet. Smoke alarm above the kitchen doorway tripping and setting off the rest of their dozen networked smokes. Circuit breaker in Maria's bathroom bagging out whenever she straightened her hair. A boy in Grace's bed—

Okay, that visit had been warranted.

But Maria could've taken care of each and every one of the minor home blips herself. Wasn't that why he'd left her with a detailed home-care cheat-sheet binder, with sections for the plumbing, electrical, and water heater? Each and every emergency call had been a ruse to get Rob back into the house. Grace was getting ready to leave for college. Another month they'd drop her off in Plymouth, and she wouldn't look back, at either of them. Nature of the world.

Maria's call had nothing to do with selling the house.

"Maria?" Rob said, his tone softening to cushion her rising panic.

"Maybe the divorce was a mistake."

"It wasn't."

Maria's footsteps echoed through the phone, and Rob pictured her heels tapping across the kitchen floor, retracing the worn path from counter to window, out of habit.

"Are we doing the right thing?" she asked.

"Yes."

"I don't know. . . ."

"Yeah, you do. Put the house on the market, Maria. You can handle this yourself."

"Okay," Maria whispered, and she ended the call.

Rob shook his head at his cell before turning it off and slipping it into his back pocket.

At the stepping-stones, Tessa toppled from her crouched position and landed on her bottom. Abby took Tessa by the hands and pulled her to her feet. Abby raised a hand in Rob's direction, and Rob waved back. Then she walked Tessa back to the house. There, Abby would play social director to her guests, make sure their rooms were spick-and-span, bake their midday snack, prep for tomorrow's breakfast. Soon, she'd add an infant to her long list of responsibilities. No matter how cute the kid—they sure were cute—taking care of a baby was a twenty-four/seven job.

Abby wanted him, but she didn't need him to fill her days.

The opposite of Maria.

Part of him wanted to follow Abby into the house, like a

lovesick stray, and lie down at her feet. Part of him wanted to get in his truck and drive in the opposite direction. Not away from Abby, not exactly, but away from the potential, his potential, to make another terrible mistake.

Tessa's mother had once sent her a postcard from Paris, a photo of a sunset blazing behind the Eiffel Tower, the famous cosmopolitan city aglow. But all Tessa could see was the man-made tower, its yellow lattice piercing, ruining the otherwise perfect sky. Electrified with artificial light, the iron monument stood as a solitary reminder of all that was wrong with her mother. For that, Meredith Lombardi had left her only child?

Tessa couldn't help but wonder whether one day her only child would stand in this exact spot and hate her, too. She could live with hatred, knowing her child would get to live with both Abby and Charlie, and see clear to heaven.

Watching the sunset behind Briar Rose was like bearing witness to edge-of-the-world magic. Standing here, Tessa could really and truly believe that any minute now a merman might climb out of the harbor and into the labyrinth, straight out of the lie Lily Beth fed Abby.

The sun slipped into the horizon, painting fair-weather clouds the hottest pink, the palest lavender, the prettiest coral. And voices, Abby's voice, carried.

Same as when Tessa had spied her on Sunday, Abby was kneeling in front of Luke's stepping-stones, her head bent in prayer. Her peach dress hugged her knees, and her hair fell down her back, glowing with the last rays of daylight.

"Why, Luke? Why did you have to climb out your window? What possessed you?" Abby's tone sounded light, too light for the question, as though she'd spoken the words so many times she'd wrung out their emotions.

But Abby's next phrase carried a choked note of fresh despair. If Tessa didn't know better, she would've sworn Abby had reached through Tessa's rib cage and yanked the query straight from her heart. "Why did you have to leave me?"

A breeze rustled the perennial garden and stirred the scent of those purple cone-shaped flowers, reminding Tessa of Shasta grape soda.

"Hey, Abby!" Tessa called across the yard, loud enough to give Abby fair warning. Loud enough to drown out the bass note of guilt pounding through Tessa's chest.

A little guilt, sure, for the "emotional blackmail" Abby had called Tessa out on last night—as if she didn't know what that meant—her little ploy to get Abby and Charlie back together. Means to an end. That guilt was Lilliputian compared to the gargantuan guilt of knowing exactly what had possessed Luke's fall.

If Tessa didn't know better, she could've sworn Abby aimed a smile straight her way, as though she were genuinely glad to see her here, a thorn in the garden.

If she were the least bit paranoid, Tessa would've thought Abby *did* know what had happened, and this—acting nice to her after *everything*—was Abby's kick-ass way of paying Tessa back.

Ever since this morning's discussion about the paving stone deficit, and Tessa's quicksilver brainstorm, Abby had been possessed with the idea. Researching the best prices for concrete paving stone kits. Estimating the cost for raw materials.

Past the arbor, fireflies flickered along the labyrinth, lighting the way. Growing up, Tessa had seen careless boys imprison fireflies in airless mason jars, and then, come morning, toss the lifeless corpses. Considering the way Abby had raised Luke, Tessa bet he'd been thoughtful, careful to punch holes in jar lids, capture the creatures for a brief show, and then letting them fly.

Abby jumped to standing, brushed the grass from her dress. "I was just thinking about you!"

If Tessa were the least bit paranoid . . .

"Heading over to Head Beach," Tessa said. "I'm not planning on staying long. Okay. See you later."

"Don't you want to try out the labyrinth?"

"Uh, I know how to walk."

"Don't you want to hear my latest greatest idea, inspired by your latest and greatest? Well, actually, Rob's latest and greatest." Abby hiccupped. Or maybe it was a snort. Either way, she didn't sound like herself. She sounded unleashed. Like some weight had lifted. Like a firefly, released and sparking.

"Um."

Abby looped an arm through Tessa's and rushed her through the arbor. Then Abby's pace slowed, and they strolled, brides walking down a church aisle.

Alternating round and spiked bushes lined the grass walking path. The stone pavers that earlier had been sitting on the sidelines now fit between the bushes. Instead of filling in the blank spaces with pea stone—what Abby had originally planned—empty spaces awaited the handprint stepping-stones.

"Aren't the bushes kind of small?" Tessa asked.

"They'll grow," Abby said. "A little more each year."

Tessa pictured the labyrinth like a time-lapse photo. The bushes tiny now in the summer months, imperceptibly bigger when the maples rained down crimson leaves, and then, end of next winter, shaking off the snow to reveal visible growth. She imagined years passing, the plantings doubling in size. And the baby, her baby, walking this path without her.

How could you miss someone you didn't even know?

"Rob knows someone," Abby said, "or at least thinks he knows someone who'll give me the concrete at cost. We wouldn't need to charge people for the kits."

A baby cost a lot of money. Wasn't that what Tessa's father kept telling her, over and over? If Abby and Charlie were going to adopt her baby—

"We could still ask people to pay to have their stepping-stones set in Luke's labyrinth."

"I don't want people's money—"

"It could go for a scholarship fund. A Luke Connors—"

"HRTA!" Abby finished. Hotel, restaurant, and travel administration. Luke's major at UMass.

"Yes!" Tessa said. Center of the labyrinth, the baby squirmed, as though casting a vote of approval. The last smidges of sun peeked out over the horizon and melted into the navy water.

Abby unlinked her arm from Tessa's and clapped her hands together. "No wonder Luke adored you! No wonder he wanted to bring you home to meet me."

"Luke wanted to bring me home?"

"Of course!" Abby said.

When Luke had mentioned spring break in Hidden Harbor to Tessa, she hadn't taken him seriously. After all, they hadn't been going out for that long. What if they didn't last? What if he broke up with her before the middle of March? What if she'd spent months daring to hope?

Tessa stepped from the labyrinth, but Abby ushered her back inside, apparently determined to retrace every step. "The way out is the way in!" Abby said, sounding a lot like Lily Beth. "Can you imagine how great that would've been? Me and you and Luke at Briar Rose?"

All the time.

"The three of us watching the sunset . . ." A glimpse of Abby's face told Tessa that Abby was paying the price for envisioning the impossible. Then Abby picked up her pace, as though trying to outrace her thoughts. "Anyway, you're here, and that's a good thing. More than I could've wished for back in February. And the fund-raiser? Touch of genius. Once Luke's friends purchase pavers, that'll give them a solid reason to come over to visit. Not just the labyrinth, but Briar Rose."

According to Luke, his high-school buddies were scattered far and wide. His best friend, Joey, went to UCLA on a basketball scholarship. Another local buddy got recruited to Michigan State. And Luke's UMass friends? A five-hour road trip to a quiet B&B on the coast of Maine wasn't exactly an ideal vacation destination. Didn't exactly mesh with the quad's spring break motto kids shouted across the Orchard Hill bowl: *Get done in the sun.*

Tessa's breathing rasped, hard and shallow. Even though she'd read about the symptom, it still came as a surprise, an insult. Yet another weird pregnancy thing, the baby taking up more and more space inside of her. "I can get the word out at UMass, help kids make the handprints on campus. Put together a kit for other friends to use and mail. I don't think many will be able to make it to Maine, though."

That didn't deter Abby's excited ramblings. "It'll be just like old times, with boys making a mess through the house, tracking mud into the dining room."

The labyrinth's pavers blended into the earth. The shrubbery, soft and amorphous in the darkness. Across the yard, Briar Rose glowed, as if the sun were shining from its rectangular windows like a lighthouse.

Abby passed beneath the arbor, continued to the perennials and Luke's stepping-stones. When she turned to Tessa, Abby's voice sounded breathless, taken by an imaginary wind. "I want you to know, I'm really glad you're here. Luke was lucky to have had you as a girlfriend."

Sweat, sudden and soaking, cooled the back of Tessa's neck, as though her body were trying to exorcise her guilt. If Tessa hadn't been Luke's girlfriend, Luke would've been here instead of her.

Sounded like shit for luck to Tessa.

Luke would've been better off if he'd never met her. If instead of veering left at the fateful dorm party, he'd veered right. Or, safer for everyone, it would've been better if Tessa had never been born.

Abby held a hand to her throat. "We work so well together. I appreciate your idea for the fund-raiser. I know this situ—"

"It's my fault." Tessa whispered; the words barely left her lips. But Abby must've heard her loud and clear. Why else would her voice cut out? Why else would the silence hanging between them grow tighter with every breath, a hand clutching at nothing?

Why else would Abby's exuberant singsong tone slip-trip into angst-riddled worry? "What's your fault, Tessa?"

The white noise of blood and oxygen, fear and desire, boxed Tessa's ears, like every other moment before a disaster.

The moment before she opened her mother's Dear Tessa note, sealed with a ruby-red kiss.

The moment before she'd let Luke inside her, with nothing to protect him.

The moment before she'd let Luke go.

Tessa could shrug Abby's question off with a giggle. *Oh, nothing. I don't know what I'm talking about.* She could make up something stupid, say she'd accidentally crushed the sand dollar Lily Beth had given her. She'd spilled syrup between the kitchen counters, inviting in a slew of ants. She'd mistaken Room 3's queen-size sheets for the full bedding of Room 4.

She could let Abby continue babbling until the praise chased Tessa into the bay.

"I'm the reason Luke fell," Tessa said. "I've heard you talking to Luke. Out here, by his stepping-stones. You want to know what happened on the day he died. I was there."

"I know you were there. You were in Luke's dorm room."

"I wasn't in Luke's room," Tessa said, drawing a charcoal-black line through the only thing Abby had thought she'd known about the day her son had died.

Abby didn't move, but the tone of her voice effectively crossed her arms and widened her stance, throwing up a barrier against Tessa. "Start at the beginning, because I obviously don't have a clue."

"Dina told me she saw Luke flirting with another girl." The blonde from Central, with the long legs. Guys called her Cherry, but not for the obvious reason. Rumor had it the girl could tie the stem from a maraschino cherry into a love knot with her tongue, making every guy on campus curious what else her tongue could accomplish. Making Luke curious.

Abby sighed, loud and annoyed. "Go on."

"I don't—I didn't like when he flirted with other girls. I was really mad at him—Sorry, sorry." Tessa was so angry she could've killed. Not Luke, but herself. How could she have been so stupid to imagine Luke would want only her? What had led her to believe she was enough?

"You weren't in Luke's room because . . ." Abby coaxed.

Tessa shivered, shoved her hands into the pockets of her shorts, squeezed emptiness. "I called Luke on it, told him I didn't want him flirting with other girls. Told him I was breaking up with him for cheating on me. Luke said he hadn't done anything wrong. Talking with another girl wasn't cheating. We argued, and, um, I locked myself in Dina's room."

"What does that have to do with—?"

"Dina's dorm room, next door to Luke's."

"Dear God," Abby said, the same plea Tessa had tossed up to the heavens that day. The same plea that had fallen flat.

Tessa's body was a series of balls. Her heart swelling in her chest. The baby pressing against her esophagus. The mass closing her throat. Tears leaked down the sides of her cheeks. "He could've made it through the window, but he begged me to take his hand. He begged me."

"Trust me," Luke had said, and then he'd slipped from her grasp. A quick jerk of movement on the way down. The crack of Luke hitting the frozen sidewalk. And then nothing.

Tessa hadn't known silence could scream.

Abby was a statue in the low light, gray and unmoving, her face impassive. "The grand gesture. Sounds like something Charlie would do. I'm so angry with Luke I could spit."

"What did you just say?" Tessa asked.

Abby nearly laughed. "Climbing from window to window to prove his loyalty. He couldn't have sent you flowers? Taken you to dinner? Something that didn't involve risking his life?"

Maybe Abby didn't understand. She couldn't blame Luke. It wasn't his fault. It was Tessa's fault. "My hand was all sweaty." Tessa's hand had been sweaty, hadn't it? Or had Luke's been perspiring? "I was supposed to pull him into the window. I wasn't supposed to let him fall. He wasn't supposed to die. Don't you understand? Don't you—?"

"It was an accident. No one's fault. That's the meaning of an accident. I don't blame you for Luke's death. I don't even blame you for being angry with him. Poor kid got all of Charlie's best features, and some of his worst traits. On one hand, Luke was loyal, Tessa. I doubt he cheated on you. But flirting? Lily Beth used to say our Luke could flirt with a rock and get it to blush. Funny thing was—or maybe not so funny—that's what I still say about Charlie. When a boy, or a grown man, flirts with other women, it's diminishing. Makes you feel not quite so special anymore. Makes you doubt what they feel for you. Makes you doubt what you feel for them."

"But, but you love Charlie."

"Everybody loves Charlie," Abby said, her tone resigned, sad, and definite.

Tessa pictured her baby walking hand in hand with Abby, Charlie the weekend daddy who visited on Sundays. No better than the way Tessa had grown up. Actually worse. What if her baby wanted his parents together, too? What if instead of giving her baby Luke's fondest wish, Tessa gave him Luke's worst nightmare? "You're not going to marry Charlie?"

Abby sighed. "No, Tessa, I'm not."

Tessa rubbed her baby bump, imagined massaging a tiny back. Who would love her baby? "Don't you want to adopt my baby?'

"With all my heart."

"But if you're not going to marry Charlie, how can I give my baby to you?"

Abby started toward Tessa, as though she might embrace her, and then she stopped short, as if she'd hit a wall. "You want me to tell you, to explain, why you should let me adopt your baby? I have only one thing to say to you. One thing only. So you'd better listen carefully. You'd better pay attention. Are you ready, Tessa?"

Tessa wanted to go back to Sunday. To sitting in the shade and letting Abby hold her, as though she were the mother she'd never had. To hanging on tight and never letting go. Tessa had thought that telling Abby about the day Luke had died would enrage her. That when Abby found out Tessa's part in Luke's death, Abby would chase her out of town and out of her life.

Turned out threatening to keep Luke's baby from Abby was the only thing that could inspire Abby's hatred.

"Are you ready to hear me, Tessa?" Abby's voice was soft but powerful, echoing into the low light. Echoing into Tessa.

"I'm listening." Tessa wanted to hide her head, to cover her burning cheeks, to run from whatever was coming her way. But she was tired of hiding from what she deserved, even if what she deserved was an impossible riddle.

"A good mother," Abby said, "always does whatever is best for her child."

CHAPTER 16

Twenty years ago, Abby had believed convincing Charlie to stay with her in Hidden Harbor was her last best chance to keep their child safe. That two parents, two sets of eyes, two sets of quick hands, provided a better safety net than one.

August had been winding down, tourists packing up their bags of found shells, banging the sand from their flip-flops, and packing away summer for another year. Still, the sun was warm, strong, and bright, and refusing to bow to the calendar's whims. If she'd held her breath, she could've almost believed she could hold back time. Dug in her heels and refused to budge. Refused to let Charlie budge. She and Charlie had gone to Spinney's, neutral battleground. Between bites of fried clams, amid the clutter of menus and wadded straw wrappers, she'd laid their revised life plan on the table, as if she and Charlie had been two parts of a whole, instead of distinct people. As if laying her heart on the table was enough to keep him from leaving her and their unborn baby.

Little had Abby known, twenty years later, she'd be at Lily Beth's cottage on Edgewater Lane in the exact same position. Digging in her heels and on the verge of losing everything.

Lily Beth stood before her kitchen sink, barefoot and wearing her blue summer robe. Instead of leaving her hair down, her usual do, she'd piled her loose curls on top of her head, in deference to the humidity. Tiny lighter-than-the-rest hairs curled at the back of her head, making her mother's neck look childlike, vulnerable. A dirty cast-iron fry pan sat on the stove. The skin of a salmon stuck to its innards and added its funk to the scent of seawater and roses, traces of sandstone incense. An old TV played on the counter, the volume down low—local weather predicting clouds moving in—but Lily Beth didn't seem to be listening. When had her mother begun the habit of keeping the TV on for company?

Abby shut off the TV.

Lily Beth turned and held a hand to her heart. Soap suds dripped from her pink dish gloves onto the floor. When had Abby's sudden appearance ever startled her mother?

When had her mother become human?

"Hi, baby." Lily Beth peeled off her gloves. Under the unforgiving fluorescent light, the veins in her hands showed, too close to the surface. "What brings you around?"

Abby pictured Tessa at a dorm-room window, her breath hanging in the winter air. Abby imagined Luke dangling from the sill, trying to sweet-talk Tessa into forgiving him for playing with her affections.

The medical examiner had told her Luke's death had been instant, that he hadn't suffered, an impossible-to-disprove pretty little lie. But what about Luke's fall? What about the descent, the shift from desperate love to the desperate need for self-preservation? Had Luke, however briefly, felt the magnitude of his own loss? Had he envisioned the gaping, empty hole he'd leave behind?

Had he, too late, realized he'd traded his life for a Spider-man grand gesture to win back the mother of his child?

Of course, Luke hadn't known about the child. If her son had stuck around, then he could've proven himself a real superhero, just by being a father to his baby.

"I'm so angry I could spit," Abby said, repeating what she'd told Tessa. This time, her feelings bled through her words, rasping her voice and getting the better of her.

"With me?" Lily Beth asked.

"Why would I be—?" Last night's visit and her frustration over the mermaid tale seemed like eons ago. "No, Mom. I'm not angry with you. It's—I'm—" That swell, that tsunami pressure swell she'd been holding at bay for months pressed, threatened. Abby tilted her face to the ceiling, and her vision blurred with unshed tears. When her gaze returned to Lily Beth, her mother shimmered, like a vision underwater. Not a mermaid, but a woman drowning. "I'm angry at Luke. I'm angry at Charlie. I'm angry at *everyone*."

Lily Beth nodded. "Baby girl."

"Mostly I'm angry at nature and genetics. And stupid, stupid boys!"

Lily Beth took a highball glass from the open shelving, poured Abby ice water from the glass pitcher she kept in the fridge. Just like the days when Lily Beth worried Abby might cry herself dry over Charlie.

"Let's go have a nice talk," Lily Beth said.

"I don't want to be nice anymore." As if to prove her point, her body responded, her jaw and neck tightening, her hands curling into fists.

"Even better." A smile tugged at the corners of Lily Beth's lips. "It's about time." Lily Beth led Abby into the great room and set her water down on the glass curio table, a container for sand dollars, aquamarine, and mermaids. Similar collections decorated the side tables, tiny sea-themed altars everywhere.

When Abby had been a girl, she'd eschewed Barbie dolls for the resin mermaid figurines, pretended she was a princess under the sea, waiting for a prince to awaken her. Years before she'd first slept with Charlie, the game had soured. She'd replaced the child's fantasy with the grander scheme of saving herself. She'd told herself Charlie had only been around for the ride. She'd told herself a lot of impossible-to-disprove pretty little lies.

"Do you remember when you told me Charlie would never change? That he couldn't help but be a shameless flirt? That he was cursed. People take one look at him, get in his energetic zone—whatever you called it—and they're powerless against his charm?"

"Which time?"

"Do you remember when I came home from school and told you I'd broken up with Charlie because he was flirting with Caroline Eastman in trig?"

"Charlie said that was impossible. He couldn't be flirting because his forever girl—you—were right beside him at the time. Nope, I don't recall that day. Must've slipped my mind. How does the story end?"

Beyond Lily Beth's glass patio doors, beneath the moon, the sea glimmered. Below the surface, those same waves were, little by little, changing the shape of her childhood beach. Abby sipped her water, let the cold soothe her temples. A poor substitute for diving beneath those numbing waves.

"Do you remember when we both noticed how much Luke looked like Charlie?"

"Day he was born. One of the two best days of my life."

"Do you remember when we took Luke for his first haircut?"

"The look on his face!" Lily Beth said, letting Abby know her mother was imagining the identical scene that played in her head. Her fifteen-month-old baby, batting his big blue eyes, playing coy, and charming the thirty-year-old hairdresser every man in town was in heat over. Word on the street had been that every full moon, the eligible men of Hidden Harbor lined up beneath her window and howled.

"Do you remember the trail of broken hearts Luke left in Hidden Harbor?" Abby asked. "All the girls who called the house crying?"

"The select few who showed up on your doorstep?"

"Yes." Tessa hadn't been the first girl who'd cried on her shoulder, only the most recent. "The day Luke died," Abby said, and the rueful smile drained from Lily Beth's face.

"The day we lost our baby," Abby added, and Lily Beth squeezed Abby's hand. "Tessa was trying to break up with Luke."

Lily Beth inhaled sharply, and her eyelids drifted shut. Her eyes flitted beneath her pale lids. Then she opened her eyes and nodded for Abby to continue. Abby's cue to share Tessa's tale, not a pretty fable you told a child, not a magical yarn, but the human complicated truth.

When Abby was finished, Lily Beth gave her a hug. Cheek-to-cheek, chest-to-chest, Lily Beth's pulse rapid-fire fluttered like the baby growing beneath Tessa's heart. "That boy," Lily Beth said.

"Why did Luke have to inherit Charlie's personality? Wasn't it enough he got Charlie's looks? No matter how many times I talked to Luke about how he should treat girls—"

"He was an eighteen-year-old boy, Abby," Lily Beth said, reminding Abby of the nature lesson her mother had tried to impart on her. Lily Beth's warning that a male's biology compelled him to try and plant his seed in as many females as possible.

And if Luke had survived the fall, maybe he could've grown out of his heartbreaking ways, instead of following in the steps of his thirty-eight-year-old father. Charlie couldn't help but perpetually charm the world. The heck with the trail of heartbreak. The heck with *Abby's* heartbreak.

"Mom, I could never marry Charlie. I don't know how I ever thought we were a good match."

Lily Beth looked to the ceiling, sighed into a grin. "I've lived to see the day! You're finally ready to leave the fantasy world behind. It's a good thing he didn't take you up on your offer last year. It's good—"

"Yesterday," Abby said, "Charlie asked me to marry him again."

Lily Beth angled Abby a sideways glance. "Why now? Does this have something to do with Luke's baby?"

Something, everything, nothing.

Abby could blame Tessa, uncover the way she'd been playing her and Charlie. Reveal the way Tessa had swept them into her whirlwind, and the way she'd been attempting to reconfigure their lives.

Or Abby could shrug, feign ignorance, and protect Tessa from Lily Beth. Mothers always protected their daughters.

"It doesn't matter, Mom. I can't marry Charlie. I don't love him." Abby shrugged. "Not that way, not the forever way. Not anymore."

Not the way she was falling in love with Rob.

Abby waited for her chest to palpitate with the thought, for the muscle in her temple to twitch, for her fingers to grow cold. All she felt was a gentle uptick of her heartbeat, and a quiet sense of peace. Considering Rob's unwillingness to discuss Luke's baby, and her unwillingness to just see what happened, that made no sense at all.

Did love ever?

"What about you?" Abby said, and Lily Beth's mouth fell slack, her brow furrowed, as if she knew what was coming next. "Why didn't you marry my father?"

Abby stared into Lily Beth's eyes, expecting her mother to, any second now, break her gaze, leave the room, and reach for the familiar tired fable.

Lily Beth smoothed Abby's hair from her face. "I couldn't

marry your father." Lily Beth blinked away tears, pressed a hand to her mouth, and then her chest. "He was already married."

Abby's chest gave two sharp out-of-sync kicks. A muscle on the left side of her temple twitched and her fingers went cold. Abby must've heard Lily Beth wrong. Because the woman she knew, the woman she thought she'd known, would never take something that didn't belong to her.

The woman Abby knew had been a sixteen-year-old girl.

Lily Beth looked down at her hands, twisting in her lap. Were Lily Beth's hands cold, too? "I'm sorry to disappoint you, baby," Lily Beth said, letting Abby know she'd read the look on her face—childish, selfish, careless with fragile emotions. Not much different from that beautiful, tormented girl who was carrying her grandchild. And Tessa had good reason to be disappointed with her mother.

Abby wrapped her hands around her mother's. All she felt was warmth. "Not disappointed. Never disappointed in you." How would Abby have known how to survive on her own with a baby, if her mother hadn't shown her the way? Lily Beth was everything to her. Mother, father, her entire family. "Did you really meet him swimming off Head Beach? Who was he? What did he do? If he was married, he must've been older," Abby said, imagining a young man of twenty-one or so, that tender age when you touch a toe into adulthood. At that age, she could almost forgive his misstep.

Lily Beth laughed. "I'll answer all of your questions, and then some. I did meet your father swimming off Head Beach, my day off from working at the Kelp Shed. That part is true."

Lily Beth rubbed her thumb nail, the way she'd buff the outside of a tumbled stone till you could see your reflection. "He was staying at a cottage nearby, one with a private beach and a view of the ocean, and so many lovely roses."

"This cottage?" Abby said.

"Uh, hum," Lily Beth said.

Abby's stomach tensed, the tug of Lily Beth's admission dredging up history, like sand from the ocean's bottom clouding still waters. Had Abby made a terrible mistake? "Did he own our cottage?"

Lily Beth didn't seem to hear her. "He told me he liked to get away to clear his head. So he'd ride his bike to Hermit Island, pretend he was alone in the world."

"But he wasn't alone for long. He met you."

"When he spotted me swimming offshore, at first he didn't recognize me as the cashier from the snack bar. He thought I was a beautiful magical mermaid—"

"From the painting in the Kelp Shed."

"Come to spirit him away from his earthly life."

According to legend, mermaids seduced unwitting young men away from their homes and to the deepest seas. But Lily Beth's story of Abby's origins had always portrayed her father as the mythical creature, the parent who'd left for his own survival. Could both versions speak a facet of the truth?

"In his earthly life, he was married," Abby said. And Lily Beth had been the fantasy, playing the part of the nymph from the sea.

How would Abby have felt if a man, a married man, had bedded her sixteen-year-old daughter? But Lily Beth's birthday wasn't until the beginning of August, the middle of the summer season—

"You were sixteen when you met my father?"

"Fifteen and three quarters," Lily Beth said, with as much seriousness as when a preschool Luke had once proclaimed himself three and three quarters. Every month mattered to a child eager to hasten the years. How much had it mattered to Abby's father?

"Mom?" Abby drew her bottom lip between her teeth,

gnawed on the spark of a thought, frissons of sharp light catching. "How old was my father?"

Lily Beth didn't skip a beat. "Thirty-two."

Not a boy-man, but a full-grown adult who ought to have known better. "He was twice your age!"

"Age didn't matter to him. We'd lie on the shore, talking for hours . . ."

When Abby had first discovered Luke was sexually active, she'd Googled Maine law, and verified that the age of consent was sixteen.

". . . He loved Steinbeck and Hemingway, *The Old Man and the Sea*."

And at fifteen, Lily Beth, old soul that she was, must've eaten up Abby's father's attention with a spoon. What girl didn't want to feel herself the equal to an older man? "When did he touch you?"

"Abigail!" Lily Beth held a hand to her throat. This from the woman who'd painstakingly explained deer mating rituals. The way the bucks pursued females, like serial monogamists. The way the does sometimes moved into a second breeding season and pursued the bucks.

Abby shook her head, but the sentiment persisted, the feeling that she was the elder, sent back to the past to protect her mother's honor. "How old were you when you first slept with him?"

Lily Beth took a sip of Abby's water. "Sixteen," she said.

Abby inhaled through her mouth, a near sigh of relief.

"We made love on my sixteenth birthday."

Abby sputtered on the exhale. Her thirty-two-year-old married father had known exactly what he was doing, the entirely intentional seduction of an innocent. Happy sweet sixteen. "Oh, Mom."

Abby had also read online that if a man of twenty or older slept with a fifteen-year-old girl, it was considered a crime. Abby was 100 percent sure that thirty-nine years ago her father hadn't Googled sexual abuse. She was equally sure he'd known the law, assuring he didn't cross the legal line some bureaucrat had drawn in the sand, and telling himself that took care of the moral implications.

Another pretty little lie.

"I thought I loved him," Lily Beth said. "I knew he was married, but I was too selfish to care."

"Selfish in love. Sounds like any other teenage girl." Hadn't Abby been selfish with Charlie, not wanting him to leave for college, but refusing to leave with him? She'd laid out a plan—her plan to have their baby in Hidden Harbor. But had she ever engaged in a back-and-forth conversation? Had she ever been open to compromise? At eighteen, had she listened to Charlie's plan?

"When I found out I was pregnant with you, baby girl, I was going to tell his wife. He said he loved me, but even then, I doubted his affections. Why hide what you loved? So I came to his house. I came here." Lily Beth's bottom lip trembled, the petulance of a girl. "I sneaked around the cottage to the beach when I knew he wouldn't be home." Lily Beth tapped her fingertips to her lips. Keeping words in or letting them out?

"What happened?" Abby asked, imagining Lily Beth stepping onto the beach Abby had always associated with her mother, with the sun in her eyes, a secret in her belly, and the power to upend a stranger's life. She imagined Lily Beth's heart clenched tight as a fist before you threw the first punch.

"I couldn't do it. I don't know what I expected, or hoped, to find. When I came around the house, she had her back to me."

"His wife?" Abby asked.

Lily Beth nodded. "She was kneeling in the sand, helping a toddler make a sandcastle. A towhead with the most angelic face. Could've been Luke's brother."

"Luke's uncle," Abby said. "My big brother."

"With another big brother or sister on the way." Lily Beth's mouth twisted. "His wife . . ." Lily Beth looked out toward the beach, as though searching for the spot where she'd last seen her. "At the time, she looked like a woman to me. But she was probably no more than nineteen or twenty. Hardly a woman. More like an older sister."

"How horrible for you."

Other people needed him more than we did. Lily Beth's day-old declaration sounded in Abby's mind, another string from her knot of riddles unraveled.

"How horrible for them," Lily Beth said. "If I hadn't lured him with my long blond hair and my siren song . . . Believe it or not, your mother was once quite a seductress."

"First of all, you're still a dish. Second of all, he seduced you."

Lily Beth turned her head and squinted, the look she got seconds before she'd reach for her phrase-clarifying reading glasses.

"If you and my father"—for the first time in Abby's life, she translated the misnomer to sperm donor—"had made love the day before your birthday, he would've been a criminal." As far as Abby was concerned, he was a criminal. "He could've been charged with the sexual abuse of a minor. He could've gone to jail for ten years. He must've known that, Mom. I'm surprised you didn't know that."

"I was sixteen . . ." Lily Beth said. "What did I know?"

Spoken with the hindsight of maturity.

As a teenager, you thought you knew everything. Then, year by year, the stockpile of what you knew for sure, what you could depend upon, dwindled. Until, Abby imagined, you died an old woman, knowing nothing at all.

If Lily Beth had thought herself an equal to a thirty-two-year-old married man, had she held herself equally responsible, a partner in adultery?

"Mom," Abby said. "Why haven't you ever dated?"

"I have you, baby. What else do I need?" Lily Beth said, the same thing she'd told Abby when, growing up, Abby had first tired of imagining an absent father who swam beneath the waves. Back when Abby had gone to school and discovered other little girls had real-life flesh-and-blood daddies, who hoisted their daughters on their shoulders above the waves and held them up high.

"I'm not talking need," Abby said. "I'm not talking food and shelter. What do you *want?* Don't you want someone to come home to? Someone to share your life with?"

"Want," Lily Beth said, "gets you into a world of trouble. When you want what you can't have—When you take what doesn't belong to you—" Lily Beth covered her eyes and cried silently into her hands, her body rocking forward with each sob.

Abby had only seen Lily Beth cry in front of her three times.

The day Abby had told her Luke had died.

The day Abby had revealed Tessa was carrying Luke's baby.

Today.

Abby's lips trembled and she swallowed through the thickness in her throat, but the melancholy refused to budge. The side table to Abby's right held photos of Abby and Luke, their faces smiling out from shell-encrusted frames, grinning beneath garlands of antique buttons, strings of tiny silver jingle bells. The side table to the left displayed older photos of Lily Beth holding Abby on her narrow hip, walking along the beach, climbing from the sand to higher ground.

Lily Beth and Abby against the world. Abby and Lily Beth.

Growing up, Abby had noticed the way men looked at her mother. Hadn't Lily Beth?

Abby touched the back of Lily Beth's hand, and she startled, as though waking from a dream. Then she caught her breath and swiped the wetness from her cheeks. Abby passed her water to Lily Beth, and she gulped it down.

"You said my father, his family, was staying here." Abby's belly quivered, ghosts moving through her. "Did they rent the cottage or . . . ?"

Lily Beth wiped her mouth with the back of her hand. "His parents owned the property. They sold it to me for a dollar." Lily Beth laughed, releasing more tears, which she ignored. "Sounds crazy, I know. But it worked out for us, didn't it?"

"What about property taxes? How did you afford to start Heart Stone? Where did you get the down payment for Briar Rose? Who was he? Where did he go?" Who'd paid for Lily Beth's clothing? Groceries? Doctors' bills? Before Abby's pregnancy, Lily Beth had offered to pay for half of her college. And, if that had come to pass, Lily Beth probably would've forgiven that, too.

From what Lily Beth was telling her, she could forgive anything and anyone, except herself.

Lily Beth unclipped her hair and it fell around her shoulders, a blanket of protection. "Give me a minute." Lily Beth retreated to the kitchen and returned with a glass of white wine, as if she needed something stronger than water. She tucked her feet beneath her, pulled closed her robe around her knees, storytelling mode. "Fire away." Lily Beth held up a hand. "One question at a time, please."

"What did my father do for a living?" Abby asked.

"He was a navy doctor. Working in Portsmouth when I met him, preparing to ship out." Another piece of Lily Beth's riddle, another truth buried in a lie. Abby's father was, had been, a healer.

He was never mine to keep. He was of another world. He belonged to the ocean.

How could a healer do so much harm? To the family he'd recognized? To the family he'd ignored?

But a thirty-two-year-old doctor couldn't have had that much money. He would've been just starting out, trying to stay afloat and care for his young family. He couldn't have afforded a second family, not on his own. Not without help.

"Mom," Abby said. "Did he give you money? Did he help you with expenses?"

"His family was well-heeled. They made all the arrangements. Money doesn't bring you happiness, but it does smooth the way. It did smooth the way to sever our connection. I took a lump sum," Lily Beth said, as though she'd won the lottery. But, no, that's not how she felt. Abby knew the look of a woman just trying to survive.

"How much?" Abby asked.

"I would've walked away. After seeing her—I couldn't let him hurt another woman."

But Lily Beth had let him hurt her.

"How much?" Abby asked again.

"More than enough." Lily Beth took a generous sip of her wine, and Abby inhaled the scent of fermented grapes. She could almost taste the alcohol. "A lot," Lily Beth said. "I was planning on living a long life."

That life could seem unceasingly long if you'd unnecessarily denied yourself the chance for love.

That had to be one of the saddest stories Abby had ever heard.

"Mama," Abby said, the term of endearment Abby hadn't used since she was a girl.

Lily Beth touched Abby's cheek.

"You deserve happiness," Abby said. "Stop denying yourself."

Lily Beth flashed Abby the same expression she'd wave in front of any man who'd tried to ask her out. The look she slipped on her face while she'd pressed a girlfriend's phone number into a hand that reached for hers. The rue-tinged smile she'd offered potential suitors in lieu of her heart.

That feeling Abby had had as a new mom, warning boys

away from her, wanting to call them back? She'd seen the outer expression of that inner turmoil on Lily Beth's face. She'd learned denial from Lily Beth. She'd learned how to hang on to the past and never let go. "My father, whoever he was—I don't even care anymore," Abby said. "I bet he was ridiculously handsome, though. Too handsome for his own good, like Charlie."

That wasn't fair. A flirt wasn't the same as a cheater. A broken promise wasn't the same as an adulterous lie.

Lily Beth nodded. "He was."

"And charming. I bet he said all the right things. I bet, at first, he made you feel all the right feelings. But he was the person in the wrong. For heaven's sake, Mom, you were sixteen years old. You were just a kid."

Lily Beth stared at Abby and then shook her head. She took the shawl from the couch back and draped the pale cotton around her shoulders, sighed in time with the white noise of breaking waves. The constant soundtrack of Lily Beth's, and Abby's, life.

Abby scooted closer to Lily Beth and tugged a corner of the throw around her shoulder. She laid her head on Lily Beth's arm, and Lily Beth took her hand.

Lily Beth and Abby against the world. Abby and Lily Beth.

Abby had always considered her mother married to the cottage on the beach, the peninsula jutting out into the Atlantic Ocean, the sea surrounding and protecting her. What if this cottage filled with stones and crystals, shells and mermaid dioramas, hadn't protected Lily Beth from the elements, but kept her prisoner to the past?

What if Lily Beth had imprisoned herself?

Chapter 17

When the person you'd built your life around was gone, where did that leave you?

If Abby lived to eighty-six, she'd have another seventeen thousand four hundred and forty-one days left to throw her arms wide, take risks, and embrace her big beautiful life. Anything less would be a sin against all she'd lost.

Anything less would be a sin against Luke.

Abby sat outside her mother's cottage, keys in the ignition, the truck vibrating beneath her thighs. Her cell phone trembled in her hands. She'd wanted to make a clean sweep of her mother's cottage, pack away the aquamarine and mermaids in satin-lined boxes, fix them with padlocks, toss the keys into the Atlantic, and watch the tides ferry them down shore. Instead, she'd left Lily Beth on the couch, traded her wine for water, tucked the throw around her, and kissed her on the cheek. Her mother was still beautiful. Her hair just as blond as when she'd been a girl, her skin clear and flawless, as though she were Sleeping Beauty, forever frozen in time, having fallen into a spell on the night of her sixteenth birthday. Someday, Abby would convince her mother to wake up, get up, and find her strength.

Right now, Abby needed to make a phone call. She'd already wasted twenty years under Charlie's curse.

Abby smiled at Rob's photo seconds before he picked up.

"Hey, there," Rob said.

She liked that whenever he answered the phone, he sounded as though he'd been expecting her call. She liked his most recent reveal: the way he treated the college guys working for him with clear instructions, concrete praise, and enthusiastic pats on the back. She liked that it was taking a long time to get to know him, and the way he shared bits and pieces of himself, instead of dumping his whole life on the table. She liked so many things about him.

She planned on learning even more.

"What are you up to?" Abby said, her fingers jittering madly. Stupid, silly hands. Now wasn't the time to hold back.

"Let's see. Left your place, showered. Time to wind down, rinse, and—"

"I miss you," Abby blurted out.

Oh, God. Say something. Say something, say something.

Rob's voice lowered, deepened, warmed her ear. "I miss you, too."

"Feel like going for a hike?"

Rob didn't hesitate. "Always."

Abby knew her plan was crazy, but she couldn't stop herself. Didn't want to. Wasn't that how it had felt when she was a teenager? The heck with danger and breaking the law. Pile on the risk. Bring it on.

Luke used to say, if you weren't pushing yourself, how did you know you were alive?

This one's for you, baby.

"How do you feel about Morse Mountain?" Not the 4,000-footers Rob was used to, not even much of a hill. But the two-mile hike brought you to Seawall Beach. And Seawall led to a virtual hill she'd yet to summit.

"When?"

"Depends. How fast can you get there?"

"Doesn't it close at sundown?"

"Not if you're planning on skinny dipping," Abby said. Rob was a good guy, played by the rules. She planned on corrupting him. "The parking lot closes. That means there'll be plenty of spaces. We meet there, and then we walk in. It's a stealth operation."

A jangle sounded from the other end of the phone.

"Rob?"

"Gettin' my keys."

Abby did a mental scan of her truck and came up with her year-round supplies: grocery bags, light-weight blanket, hat, pair of gloves, and two ice scrapers. "Wait!"

"Yes, ma'am."

"Could you bring a couple of towels?"

"Done. See you in ten."

Seven minutes later, Abby pulled onto Morse Mountain Road and found Rob's truck in the otherwise empty lot, waiting for her.

She cut the engine, and the canopy of trees dimmed the moonlight. They'd have better luck on the beach, where the clouds weren't expected to roll across the waxing moon until much later.

Abby thudded her door shut, and Rob shot through the low light. His hands found her waist, eliciting a tickle. The tension started in her belly and bubbled through her chest. He lifted her so her back was up against the driver's side door, pressed his chest to hers. Beneath her truck, the heat shield pinged and popped.

Abby couldn't stop smiling. She touched his cheek, smooth from his shower, inhaled the menthol of his skin. The part of her brain with no impulse control wanted to taste him, memorize every inch of his body with her tongue, and then bring him home to test her memory. "Glad to see me?"

"Little bit." Rob's lips captured hers and pressed the shape of a smile into her mouth, the taste of mint and sweetness. His breathing promised energy at the ready. His hips held back.

Abby had the urge to slide her hands to his buttocks and pull him in until nothing was left between them. Toss him into the backseat of her truck. First, she had a river to cross, one item to scratch off a very long bucket list. And then, on neutral turf, after a cooling swim, miles away from the demands of Briar Rose and Tessa, far away from the constraints of Rob's office-apartment, she needed to talk. Rob needed to listen. She slipped a fisted hand into the pocket of his shorts and dropped her truck keys on top of his.

Rob pulled away, chuckling. He fished the keys from his pocket, slung a daypack from his shoulder, and zipped the keys into the front compartment. "Using me to carry your stuff, are you?"

Abby took his hand, gave it a squeeze. "Yup, that's right. I'm totally using you. I don't like sneaking around in the dark alone." Abby got the cream-colored cotton blanket from the backseat of her truck and fit it into Rob's pack alongside two towels.

Rob kissed the top of her head. "You're so much fun."

Abby Stone? Fun? She liked the sound of that.

"You'd better stick by me," Rob added. "Brought along a headlamp."

"Shh. After we pass by the guard booth."

The cicadas hummed a roadside backbeat. At first, she felt awkward, their legs groping through murky light, each step unsure. Then they fell into a rhythm. No one was there to block their path. No guard manned the parking lot booth. No flashing blue lights. No barbed fence to bar their entry.

Just the same, Abby's pulse kicked up, ticking in her ears.

Her arms prickled with the knowledge she was getting away with something, living on the edge.

Living.

Rob, her partner in crime, tickled her palm with his finger.

No wonder Luke had loved sneaking out at night. Under the cover of night, anything could happen.

You could hike into a closed-after-dusk conservation area and break the law.

You could escape out from under the yoke of a childhood dream and reach for something real.

You could risk your heart.

Rob stopped, dug a headlamp from his pack, tested it. Dead. "How's your night vision?"

"Pretty good right now. But I heard clouds are heading in later tonight." Abby smiled at the absurdity of her hiking in a sundress and without a headlamp. Of Abby Stone going out without making sure she was 100 percent prepared for every eventuality. As if you could ever prepare for the unknown.

She'd buried that notion with her son.

Rob put away the headlamp and reclaimed her hand. They started down the path, following moonlight through the thick woodland growth. "Another hailstorm?"

"You never know what you're going to get."

"True enough." Rob's voice trailed off, as if he were mulling over that particular thought.

He smacked his forearm.

"Wha—" A buzzing sounded against her ear, and then a prick behind the lobe. She slapped her neck. Her fingers came away tacky with blood. Mosquitoes swarmed in the light before them, one vibrating body. "Would you happen to have insect repellent in your bag of tricks?"

Another skin-on-skin smack, and then Rob's voice skipped on a chuckle. "Nope."

"Then I hope you're ready for a two-mile run."

How could she have forgotten insect repellent? She'd walked the trail enough times in the light of a humid day to know that even with a thick layer of protection, you came away scarred and itchy. She and Luke used to call the marsh-side trail the mosquito swamp, a nod to the fire swamp in *The Princess Bride.* In eighty-degree weather, nighttime would do little to hamper the insects' appetites for blood.

But when she'd called Rob with her idea to go for their hike, she'd had two thoughts in mind: surviving the hike through the woods, and what she'd planned once they arrived at the beach.

Turned out when every moment dripped with potential, you didn't waste precious time planning for an uncertain future.

"Rob?"

"Yeah, baby?"

Mosquitoes flitted around her grin. Last time he'd called her *baby,* they'd been making out on his bed. The details were dreamlike and sketchy. But the way she'd felt? Wide-awake double rainbow.

Abby grabbed Rob's hand, infinitely grateful she was wearing sports sandals and not the teeter-totters she'd attempted on their dinner date. "Ready to make a run for it?"

"I was born ready." Rob cracked up, Mr. Reserved laughing at his own joke.

Despite his attractiveness, Rob wasn't a player. Not even a monogamous player, like Charlie. When she'd first spotted Rob, his energy had been directed at his daughter, Grace. Then his energetic field, or whatever Lily Beth called it, had reached out, tapped her on the shoulder, and pulled her in close.

Rob held his pack before him to secure the zipper, making Abby think of front-facing baby carriers. And then, strangely, a sea horse, the only creature where the male of the species carries the young. Weren't sea horses also one of the few animals that mated for life?

Abby widened her smile long enough for a mosquito to sneak into her mouth.

She scraped the interloper off her tongue. "What are we waiting for?" Abby said, and they started off at a jog.

Their feet pounded on the asphalt and gravel. Moonlight cast the pines and low-lying shrubs into a black-and-white photograph. The wind of movement blew her hair behind her. Her legs pumped to keep up with Rob. Her heart pumped to keep up with her legs. No hope of turning back.

A memory bubbled up through the darkness, natural as a breath. She'd brought seven-year-old Luke on a daytrip to Whale's Tale Water Park. And much to her horror, he'd been tall enough to ride on the Eye of the Storm, even though it was clearly meant for older kids.

Not wanting to let Luke go alone, she'd taken her turn in line before him, holding down her own fear. For Luke, she'd given over control to the Eye of the Storm and shot down a fifty-degree enclosed tube that shoved her out into the light, where she'd spiraled in circles before hitting the water.

Later, safe at a picnic table, Luke had scarfed down two burgers and a grape soda. Just watching Luke eat had upended Abby's stomach. "Weren't you scared?" she'd asked him.

Luke's grin had stretched a purple mustache across his upper lip. "Yeah," he'd said. "That was the best part."

Abby and Rob shot out of the woods and onto the path that ran a straight line through the first of two salt marshes. A cement form-covered wooden bridge spanned the Sprague River. Tides moved beneath their feet. Her calf muscles burned, her lungs struggled for air. When was the last time she'd gone for a run, not counting a dash to Shaw's to replenish the fridge and pantry or Reny's to stock up on batteries and bulbs? When was the last time she'd given herself a day to just be?

Their feet pounded across the wooden bridge, padded back onto the path. Rob's breath huffed beside her. The steady beat of their shoes fell in sync. Just when she thought she'd gotten the hang of it, the trail steepened, making her work for every step.

She paused at the top of the hill, hands on hips, breathing hard. "I need a break!"

Rob jogged in place, his breath only marginally affected. "How much farther, do you think?"

It amazed Abby that avid hiker Rob had lived forty-five minutes away for the last ten years, and yet never ventured the easy—if you were walking—stroll to Seawall Beach. It amazed Abby even more that she couldn't remember the last time she'd carved out the time to make her way to the hidden gem.

A slap in the face to Luke, who'd reached for the world, and had it snapped from his fingers.

" 'Bout halfway?" she said, sure of nothing.

"Great! Then we're almost there!" Rob tugged her arm, pulling her along.

"Time out!" she said, but the words tangled in her throat, forced back down by the need to breathe.

Sooner than she'd remembered, the trail veered to the left, sloped gently downward, and crossed the second marsh. Through the last stretch of woods, she finally hit her stride. With Rob beside her, life surged through her muscles, and every responsibility fell away.

The path narrowed. Beneath their feet, the beat changed from the hard thud of gravel and asphalt to the soft give of sand. Then they ran through the roped-off dune grass and broke onto the wide-open expanse of Seawall Beach.

Not bright as day, but close enough.

The nearly full moon shone down from a clear sky, seeming brighter because of the threat of clouds. The ocean growled, roared, bellowed, so much louder than the gentle seaside lull that rocked her to sleep. The waves whipped the shore, evidencing the notoriously strong undertow. And when she tilted her head back, a few glittery pinpricks of stars greeted her, the rest obscured by the candle blaze of the moon.

Abby imagined Luke's child as a full-cheeked three-year-old girl, kneeling on one of Abby's dining room chairs, her face a study in concentration as she squeezed Elmer's glue onto black construction paper and dumped a tube of glitter on its head.

If Abby got a second chance, she'd welcome the whole glorious mess of childhood with open arms.

Sweat cooled her face and trickled down her spine. She inhaled through her nose to catch her breath. Ocean air cooled the back of her throat.

Rob touched her shoulder, his voice clear, as if they'd gone for a casual stroll. "Fantastic."

"Told you so." Abby expected to see Rob's face in profile as he gazed toward the ocean. Instead, he was looking her way, close enough to see inside her. He handed her a water bottle from his pack and then drank from the same bottle.

Rob zipped the water back in his pack and took her hand. He swung their hands between them, and they walked along the hard-packed sand. Roaring ocean, bright moonlight, and the right guy. All she needed was a dip in the Spirit Pond-fed Morse River and the guts to find her voice.

"Ex finally put the house on the market," Rob said, beating her to it.

"Really?"

"Yup, looks like I won't have to live in my office forever."

"Time to look for something more *permanent?*" Abby's mouth tingled, same as years ago when she'd readied herself to slide into the Eye of the Storm.

"Could be," Rob said, as vague as Tessa's ever-present shrugs. Clearly Rob's ex was having trouble letting go of Rob.

Was Rob having trouble letting go of his ex? Were both Tessa and Rob stringing Abby along? Reining her in so they could cut her loose?

At least she and Tessa had made their wishes clear to each other. Nothing more for Abby to do but wait and, like any good parent, hope and pray the child would do the right thing.

That was the hardest part.

Up ahead, their destination shimmered and snaked its way to the Atlantic Ocean. She shivered at the thought of baring herself and submerging.

She'd taken him this far, she might as well go all the way. She owed him that much.

She owed herself.

If they were going to have any sort of future, she had to chance telling him the truth. If she wanted him to understand she wanted a future, she had to tell him.

"I, um, spent some time with Charlie yesterday."

Half a second passed, enough time for waves to rush the shore. Enough time for Abby's blood to rush through her veins and crash through her ears.

"Oh-kay," Rob said, but his tone begged to differ. His pace slowed, and his stomach muscles tensed beneath her fingers.

"He asked me to marry him."

Rob stopped walking, and turned from her embrace. "If this is your idea of letting me down easy, it's going to be a really looong walk b—"

"I'm not going to marry him," Abby said, but Rob didn't budge. "I mean, I can't marry Charlie. He only asked me because of the baby, and because Luke always wanted us together. What child doesn't want their parents together?"

"Can't argue with that."

Abby rolled her lips in between her teeth, glanced at the moon, and mentally kicked herself. They were supposed to swim first and then talk about how they felt about each other. She wasn't supposed to dig into his soft places and draw blood.

Rob lengthened his stride and doubled his pace, putting quick distance between them. "Hey," she said. "Hey! I don't love Charlie!"

No, she loved Rob, the guy running away from her. Story of her life. She jogged through the color-softening moonlight, feeling like the sandpipers that chased the Seawall Beach tides dawn to dusk. The silly birds would scurry toward the ebbing current, and then turn on a dime and hurry away from the approaching swell.

Didn't they ever get sick and tired of the game? Didn't all the back-and-forth with no progress make them want to scream?

Abby sprinted up behind Rob and socked him in the arm.

"Ow!" he said, a chuckle in his voice.

So she punched him a second time.

"Okay, that one actually hurt." He rubbed his arm, slowed his pace.

"What do you care if I marry Charlie? You're the one who wants to just see what happens. You want us to continue dating, and then what? If I adopt Luke's baby, you're going to disappear from my life?" A dark current swelled in Abby's belly. This wasn't how she'd envisioned their conversation playing out, but she couldn't stop herself, as if she were a deep-water wave, gathering energy and refusing to break. She deepened her voice. "Uh, sorry, lady, been there, done that, so through with the kid thing."

The Morse River beckoned. At low tide, the waters were as gentle as a tidal pool. At high tide, more dangerous than the ocean into which it flowed. Her stomach tensed around the realization she hadn't consulted the tide charts before embarking on this mission. Adrenaline rushed in with the clear understanding she couldn't care less about the potential for disaster.

Rob eyed her, should-I-stay-or-should-I-go all over his face. "Abby—"

"You're going to leave me for doing the right thing, because it doesn't fit in with your life plan?" she said. "Well, I have news for you. Life is hard! You can do everything right, live your life for your son. Then one day while you're paying the bills, the phone rings, and a stranger is telling you he's gone, and there's nothing you can do about it. And none of it makes any sense! Day after day, it continues to *not make sense*. And you're left all alone with your anger. But there's nothing you can do about it, because the one person you really want to haul off and yell at is dead!"

Abby's hands shook. Her fingers clasped the thin cotton of her sundress, digging into her chest. Her bottom lip hammered with the aftershock of her words.

They'd stopped walking. When had they stopped? Rob stared at her, a still presence, as though he were part of the beach itself, raised from the sand. His mouth worked around something unspoken, and he kept swallowing. He rubbed her arms with either hand, the tips of his fingers raising goose flesh.

She was sweating, her dress clinging to her body, but her teeth chattered. "What am I doing here?" Not here on Seawall Beach, but here on Earth. "Why am I alive while Luke—?"

Rob's mouth pressed against hers, swallowing her hurt. She whimpered, and he kissed her harder, pulling an ache through her center. Tears swelled in her throat and leaked down the sides of her face, an endless stream.

"Don't cry." He kissed her cheek to ebb the flow, his face distorted and blurry.

The sand and the sea were all she'd ever known, her home base, touchstone, and guiding light wrapped up in a blue satin bow. After Luke had died, nothing felt quite the same, the beauty brushing the surface, but not sinking into her soul. She'd look past the sparkling sands with warm glints of glitter and see a landscape of crushed shells. The glorious waves went from comforting to repetitive. And the once-magical sky? The place she sought her son.

"I need this world to feel like home again," she said, not caring if she sounded crazy, hoping against hope Rob would understand.

He brushed her hair from her face, and the swallow-sound came through his voice. "Tell me how I can help you. Tell me what you need," he said, his tone reminiscent of the day they'd first discussed the labyrinth project and his eagerness to get to the center of what she really wanted.

The day she'd begun the sure, steady fall for Rob Campbell.

Today, she needed to wash clean. She needed to return to the sea. She needed to go home.

"Close your eyes," she said. Rob flicked his gaze to the river, and a twinge at the corner of his mouth told her, yes, he understood.

Still smiling, Rob covered his eyes. She swiped the tears from her cheeks and slid the spaghetti straps from her shoulders, pushed the fabric past her hips. Stepped from her sundress, like a hermit crab vacating its outgrown shell. Abby had heard local lure about skinny dipping in the Morse River, even passed along the suggestion to the guests at Briar Rose. Yet, she'd warned Luke not to try it.

Probably making the notion all the more attractive.

She set her bra and underwear on her dress. "I'm swimming across, so as soon as you hear me splash the water, you can join me. I promise not to peek."

His grin widened, a flash of white. "I'm not at all concerned."

Low tide, and the river barely moved. She waded through the squishy, sucking sand that had reminded her and Luke of lightning quicksand from *The Princess Bride.* When the river hit her waist, she dove below the surface. A splash. A split second of panic. And then total sensory overload. The cold water numbed her skin, boxed her ears. Salt water clogged her sinuses, and she stared into the watery darkness. Nothing but life beating in her throat, and the exertion of her arms pulling her upward, upward, until she broke through to the surface and swam for the opposite shore.

She gulped the air, called to the dark figure standing waist-deep in water. "Woo-hoo! Dunk in, the water's fine!"

"Where are you?" A seed of panic rode on his voice, threatened to grow. She'd never heard him sound that way before.

Abby splashed the water before her, counting on her movement, the reflection of moonlight. "Swim toward my voice. I'll meet you in the middle. Marco!" she called, instantly regretting her choice of a game where, after each shout-out, you were supposed to change your location to evade a closed-eyed pursuer. The game had caused her five-year-old son to melt down in swim class, after the closed-eyed kids had challenged the mothers and lost.

Hours later, Luke had refused to sleep alone, convinced if he shut his eyes, Abby would slip away from him.

Abby hadn't thought of that day in years. Now, the memory felt as close as the salt water that buoyed her. The way Luke's tears had molded the lashes on each of his eyes into three dark-blond spikes. The way his eyes had glistened, huge blue caricatures. Against the peach-soft curve of his cheek, the way his tears had tasted like the ocean.

Abby licked the salt from her lips.

"Polo!" Rob called.

Abby swam the rescue stroke, head up so she couldn't miss him. "Marco!"

Rob approached, his head and torso cutting through the water, kicking up a blue-black wake.

Then, a few feet away, he surface dove. The water barely rippled in his place, making Abby wonder whether she'd dreamed him. Whether he was nothing more than a figment of her seawater imagination. The same imagination, sending her pulse into overdrive. Her—

A sharp tug on her leg. Abby yelped, and Rob's head and shoulders sliced to the surface. "Shark attack!" Rob said, breathless.

She swam closer and came to standing in shoulder-deep water. When she touched his smile, he kissed her fingertips. Her mouth found his, and she closed her eyes. Pulled his lower lip into her mouth, nibbled. Let the gentle tides sway them ever so slightly. When she opened her eyes, he brushed his lips against the edge of her ear and she shivered. "Let's warm up," he said, his voice thick. "I'll get a towel, and then leave one for you. Eyes closed, of course," he said, without an ounce of sarcasm.

If Rob had been any other man, Abby would've thought he was joking. If he'd been any other man, she wouldn't have trusted him.

They swam, two parallel rescue crawls, until they approached the shore. Abby kneeled in the water and covered her eyes, probably grinning wider than Rob had when she'd insisted upon the same move. She couldn't help but imagine his bare white bottom walking along the beach. Considering how nice he looked in jeans—

The sound of Rob unzipping his pack. And then, a moment later: "You can open your eyes!"

Rob stood on the shore, hands over his eyes, same wide white grin from earlier. The striped towel tied around his waist reached to his calves and showed off his sculpted-from-yard-work chest, as though he were posing for a calendar featuring hot landscape architects. Pretty much the last thing on Earth Rob would consider doing. Off to the side, Abby's backseat emergency blanket covered the sand, and a second striped towel sat at its near edge.

If Rob had been any other man, Abby would've thought her imagination had gotten the best of her, conjuring the gentleman of her dreams.

Abby climbed from the river, her skin comfortable in the warm air. She unfurled the towel, secured it at the chest, and lowered herself to the blanket. A giggle rose from her center. "You can open your eyes now." *Honey.* She'd nearly called him *honey.*

"Oh!" Rob sat beside her, bumping her hip. His pale eyes glowed from beneath dark, wet lashes, and an easy smile played on his lips. Ribbons of clouds laced the moon. Its reflection sketched a curved white path across the waves.

When Rob wrapped his arm around her, she laid her head on his damp shoulder. Exactly the way she'd imagined this scene. She sighed, the ocean having aptly cooled her head and mood. All the beauty seeped into her soul, stirring energized contentment. There was no other place she'd rather be. Just like the old days. A few moments to soak in the atmosphere, and then she and Rob would have a real conversation about her adopting Luke's baby. What it would mean to her life. What it could mean for him, if he wanted a future with her.

Rob kissed the top of her head, and his words, light as a sigh, ruffled her hair. "I love you, Abby."

Abby made a sound at the back of her throat, a sharp *ha* of shock rushing out of her. "What?" she said, although she'd heard him. Clear as the clang of a bell buoy piercing the night, she'd heard every word.

But what did love, Rob's love, mean?

The only other man who'd ever declared his love for her was Charlie. And love, Charlie's love, hadn't convinced him to stay.

Abby lifted her head. A trace of surprise stiffened Rob's features, as though love had blindsided him and he wasn't sure what to do with it. Because he was scared, unsure, or unsure of his love's meaning?

Then Rob swallowed and blinked, and a broad smile shone through his eyes. He nodded, as if he'd just had a conversation with himself and come to an agreement. He caressed the wet curl lying at her shoulder and licked his lips. "You're a beautiful person, Abby. And, yeah, I love you."

She wanted to take him to task and ask him what he meant by that. Did love mean he couldn't live without her? That he'd change his life for her, rewrite expectations for his over-forty years? Or was love simply an expression of appreciation for a woman he could take or leave?

She could live without Rob Campbell, but, heaven help her, she didn't want to. And she'd be damned if she went to her grave not telling him the way she felt.

Rob tilted his head, brushed tears off her cheek with his knuckles. "Baby—"

"I love you, too," she blurted out in a *ha* of surprise, same as when she'd been at the receiving end of the declaration. She held his face between her hands. "I love you," she repeated, and she kissed his smiling lips, swallowed down all of his sweetness. Let herself feel the beauty of Rob's love, the beauty of this life, fully and deeply, with no expectations for a future.

Be here now.

Rob ran a hand down her back, and they lay on their sides. Face-to-face, nose-to-nose, she memorized the topography of his ocean-cooled back, the broad expanse, the ropes of muscles at either side, the scrapes and scars that defined him. Rob opened the top fold of her towel, and his gaze washed over her, rushed heat down her body. Then he lay back down, stroked her face, and folded her in a kiss. His chest warmed hers, his pulse thrumming through her, melding with the ocean roar.

Abby took Rob's hand from her hip and moved it to her chest. "I won't break," she told him. And when he cupped her breasts, when he traced each nipple with first his fingers and then his tongue, and her body answered, she knew she'd spoken the truth. She wasn't broken. Not anymore.

She unfolded Rob's towel, unleashing him, and he sprang to life between them. The ache between her legs blossomed, her whole body wanting him fully and deeply inside her. She ran a hand over his hip, down his belly, into the warmth between his thighs. Then she traced the length of him with her fingertips and found her voice. "Happen to have a condom in that pack of yours?"

Rob leaned his forehead against hers. "Got a few in the first-aid kit for emergencies. This qualifies," he said, and he scrambled over to his pack, his white bottom even cuter than she'd imagined.

Moments later, he returned and unrolled the condom onto himself. Up on one elbow, he brought a strand of her hair to his lips. His hands trailed across her chest and down her body. She shivered, but perspiration prickled her brow. "I want to make you feel good. Tell me what you need," he said, for the second time that night.

If Rob had been any other man—

Abby covered his hand with hers. "Just you. All of you."

Rob knelt over her, and her body angled to him. And just in case this was all she got, she took a snapshot. Told herself to remember the smile on his face, the way his soft gaze held hers. The way his gorgeous body blocked out the moon as he lowered himself with care onto her, making sure not to crush her with his weight. The soft sands cushioned her back on one of the most beautiful beaches in the world. The waves lapped the shore, the ocean air caressed her skin, and she guided him inside her, all the way to her soul.

"Honey," she whispered. "That feels really good."

Then, holding hands, they moved to the rhythm of the tides and brought each other the rest of the way home.

CHAPTER 18

If anyone cared to ask, Tessa could've identified the three most stressful days of her life. The day her mother had run away from home. The day Luke had died. And today.

All of them involved losing someone she loved.

Tessa could bet her life that if she had a Cutters Anonymous sponsor, she'd tell Tessa that in times of extreme stress, she should close her eyes and go to a place where she was safe and loved and forgiven for all her sins. The sponsor would probably tell Tessa that if she'd no clue where to find such a place, she should, instead, find a healthy means of distracting herself from what she really wanted.

But how could you resist when relief was just an arm's or a thigh's length away?

Two hours ago, Abby had stormed out. Well, not really stormed. But right after Tessa had risked telling her about the day Luke had died, Abby had jumped into her truck and sped from the driveway. Abby had told Tessa Luke's death wasn't her fault. But Tessa knew better than anyone that actions spoke louder than words. When someone hated you, they did everything in their power to put road—or air miles—between you.

Since Abby had been gone, Tessa had switched a load of

towels from the washer to the massive front-load dryer, and then folded the white cotton, reveling in the warmth, the fresh scent that reminded her of Abby. She'd consulted the blackboard menu and then prepared the egg batter for tomorrow morning's French toast. She'd sliced oranges for garnish, set the coffee makers to auto.

All the while Tessa's thighs ached, physically ached, vying for her attention.

Tessa hurried into Abby's apartment, careful to close the pocket door behind her, and then swung into Luke's room. Faced the photo above Luke's bed.

"What am I doing here?"

Sadie padded into the room and stared up at Tessa with her big golden eyes, meowed three times, and then jumped onto Luke's bed, as if the cat were trying to communicate an answer to Tessa's question. If she hadn't already known, that should've told Tessa she was stark raving bonkers.

"Sorry, Sadie." Tessa snapped up her handbag, dashed into Abby's bathroom, and slammed the door behind her. She slid the slide lock into place. The *click-clack* of metal against metal notched her pulse, energized her fingers. She was just going to look at it. Anything else would be stupid, pathetic, and shameful. Wasn't that why she'd kept it in the first place, the way former smokers kept one cigarette to remind themselves how far they'd come and how much they had to lose?

She unzipped the inside pocket of her handbag and eased a square of silk scarf onto her lap. The smooth, cool texture enticed her fingers, but the design she'd purposely chosen—red flowers blooming on silk pale as her skin—was supposed to warn her away.

Instead, her thigh went into overdrive, and the design urged her forward.

She sat on the toilet cover, unfolded her mother's silk scarf to reveal a single, shining, silver razor blade, sparkling like a jewel. The blade was supposed to scare her, resurrect the memory of physical pain and scarring.

Instead, her throat tightened in anticipation of how good it would feel to part her skin with the blade and give herself a blissful moment of relief. First thought? She was sick and disgusting. Second thought? She wanted Abby to come home. Third thought? She'd driven Abby away. Sobs rippled through her body, forceful as tides on the open ocean. She clamped her hands over her mouth, and the pressure, pounding pressure, built in her chest.

She took deep breaths, the kind the OB/GYN made her do whenever she went for her monthly visits. Then she pinched the blade between her thumb and forefinger, waved it over the scars on her leg, gritted her teeth, and chucked it into the trash can. Metal on metal, the blade clanked to the bottom of the empty pail.

The baby turned inside her belly, as though it knew what she'd almost done, and she flashed hot. Bile bit the back of her throat. She'd told Abby she didn't cut anymore. She'd promised.

First thought? She wanted to go home.

Second thought? She didn't know where home was anymore.

Wasn't home the place where you were supposed to feel safe, loved, and forgiven?

Fifteen minutes later, for lack of a better plan, she hit *Home* on her GPS and headed in the opposite direction.

Tessa parked in the far lot of Head Beach and made her way through the narrow beach-grass path. The moon shone down on the beach, bright enough to throw shadows. Not quite a full moon, she could see that now, but she wouldn't have known on her own. If Abby hadn't taken the time to explain the phases of the moon, Tessa would've thought she were imagining the asymmetry. She would've assumed the fault lay in her skewed vision. She would've believed the fault lay in her.

Waves broke—low tide, she was guessing—and blue reflected off the water. She should totally paint this scene. Her shadow thrown to the side, the subtle deep shades of water, the way moonlight mimicked the low light of a dorm-room desk lamp turned to the wall for nighttime romance.

Wish you were here, Luke.

Just past the Kelp Shed, about twenty kids gathered in a semicircle on beach towels. Half a dozen kids finished the circle on a piece of driftwood. A long-haired guy at the edge of the driftwood played "Like a Rolling Stone" on his guitar, while the kids sang along, loudly and badly, to the refrain. Even from a distance she could see the configurations of couples, the party game of hooking up. If she turned back now—

"Oh my God, it's Tessa! You came! Hurray!" Hannah shot up from the edge of the driftwood bench and raced across the sand. She skidded to a stop and threw her arms around Tessa's neck, nearly knocking her off balance.

"You have got to meet Jake!" Hannah said, letting Tessa know last week's guy hadn't yet morphed into an exclusive boyfriend thing and she'd resumed her mission. Even if Hannah wasn't clutching a can of Bud, even if Tessa hadn't heard the wildly exuberant singing, the fumes would've announced the second most popular activity on the beach. Getting totally faced.

"I'm so glad you came!" Hannah said.

"Sorry I missed the fireworks." She'd stay for ten minutes, get in the car, and put distance between herself and Hidden Harbor. By the time she crossed the state line, they'd forget about her—Abby, Charlie, Lily Beth, her whole Hidden Harbor family. Out of sight, out of mind. Even Rob, Abby's boyfriend, would be relieved to have her gone.

Rob was Abby's boyfriend.

How would Tessa have felt if a stranger had come to Amherst and asked her to choose between Luke and their child?

How could Tessa live without either of them?

Hannah slung an arm around Tessa's waist—no small feat—and led her toward the circle of kids. "The fireworks haven't even started yet. Isn't this the most amazing night? You look so pretty." Hannah fingered the thin French braid weaving through the front of Tessa's hair. "You've got to meet Jake's friend Derrick. He's an artist, like you. Actually, a musician. But that's the same, right? Painting, music." A cooler sat beside the driftwood. "Want something to drink?"

Tessa couldn't help but grin. Was that how she'd acted, powered by beer, buzzing to the max? She wouldn't mind the symptoms of intoxication. The life-is-good, love-you-all, and everybody-loves-me feeling that bathed your brain, hand in hand with the alcohol. Then you woke up with a wicked headache and nothing but regret. "Do you have anything non-alc—?"

Hannah took Tessa's hand and dragged her to the center of the circle, making Tessa think of the childhood game of the farmer in the dell. And she was the cheese. "You've got to meet everyone. Everyone, this is Tessa!" Hannah said, and then she started around the circle, ending the introductions with Derrick, as though he'd been the intended destination.

"Tessa!" Derrick gave his guitar a strum. "Beautiful name for a beautiful girl."

Tessa laughed, despite her instinct to roll her eyes. As if Derrick couldn't tell she was hugely pregnant, on her way to becoming a pregnasaurus. The made-up word she and Dina used for a big-as-a-dinosaur pregnant woman. Tessa would find a spot away from the guitar dude, bide her time—

Derrick set his guitar down and got up to greet her. Snug jeans, bow-legged cowboy saunter, plain white T-shirt, some kind of red tattoo on his forearm. He shook wavy, dark, shoulder-length hair from his eyes, smiled with lips a little too full. She took his outstretched hand, an opportunity to glance at the tattoo: heart on his sleeve. A little corny, too on the nose. Plus, something about the tattoo seemed artistically misplaced and wrong.

"Can I get you something to drink?" Derrick said.

"I can't—"

"A bottle of water?" His dark eyes met hers, and understanding curled the edges of his mouth.

"Thanks," she said, her throat suddenly dry, now that relief was at hand. She hadn't thought to bring water with her for the drive back, hadn't considered that if she was already tired, she'd be exhausted before she was halfway to Amherst. And what if she ran out of gas? What if she put her baby in danger?

What kind of a mother was she?

She imagined heading back to Briar Rose, walking through the door, and pretending nothing had changed. She knew better than anyone that some things, once released, you couldn't take back. And once you'd broken a heart, the reasons didn't matter.

Maybe if Luke hadn't died she could've talked to him about how much it hurt when he flirted with other girls. If he hadn't died, maybe she could've grown up a little and controlled her instinct to escalate each and every conflict into a full-blown melodramatic ordeal.

Sometimes her father was right.

Derrick fished through the cooler and pulled a slippery plastic bottle through the brown glass and silver cans. "My sister didn't show from behind either. Carried my nephew in the front. Cutest kid on Earth and wicked smart."

"Really?" Tessa twisted the cap, took a sip, smiled. Could guys like babies? Was that even possible? First time tonight, the fronts of her thighs relaxed, the fire-scream downgrading to a warmth-tinged imperative. Most guys she talked to these days avoided the subject of her pregnancy like the plague, all the while staring at her boobs. She'd even overheard a group of guys from the rugby team talking about her after she'd walked by them in the Campus Center, comparing her rack to the cafeteria's milk machine.

As if she hadn't already felt like a deformed freak.

"Hannah told me you're an art major and painting's your thing," Derrick said. "What do you like to paint?"

"People, mostly, but I'm thinking to try my hand at landscapes."

"Casco Bay's like that. It changes you artistically."

"Changed you?"

"Oh, yeah. Used to go for classic rock. I play for a cover band, The Great Pretenders. That's my full-time gig. But I've been totally getting into folk rock. And, uh, don't let it get around, but I've been trying my hand at art, too. Cross-training."

"You paint?"

He shook his head, and gold hoops showed through his hair, three on each lobe. "Sketches, mostly. Not great, just for fun. But I've been, you know, getting lost in the zone. Know what I mean?"

"The zone where you lose track of time?" she said. "And before you know it, you've created something altogether different than you intended?"

"And way better," Tessa and Derrick said in unison, and the bliss of being understood washed through Tessa like a salve. When his white teeth flashed, her stomach muscles automatically tightened, as though she had any hope of holding her stomach in. As though she were just an ordinary girl trolling for a summertime hookup. As though she could ever forget Luke.

Luke hadn't understood her explanation of the zone until she'd likened it to sex. Then he'd totally gotten it.

Wish you were here.

The air shifted, warmed, as though Luke were standing beside her. And then the sensation retreated, quick as the tides.

Derrick sipped his beer. When he placed his hand on her shoulder, she stiffened, held her breath. "Hey, wanna lose the crowd?" he said. "I've got prime seats for the fireworks."

"I'm, uh, here to see Hannah." Over at the driftwood, Hannah and Jake were playing a mad game of tonsil hockey. Crazy, but Tessa wanted to dash over there, yank Hannah away from the lip-lock, and tell her she should have more respect for herself. Don't give anything to a boy until he'd earned it. Know your worth.

Even nuttier? She wished she could switch places with Hannah. Go back six months to when she'd only thought she'd had problems. Back when she'd only had herself to worry about.

"Doesn't look like she'd notice." A chuckle danced across Derrick's voice. Making fun of Jake and Hannah's PDA or suggesting they make their own good time? He slid his hand from her shoulder, but his gaze held hers, sending a flicker through her brain: the image of kissing Derrick.

Right. What kind of nut job would want to kiss a pregnasaurus?

Luke would've.

He would've rested his head on her belly, awaiting the inevitable fetal gymnastics. He would've made his hands into a megaphone and, via her belly button, praised the baby for a job well done.

He would've wanted to keep their baby.

Derrick leaned in and pointed down the beach. "See those rocks over there? Best seat in the house," he said, his voice turning singsong, and she could imagine him wowing a crowd, drawing them into his zone. "Closest to the action. Or we could hang with Hannah and Jake . . ."

"I see your point."

They passed by the circle of kids, the rumble of conversations, girls slung across boys. A double row of brown bottles circled around a pyramid of silver-can empties, somebody's idea of beach party art. How many of those empties belonged to Derrick?

His chest was broader than Luke's, and his hips rolled when he walked. He looked dangerous, edgy, exciting. Just the kind of guy she would've gone for before she'd met Luke. Before she'd learned you couldn't really judge a book by its cover. Multiple piercings and layers of makeup hadn't made her confident inside. And Luke, with his short hair and pastel polo shirts, had given her the biggest challenge of all. Abby wasn't the only person who yelled at Luke for his stupid stunt.

Edge of the rock wall, Tessa set down her bottle of water, and her hand went to her belly. Her gaze cut to the kids on the beach. She should go back.

Derrick placed a hand on the exposed skin of her lower back, and she startled. "Watch where I step," he said.

She should say good-bye to Hannah. She shouldn't—

"I'll go slow," Derrick said, and then took off, pushing Tessa to either follow in his footsteps or get left behind.

She climbed through the sepia-toned moonlight. Strange beach, uneven light, uncertain footholds. Her movements slid across the rock surface, fluid and gliding, the way you moved in a dream. Derrick jumped across a crevice, nailed a solid landing. Tessa mimicked his motion and underestimated the distance. Her toe caught in the crevice. Adrenaline raced through her body as she lurched forward and landed on her knees.

"You okay?" Derrick knelt beside her, his face inches away.

Tessa made herself smile when she really wanted to cry. "Nothing hurt but my pride," she said, although she was sure her throbbing knees would disagree.

Derrick held out his hand, and she let him help her to standing. "Center of balance," he said.

This time, she smiled for real. "Your sister?"

"Who?"

"When she was pregnant?"

"Oh, yeah. Definitely," he said, but she couldn't see his face.

Adrenaline from her fall lodged in her throat. "What's your sister's name?"

"Hannah."

"That's a weird coincidence." Or the first girl's name that popped into his head that wasn't hers. What were the chances? What did she really know about Derrick?

What if everything he'd told her about himself was a lie?

Tessa had played that game before in high school. She and Dina had gone to frat parties at UMass and managed to convince half-in-the-bag boys they were eighteen-year-old French exchange students, instead of local jail bait. Then, when the attention had turned serious—boys scrambling for available bedrooms—they'd excused themselves to the restroom and run for their lives.

Tessa glanced back toward the beach, but the darkness had swallowed the circle of kids. Clouds moved across the sky, lacing the pink moon. The climb looked even steeper in hindsight.

"Take my hand." Derrick was all at once standing beside her.

Long tan fingers, a hammered silver ring on his forefinger. Not Luke's jewelry-free hand, with the broad knuckles, the smooth backs, calluses marking the spots where he held pens and pencils. When he'd touched her, he had the hands of an artist, memorizing through his fingers. But she'd seen Luke's athlete's hands propel him through lap swim at Boyden Gym, Luke's early-morning wake-up workout. She'd watched from the sidelines, when Luke played pick-up basketball and stole the ball from much taller opponents. She'd felt his hand hold on for dear life.

"I won't let you fall," Derrick said.

But he already had.

"I need both hands for balance," she said. A fact he'd already know if he knew about center of balance from his so-called sister. Wouldn't he?

Slow, careful placement of her feet. Clouds that moments ago had laced the moon now obscured it. Just a tiny slip peeking above the clouds, as though the moon were rising at the horizon.

Derrick turned to her from a few rocks away, three more jumps and scrambles. "Almost there, Tessa!"

She inhaled the briny air, slid down a craggy boulder, and then climbed to where Derrick was facing the open ocean. She took half a step back from the edge, too late to escape vertigo.

About twenty feet down, stratified rocks jutted from the ocean in vertical layers, instead of horizontal, evidence of the plate tectonics she'd learned about in her fall earth science class. Maybe one hundred feet from the outcrops, it looked like a second set of vertical rocks pierced through the ocean, but it was really more of the same, the other side of a crack in the tectonic plate. In between, the ocean rushed in, further wearing away volcanic rocks, shale, and limestone.

She'd gotten an A on the final exam.

She clamped one hand on Derrick's arm, the other across her belly. "Wow."

"You okay? We should sit down." He guided her to the nearest outcrop and then sat down right beside her, facing away from the ocean. His jeans rubbed her bare leg, and his cologne tickled her nose. Something pine and artificial that didn't mix with artsy. Didn't mix with Luke either, who never wore fragrance, artsy or otherwise. Luke smelled naturally yummy, as good as a fresh-baked blueberry muffin.

The rocks darkened. Derrick pointed to the left as the first firework shot into the night sky, sparked into a white chandelier, and curled to the ground. He crossed his legs and rested a hand behind Tessa. "Nice!"

Tessa and Luke had never watched fireworks together. They'd never sat along the Maine coast, like this, or even out on the UMass football fields, staring up at the fire and wonder. They'd never even camped out, or stood in the Orchard Hill Bowl after dark, and thrown their heads back, seeking the stars.

Purple fireworks whirred into the sky. Explosions sparkled, shook, and shimmered, like a sky full of stars.

Luke.

Derrick wound his arm around her and rubbed her shoulder.

Tessa held her breath and kept her face turned to the sky. If she didn't look, she could ignore the foreign feel of his ring against her flesh and pretend he was Luke. Pretend she'd come to visit him for the summer, and he'd taken her here, to Head Beach because—

Derrick turned toward her, blocking the fireworks and, more importantly, ruining her fantasy. He brushed his long hair from his eyes. His gaze moved between her eyes and her lips, quickening her breath, because she was trying not to cry. She widened her eyes, refused to blink. Not much of a come-on. But Derrick angled his head and kissed her anyway.

If she closed her eyes, she could hide her tears and pretend Luke was kissing her. He tasted of beer, which Luke liked. And he'd grown his hair long on a dare, which she liked. They hadn't seen each other in a week. That was why he was kissing her too hard. His teeth bumped hers. He'd never done that before. And right out of the gate, his breath came uneven and loud. He pulled at the hair at the back of her neck and then leaned forward until she was lying down, spikes of uneven rock pressing into her back. His fingers skimmed her breast. His ring brushed—

Tessa clamped her lips shut and shoved Derrick's chest with both hands. "Get off me!"

"What the fuck?"

Luke had never sworn at her.

"What do you think you're doing?" she said.

"Relax," he said. "It's no big deal. C'mon." He chuckled, and the sound grated across her nerves, cramped her stomach. "We were having fun. What's the matter with you?"

"What's the matter with me? What's the matter with you, pervert! I'm pregnant!"

"Yeah? So? It's cool." Derrick edged closer. He touched the hair fallen across her chest, and she smacked his hand. "Geez!" he said. "It's not like you can get any *more* pregnant."

Her mouth fell open. "Are you kidding me? Just because—? You thought—? That's why—?"

Derrick huffed. "Don't get all snooty. You were into it. You knew where this was going."

"No, I didn't." This wasn't like the games she'd played in high school, leading college boys on only to run away. She'd grown up. She'd been in love with a college boy. Now she was all alone, and lonely. So. Freaking. Lonely. "I was just looking for a friend," she said, her voice sounding more like a request than a defense.

Derrick edged closer, and he lowered his voice into the sweet range. "Tess-ah." He dragged out the syllables, but he still didn't sound like Luke. "We can be friends. Really, really good friends." He trailed a hand across her hair, down to her shoulder, the red heart-on-his-sleeve tattoo heading for—

She clamped a hand around his heart. "It's on the wrong arm." She let out a laugh, skimming the top off the tension in her throat. "I figured it out."

"What?" Derrick said, forgetting to sound sweet.

"The heart pun. Your stupid tattoo. A line goes directly from your heart to your left hand. Your left, not your right."

Behind him, the finale lit up the sky with red, white, and blue fireworks, the whirring sounds constant and relentless. Derrick wrenched his heart—wrist—away from her. "My tattoo's not stupid."

"Sorry?" she said, although she wasn't. Then she watched his stupid bowed legs take off across the ledge, jumping from rock to rock. She bet he wasn't even a professional musician. Probably taught himself to play two or three songs so he could lure girls, put on a fake show. "Loser!" she yelled after him, but he was already gone.

The last firework popped and fizzled, leaving nothing but gray clouds hanging in the black sky. A cheer went up from the crowd on the beach, the sound far away and ocean-muted. She stood up and turned in a circle. Nothing but a sea of rocks in every direction, faint shapes marking the darkness.

"Oh, crap. Crappity crap."

She sucked air, and it tangled in her teeth. Her thigh hummed, and she distracted herself by cradling her belly. "We're okay. We're okay. Calm down. I've got you. We're getting out of here. It's that way, I think."

She sat down on the rocks and slid to the adjoining ledge. Then, arms out for balance, she stepped across a few more rocks. Step, sit, and slide. She repeated the process until the rocks angled sharply downward, reminding her of the beginning of the climb from the beach. But she couldn't see the sand, not yet. No moon showed in the sky, nothing but a few stars, flickering weakly through the clouds.

"I wish you were here, Luke. I miss you so much," she said, and the catch in her voice quickened her heartbeat. Her foot slipped on something squishy. What the heck? Seaweed at the edge of the beach? *Yes!* She inhaled, and her throat relaxed.

"I want to go home." She leaped toward the beach, and her throat clenched around a too-long hang time, the ocean coming into focus.

She was falling into the crack in the stratified rocks, the tides rushing up to submerge her.

"Please, God," she said, and the water swallowed her plea.

CHAPTER 19

Abby should've paid more attention to the cat.

Sloppy drunk with each other, Abby and Rob stumbled into the private quarters of Briar Rose. Abby's legs shook, her thigh and calf muscles on fire from their run from Seawall Beach back to the Morse River Road parking lot, the love they'd made on the beach, and the plans she had for Rob once they broke through her padlocked-against-men bedroom door. She wanted to fling the chenille throw pillows onto the floor and tear off the coverlet. To yank down the top sheet and invite Rob into her sanctuary of lavender-scented cotton and firm support.

She wanted to free herself from safe, solitary confinement.

Abby took Rob by the hand and tiptoed through the darkened living room, fearful sound or light could break their love spell. One wrong move and—

Sadie dashed across her path, as though the cat were reenacting her long-ago Luke-inspired morning ritual of running in circles. "It's okay, Sadie. It's only Rob."

"Only?" Rob wrapped his arms around her from behind and nestled his mouth in her neck, heating her skin all the way to her toes. She arched her back against him, and he slid a hand to her breast, making her wonder how the heck they were going to make it to her bed.

Sadie stared up at them and released three plaintive mewls. Then the gray tabby dashed back down the hall, continuing her nighttime exercise.

Abby scowled after Sadie.

What in the world?

Rob ran a thumb across Abby's nipple, sending an ache to her throat, a pang between her legs.

She led him the rest of the way to her bedroom, and they stepped over the threshold. No big band music greeted them, no trumpet sounded. Just the sweet, peaceful feeling of rightness settling into Abby's gut. "I think Sadie's glad we're home."

Rob pressed her against the wall, the hard edge of his jeans rubbing between her legs. "She's not the only one. Didn't think I was gonna make it in my truck."

"Thinking about me a little?"

Rob played with a lock of her hair. The seawater-coiffed strand crunched in his fingers. "Only thing I was thinking about."

During Abby's drive back, she'd replayed their love making, their love confessing, daring herself not to worry about tomorrow. In between the replays, she'd fantasized about a roadside ladies' room. "Can you hang on a couple more minutes so I can freshen up a bit?"

"We'll shower later," he said, making her envision water running down his chest and sluicing across the perfect mounds of his firm buttocks.

Not helping the situation.

"Ladies' room break?" she said, and Rob backed off so she could duck out from under his arms. She tossed her cell and truck keys onto the dresser. "Promise I'll be fast."

"Promise I'll be waiting," he said, arousal hooding his eyes.

Abby jogged across the hall to the bathroom, and skirted Sadie a second time. Tessa had probably gotten the old cat worked up with her extensive between-the-bathroom-and-the-bedroom getting-ready-to-go-out routine. All that opening and closing of doors used to bother Abby when Luke had been the offender. Now the creaks and bangs meant she wasn't alone.

Abby used the toilet, as fast as humanly possible, and washed her hands. She shook her head at her reflection in the mirror. Crunchy-tight curls framed her sweaty face. But her cheeks glowed, as if she'd spent hours under the sun rather than bathing in a river and moonlight. And she liked the contented smile on her face. Who knew how long this thing—love—with Rob would last? Her eyes moistened. No, she would not go there. She refused to waste time on sadness.

Abby blew her nose and threw away the tissue. Light reflected off something metal in the bin, and she bent to get a closer look.

Her thighs twitched and she sank to her knees.

With weak fingers, she picked up a silver razor blade. A replacement blade for a man's shaver. Not the kind she used. Not the type Tessa would need for the pink disposables she left lying around the tub.

The kind of blade Tessa might use if she were cutting herself again.

Abby stood and examined the blade under the light. No blood showed against the sharp edge, but Tessa could've washed it clean, she could've started to cut and then—

Abby imagined blood oozing from a pale scar on Tessa's thigh.

Abby tossed the blade back into the trash and ran into Tessa's room. The bed was made, the room empty. Would Tessa cut herself and then go out for the night, as if nothing had happened?

How many nights had Abby spent fighting the darkness, only to get up, tie an apron around her waist and a smile on her face?

Abby re-played their last conversation in her head. Tessa's distress over Abby's admission she couldn't marry Charlie. Tessa's threat to keep the baby from Abby. And then, from between clenched teeth, Abby had retaliated with a riddle: *A good mother always does whatever is best for her child.*

Abby was definitely her mother's daughter.

And the last time she'd seen Tessa, the girl's face was lit with anger and confusion, similar to the way Abby reacted to Lily Beth's fables and wordplay. The difference was Abby had never taken her frustration out on her flesh. "Poor baby," Abby said, referring to Tessa.

Abby was expecting to find Rob naked and reclining in her bed. Instead, he was sitting in her club chair, fully dressed. He'd turned the side table lamp on dim. He lifted a piece of note paper from beneath the light and handed it to her, his lips set in the simultaneous up and down curl of apology.

Dear Abby,
Went back home. I'm sorry.
Love,
Tessa

How could Tessa have gone home? Her home was here.

Abby covered her mouth, shook her head. "I messed up. I should've offered to take Tessa and the baby in for a few years, same way my mother helped me. Now I'm going to lose both of them. Oh my God. What kind of a mother am I?"

"You're not her mother, Abby."

"Doesn't matter. I'm the closest thing to a mother she has." Abby blew out a breath, and her gaze darted around the room.

"Think, Abby, think." She drummed her fingers on the dresser, but they couldn't keep up with her pulse.

Rob stood and handed Abby her cell from the dresser. "Try her cell."

"Thank you. Yes. Right. Logic." The call went immediately to voice mail. "It's off." She laughed, the type of giggle that threatened to whir out of control. "Probably left her cell on overnight in her car again."

"Try her father."

"Gosh, no. He's an ass. Plus, what could he do at this point? I'll have to go after her." Doing something was almost always better than sitting still.

Rob stood up, probably to try and talk sense into the crazy momma she'd become. "I'll drive," he said, volunteering for the mission.

"I'm fine. I've driven to Amherst before." Not alone or at night, but that was beside the point.

"Then we'll take turns," he said, but she didn't believe him. "We'll start fresh, first thing in the morning."

"I could *get there* by morning. Besides, it's not even that late yet. If she'd gone to the party—wait a minute! Hannah invited Tessa to a party on Head Beach. She could still be there." Abby scrolled to *Hannah* on her cell. After three rings, the call went to voice mail. She answered Rob's gaze with a frown and shook her head. "Hannah, it's Abby. I'm looking for Tessa. If you see her, have her call me right away."

"She'd go to a party on the way out of town?"

"She promised Hannah," Abby said, thinking of Tessa's mother, and the broken promise that had crushed Tessa. Mothers weren't ever supposed to leave their children, or give up on them. "It's worth a shot." Abby snapped up her keys from the dresser.

Rob covered her hand with his. "I'm still driving."

"I'm still fine," she said, and then her pulse thrummed an erratic beat all the way to the parking lot at Head Beach.

"There's her car!" Abby said.

Rob hit the brake, and Abby jumped from Rob's truck.

"Wait a sec—" he called, but she was already racing toward the familiar dune grass trail. He caught up with her, and they slowed to a race walk.

Out on the beach, disembodied voices tweaked her ears. A group came into view, sketchy gray-on-black outlines you'd see in a dream. Or a memory.

Nineteen years ago, Abby had walked the same path along this beach and come upon the same type of group. For a few precious hours, she'd pretend she was just single, rather than a single mom. She'd pretend she'd nothing to worry about, other than sidling up to a hot guy and getting a little much-needed attention. The kind that made her feel special and loved and needed.

Until the next day, when she'd feel nothing at all.

A couple dozen kids sat in a circle, with subgroups of three or four, but the predominant configuration was two: a boy and a girl wound around each other. Off to the side, a boy sat on a cooler, guitar by his feet, beer in hand.

She didn't see Tessa.

The group quieted, and a few of the wound-together couples disengaged. Wasn't that—?

"Hey, Abby! What's going on?" Hannah called to Abby from her perch, sitting atop driftwood and some boy's lap. Her voice sounded casual, but she jumped from the lap and rearranged her off-kilter top.

"Where's Tessa?" Abby ran her gaze over the crowd, pausing at the few girls whose faces were pressed to boys. None of them was Tessa.

"Uh, she went off with Derrick." Hannah turned toward the kid sitting on the cooler, pounding a beer.

"Are you Derrick?" Abby asked.

The boy set his beer on the cooler and wiped his mouth with the inside collar of his T-shirt. "That would be me." He stood up and took his time walking over to them. Half in the bag from beers or full of himself? Then he stopped too close to Abby and fixed his unapologetic gaze on her breasts.

Abby took a step back.

Rob took a step toward the kid and widened his stance.

"Where is she?" Abby asked.

Derrick shrugged and ran his tongue over his lower lip. He rubbed at the side of his neck, and his head swayed. "Beats the hell out of me. We were watching the fireworks over on the rocks, and then I came back to the beach."

"You left her there?" Abby said. The rocks were tricky to navigate in the light of day. Even if you weren't pregnant and knew the coast. Even if the night wasn't half a shade lighter than pitch. Even if you didn't already feel all alone in the world.

Chills ran across Abby's shoulders and down her arms. Pressure built behind her eyes. And the smell of the ocean sharpened in her nose, on her tongue. Abby hadn't sensed the moment Luke was in trouble. But she was certain she was in danger of losing her girl.

Hang on, baby.

Rob glared at the kid. "You brought Tessa up to the rocks and then came back without her?"

Derrick tossed his hair from his face and stumbled a bit in place. In the bag *and* full of attitude. "Hey, man, I thought she was following behind me."

"Hey, man, that's bullshit," Rob said, the first time Abby had heard him curse.

"Describe where you were," Abby told Derrick. She wasn't about to follow some drunk clown out onto the coastline rocks in the middle of the night. She hadn't done anything that dumb in half a lifetime.

"I dunno, rocks. We were hanging out above the funky vertical rocks."

"Vertical?" Rob said.

"Stratified," Abby said. "I know what he's talking about. Surprisingly."

The sky brightened enough for Abby to make out Derrick's tattoo. Heart on his sleeve, as if he were sensitive about anyone but himself. "Let's go!" Abby said, and then she and Rob started off toward the rocks.

"Tessa!" Abby called.

Rob's deep voice cut through the darkness. "Tessa!"

"What if she can't remember which way she came?" Abby said.

"She'll find her way," Rob said, his tone sincere and self-assured. "She made it to your doorstep. Girl's resourceful."

"True enough," Abby said, but her chest ached, and every inhalation stopped halfway to her belly. When she found her girl, she was going to give her what for, really lace into her.

Don't you ever scare me like that again!

Then Abby would make sure that infuriating girl understood how much she loved her, and her baby. Abby would make Tessa understand she couldn't live without either of them.

They were at the coastal rocks, staring up into the steep and uneven climb.

When Luke had been fourteen, she'd chased him to this beach and found him with a beer in his hand, an arm looped around an older girl. By the time Luke turned sixteen, Abby had given up the physical chase, letting him go out with staunch warnings about designated drivers and staying away from the water. Just in case specifics didn't fit the bill, Abby would tell him not to do anything stupid.

Some good that had done her.

Tessa was just like Luke. There was nothing Abby could do to protect her.

Abby's back convulsed. She doubled over at the waist, and the air rushed out of her. "Muscle twinge."

Rob massaged her lower back, digging his fingers into the crimp. "I'll find her," he said. "Wait here, and I'll bring Tessa back to you."

Abby inhaled, slow and deep, around the pain. She straightened, and forced lightness into her tone. "You'd never find your way without me," she said. "Without me, you'd be lost."

Then, one foot in front of the other, she led him into the darkness.

When you're going through hell, keep going.

In the background, the tides beat the shoreline ragged while, forefront, the famous Winston Churchill quote played in Rob's head. Wasn't that the philosophy Rob's father had adopted back when Mom had gotten the dire brain cancer prognosis? A team of oncologists, neurologists, and other white-coated -ologists sat Rob and his folks down and explained Mom's options. Best-case scenario: surgery, radiation, and chemo would cause a host of further medical horrors and prolong Mom's life a few months.

A few more months where she'd still seize, go slowly blind, and lose control of all bodily functions.

Dad had left the office acting as though they'd received good news, as if he hadn't listened to a word the doctors had said. As if Mom's last wishes—to halt all treatment and die with dignity—hadn't even mattered.

Sometimes forward movement only looked like progress.

Abby moved through the darkness, climbing from rock to rock, swift and sure. "Tessa!"

When no answer sounded across the ledge, Rob added his call to the mix. "Tessa!" He wished to God there was something more he could do to help Abby. Five years ago, he'd sent out the same plea. Next day, Mom had phoned with a lawyer's name and an appointment to sign over her power of attorney.

Not the answer he'd been hoping for, but an answer nonetheless.

Abby paused and made blowing noises, three scraggly huffs.

Rob massaged her shoulder blades until her breathing softened and she resumed the hike.

"I'm okay," she said, the thing she said when she wasn't.

Moments ago, he'd seen her bend under the weight of her fears. And then, just as fast, he'd seen determination claw its way to the surface. He'd seen the face of the woman he loved and admired.

When was the last time he'd felt that way about his ex? Years before the divorce. Years before Mom got sick. Mom's cancer was the last of many relationship stressors Rob had refused to discuss with Maria, the beginning of the end of their disintegrating marriage.

He had no one to blame but himself.

Abby came to the end of the line, or at least to the place she'd decided to halt. Rob rested his hands on her shoulders, and she tilted her head back. She looked left and right, as if she sought Tessa in the sky. "Help me out here, Luke," Abby said, and a chill skittered up the back of Rob's neck. He closed his eyes and kissed the top of Abby's head.

How would he manage if he'd lost Grace? He didn't want to ever find out, but he strongly suspected he wouldn't cope nearly as well as Abby. Most mere mortals didn't deal with adversity half as well as the amazing woman in his arms.

Below them lay the vertical rocks the asshole kid on the beach must've been talking about, a seawater alleyway. And then, as far as he could see, the craggy shoreline continued.

Abby put her back to the ocean. Tremors rippled her

shoulders. "There's so much coastline. So many ways she could've gotten lost." Abby shook her head, her jaw set tight. "Earlier tonight, she told me she thinks Luke's accident was her fault. Then she told me she's still considering giving Luke's baby to someone else."

"Why would she do that?"

"I know it doesn't make any sense. But she was upset, and we argued. And then that boy, that stupid boy . . . What if she hurt herself? What if—?"

"She's fine. She wouldn't hurt herself."

"Survivor's guilt," Abby said, and her knowing eyes shone through the darkness. "I've been there. It's not a pretty place."

Rob couldn't stand the thought of Abby feeling that way, not even for a second. He couldn't stand the thought of not being able to help her, even in hindsight.

"Tessa wouldn't hurt herself," he repeated, but he could tell from the tilt of her head that she wasn't convinced. "She wouldn't hurt the baby," he added.

Abby straightened. "You're right. Tessa loves that baby."

"Besides, she's too fiery to let a little darkness get in her way. She's a survivor, like her—She's like you, Abby."

If they found Tessa—when they found her—he and Abby would sit down and talk about her plans to adopt her son's baby. The least Rob could do for the woman he loved. Who cared if the so-called timing wasn't right? Was there ever a good time to have a baby? The tiny creatures took over your home, your every waking moment, and wended their way into your heart. Grace made Rob's life worth living.

Abby made his life worth living, too. Any child, or grandchild, of hers came with the package.

Let's just see what happens.

Yup, sometimes he was an ass. A little unsure and a lot scared as hell. And yet, Abby hadn't given up on him. She was gunning to be heard, determined to make him listen.

The fiery blonde packed a punch when she was ticked off. When he'd ticked her off.

He wouldn't let this thing, this amazing relationship, with Abby die from neglect. This time, he wouldn't screw up.

"We'll find her. Let's keep going." Rob motioned with his head to the right. "If she was disoriented, maybe she got turned around, and headed the wrong way up the coastline instead of back to Head Beach."

"Uh, uh. No." Abby turned back around and faced the overhang. "We stay here."

"Like hugging a tree?"

"Exactly. We hug this spot and wait for Tessa to come back to us."

Rob wrapped his arms around Abby. They stared down the sharp incline to a V in the rocks, where the tides seemed to rush in and out simultaneously. He'd never had a problem with heights. But a healthy respect for the power of the ocean kept you alive. "Okay, baby. Your call."

Sometimes making progress only looked like standing still.

The force of the fall propelled Tessa into the ocean, as though she were doing a pencil dive. She held her breath, diving deeper and deeper through cold and darkness. Her arms flailed through the water, trying to halt her descent. Her eyes widened, focusing on nothing. Adrenaline filled her chest, backed into her throat.

Was this how Luke had felt when he was about to die?

She touched a hand to the baby, imagining it floating in its own ocean. Just as dark, but warm and safe and—

Her feet hit bottom, and she pushed toward the surface. Pulled and pulled upward. Her lungs aching for air. Her jaw clenched against the building pressure.

She gasped to the surface, sucking in a greedy breath.

Rocks on either side of her, the tide swayed gently toward the open ocean. She treaded water, her belly a firm, tight ball beneath her palm. "We're okay, we're okay. We're—"

A wave smacked her in the face. She swallowed a mouthful of water, sputtered, coughed, tried to catch her breath around—

Another wave barreled over her, pulling her under. She needed air, now. The baby. Air. Inside the wave, she somersaulted, over and over, her arms ineffective against the pull of the tides.

Please, no, my baby.

Pressure built inside her chest, her cheeks, her head. She squeezed her lips together, barring the ocean.

Something dark moved outside the wave, a flash of a fin. And then Tessa saw her: a little girl of about two or three, with long dark hair and gray-blue eyes. Tessa knew that face. She knew her. Knew her and loved her.

She loves me.

A smile filled Tessa's body, a sweet wash of joy like she'd never felt before, and she relaxed inside the wave. Relaxed inside the love. Relaxed and let her body go slack. Even if she made it home, she'd never be the same again.

For the first time in her life, Tessa stopped fighting.

Abby clutched Tessa's hand, the two women holding on to each other for dear life.

Tessa reclined halfway on the examining table. Tears streamed down the sides of her face, but she didn't make a sound. As instructed, she pulled her hospital johnny up to reveal her swollen belly.

Rob stood to Abby's left, beaming a soft-serious gaze at Tessa. Tessa had asked him to stay. "Warm enough?" he asked. When she didn't answer, he tucked the blanket around her feet.

The ER nurse, Bonnie, wrapped two straps around Tessa's belly. Then she tucked loose bangs back into her dark ponytail and held up two white discs. "I'm going to attach the transducers to the straps. The top transducer picks up contractions. Hopefully, you're not having any of those." Bonnie looked to Tessa and offered her a nod-grin, but Tessa's gaze was trained on Abby.

"Top disc is for contractions that she's not having," Abby said. "Gotcha."

"Bottom disc monitors your baby's heart rate," Bonnie continued. "Normal rate's one-twenty to one-sixty beats per minute."

"Baby's heart rate one-twenty to one-sixty. Excellent."

Because of Tessa's fall and the associated risk of placenta abruption, the ER doctor had insisted on a CTG, or non-stress test. But who wouldn't be stressed after Tessa's ordeal?

Shortly after Abby's decision to stay put on the ledge, Luke had answered her plea for help and delivered Tessa onto the seaweed-covered rocks. Rob had carried her up over the rocks and back to the beach, as sure-footed as a local. Abby might've believed Tessa was perfectly fine, if it hadn't been for her insistence that a merbaby had led her from the grasp of a killer wave to the safety of shore. More likely, Tessa had sighted a baby seal. Dark haired and a few feet long, the adorable mammal approximated the description Tessa had given for the girl in her oxygen-deprived hallucination.

"The baby didn't move in the ambulance," Tessa whispered.

A pinprick of tinnitus wailed in Abby's left ear. Abby sweetened her voice, and the screaming in her head softened, too. "That doesn't mean a thing. Car rides always soothe babies to sleep. When Luke was an infant, we'd go for a nap ride around Hidden Harbor every day at noon."

Tessa searched Abby's gaze.

Abby held her ground, but her chest drummed as though hundreds of tiny fists were trying to punch their way out.

Rob swung in for backup. "Used to take my daughter, Grace, for a nap ride after dinner," he said, and Tessa gave the barest hint of a nod.

Bonnie pushed her glasses onto the bridge of her nose and offered Tessa a smile that looked more pained than encouraging. "Big screen above the monitor will show two lines. Top one's for the baby's heartbeat. Bottom's for contractions. Same lines will print out on the graph paper beside the monitor." Bonnie tapped the left side of the monitor screen. "Baby's heart rate, right here." She squeezed a loop of blue gel onto the first transducer and positioned it against Tessa's abdomen. Tessa shivered and shut her eyes.

"Sorry," Bonnie said. "Goop's always chilly."

Especially if you'd just raced by ambulance from the frigid Atlantic in Phippsburg to an ER in Brunswick.

Bonnie affixed the second transducer and readjusted both.

Since Tessa's eyes were closed, Abby filled her cheeks with air. Rob's exhalation echoed from beside her.

Help us out, Luke.

Bonnie fussed with the monitor's controls, and the baby's heartbeat filled the air, evidence of a beautiful creature floating underwater, not unlike a merbaby. Did that mean he or she was safe and sound?

Tessa squeezed Abby's hand, but she kept her eyes closed, her expression tight. "What's the baby's heart rate?" she asked, proving that she'd been listening all along.

"One hundred and thirty-five beats per minute," Bonnie said, her voice suddenly melodic. "See here?" She pointed to the flat line scrolling across screen. "No contractions. None. Nada."

Abby checked the monitor and screen herself. The number 135 next to a blinking heart, and no measurable contractions.

She released an easy breath. "Open your eyes, baby," she told Tessa.

Tessa blinked her eyes open, but her expression didn't change. Then Tessa's hand went to her belly, and her eyes finally brightened. Tears slid into her mouth. "I felt the baby turn. I felt it!"

Thank you—

"Thank you, Luke," Tessa said, and she looked to Abby.

Abby's stomach trembled. She couldn't be prouder. Her son was watching over his family.

Bonnie held the graph paper in her hands. "Everything looks good. I'm going to let this run for another fifteen minutes and pop back in to check on you before we head over to talk with the doctor."

Thank you, Abby mouthed.

Bonnie nodded and slipped out the door.

"Can I have a hug?" Tessa reached her arms out to Abby and folded them around her neck, same way Tessa had held on to Rob when he'd carried her to the beach. All it took for Abby to let a few tears fall. Tessa cried soundlessly into her shoulder, same as Luke used to do when he was little.

When Abby angled her head to Rob, his eyes were wet, and a muscle twitched along his jawline. Big sensitive guy loved babies. Another checkmark from the way-back Abby-and-Celeste ideal-guy list.

Rob passed Abby a box of tissues. She wiped her face and then used another tissue to dab Tessa's cheeks.

"I shouldn't have left the way I did," Tessa said. "I'm so—"

Abby held up a hand. "No more sorry's. I'm sick of being sorry. But, yeah, you shouldn't have left the way you did. In fact, you shouldn't have left at all."

"Abby—"

"Let me finish."

Rob stepped aside. "I'll leave you girls alone."

Abby grabbed his hand. "You need to hear this, too," she told Rob.

He brought her hand to his smiling lips. "Yes, ma'am," he said, and a fresh batch of tears pressed behind her eyes.

Abby turned back to Tessa. "You were right. I had it easy when Luke was born. Lily Beth took us in. I never even asked for her help. She's my mom. We pulled together. That's how families work."

Abby looked to the ceiling, not seeking Luke this time, but trying to regain some semblance of composure before she flung herself over another ledge in her life. "Tessa, I want you to stay. Not just this week. But—well, however long you need. I want you and the baby to live with me. You're part of the family now. We pull together."

"Thank you," Tessa said, but she looked more dazed than happy. She looked as though she had something to say that she dreaded.

A tickle irritated the back of Abby's throat. She hadn't imagined Tessa saying no. She hadn't considered she could still lose both Tessa and the baby. "You don't have to decide today, or this week," Abby blurted out. "We'll go home, get some rest. You can think about it. Whatever you need."

Abby caught Rob's gaze. His rejection she'd considered. That didn't stop the tickle in her throat from coating her mouth with cotton. "Sometimes the situation's not ideal. Sometimes, when you're a mom, you can't have it all. Not all at the same time anyway," Abby said, and her chin quivered. Stupid, silly chin. Now wasn't the time—

"I'm not going anywhere," Rob said. "I'm staying right here."

"Right," Abby said. "I asked you to stay in the room."

"I'm not talking about this room. I'm talking about us." Rob shook his head. "I'm so bad at this. I'm trying to say I'm not leaving you."

That sounded suspiciously like what Charlie had told her before he'd packed his bags and left for college.

"Don't say something unless you mean it," Abby said.

Rob grinned, but his eyes were still wet. "I might be slow, but I know what I want."

Enough with the skirting talk about their relationship. Enough with the circle dance. "Which is?"

Rob didn't hesitate. "You."

"The baby—"

"With or without the baby. I want you, if you'll have me."

Abby loved Rob's bright blue eyes, and the way they turned down at the corners, even when he was happy. She loved his tiny star-shaped scar that proved, even in sleep, he was always listening for his loved ones and ready to run to their rescue. She loved all of him.

"Hate to interrupt your plans for a lovefest," Tessa said. "But I know what I want, too. I know what I want for my baby." Her voice sounded strong, with the take-no-prisoners, entertain-no-argument certainty of a decision made.

Abby's legs softened beneath her. She gripped the examining table, and forced a smile.

Rob's hand lighted on her shoulder, a preemptive strike to keep her from splintering into a million pieces. The music of the baby's heartbeat sounded through the room, sunk through her skin and into her soul. More than enough to make her grateful. But still . . .

Tessa gazed at her with eyes far too old for a nineteen-year-old.

Same thing people used to say about Abby at that age. Likely the same had once been said of Lily Beth.

"When I first found out I was pregnant," Tessa said, "I considered keeping the baby. But then I got scared."

"I know, sweetheart. I can help you. You can live with me."

"No, I can't. I wouldn't do that to you."

Abby swallowed against a wave of sorrow threatening to knock her down and spin her in circles. Rob rubbed her shoulder. Whatever Tessa decided, Abby would be fine. Not today, maybe not even tomorrow. But she wasn't broken. Life was hard, but she would not break.

Tessa laid her hand over the lower-belly transducer, as though protecting the baby's heartbeat. "Even when my mom still lived with me and my dad, she wasn't exactly maternal. I didn't have anyone to show me how you were supposed to mother a kid. I never had anyone mother me. Until you, Abby." Tessa shrugged, but the expression on her face brooked no compromise. "I'm not going to live with you, and I can't give you my baby. Do you want to know why?" A coy grin played at Tessa's lips.

That made no sense. Tessa wasn't trying to emotionally blackmail Abby anymore. Abby had stood strong and laid everything on the table. She'd laid herself bare. Now all she needed was Tessa.

Rob's hand stilled on Abby's arm. He edged closer. The heat of him warmed her back.

The baby's heartbeat thrummed through her chest, good and strong.

For a second, Abby couldn't move. Then she managed to raise one shoulder in a shrug.

That only widened Tessa's grin to a full-fledged megawatt smile. "A good mother always does whatever is best for her child," Tessa said.

Second time today, Abby wanted to take Tessa to task and give her what for. Really lace into her.

Don't you ever scare me like that again.

Instead, Abby nodded and returned Tessa's impish grin.

You raised your kids, tried to teach them everything you

knew, and then you stepped aside and hoped they made the right decisions.

Tessa was going to raise her and Luke's baby herself. Her life wasn't going to be easy. But she was strong. She was a survivor. And her girl was going to make a great mother.

Abby had no one to blame but herself.

CHAPTER 20

Thanksgiving morning at Briar Rose, and the guest quarters were closed for the family holiday. The aromas of turkey, sweet potatoes, and cranberries filled the air, and the labyrinth awaited its heart.

Abby looked to the skies for guidance, low and dark and threatening to stay. The rain had finally let up, the moderate downpour dissipating to a moderate mist. Tessa bundled Daniela in her pink fleece bunting, the shade identical to the streaks framing Tessa's face. The exuberant feminine color complimented both mother and daughter and brightened the day.

Abby picked her granddaughter up from the entryway couch and secured the baby against her shoulder. The infant's thick, dark hair poked out from the bunting's hood. Daniela held her head upright, strong for her age. Her gray-blue eyes focused on Abby's, stirring up a well of emotion. Sadness-edged joy, but joy nonetheless. Time was taking the sting from her loss, but she'd never stop missing her son, never stop wishing he were here.

Maybe someday Abby would be able to look at Luke's photo albums. Someday she'd like to show his daughter the tan-from-outdoor-play kid with the Band-Aids on his knees and the daredevil smile. The boy who'd trick-or-treated as Spiderman three Halloweens in a row. For now, telling Daniela about her young father would have to suffice.

Abby would have to rely on the inexactitude of memories.

Rob took the most important stepping-stone from the dining table by the slider and they headed out to the yard. The cool mist numbed Abby's cheeks, the final month of autumn making itself known, but the hot little bundle she carried kept her warm.

"She's got your best features," Abby told Tessa, "and Luke's." Abby kissed the top of Daniela's head and inhaled the fresh newborn scent, all milk and powder and possibility.

As soon as Abby raised her lips, Rob leaned over her shoulder to drop another kiss atop the baby, a raining down of blessings. "She's a beauty, just like her grandma," Rob said, emphasis on *grandma*.

Abby slid Rob a faux look of annoyance—he was having way too much fun with her new title—but she couldn't keep the grin from overriding her scowl. A visiting grandbaby in her arms, an engagement solitaire on her finger, and her very own landscape architect living on-site.

Right guy and right-enough timing.

After she'd turned down Charlie's marriage proposal and told him about the proposal she'd accepted, he'd kept a low profile. Abby had invited him to Thanksgiving dinner, knowing he'd put aside his discomfort and come out of hiding for their granddaughter. Charlie loved her as much as she did.

Lily Beth would join Abby in the kitchen within the hour. Grace and her boyfriend, Tyler, would make their way over for dessert, completing their blended family. Last summer, Grace had been wary of the new woman in her father's life, but yesterday's visit with Daniela and Tessa had broken through Grace's reticence. Like her dad, Grace was well worth the wait.

Tessa beamed at Abby, pride that cut both ways. "I kind of

think Daniela looks like you," Tessa said. "And, hate to say it, but a little like my dad. But that's only when she has gas."

Abby laughed. "How's Noah doing?" According to Tessa, she, Daniela, and Noah had celebrated an early Thanksgiving. Today, the professor was dining with his colleagues.

Six weeks ago, Abby and Lily Beth had made the trek to Amherst. Tessa had wanted them in the birthing room. Even Lily Beth had been impressed by Tessa's fortitude, her willingness to get down to business, no whining and fussing and carrying on. Twenty-four hours after the first labor pains, Daniela made her appearance.

One look at his granddaughter, and Noah was smitten. According to Noah, that's how he'd felt the first time he'd laid eyes on Tessa. That was how he felt about her still.

Tessa shrugged, an old defense, but her smile remained. "He's becoming strangely paternal. It's a little freaky. He made me call him from every rest stop on the way here yesterday so he could talk to Daniela. Not me, her! He jumps out of bed when she cries for me at night. I told him he doesn't need to get up, but he says he wants to. It's not like he can nurse her or anything."

"Tell him to watch out for the dog," Rob said.

"What dog?"

"Oh, sorry, puppy on the brain." Rob winked at Abby and kissed her on the cheek.

"Huh?" Tessa said.

"It's like baby on the brain," Abby said, "except with a dog. Rob wants us to get a golden retriever after we tie the knot."

"Aw, cute," Tessa said.

"Not helping," Abby said.

"What? You don't want a puppy?"

"We're talking about it," Rob said. "In negotiations. Abby's still miffed Sadie likes me better than her."

"Hey!" Abby told Rob. And then to Tessa, "It's true. Can't say I miss waking up with her toosh in my face, though."

The bare-of-bloom perennials—including new hostas, roses, and black-eyed Susans—lay dormant, awaiting the blanket of first snow. Tessa had already promised to return for that impressive show. She'd promised to paint the labyrinth each and every year, each and every season, charting its growth along with her daughter's. And in between, Abby and Rob and whoever wanted to tag along, had promised to make pilgrimages to Amherst. Abby had even promised Rob she'd try winter camping. A trial run in the yard, and then, if she survived, she'd consider tent camping with him in the White Mountains.

About time Abby took some time off from the B&B and remembered how to live.

The great maple shade tree was bare, having given up the last of its crimson and gold leaves weeks ago, and the hard lines of the branches stood out strong against the gray skies. Luke's original three stepping-stones hadn't changed. Now and again Abby still placed her hands in his. Then she'd pick herself up off the ground and continue along the seven-circuit path.

Single file, they passed beneath the arbor, Tessa leading the way. Abby had expected her to rush. Instead, she walked slow and sure, as though savoring every moment.

Her girl was wise beyond her years.

Daniela turned her head into Abby's shoulder, her mouth opening and closing against the light-blue nylon of Abby's down vest. Abby stroked Daniela's cheek. "Sorry, little one, you're not going to find any milk here."

"She's rooting?" Tessa said. "I just nursed her half an hour ago."

"As I recall, you time from the beginning of the previous nursing, not the end."

Tessa snorted. "Great. I'm going to have to nurse her in class. I'll be the only sophomore with a baby hanging off her boob."

"You'll figure it out," Abby said. Tessa was planning on going back to school next semester. She and Daniela were living with Noah. He'd agreed to babysit a couple of days a week. The other two days, Daniela would go to "school," the on-campus childcare center.

"The stepping-stones look amazing!" Tessa said. "I didn't realize we'd sold so many."

Since the summer, the dotted line of stepping-stones had filled in between the privets, growing end-to-end solid. "Thanks to your on-campus fund-raising," Abby said, "and Rob planting the stones. Oh, and the first scholarship fund essays are trickling in. Remind me to show you later. And bring tissues." Abby had decided upon the essay's theme: What would you do if you knew today was the last day of your life?

Strange, given the fact that those same students sought careers in hospitality, caring for others? Abby thought it perfectly appropriate. How could you treat others to a vacation experience, a comfortable room, a hot home-cooked meal, if you didn't first know how to live?

In the center of the labyrinth, Rob set the heart-shaped stone in the ground he'd dug out and prepped with soft sand. Special stone from a special little girl had made quite a journey, starting in Hidden Harbor, where Abby and Lily Beth had rimmed the heart stone with Luke's sand dollars. Then, in Amherst, Tessa had pressed Daniela's tiny handprints into the wet concrete and etched her name.

Now, the heart stone returned, full circle.

Daniela continued to root on Abby's shoulder. The warm, wet pool of drool darkened the down vest. Abby handed Daniela to Tessa, and Tessa gave Daniela her finger to suck on, buying a few minutes before the next nursing.

They didn't have much time.

Abby and Tessa joined Rob on the ground before the heart-shaped stone. Just like they'd planned, Tessa unfurled Daniela's tiny right hand and pressed it into her handprint. "Daniela Lombardi Connors." Tessa brought her daughter's hand to her lips. "She's so yummy! I can't stop kissing her."

Abby bent her head to Tessa's. "Why resist?"

The mist had finally stopped. Droplets were drying on Abby's face without the associated chill.

"Ladies," Rob said. "Check it out. Over the bay."

"I know. The mist—oh," Abby said.

A double rainbow arched over the water, the colors faint and then deepening before their eyes. Deepening and taking on a rich, saturated hue.

"It's Luke," Tessa said, her voice full of awe. "Your daddy," she told Daniela. Tessa glanced at Abby, and Abby nodded, getting the reference from the song "If I Die Young."

Luke was shining down on his mother.

Abby would've liked to have believed her son lived in the rainbow, his soul dwelling in the color spectrum of refracted light, but she knew better. She knew the truth.

You okay? Rob mouthed, and Abby nodded. He wanted to save her from sadness. She was just grateful he'd chosen to come along for the journey. Abby raised her gaze to the sky, not caring whether tears fell freely.

For one more minute, one more precious minute, Abby, Tessa, and Rob huddled together on the November-hard ground with Daniela between them. Abby knew for sure she heard Luke's voice in Daniela's coos. She saw her son's determination in his daughter's gray-blue eyes. She felt his love radiated through Tessa and Daniela. And even though Luke had never met Rob, Abby believed Luke would've approved of her choice. Her son, her sweet, sensitive son, had wanted her happiness.

What would you do if this were the last day of your life?

This. This and nothing more.

A READING GROUP GUIDE

WHAT'S LEFT BEHIND

Lorrie Thomson

ABOUT THIS GUIDE

The following discussion questions are included to enhance your group's reading of *What's Left Behind*.

DISCUSSION QUESTIONS

1. At the beginning of the story, Abby is still angry with Charlie because he left for college when she was pregnant with Luke. How do her feelings about that time in their lives change by the end of the story? As a teenager, do you think Abby was fair to Charlie?

2. For years, Lily Beth told Abby her father was a merman who returned to the sea for his own survival. What makes Lily Beth think Abby is finally ready to know the truth about her father? Who do you think Lily Beth was trying to protect with her fish tales?

3. In what ways does Abby see herself in Tessa?

4. How does admitting Luke's faults help Abby move forward and let go of Charlie?

5. Charlie says that Abby "holds a grudge like nobody's business. She never forgives." Do you think this is true? In what way does Tessa's father, Noah, hold a grudge and never forgive? How does this impact his relationship with Tessa?

6. At The Cove, Abby reasons that Charlie is proposing for selfish reasons. Do you agree?

7. Near the end, Abby surmises that when she tells Daniela about her young father, Luke, she'll "have to rely on the inexactitude of memories." How does this theme weave throughout the story? Give examples of how the novel's characters remember the same events differently.

8. In Chapter 1, Abby says Lily Beth's motto is, *Whatever doesn't kill you makes you stronger.* Farther along in the story, Abby catches Lily Beth off guard, and Abby wonders when her mother became human. Do you think Lily Beth was ever as strong as Abby once believed?

9. Abby's bed-and-breakfast is called Briar Rose for the heirloom roses taken from Lily Beth's cottage. After learning the truth about her father, Abby likens Lily Beth to Sleeping Beauty. How does that fairy tale color *What's Left Behind*? How is Abby also like Sleeping Beauty?

10. At the beginning of the story, Tessa believes her options are to keep the baby, give the baby to Abby, or give the baby away to a stranger. Discuss how and why Tessa's options evolve throughout the story.

11. How does Abby help Tessa see herself differently?

12. How does Abby change the way Rob views the disintegration of his marriage? In what ways is Abby similar to and different from Maria?

13. How does Tessa affect Rob's relationship with his daughter, Grace?

14. How is Abby's relationship with Rob different from her childhood romance with Charlie? How does Luke's death ultimately make her want to risk her heart with Rob? How does Lily Beth's revelation likewise impact Abby and Rob's relationship?

15. Abby sees Rob as mature. Do you agree?

16. In what ways are Abby, Tessa, and Rob all holding on to the past?

17. Do you know anyone who has cut herself/himself? If so, how has that influenced the way you feel about Tessa? Are you more or less sympathetic toward her?

18. Abby has never cut herself. But what are the lesser ways she's harmed herself? What is she addicted to?

19. Even though Rob hasn't lost a child, in what ways is he grieving?

20. Discuss how Rob's mother's death and his estrangement from his father tie into the theme of hiding behind fantasies.

21. At the beginning and nearing the end of the story, Abby asks, "When the person you'd built your life around was gone, where did that leave you?" Discuss Abby's two very different answers to this question.

22. How is the labyrinth symbolic of the characters' emotional journeys? How does the labyrinth project impact all of their lives?

Celeste's Sugarcoated Lemon Blueberry Muffins

2 cups flour
⅔ cup sugar
1 teaspoon baking powder
1 teaspoon baking soda
½ teaspoon salt
1 cup plain yogurt (not Greek style)
Juice of 1 lemon
¼ cup butter, melted and cooled
1 egg
2 teaspoons grated lemon peel
1 teaspoon vanilla
2 cups wild Maine blueberries

Glaze
½ cup sugar
Juice of 1 lemon
1 teaspoon grated lemon peel (optional)

Preheat oven to 400 degrees. Grease twelve regular-size muffin cups or thirty-six minis.

In a large bowl, whisk together flour, sugar, baking powder, baking soda, and salt until blended.

In another bowl, stir together yogurt, butter, egg, lemon juice, lemon peel, and vanilla until blended.

Make a well in the dry ingredients. Add yogurt mixture. Stir until just combined. Fold in blueberries. (If you must use frozen blueberries, thaw and drain before folding in.)

Spoon batter into prepared muffin cups. Bake regular-size muffins 20–25 minutes and minis 12–17 minutes or until cake tester comes out clean.

Remove muffin tin(s) to a wire rack. Let cool for 5 minutes.

While muffins cool, stir sugar and lemon juice together for the glaze. If you want extra lemon flavor, grate a teaspoon of lemon peel into the mixture.

Remove muffins from cups. Spoon or brush glaze over hot muffins. Let cool before serving for a crunchy sugarcoated topping.